SNOW IN W

Margaret Bacon was educated at The Mount School, York, and at Oxford, where she read history. Married, with two daughters, she now lives in Wiltshire. She has written several novels, a travel book and a children's book.

signed by author

With best wishes,

Margaret Bacon

25th. March, 1993

By the same author

Going Down
The Episode
Kitty
The Unentitled
The Package
The Chain
The Kingdom of the Rose
The Serpent's Tooth

Travel

Journey to Guyana

For children

A Packetful of Trouble

Snow in Winter

by Margaret Bacon

HILL HOUSE PUBLICATIONS

First published in Great Britain in 1978 by
William Collins, London.

First published in this edition in Great Britain
in 1989 by Hill House Publications, Highworth,
Wiltshire SN6 7BZ

British Library Cataloguing in Publication Data

Bacon, Margaret
Snow in Winter
I. Title
823'.914[F]

ISBN 0-95135-651-8

Cover illustration by Charlotte Knox
Cover design by Jayne Brooks

Printed and bound in Great Britain by
Redwood Burn Ltd., Trowbridge, Wiltshire

Part One

Chapter One

A great stillness hung over the dale. The distant fells slumbered in a haze of blue heat, while on the nearer hills the limestone scree quivered under the glare of the afternoon sun. Even the sheep were silent as they lay like boulders against the dry-stone walls. The beck, usually a quick and lively stream, crawled sluggishly down to the village, exposing muddy banks baked hard. The lane which wound its way between hills up to the dalehead was a grey ribbon of dust.

The village was deserted: from the church at one end to the Newboulds' farm at the other, nothing moved along the shimmering high street. In the centre, where the road widened and forked to embrace the green, the doors of The Curlew were closed and on the bench outside only a cat lay sleeping. In the village shop on the other side of the green, old Drinkwater sat on his high stool, surveying his merchandise with hooded eyes. Gaunt and watchful, he perched there in his black suit like a bird of prey; no customers came to disturb his vigil.

Beyond the green the village narrowed, as a stream does below a pool, and its houses faced each other across the narrow street, like rocks on their opposing banks. For they seemed always to have been there, these little houses whose walls were built of local stone and whose slab floors were made of slate from the quarry over the hill. They were part of the landscape like the lanes and the beck and the dry-stone walls, which had straggled up hill and down dale for as long as anyone could remember.

The Newboulds' farm was at the far end of the village, a little apart from the other houses and occupying the corner made by the lane turning up to the head of the dale. It was a long low building of grey stone, one end being the dairy and the other the farmhouse. George Newbould was in the dairy now, ladling milk from a churn into a blue and white jug, while his three-year-old niece sat on her haunches watching him. She was a solemn-looking child, who observed the world with big brown eyes, but did not find it necessary to comment upon it.

She watched her uncle now, as he filled the jug to within half an inch of the rim, as meticulously as if he had been filling it for a customer on the morning milk-round. She watched him rinse the ladle and return it to its place next to the larger one on the rim of the can. Then he picked up the jug of milk, and glanced down at his niece to show her that he was ready to go, for he was not a man who used words needlessly.

She jumped up and followed him out of the dairy, hesitating for a moment in the doorway, taken aback by the blinding glare of the sun. Then she set off after her uncle along the cobbled front of the house; the rounded stones felt hot as they pressed up into the thin soles of her sandals. Then she was in the kitchen and it was pleasantly dark again like the dairy and the slab floor was cool under her feet.

Her cousins Derek and Chrissie were already sitting up at the table and her aunt was moving quickly about, carrying things. She was a sharp-featured little woman, quick and abrupt in everything she did. She seized upon her niece now and tied a bib under her chin. Then she yanked her up on to a chair on which she had already placed a hard, thick cushion which gave Nell precarious height. Nell waited until her aunt and uncle had sat down and Uncle George had said 'For what we are about to receive, Oh Lord make us truly thankful', and then methodically set about eating the ham and salad which her aunt had put in front of her.

Nobody spoke much, partly because it was too hot and partly because it was not their custom.

When they had finished their tea, Derek and Chrissie went out to play.

'Half an hour, mind,' their mother called after them, 'then you come back and do your homework; I'll have the table cleared by then.'

Nell slipped down from her chair, the cushion slithering after her. She collected her doll from where she had left it on the dresser and went and sat on her stool by the empty grate. Behind her she could hear the sound of more tea being poured, of chairs being pushed comfortably back and plates being moved to make way for elbows. She knew from these little sounds that her aunt and uncle were going to talk, just as she knew from the preliminary wheezes of the grandfather clock when it was going to strike.

'You've read Patrick's letter?' she heard her aunt ask.

'Ay.'

'Looks like he's off, then. Gone for the rest of war, likely.'

'It's hard on t'little lass. They ought to be given leave before they go like that.'

'Maybe he was.'

'Nay, he'd have come.'

'Maybe.'

More tea was poured. In the hearth a trickle of soot pattered down on to the newspaper which was stuffed up the chimney.

Liz Newbould sighed. 'And what was in the brown one?'

'Ministry,' her husband told her gloomily. 'Upping the percentage we've got to plough. They're daft; it'll ruin good pasture, all this ploughing. I'd like them to see the stuff we turn up. There's not more than an inch of soil on those hills.'

It was a long speech. He sat back, tired, and drank his tea.

'Townfolks,' his wife agreed.

The grandfather clock wheezed, was silent and then broke into rapid striking.

George Newbould waited until it had done, then got up and stretched. 'Ay,' he said, looking at the clock as if it had addressed him personally, 'time for milking.'

After he had gone his wife set about clearing the table, moving briskly between the kitchen and scullery. Nell watched her. On the opposite side of the hearth was the empty chair where her mother used to sit. It was as well, she reflected, that it had been her mother who had died and not her aunt, for her mother had never done anything, at least nothing useful like cooking and washing and clearing the table. She had always been there, in bed or in the chair, but never actually moving about. It was always her aunt who was busy. If Aunt Lizzie died, whatever would become of them all?

She looked anxiously at her aunt, who was vigorously sweeping crumbs off the table-cloth and seemed in good health, and then she slid off her stool and went and attached herself to her aunt's skirt, gripping a fistful of it near the hem. Her aunt took no notice, but went on her brisk way into the scullery, her niece following in her wake like a small tug.

'Top-and-tail'll do tonight,' Aunt Liz said, rubbing Nell's face hard with a flannel. 'By, but you've caught the sun, that you have.'

It was true: her face and legs burned. She noticed with interest a clear white line round her ankles where the socks had reached. The bathroom linoleum was pleasantly cool under her bare feet. The sun streaming in through the skylight made a small bright square on the dark green. Into this she carefully fitted her feet and looked down at them with satisfaction. Then, with everything else, they suddenly disappeared from view as her aunt pulled her nightdress without warning over her head.

'There, that's you done,' Aunt Liz said, and taking her by the hand hurried her out on to the landing. The passage to her room was cool and dark and smelled of old wood and furniture polish. She shared a room with Chrissie, or rather she had a little bed under the window in Chrissie's room. She liked her bed, which had a patchwork quilt; somehow in the whole house her bed seemed to be the only thing which really belonged to her. Under it she had a small red case which belonged to her father, inside which were his letters tied up in a bundle with blue string, all in order. In them he told her about the house they would have when he came out of the army, how they would live together, the two of them, after the war, but until then she must be very good and do everything that her aunt and uncle told her. The letters had all been read to her and in reply she had sent him drawings enclosed in the adults' letters; usually they were drawings of houses.

'Kneel down now,' her aunt ordered, and she knelt obediently and folded her hands together as her aunt said the Lord's Prayer and asked God's blessing on each member of the family in turn. Aunt Liz made her requests brusquely and scarcely paused for breath before adding, 'Now into bed with you,' so that it was not clear if it was her niece or her creator that she was packing away for the night. Then she gave Nell a quick peck on the cheek and went out.

Nell lay listening to the familiar sounds from downstairs; the thump of books as Derek unloaded his satchel on to the kitchen table, the drone of Chrissie reciting something foreign, the noise of china and cutlery as Aunt Liz washed up in the scullery, the clash of metal against stone as she turned the washing-up bowl upside-down in the sink when she had finished. Outside the window Nell could hear the occasional hum or buzz of an insect, and then, as a slight breeze got up, the gentle scraping of the climbing rose against the window pane. The scent of stock and mignonette wafted up from the flower-bed at the foot of the wall. Sometimes she heard the lowing of cattle in the field behind the house and now and then the distant bleat of sheep on the hillside. The sounds and smells of the countryside filled her being, laying down layer upon layer of memory, below the level of all change, so that for the rest of her life when she smelled the sweet scent of evening flowers or walked between hills and heard the distant call of sheep, she felt at one with herself, although she did not remember why.

As she lay in bed now, listening intently, the present slipped into the past, and she felt again the hot cobbles under her feet, remembered the soap-and-lino smell of the bathroom and the old polished wood on the landing with its uneven floor which had creaked as she walked along it with her aunt. She felt again her aunt's work-roughened hand in hers and heard her sharp voice praying.

'God bless Daddy,' Nell suddenly commanded, her voice as peremptory as her aunt's. Then she fell asleep.

Chapter Two

Patrick Thorpe jumped down from the train at Bragton Station and strode across the platform. Heads turned. He was tall and very handsome. Two years' campaigning in North Africa had left him bronzed and fit. When people saw men like Patrick Thorpe in uniform in 1943 their spirits rose.

Conscious of the attention he attracted, he did not exactly swagger, but rather walked with a more self-conscious purposefulness than the situation required. He was, after all, only going to cross the road to catch the bus, and there was plenty of time.

He had so much time, in fact, that he decided to go and have a drink, as a result of which he missed the bus. There was an hour to go before the next one, which gave him time to buy a present for his daughter, which he had intended to do in London but had forgotten.

She must be five now, he calculated, as he looked at dresses in a shop window, but he had no idea of her size. He walked slowly on and came to a bookshop. She had started school, he thought as he turned over the picture-books, so presumably was learning to read. But he was afraid of getting her something either too difficult or too babyish, so came out without buying her anything. There didn't seem to be any toyshops in Bragton. In the end he bought her an exotic rose made of fine linen and highly scented with sophisticated perfume. It reposed in a cellophane box and the assistant who handed it to him envied the woman who would receive it.

He had time for another quick drink and then caught the bus to Netherby. He stared out of the window as the bus made its way out of the town and on to the open road. What hard countryside it is, he thought, watching the grey walls and bare hillsides slip by. Hardly any trees. He preferred something more lush himself; the kind of wooded slopes and gently undulating parklands you got in the south. The people up here were hard, too, he thought, stern and unfriendly like the land they lived in. Interesting the way people are formed by the surroundings. Not that Madge had been like that, not at all. Nobody could have been less like her sister Liz than his Madge. She was gentle and vulnerable, he thought with longing. She was soft and rounded, whereas Liz was all sharp edges.

The bus slowed and turned off the main road and began the long winding trail into the village. He hadn't been here since the day he came on compassionate leave for his wife's funeral. Before that he had been only once; he had brought his wife and baby here when he was called up. At least he would know they were safe up here with Madge's sister and her family, he had thought, whatever happened to him. For they had all assumed that he was the one whose life was in danger; they had not known of the enemy within her body.

Patrick Thorpe thought of these things as the bus approached his sister-in-law's home, and he would have given anything for a bottle of whisky.

Liz opened the door to him.

'You're late,' she stated as he stepped over the threshold.

'I missed the bus.'

All the same, she welcomed him kindly and his room was prepared for him.

'I'll just brew the tea,' she said. 'It's all ready.'

He thanked her and again thought longingly of whisky.

'You'll be able to meet her out of school in a few minutes,' she said as she poured out his tea. 'She'd like that.'

'How is she, my little Eleanora?'

'Nell? She . . .' She hesitated. 'She frets.'

'For her mother still?'

'No. For you.'

'For me?' He looked at his sister-in-law in amazement. 'But she doesn't even know me.'

'All the more reason,' she said.

The village school was a Victorian building, ecclesiastical in style, with long narrow windows high up in the wall, and lavatories at the far end of the playground. The heavy double doors were still closed when Patrick arrived. He stood deciphering the carving above the door which proclaimed that the school had been built by a local benefactress called Adelaide Symons in 1836. Suddenly a bell rang and the latest beneficiaries of this lady's charity swarmed out into the playground.

A little girl with long dark hair stood for a moment on the steps. She saw him and sprang forward, colliding with a group of children. 'It's my daddy,' he heard her shout. 'I said I had a daddy, I said I had.'

She shot like a bullet across the yard and hurtled herself into his arms. The words had shocked him; indeed it seemed as if a bullet had grazed his heart. He clung to her. The words *I must never let her down* came into his mind, unbidden.

He could not take his eyes off her that evening; she was so vibrant with life, his daughter. Everything she did seemed like a celebration. Not that she was noisy or wild with it, just quietly, intensely alive and feeling. The two older children, who came in later by bus, were noisier, talked more and argued, but they had none of her inner fire. Patrick Thorpe observed this with some satisfaction. It pleased him that his child was cast in a different mould; after all, she came from the south, she was in a way destined to be a city child, though of course it was good to have country joys too, he conceded; but she was not a child of the soil the way her cousins were.

'Calm down now, Nell,' Aunt Liz said after tea. 'You're overexcited. It'll be tears before bedtime.'

'Oh no, Auntie Liz, I *promise*,' her voice was positive; how could tears enter into the scheme of things on this day of days?

'Shall we go for a walk this evening?' Patrick asked when the older children had finished their homework.

Nell jumped up.

'I think it's daft,' Derek objected, 'the way townsfolk want to walk in the country.'

'That's enough,' his father said. 'You'll go for a walk with your uncle.'

Derek did not argue, but made it plain that he consented with ill grace. 'Farmers are walking all day,' he pointed out. 'They don't have to do it for exercise.'

'Look sharp,' his mother told him. 'Your boots are outside the door.'

'Show your uncle where we've lately ploughed,' his father told him. 'You wouldn't credit the rubbish we've turned up, Patrick.'

They walked up the lane behind the house, the two older children running ahead, Nell holding her father's hand, dancing along at his side and every now and then glancing up at him to make sure he was really and truly still there. They came to a newly ploughed field. Great rocks and boulders had been turned up by the plough.

'It's daft,' Derek said knowledgeably. 'It's grazing land, is this, and it'll take years to get it right.'

'We have to grow as much food as we can,' Patrick pointed out, 'because of the war.'

'Them as made war should have thought about that,' Derek said darkly.

Patrick smiled to himself; the boy evidently modelled himself on his father. All the same, it was true: the soil on these hills was so thin that everywhere the limestone broke through it, like the bones of the world showing through the thin skin of earth.

He breathed deeply. It was a perfect evening, everything calm. Clouds drifted gently across the sky, their shadows moving slowly over the green hillsides. The child at his side wore an expression of pure bliss.

'Enjoying it?' he asked her.

She had no words, she wasn't used to saying what she felt

because it was something the Newboulds never did. She thought for a while and then said carefully, 'Yes, thank you. It's being a lovely walk, isn't it?' He agreed that it was and she felt pleased with her first attempt at grown-up conversation.

Derek and Chrissie stopped at the top of the hill and were looking through a gate. A sheep stared back at them. As Nell and her father caught up with them, Derek turned to his sister and said, 'Do *you* know what it is, Chrissie?'

Chrissie shook her head.

Patrick looked from one child to the other with disbelief. He had known that country children were a bit slow on the uptake, but this really was incredible.

'You tell them,' he said to his daughter.

Nell shook her head.

'It's a *sheep*, of course,' Patrick cried out, half mocking, half exasperated.

It was the children's turn to look with disbelief. They stared up at him in silent wonder and then Derek broke out in a great peal of laughter.

'It's a *sheep*, he said, a *sheep*,' roared Derek, breaking into a kind of clod-hopping dance in his heavy boots.

Chrissie, always much more aware of the proprieties than her brother, looked embarrassed. 'I'm sorry, Uncle,' she said politely, 'but you see it isn't a Dalesbred, nor a Swaledale, which is what our dad usually stocks.' She hesitated. 'It could be a Masham, but I'm not rightly sure. That's what Derek means.'

Derek evidently meant nothing of the kind for he kept up his rough laughter and clod-hopping dance. 'A sheep,' he repeated, 'a sheep. By gum, that's clever,' he added, varying his refrain as he watched his kicking feet with more admiration than their finesse warranted.

Suddenly he found, to his surprise, that instead of the ground and his feet upon it, he was regarding the blue sky. He was staring fixedly up at it and the back of his head felt uncomfortable. He realized, with astonishment, that it was Nell who had butted him in the stomach and sent him flying backwards. Even now as he looked up at the unexpected sky, his view was darkened by her furious little face. Her mouth was wide open and she was shouting, 'Be quiet, you, or I'll bash you, I will.' In her hand she was holding a stone which she had evidently snatched from the top of the dry-stone wall.

'I will, I will,' she continued, waving the stone threateningly above her head.

'It's all right, Eleanora,' Derek heard his uncle say, the name sounding strangely inappropriate to the small dark fiend that straddled him. Then, to his relief, both child and stone were removed from their close proximity to his face. His uncle held out his hand to help him to his feet, but Derek had a strong sense of dignity even in the midst of humiliation and got up without assistance. He strode on ahead and, after a moment's hesitation, his sister followed him.

'It's all right, Eleanora,' her father said again, taking her hand after he had carefully replaced the stone on the wall. 'It was only a joke.'

Her face was still working with rage and misery; there were angry little red patches on cheeks which had otherwise gone very white.

'It was funny,' he went on. 'Derek was right to laugh. You have to learn to take a joke against yourself, you know.'

But it wasn't a joke against myself, it was against *you*, she wanted to protest, but couldn't say a word in explanation of her grief, nor tell why it was intolerable, so continued on the ruined walk in silence.

Chapter Three

The speed with which Nell learned to read was a matter of wonder not only to the Newboulds but also to Mrs Blunt who taught her and who confided to her aunt that she had never had a child pick it up so quickly. She could only suppose that Nell wanted to get at the big fairy-story book which was reserved for those who could read to themselves as an inducement to those who preferred to let others do their reading for them. But she was wrong. Nell's goal was not the book, it was her father's letters: more than anything in the world she wanted to read them for herself. It wasn't that her aunt did not read them clearly or willingly enough when they arrived each week. It was just that she wanted them to belong entirely to her, to possess them without other eyes having asserted their priority over them. She carried them now unopened upstairs, sat down on her bed by the window and very carefully read each word. His easy round writing presented no problems. She replied by return of post, usually drawing a picture of the house they would share when the war was over – for he always said that they would live together when the war stopped – and kept his letter by her, rereading it although she soon knew it by heart. Only when the next one arrived did she add the old one to the bundle tied with blue string and replace them all carefully in the little red case under the bed.

Apart from reading she had few skills. She showed no sign of being good with her hands like Chrissie who could knit and sew very well for her eleven years, and who already helped her mother about the house, cooking and washing-up. Chrissie was tall for her years and well made. Her face was much plumper than her mother's; it was a pretty, good-humoured face which Nell liked to look at. She enjoyed the comfortable feel of her cousin when she picked her up and hugged her when she fell, and the soothing tone of her voice when she took the infuriating tangle of wool that always developed when Nell tried to knit and said, 'Here, let me show you how', and made it all come right.

She couldn't remember her cousin Chrissie ever saying anything nasty. At least, not on purpose.

It was a different matter with Derek. Not that he was spiteful, just that he never minded laughing at things which might hurt and always said the first thing that came into his head. There was something clumsy about him, though like his sister he was good with his hands and already helped his father on the farm. He was dark and thickset and sharp-featured like his parents. Nell was afraid of him. He was an additional reason for wanting the war to end.

There were other reasons too, for the war had meant fear for as long as she could remember. It wasn't that she was afraid of anything like faraway Germans; the war brought other terrors near at hand, like the blackout and the Home Guard and evacuees.

She was not afraid of the dark, in fact she rather liked it. But she was made uneasy by the fear that beset the adults that they would be found guilty of letting a chink of light escape from doors or windows. Nobody ever said exactly what happened if you did, but there was no punishment which might not be conceived by men called Air Raid Wardens who had absolute power in these matters. The Home Guard too were an ever-present danger with their manoeuvres and the terrifying noise they made in the village hall. Once they even reversed a vehicle into Mrs Martin's house on the green, making a huge hole in the wall and opening up her sitting-room for everyone to see. Nell never forgot the sight of the jagged yawning gap in the thick wall and the dust all over the room and the great lump of mortar on Mrs Martin's grand piano. Nobody but the Home Guard would have dared to do that to Mrs Martin, the terror of the village, of whom even the vicar was said to be afraid.

But of all the terrors inflicted on her by the war, the evacuees were undoubtedly the worst. There had been a few of them there when she first started school but the second wave moved in a few months later. They came unheralded and took over the playground with scant regard for the rights of its former occupiers. When she heard on the wireless of the enemy occupying foreign countries, she always pictured them swarming in like the evacuees.

The Hitler among them was a boy called Alf, from Southport. She always tried to keep out of his way and make herself too little and inconspicuous to be worth his notice. She suspected that it was Derek who had told Alf that she was afraid of worms. Everything else in the animal kingdom she liked; she wasn't even afraid of things that might hurt you, like wasps. But worms filled her with horror and disgust. One day she found herself alone in the playground with Alf between her and the door through which the others had just passed. Alf was dangling from his hand a great fat wriggling worm. She saw him recognize with delight the terror in her face; she was doomed.

He waved the worm in front of her nose. It was fat and mauve and had a thick grey band around its middle.

'Are you 'ungry?' Alf asked, grinning with enjoyment of her terror. 'Like a nice worm for your dinner?'

Behind him, on the other side of the door, she could hear the blessed hum of voices in the schoolroom. To be safe inside there seemed like heaven.

'No thank you,' she said politely, placatingly. 'You are funny,' she added, remembering that sometimes it worked if you pretended that you thought they were only joking. It didn't work with Alf.

'Funny, am I? Then I'll tell yer what. I'll pull down yer knickers and shove it up yer bum.'

He lunged at her, but with courage born of desperation she suddenly lashed out at him, thumping him on the chest so hard that she fell against him, feeling his brown jerkin rough against her cheek. Then she turned and fled down the path before he could recover from her change of attitude.

She dived through the gate, slipped on the steps and fell into the road. The postman was doing his round, and she landed in front of his wheels. He fell off his bicycle and there was a lot of clattering and some blood. Mrs Blunt came out, shouting questions and reprimands. Nell expected to get into trouble for leaving the playground and running out into the road, but for some reason she did not get the punishment she deserved. With the utter inexplicability of adults, Mrs Blunt helped her gently up, petted her and put a plaster on her knee. She even gave her a drink of water for looking pale. Then she sent her home early with a note for Aunt Liz.

She seemed to be quite a heroine. The postman called to enquire after her and brought her some sweets. Aunt Liz removed the plaster and substituted for it a much more impressive-looking bandage. She was terrified of going to school the next day but couldn't of course tell them about Alf, so pretended she felt dizzy and was allowed to stay at home. She hoped to keep up this pretence until the end of the war, but after three days her aunt sent her back to school.

She managed to keep out of Alf's way until playtime when, as she sat momentarily alone on a bench in the yard, he came up to her and sitting down next to her, muttered, 'Thanks for not tellin' on me. Th'art a grand lil lass,' and he put his big red hand on her undamaged knee and his fingers were fat and mauve like worms with grey bands at the knuckles. She stared at them in growing horror and then, grinning to hide her fright, ran off shouting, 'S'all right,' hoping that he would not see how her legs wobbled with fear.

Although she was no longer quite so afraid of the evacuees, it was nonetheless a relief when they began, one by one, to return to where they had come from. The war, it seemed, was likely to be soon over. She hardly dared hope; she tried not to let herself even think the words. But at last, on a June evening, it happened. They sat in a semicircle, her aunt and uncle, her cousins and herself around the wireless, concentrating on its shiny wooden presence and listening to the voice of the man who said 'the War in Europe is over'. It was a measure of the gravity of the occasion that even the children did not whoop or shout, but listened, ears strained, to everything else that was said on the subject. Only then did Derek and Chrissie dash off to make sure that their friends knew. Uncle George said, 'It's over then,' and Aunt Liz went to put the kettle on, but seemed to walk more lightly than usual.

Nell neither spoke nor ran out after her cousins. Conscious of a marvellous kind of inner stillness, she went quietly upstairs. She collected her clothes from the cupboard and put them on the bed. She took the last letter from her father and arranged it in the bundle, retying the string, for there would not need to be another. She took her dressing-gown from the hook behind the door and her nightdress from under her pillow. When she had put everything ready, placing as much as possible in the little red case and leaving the rest in a pile beside it, she sat down on her bed to wait.

It was dark when her aunt came and found her.

'Whatever are you doing up here so quiet?' she asked.

'I'm ready,' Nell told her. 'Please, could I have a carrier bag?'

'What for?'

'The war's over,' she explained patiently. 'And I can't get everything into the red case.'

Liz stared at her for a moment. Then she came quickly across to the bed.

'It'll take time,' she said.

'What will?'

'For the war to get itself properly over.'

'But it *is* over.' Her voice sounded desperate.

'But the soldiers can't leave the army all at once. It might be quite a while before your father can be spared – demobilized they call it.'

'Why?'

'Because it's the opposite of mobilized, I suppose.'

'Oh,' Nell said, though that wasn't what she had meant.

'Tell you what, there's going to be a victory celebration – the biggest bonfire you've ever seen, up on top of Westerbirt, and we'll all go up. You'll like that. It's next week, one evening.'

'Say Daddy came when I was out?'

'He won't,' her aunt told her flatly. 'Now you'd better put everything back where it was,' she said, picking up the dressing-gown and returning it to its hook. 'Make it all nice and tidy.'

Nell turned her face away. She did not cry, but her face was white and pinched.

'Can you manage?' her aunt asked, from the doorway.

'Yes, thank you.'

And she did manage, because she had no option.

Chapter Four

The winter of 1947 was as cold as anyone could remember. The roads into Bragton were blocked with snowdrifts so that Derek and Chrissie could not go to school, and even Nell had one day off when her aunt decided that the weather was too bad for her to go out. They had a paraffin heater burning day and night on the landing and various little lamps under pipes to stop them freezing. But nothing stopped the lavatory from freezing up; every morning Uncle George had to melt it with a blowlamp.

Outside it was magical; the grown-ups might grumble, but to Nell it was pure delight. At first the snow fell heavily and evenly, mantling village and hills alike. Then the wind swept the snow off the hillsides, piling it up in corners, whipping it up against the walls and leaving great clear patches in the middle of fields. In the lanes the snowdrifts were six feet high at least and carved by the sculpting wind into marvellous shapes. Nearer home she got to know the individual drifts. In the paddock behind the back garden was a huge one whose great overhanging crest of snow hung perilously forward like a frozen wave, for the wind had cut all the snow away from the base; it seemed miraculous that it could stay like that, unsupported and yet so fragile.

The snow made a deep frame round her bedroom window and every morning she peered out anxiously in case it had all melted in the night. But frozen week followed frozen week and still the snow remained. On a bright morning it was brilliant, the crystals sparkling each with its own distinct colour. On less sunny days the snow had a softer, more uniform glow and in the evening it would turn slate-blue with cold. There weren't many trees, but every twig and every evergreen leaf was thickened and frozen hard. In the breeze they jangled and tinkled like bells.

The thaw came like a defeat. The trees dripped miserably and the top of the snowdrift in the paddock crashed down. Nell went outside and stood watching helplessly; the air was filled with little crackling sounds as the snow disintegrated all around her. Everything was being spoiled and she could do nothing to save it. She ran indoors trying not to cry.

In the evening they heard what sounded like thunder. Then they realized that it was great cascades of snow thudding down off the roofs of the farm and the outbuildings.

'It's dangerous, is that,' Uncle George said. 'I must go and clear it.'

He took a broom and a spade to loosen the snow and went to get a ladder.

'It'll kill him if it catches him on the ladder,' Chrissie said, in a rare display of nerves.

'Your dad knows what he's about,' Liz reproved her.

Nell almost hated her uncle for conniving at the end of the snow. She went to bed early, dreading the morning. When it came she had to force herself to pull aside the curtain and look out.

She could hardly believe her eyes. The world had been reprieved. Gently and silently while she slept the snow had fallen, covering up the works of man and undoing all her uncle's efforts on the roof. Instead of the messy green slush she had expected to see, the hills and fields were again covered in deep and satisfactory whiteness.

'Drat the snow,' Aunt Liz said, clucking her teeth disapprovingly. 'And after all that going up on the roof, too.'

'Never mind,' her uncle said philosophically. 'It's good insulation, like. It'll keep the bedrooms warm.'

Nell liked that: it was nice to think of her bedroom kept warm and cosy under its soft blanket of snow.

'There's a letter from your dad, Nell,' her aunt said.

Nell did not move; she sat with her porridge spoon in mid-air, her eyes not leaving her aunt's face.

'He's coming next Friday, if it suits. Just to stay the weekend,' she added, answering the unspoken question in her niece's eyes.

Nell knew, of course, that he was out of the army. Two months ago he had written to say that he was demobilized.

This time she had not gone upstairs to pack; she had learned caution.

He had continued to write to her every week and she knew that he was busy looking for a house for them, because he had told her so.

'Can you answer it for me, Nell?' her aunt went on, handing her the letter. 'Tell him it's all right and we'll expect him at the time he says.'

She went upstairs to her bedroom. She stared out at the snow, hardly able to believe what had happened. On such a morning to have such news! She read the letter carefully; it was to both of them really and she knew that her aunt wouldn't want it, so after a moment's thought she put it with her others in the red case. Then she settled down to answer it. Writing carefully and laboriously she gave him her aunt's message. She said that she hoped he would find a house soon, so that she could come and live with him. She wrote two pages and then put the letter in an envelope, got a stamp from her aunt and went to the post.

The snow-plough had been through the village. She walked between the great chunky cliffs of snow that it had piled up on each side of the road and her footsteps made no sound. Everything was muffled and still. If only it stays like this until he comes, she thought.

It did. It meant that his journey took twice as long as it should have done, and when he finally arrived off the last bus from Bragton, he was chilled and exhausted. For a moment as he stood on the doorstep, silhouetted against the blackness of the night, she saw him as a stranger. His face, drawn and pinched with cold, looked older and yellow. It was the first time she had seen him out of uniform and he was smaller than she had remembered. She rushed across to him and, as she hugged him, his coat and face felt unbelievably cold.

There was something almost protective about the way Uncle George put an arm round his brother-in-law's shoulder and drew him inside the kitchen.

'By gum, tha' looks right frozen, lad,' he said, kicking the door closed behind him.

They sat him down in a chair by the fire and Aunt Liz bustled about getting him a hot drink and something to eat. Nell sat on a stool by his side and rubbed his cold hands. She was allowed to sit there talking to him although it was long past her bedtime.

The next day was disappointingly misty.

'It'll get out,' Uncle George told her at breakfast.

'Are you sure?'

'Ay, it'll be sunshine by ten o'clock.'

'And will it last all day?'

'Ay, it'll last while three o'clock this afternoon.'

Uncle George always knew about the weather. Sometimes on lovely mornings he would predict rain almost to the minute. He couldn't explain how he knew; it had to do with how the hills looked and the animals behaved, and how he felt in his bones.

'We could go out all day, then?'

'You could take a picnic,' her aunt surprisingly agreed.

'A picnic in February!' Derek put in contemptuously. He thought that picnics were silly even in the summer. Fortunately both he and Chrissie had exams so nobody even suggested that they should go too.

So they set off, the two of them, with provisions for the day, and it was like an adventure into a strange land. There had been a slight thaw in the night, followed by frost, so more icicles had formed on the walls of the farm and the road outside was icy. The roadman was busy spoiling things by spreading grit, but the lanes he would not spoil.

It was up the lanes that she and her father walked that Saturday. She hardly stopped talking, so if he was quieter than he had once been she did not notice. The snow in the lanes had melted to form long pools in the ruts, which had then frozen over. The ice cracked and crunched under their feet as they walked. The air was as still and cold against her cheeks as packs of invisible ice.

'It hurts your teeth when you talk, have you noticed?' she asked.

'Pull your scarf up over your mouth like mine.'

'Oh, I don't mind.'

'Are your hands warm enough?'

'Yes. Aunt Liz knits gloves which go underneath and then mittens a bit bigger to go on top. Look.'

She began peeling off one mitten, but he stopped her.

'I'll believe you. Keep them on. She always knits for you, does she?'

'Oh yes. Chrissie does, too. She made my jumper. I told you in my letter.'

'Ah, the one you drew. They're kind to you, aren't they,

your aunt and uncle?'

'Of course they are,' she said, and laughed; it seemed such a funny question. Then she added, 'I'm kind to them too, I think.'

'I'm sure you are. You all get on very well and I'm glad of that, because . . .' He hesitated.

She waited, but he changed the subject.

'Which is your favourite lesson at school, Nell?'

She considered. 'I like band best,' she said. 'And then I like poetry.'

'What's your favourite poem?'

'It's about a little old lady and more than anything else she wants her own little home to live in. Shall I go on?'

'Yes.'

'You see, she hasn't a home. Not one of her *very* own. And she wants one more than anything. You *know*, how you do?'

He looked down uneasily at her eager face, cheeks flushed pink by the cold wind, dark hair tucked into a woollen hat.

'And she describes her little house and it's ever so homey. She wants a dresser with her own plates and things on it, "speckled and white and blue and brown". I like plates like that. But I'd have a bit about my bed if I wrote that poem and it would have a patchwork quilt.'

'And what's your *second* favourite poem?' Patrick interrupted.

'Oh, that's my second favourite as well, and my third and fourth and on and on for ever.'

She began to dance. 'Because we'll have a house one day and it'll be just like that, won't it?'

'Yes, my darling, it will be just exactly as you want it.'

She was silent, drifting along, basking in his words. Then she sighed deeply.

'Will it be *very* long?' she asked.

'Well,' he replied carefully. 'These things take time . . .'

'What things?'

'Finding the right house, finding the money, arranging the purchase, all sorts of legal complications which little girls don't understand.'

'Ye-es, but really it all *starts* with just wanting it, doesn't it? Then you make all those other things happen?'

'That's true.' He sighed. 'Yes, that's very true.'

'So it shouldn't be long?'

'No. Meanwhile you are quite happy here with your Newbould relations, aren't you? They seem very kind to you.'

'Yes.'

'That's the spirit.'

The word seemed to remind him of something.

'Shall we have our picnic now?' he asked. 'I expect you'd like a drink.'

She thought about it.

'Yes,' she said. 'I'm thirsty.'

There was nowhere fit to sit down, so they climbed up the bank and crouched on their haunches in the lee of the wall. All around them the deep snow sparkled brilliantly under the ice-blue sky. He undid the picnic. There was a flask of tea, which he poured for her, but he himself had a cold drink from a big bottle. In fact he had three, while she drank her one cup.

She took off her mittens to eat the sandwiches, balancing them on her knees, covered by the thick brown stockings. Below them, in the lane, a little stream was still iced over, but they could see the water moving underneath it.

'Could fish live under the ice?' she asked.

'I think so. Though they'd need oxygen. No, I suppose they couldn't live long.'

'We'll ask Uncle George,' she said casually. 'He knows everything.'

He looked at her, surprised at this view of his brother-in-law.

'Well, about that kind of thing,' she qualified. 'And you must be right because there aren't any fish, are there? Just plants.'

Long weeds were drifting in the water under the ice. They looked very clear and delicate.

'It's like Mr Bartholomew's,' she said.

'Why?'

'You know, under his glass case. He's the jeweller in Bragton.'

She often forgot that her father didn't know everything about her world. Only the things she wrote in her letters, and she hadn't thought to tell him about Bartholomew's shop with its watches and rings and precious stones set out on green velvet, in a big glass box so that you could see but not touch, like strange creatures in an aquarium.

When they set off again he asked her once more about how kind her relations were to her. It puzzled her: everybody knew how kind the Newboulds were.

'People in the village say that nobody's kinder than Auntie and Uncle,' she told him. 'Mrs Blunt said that because of Darky.'

'Who is Darky?'

'You know, the tramp. He doesn't have a home, he just walks about and sleeps outside in the summer and in barns in the winter. Everybody knows him; he used to come often before the war and Uncle George always let him have the barn. But one day when he came it was sheep-dipping. You know how all the others use Uncle's sheep dip?'

He didn't know.

'It's up at the back by Chisholm's Gap,' she explained. 'Well, the farmers had their sheep up there for dipping, you know how they do to get the lice out before they're shorn?'

He nodded. It shocked him a little, her casual reference to things like lice.

'Well, some of the lads thought they'd dip old Darky too, because he was never very clean, so they took him and held him in the dip.'

'Good Lord!'

'They didn't mean no harm ...'

'*Any* harm,' he corrected.

'That's right, they just wanted to clean him up a bit, they didn't put his head under or anything. But they didn't know he had sores all over him. The arsenic in the dip got into him and he was very ill.'

'What a murderous lot of people you live among!'

'Oh no, really, they didn't want to hurt him. But what was special was that when Auntie and Uncle knew, they took him out of the barn and brought him home and nursed him till he was well.'

'He was in the house with you?' His voice was disapproving.

She nodded. 'Mrs Blunt said anybody else would have dumped him at the Poorhouse where he belonged.'

It happened exactly as Uncle George had foretold; just before three o'clock thick clouds rose up from behind the hills and the air lost all its brightness. It was as if a hand had been put over the sun.

They were nearly back in the village by then. Knowing that they hadn't much more time alone, she broached the subject that had been in her mind all day, but which she hadn't liked to mention because it was too important.

'Even if we haven't got a house yet, can I come and stay with you?'

'Yes, I think it could be arranged,' he said. Then he hesitated and added, 'I'm going into digs shortly and I expect you could come and stay for the odd weekend.'

She had expected it would be for longer than that, for the school holidays perhaps, but she was so pleased to have a definite promise that she didn't press for more.

They did not talk after that, the evening air was cold and damp and raw: they kept their mouths shut against it and concentrated on keeping warm by swinging their arms and stamping their feet as they walked down the lane to the farm.

It was an evening intended by nature for sitting round the fire. She was sorry when her father went out after supper, but she was tired and easily persuaded by her aunt to go to bed early. She was asleep before Chrissie came up.

She awoke to hear a considerable noise, shouting, and a queer kind of singing. She lay very still, listening. She was used to the familiar noises of the house, even sounds from the village street, but this she had never heard, except something a bit like it on Victory night, when, after the bonfire on Westerbirt, the men had celebrated late in the village pub and sung afterwards in the streets and her aunt and uncle had said it was a disgrace. This noise was a bit like that, though not nearly so loud.

She whispered her cousin's name, but Chrissie did not stir; Chrissie could sleep through anything.

She heard her uncle's voice, then her aunt's. Something like a large animal seemed to be bumping about in the kitchen and once there was loud, wild laughter. Instinct told her that there would be trouble if she appeared on the scene; grown-ups bestow guilt on children who witness anything they don't want them to see. So she just lay and listened.

The sound diminished and she was drifting off to sleep when she heard renewed noises on the stairs, bumping and sudden snatches of song and loud remarks which she couldn't make out, and her aunt's voice talking much more quietly than usual, soothingly as she did to sick animals sometimes when Uncle George brought them into the kitchen to be nursed. But what kind of sick animal could it be that they would bring upstairs?

They were going the other way, towards her father's room.

Suddenly she feared for him, didn't want him disturbed by this trouble, whatever it was. He was worried enough already. She slipped out of bed and crept over to the door. It was slightly open, she didn't need to push down the catch which always clattered. She inched it open and slid her head and shoulders round the door, keeping the rest of her body in the bedroom ready for a swift leap back into bed. Her aunt and uncle, she could just make out by the light at the top of the stairs, had their backs towards her. They were half carrying, half propping up something bulky between them like a huge parcel. It went through her mind that it might be some surprise present for one of the children, but there was something about the way they moved which wasn't cheerful enough for that. Almost immediately the fear came to her that they might be involved in a dreadful crime: perhaps it was a great sack of stolen goods they were dragging along, something to do with the black market, she thought, her eyes starting out of her head.

Then she saw that the sack had legs, little tiny ones. No, they were bent up under it, trailing. Slowly, as her eyes grew accustomed to the dim light, she made out the head, which was lolling forward, but unmistakably a head, she realized now, making out the bump of the nape of the neck. With horror she saw that they were dragging a dead body along the landing. She screamed.

They turned. In fact they all three turned at the sound, because it was not a dead body after all. It was a live, crumpled heap of a man and the head, when it turned to her, was her father's.

It seemed best to Nell, next day, to go along with her aunt and uncle's inexplicable belief that she didn't remember anything of the previous night's excitement. Her father was still in bed at breakfast-time and no reference was made to him except to say that he was lying in because he was overtired. No, he wasn't ill, they reassured Nell, just a bit poorly. He'd had a tiring journey from London, and then a long walk yesterday. Many soldiers were exhausted by the war, and must be looked after and allowed to rest. Uncle George even made an unusually long speech about what the rest of us owed the men who had fought for us against the Germans, which was unlike his usually short but strongly expressed views about the farmers winning the war.

She was allowed to take a cup of coffee up to him later that morning. She went into the darkened room, put the coffee down by the bed and drew back the curtains. It was another brilliant morning; the sun would be bound to do him good.

'Close the curtains,' his voice said grumpily. 'I can't stand the light.'

She closed the curtains and crept out.

He stayed in bed all day and she did not go up to his room again, fearful of his irritation.

He was better the next day and able to travel back to London. The bus into Bragton left at half past eight, so she was able to see him off before she went to school. It was a raw and sunless morning as they walked through the village to the bus stop. He looked pale and didn't talk much. She worried about his health; she couldn't ask him about the strange attack because he thought she didn't know about it, but she did say that she hoped he looked after himself in London, and suggested, without much hope, that she might perhaps come and cook for him. She was desperately afraid that he would be taken ill again and have nobody to care for him.

'In your digs, will you be all alone?' she asked.

'No, it's a big house, and the landlady lets off rooms. We share the bathroom – you know the kind of thing.'

She didn't, but nodded.

The bus shelter was a little stone building, deeply thatched now with snow. They went inside and stood stamping their feet. It was only marginally less cold inside than out.

A farmer and his wife drove past and waved to Nell. Their car crunched slowly along the road, the chains on its wheels cutting diamond patterns in the snow. Then the roadman came along pushing a wheelbarrow full of grit. He greeted Nell cheerfully.

'You seem friends with everyone in the village,' her father remarked.

'Oh yes, I am.'

'You feel at home up here, then?'

'Oh no,' she said in surprise. The people in the village were her friends, of course, and as familiar to her as the surrounding hills and lanes. But it wasn't home. Home was something quite different. Home was where he was.

Soon he would be gone; she stared at the bend in the road where it disappeared round the corner by the high wall. At exactly that point the red bus would appear like an enemy to take him away. She did not take her eyes off the corner, not wanting to be taken unawares.

'But you are happy here?' her father insisted.

'Yes.'

'Because you see it will take a little while to find the right house for us. It's very difficult to find anywhere to live in London.'

'Then we could live somewhere else where it's easier.'

'There's the question of work, you know. I have to live where the work is.'

'Oh yes, I'd forgotten.'

She was silent, ashamed of revealing her childishness.

'But I'm still trying very hard, Nell. Really I am. Please don't think I'm not.'

She glanced up at him, startled by the desperation in his voice; of course she knew that he was trying; didn't he always tell her so in his letters?

'I'm doing everything I can,' he went on, looking anxiously down at her.

She shouldn't have taken her eyes off that corner of the road. The bus seized the opportunity to creep up on them, so that it was suddenly there, grinding to a halt by the bus shelter, hissing steam out of its radiator.

Almost before she knew what had happened, her father had kissed her good-bye and climbed aboard and she was standing alone by the roadside while the bus, still grinding and hissing, carried him away out of sight.

Chapter Five

Weeks turned into months and months to years; the bundle of letters grew fat and unwieldy and had to be divided into two. Letter after letter told her how hard he was trying to find a home for them, but something always seemed to go wrong. A house would seem perfect and then turn out to have unsuspected disadvantages. Or he would find a house which he really liked, only to discover at the last moment that it was already sold. Meanwhile he had moved into his rooms, all right for himself but not suitable for her. She must stay where she was for just a little while longer; the sort of home they were going to have together was worth waiting for, he said.

So she waited, and when he came on brief visits he told her how pleased he was that she was managing so well and seemed so happy with the Newboulds. Then he went away again, promising that it would not be long now before they had a home. He promised, too, that he would soon be in new digs where she might come and stay.

She was eleven when the invitation finally came: there was a spare room available at his digs for a weekend a fortnight hence, he wrote, and if the Newboulds agreed she could come and stay in it.

'Oh, Aunt Liz,' she burst out when she opened the letter, hardly able to believe its contents. 'I can go, can't I?'

Her aunt took the letter in silence. She handed it across to her husband and they looked at each other without speaking.

Then at last George said, 'It's not fitting.'

'What isn't?' Nell asked, thinking he was referring to her clothes.

'Going to his rooms, like,' George continued to his wife as if Nell had not spoken.

'Oh, *please*,' Nell begged, almost in tears.

'And think of the journey,' added George, who had never been more than fifty miles from home.

'We'll talk about it later, your uncle and me,' Aunt Liz said firmly, and Nell knew that she was reproving her husband as much as her niece.

They did talk about it later. She heard their voices in earnest debate when she was in bed; her uncle's deep, slow sentences, her aunt's short quick replies. It was impossible to tell if they were disagreeing or not: Uncle George never sounded argumentative and Aunt Liz always did.

Nothing was said about it next day. It was a Saturday and she made herself as helpful as possible. She knew that her uncle was already worried because it was a wet summer and the hay harvest was difficult to get in. Often they would work in the fields all day turning it, cocking it up ready for gathering in, and then it would rain in the night, and they would have to go back and strew it all out again to dry the next day.

But today was the third hot day in succession; the first time such a thing had happened in weeks.

'I can help with haymaking all day, Uncle,' she offered virtuously at breakfast.

Her uncle nodded. 'We'll get that Fellscale field in today,' he told her.

'You'll get good help, being Saturday,' Liz remarked. 'The Philbys'll likely come.'

Nell was glad to hear that; the Philbys had a daughter of her own age, as well as a baby. Mr Philby was a schoolmaster in Bragton but he came of farming stock and, like other village families, they helped whenever they could with the haymaking.

All day long they toiled under the blazing sun, the men lifting great forkfuls of hay up on to the cart, where Uncle George stood engulfed in it, the women drawing it up into great stooks made out of piles which the children had formed from the twisted rows of hay. Nell's job was to drag a great wooden rake up and down the field, diligently scraping up all the scraps of hay that her elders had missed.

The hot, dusty day crawled past; her arms ached, her throat was dry and her head throbbed, but she was determined not to give in. She wanted her aunt and uncle to see how grown-up and capable she was; certainly capable of going on a train to London for the weekend. The trouble was that her aunt was so busy seeing to food and drink for everybody, and her uncle was so busy with his hay, that she feared neither of them had even noticed her efforts.

Meanwhile the Philby baby slept peacefully in its pram under the trees.

They joined it there in the evening when Liz and Chrissie brought the supper along from the farm, spreading out cups and plates of sandwiches, custard pies and great cans of tea and beer on the grass under the trees. The helpers ate ravenously; it was their only payment and it was generous.

'We'll be through in an hour,' George said, as they got up, rubbing protesting muscles and joints.

'You can come back with me, Nell,' Aunt Liz said. 'You'ye done enough.'

She would have liked to insist on staying, but she was so tired she wondered how she would even walk back to the farm. So she helped her aunt gather up the dishes and tins and they set off together, accompanied by Mrs Philby and the baby, who screamed in protest as the pram bumped up and down across the uneven field.

At the gate they went their separate ways; Aunt Liz waited until Mrs Philby was out of sight and then said almost casually to Nell, 'You can go to London. Mrs Blunt's new assistant is going that weekend and you can travel with her.'

She couldn't believe it.

'Are you sure?' she whispered.

'Yes. I went to see her this afternoon and arranged it.'

Still it wouldn't sink in. Yet it was all so incredibly simple; once grown-ups wanted something they just went ahead and arranged it.

It was the first time she had been on a long journey. She had been on a coach to Morecambe once to see 'Iolanthe' at the theatre and once she had been to Leeds to the pantomime. But this was a different matter altogether and required the loan of her aunt's big case to put her clothes in, and the taking of a packed lunch because it was such a long journey.

Mrs Blunt's husband took them to Bragton Station in his car and Aunt Liz and Chrissie came just for the ride. She felt sorry for them, left behind on the station platform as she waved rather grandly, aware of her importance as a traveller.

Fortunately Mrs Blunt's assistant was not a talkative kind of person; having explained to Nell that there was a lavatory down the corridor if she needed it, she settled herself to read. Nell had brought a book, but let it slip down on to her lap as she gazed at the countryside which flew past the window in an altogether unexpected manner. That must be the other side of Westerbirt, she thought, seeing an unfamiliar hump, and over there must be the far end of Cumberscale. Somehow she seemed to be seeing her world from the back.

The green and grey countryside slid past the windows and soon she was out of sight of any familiar landmarks. It struck her for the first time that her world, which seemed so immense when she was in it, was really very small. Now she was catching glimpses of other worlds; a woman glanced up at the train as she took her washing in, a boy on a bike pedalled furiously to keep up with the train where the road and rail ran parallel. She could see his flushed face, almost feel the pain in his chest. His world was that stretch of dusty road and his bike.

Between worlds there were long stretches of open countryside and telegraph wires that dipped strangely up and down, up and down. Another train rushed past them; the people on it looked not quite real as they sat there, moulded into their seats one behind the other in their separate compartments. They didn't know how funny they looked as they sat like that, each in his own little world.

It was certainly not a time to be reading *The Tale of Two Cities*.

The hours flew past; she ate her lunch absent-mindedly and afterwards couldn't remember doing so. Rows of houses appeared; in their back gardens some of them had lines of clothes which were hanging so close to the train that she felt she could lean out and touch them. In other back gardens children were playing; she wondered what it was like to live almost on a railway line.

Now that they were approaching London she could feel excitement rising in her like pain. The size of the place amazed her; the miles of streets, the jungle of roofs, of sheds, of warehouses. The railway lines crossed and recrossed and seemed to form patterns before her eyes, like a huge cat's cradle. The train stopped and seemed to wait for an age outside the station. Mrs Blunt's assistant put down her book and talked vaguely about London, her mind evidently not on what she was saying. It was a relief to both of them when the train lurched forward and a few minutes later they drew into King's Cross Station.

'I'll stay with you until we find your father,' Mrs Blunt's assistant said as they got off. 'Then on Sunday morning I'll look out for you just here by the barrier.'

'Yes, thank you,' Nell said, peering about.

There were such crowds of people waiting that it seemed hopeless to expect to find any one person among them, but suddenly there he was waving, and she hurried to him with Mrs Blunt's assistant, who stayed only a moment and was obviously anxious to be off.

Nell looked more closely at her father. He was different, much paler. When he hugged her she noticed that he had a very funny smell. He was thinner, at least his face was, and his clothes looked loose on him.

She held tightly to his hand as he took her out of the station and on to the bus, for she was afraid of being lost in the immense crowd that pressed against them. The bus was packed too, and they had to stand and could not talk properly. He asked her about the journey. She remembered the pleasure and excitement of it, all the newness, but couldn't put it into words, so just said, 'All right, thank you.'

'Long journeys are pretty tedious,' he agreed, and she couldn't even try to explain because the bus was swaying so.

They got out at a stop near some shops and he took her up side streets until they came to a very old-looking house, dirty and in need of paint.

'Welcome to Number Thirty-One,' he said. 'Home sweet home.'

His room was on the top floor, up two flights of stairs. He showed her which it was and then opened the door across the landing into the room which was to be hers. She looked around it appreciatively: her very own room. Temporary, maybe, but nonetheless her own.

He smiled down at her. 'You unpack,' he said, 'and I'll make a cup of tea.'

She put her things on the bed. A drawer had been left open so she filled that. When she opened another it was full of somebody else's clothes, so she shut it quickly and stuffed everything into the top drawer and then went to rejoin her father.

His room seemed to be a bit of everything; it had his bed in it and chairs and a table covered with books and papers. It had a gas-ring upon which the kettle was boiling, and he had laid a meal for them on a card table by the electric fire.

He showed her the bathroom, which seemed to serve as a kitchen as well, for it contained a collection of pans and dishes as well as several toothbrushes in mugs and old jars. It smelt damp and greasy.

'It's a lovely evening,' he said after they had eaten sardines on toast, and iced buns. 'How about a stroll?'

'Oh, yes,' she said, jumping up and running over to the window; below them for miles and miles lay a great expanse of houses. Always in the distance she could hear the roar of traffic like some great animal waiting. She was impatient to be off.

The card table and a large part of the room were littered with the remains of their supper. 'Should we clear up?' she asked doubtfully.

He glanced about him. 'No, let's leave it,' he said.

She thought of how meals were always cleared away in a

great rush by Aunt Liz and laughed because it seemed somehow wicked to leave this mess.

She had expected London to be big, but nothing that anyone had said had prepared her for what it was really like.

'Which bit is *really* London?' she asked as they set off.

'All of it, but it goes on for miles and then it straggles off in all directions into the suburbs. But I'll take you to the part which really means London to me.'

On the bus he asked for Westminster Bridge. They sat upstairs and she gazed at the houses and endless streets and was amazed at the number of people still walking and driving about, even though work must be over for the day and the shops shut long ago.

They got off the bus and he showed her the Houses of Parliament; she stared in awe at Big Ben. She was really here, standing with her father looking at Big Ben. Quietly she reached down and pinched her leg. Then fearfully glanced up again: Big Ben was still there.

'Can we wait until nine and hear it strike?'

'Of course. Anything you like. It's to be your treat, this holiday; we'll do exactly what you want.'

She wished he didn't look so sad.

They walked half-way across the bridge, and stood, leaning on the parapet looking at the Houses of Parliament. He talked to her about it, pointing out the terrace overlooking the Thames.

'Liquid history,' he said, and she marvelled.

At nine she stood staring up at Big Ben. As she watched the great clock face, she heard its booming voice. When it had ceased and the air no longer tingled with the echo of it, she stood there unable to break the silence. In the kitchen at the farm they would have heard that same sound on the wireless, yet she was actually here. She felt as if she was at the centre of the world.

They took another bus to a square with a fountain in it and a hot-dog stall at one side. He bought one for her and then they sat on a seat while she ate it.

'They're lovely, these London squares,' he said. 'Oases of green and quiet in a desert of streets.'

She saw what he meant in a way, but she liked the streets all the same.

'What do you usually do in the evening?' she asked him.

'Oh, I have a few friends, you know,' he said casually.

She sensed he did not want any more questions on this theme.

'I say,' he said, getting up suddenly, 'I meant to get some cigarettes. You don't mind if I pop into that pub on the corner, do you, Nell, to get a packet?'

She didn't mind, of course she didn't. They crossed the square and walked towards the pub.

'You wait here,' he said. 'Children aren't allowed inside. Shan't be a second.'

She waited for what seemed a great many seconds. Then she got tired of standing still and began to walk a little way up the road and back again. She had done this a few times when somebody touched her on the shoulder. She turned and smiled. But it was a stranger.

'Hello,' he said. 'Care to come for a drive?'

She stood, petrified.

'Got the car ready,' he went on, pointing to a sports car parked at the kerb.

'No, no,' she managed to whisper, stepping back.

'Oh, come on, don't be a spoil-sport,' he insisted, and his voice was urgent.

She looked frantically about. There had been so many people about a moment ago, but now the square was suddenly deserted. Even the hot-dog man had packed up his stall and departed. There was nobody to turn to for help.

He reached out his hand towards her and the feel of it horrified her into action. She bolted for the pub and managed to push her way through the revolving door, though she had never seen such a device before.

She found herself standing in a small dingy hall with several doors leading off. There was nobody about, but through a glass door she saw her father. Only he was not buying cigarettes. He was drinking. He was holding the glass tipped back so he did not see her. As she watched, he put it down and ordered another. She watched it being poured, then she went outside again to wait. The man with the sports car had gone. Soon afterwards her father reappeared. He was flushed and carrying a packet of cigarettes, which he held out smilingly like a peace-offering.

'Sorry to be so long,' he said. 'It's queues for everything nowadays. What do you want to do next?'

She shook her head.

'What do you do at home now?'

'Go to bed,' she admitted.

'Good Lord, I quite forgot old bedtime! Back home with you, young lady. We'll do it in style, eh? Take a cab.'

He made a few unsuccessful attempts to hail a taxi and in the end they caught a bus.

It was eleven o'clock when they climbed up the two flights of stairs to his room. The supper dishes were strewn about as they had left them and everything looked horrible. In the bathroom there were saucepans on the edge of the bath and an empty sardine tin in the basin. Suddenly she thought of the cool order of the Newboulds' kitchen and it all seemed so unfair that she wanted to cry.

'Bed with you,' her father said cheerfully, and she kissed him good night quickly and crossed the landing to her own room.

She slept until midday. Even then she might not have woken had she not heard voices on the stairs followed by loud knocking.

She went to her door and looked out; whoever it was had just gone into her father's room. She dressed, washed quickly and went across the landing.

Her father was still wearing his dressing-gown. Two visitors had arrived who were introduced to her as Douglas and Ian, army friends of his. Each of them had a full glass, as did her father.

'Douglas and Ian usually come round on Saturdays to cheer me up,' he told her apologetically.

'That's right, Nell,' Douglas said, putting an arm round her shoulders. He was the older of the two men, in fact he was almost bald although he had a thick moustache. 'We keep an eye on your old man for you.'

'See he doesn't get up to any tricks, eh?' Ian said, and shouted with laughter. He was tall and had a way of throwing himself about and talking very loudly.

'He's very proud of you, my dear,' Douglas said. 'If we drink to our Little Gels, he'll always raise his glass to the best little girl in the world – you.'

'How old are your little girls?' she asked, hoping they might come round to play if their fathers intended to stay.

The visitors laughed again. 'Older than you, my dear,' Douglas said.

'Or we'd be in serious trouble, eh what?'

There was more loud laughter and exchange of winks and nods.

'Well, what are the plans for today, Patrick?' Douglas asked at last.

'I thought I'd take Nell to the Tower, perhaps, or Kew – there's not much left of the morning, though.'

'How about painting the town red, eh, you and us and your little gel?'

'How about bringing the old jalopy round, Doug? And we'll have a teararound.'

'But . . .' Patrick began.

'No buts. No trouble at all. You'd like that, wouldn't you, Nell?'

'What's a jalopy?' Nell asked.

They all laughed again and shortly afterwards the two men left, promising to return after breakfast, which was the same as lunch.

The rest of the day was confused. The jalopy turned out to be nothing more than a rather elderly car which Ian drove in a way that even Nell could see was wild. First of all they went by the river and had a drink. But they kept setting off for other places. Douglas and Ian would say, 'Let's go up West,' or 'I know, let's go to Joe's place,' and all these places seemed to have some magical attraction, until they actually got there, when the promise was somehow never fulfilled. So they would say, 'Never mind, we'll go to Sam's place,' or somewhere else, and off they would set again.

At one such place they were joined by two ladies and the six of them discussed at length where to go for a meal and at last decided on a pub which one of the men knew the proprietor of, only when they got there it turned out to be a different pub or a different proprietor, so they had a drink instead and decided they weren't very hungry after all. Nell was starving, but managed to eat a bowlful of potato crisps and felt better.

At about ten o'clock they set off to a little Italian place that one of the girls knew in Soho where they did marvellous late-night snacks. Ian was driving, Nell was on her father's knee in the passenger's seat and Douglas was with the ladies in the back.

Ian had just emerged from the pub car park and shot off with great speed down the road, when the accident happened. A car coming the other way suddenly appeared almost face to face with them. Ian swerved sharply, mounted the pavement and hit a lamp-post. Nell was thrown forward against the windscreen and knew no more.

She recovered to find herself sitting on the pavement. The man from the other car had got out and was shouting at them, the two ladies were walking away as if they were strangers. Her father was holding a glass of water up to her mouth. She drank gratefully and felt better; the scene was becoming less blurred. She could now hear the words of the man who was shouting. 'What the bloody hell were you doing on the wrong side of the road?' he kept repeating.

'I don't know what you've got to grumble about,' Douglas replied. 'You've no damage at all that I can see. Take a look at our car.'

'Not safe on the road, you're not,' the man went on as if he had not spoken. 'That child could have been killed, you know that?'

'Oh God, oh God,' her father said, and turned away to be sick in the gutter.

'You ought to be reported, you ought not to be allowed loose.'

'Look, old man,' Douglas put in, walking across the road and taking a wallet out of his pocket. 'No need to go to the police about this little matter . . .'

'Stuff your bloody money,' the man said. 'You murdering lot of drunken bastards,' and he turned, ran back to his car and drove off.

'I think we ought to do a bunk too, old chap,' Douglas said. 'It won't look too good to the police, you know. You smelling like a brewery and the car wrapped round a lamp-post.'

'The damage could be worse,' Ian said. 'Sid'll fix the lamp in a jiff. We've been bloody lucky if you ask me.'

'How's the little gel, eh?'

He turned Nell's head upwards and looked at it. 'Quite a bump on the old forehead, what?'

Her father looked up from the gutter.

'She could have gone right through the windscreen,' he said softly. 'She could have been maimed for life. She could have been blinded.'

'But she *wasn't*, old chap.'

To her horror, her father put his face into his hands and began to sob. His shoulders shook and terrible sounds like tearing linen came from his throat.

'Never mind, little gel,' Douglas said, observing her, 'it's only the drink. He'll be as right as rain tomorrow.' He turned to Patrick. 'Cheer up, old man, all's well that ends well.'

'Come on, for Christ's sake,' Ian put in. 'It's my car and I'm not crying.'

'Little gel has a bump and jalopy's lost a lamp,' Douglas said soothingly. 'No damage done.'

Patrick seemed to pull himself together by a great effort and they all got back into the car, only this time Nell was in the back seat with her father.

'You'll have some adventures to tell your cousins, won't you?' Douglas said, turning round to smile at her.

She smiled back; her head was feeling better though it throbbed wildly if she moved it about. But her father was worse. He did not speak a word in the car and when they got back to the house, Douglas and Ian almost carried him up the two flights of stairs.

'Phew, good job nobody's about this peaceful evening,' Douglas said as they finally reached the bedroom. Then to Nell he added, 'Don't worry about your dad, little gel, he'll be better when he's had a drink.'

'I could make a cup of tea,' she volunteered.

'He needs something stronger,' Douglas assured her. 'We all do.'

Her father nodded towards the wardrobe and when Douglas opened the door, she saw, to her amazement, rows of bottles among the clothes. It looked like a shop.

Douglas poured out three glasses. Her father drank his straight down in one gulp, and, to her surprise and relief, seemed better.

'Bedtime, Nell,' he said with surprising firmness. 'Remember we've to get you to the station tomorrow.'

'What's the plan?' Douglas asked.

'I've asked the local cabby to call at ten, he's a pal of mine; the buses are a bit few and far between on Sundays and you can't always get a taxi.'

Her relief was enormous; he seemed quite back to normal.

'So it's all under control?' Douglas insisted, and she realized he was making sure for her and was grateful.

'Yes, I arranged it last week when I saw him.'

'Good for you. Then we'll love you and leave you.'

'Oh, have one for the road,' Patrick said.

They hesitated.

Nell waited, watching, willing them to go.

But they stayed. 'Oh, just a quick one then,' Ian said, and Douglas, who had in fact turned to go, turned back.

She said good night and left them. She stayed awake a long time and when she did at last fall asleep, they were still talking and laughing in her father's room.

She awoke early but did not get up until eight, afraid of disturbing her father too soon. Then she dressed, observing when she went to the glass that the bump on her forehead had turned an interesting shade of blueish-green, rather like a blackbird's egg. She felt it gently, and then tested her head by moving it from side to side and discovered that it did not hurt badly unless she moved it fast; otherwise it just throbbed quite pleasantly.

When she was ready she crossed to her father's room. She knocked on the door, and, when there was no reply, pushed it gently open and went inside.

The back of the couch was towards her and her father had evidently spent the night on it fully dressed; she could see part of the shoulder of his suit bunched up along the back. But what transfixed her with horror, what would have made her scream, only she was so frightened that it came out as a mere yelp, was the sight of his hand. His arm was hanging down over the side of the couch, and the hand which projected from the bottom of the sleeve hung so limply there, the fingers curving towards her so lifelessly, that it seemed like the flesh of the dead.

She stood staring, aware of her eyes and her throbbing head. Suddenly he snored, the shoulder shifted and the hand flicked slightly. He was unmistakably alive. Almost sobbing with relief, Nell ran across to the couch. He was still sound asleep, his head tilted back and his mouth open. Empty bottles were strewn about the floor. She stepped over them and touched his forehead, saying his name a few times, but he did not wake. She wondered what Aunt Liz would have done and decided that she would have made some tea. So she took the kettle and filled it in the bathroom and made a pot of tea. She poured him out a cup, and set it down on a table which she placed by his head. When he still did not wake, she brought herself a tray with bread and butter and sat beside him eating her breakfast, watching him carefully all the time.

As a dog watches, so Nell watched her father. He did not stir.

The taxi came early. She heard it stop outside and went to the window to let the man know she was coming. It was raining hard. He waved up at her. She waved back and smiled, conscious of herself as he would see her, a little girl waving cheerfully from an upstairs window. Then she turned back and looked at the reality of her father sprawled across the couch and the bottles on the floor. Oddly enough it seemed to her that it was her own breakfast tray with its sticky knife and buttery crumbs which looked sordid and untidy. She took it away quickly and washed up. She tidied the room, putting the empty bottles in the bin. Then she threw away her father's tea and poured him out a fresh cup, against which she propped a note, saying *I didn't want to wake you. Thank you for a lovely time. Lots of love, Nell.* Then she kissed him good-bye and ran downstairs.

The taxi driver did not seem surprised that she was alone. 'I thought he might be sleeping in on a Sunday morning,' he said. All the way to the station as they drove through pouring rain down empty streets, she worried about paying him, for although she had money in her purse, she did not know how she should broach the subject or what to do about tipping. To her relief, however, when they reached the station he turned to her and said, 'Don't worry about paying me. I'll see him myself. I bring him home a few nights most weeks.'

She was glad to think that her father had a friend like that in London. She preferred the taxi man to Douglas and Ian. She thanked him and was getting out when he said, 'I'll show you where your train goes from,' and got out with her. She was grateful to him; he even carried her case. A policeman approached, very tall and with a great hooked nose, wearing an oilskin cape. 'Can't leave the car there, mate,' he shouted.

'Well, I'm not bloody taking it with me,' the taxi man shouted back. 'It'll bloody stop there until I've seen to the lady.'

She walked beside him, proud of the chivalrous way he had called her a lady, but at the same time pretending that she hadn't heard, and avoiding looking at the policeman who was bearing down upon them, with his black cape flapping angrily.

'Silly old crow,' the taxi man said cheerfully, leading the way into the station.

At the barrier she saw Mrs Blunt's assistant.

'I'm all right now,' she said. 'Thank you very much. I hope the policeman isn't cross.'

'I'll soon sort him out, the old buzzard,' the taxi man said, and he rubbed his hands as if in pleasurable anticipation of the encounter.

To her relief Mrs Blunt's assistant did not press her for information about her weekend; her enquiries, minimal and easily answered, were obviously made out of courtesy and not curiosity.

All the same, as she settled down in the train, Nell felt a kind of detached surprise at herself: she had parried the questions so easily, as if they concerned somebody else. Her real self seemed to be frozen, incapable of feeling.

She stared out of the window as the train moved out of the station: once again she was watching the great cat's cradle of railway lines crossing and recrossing, the sheds, warehouses, and then the streets of houses slipping past and giving way to open fields with telegraph wires going up and down, up and down. Suddenly the contrast between what she had been expecting when last she saw these wonders, and what had actually happened, struck her like a savage blow.

She gasped aloud at the pain of it. Mrs Blunt's assistant looked up, so she quickly excused herself, slipped out of the compartment and down the corridor to the lavatory. There she locked herself in and leant back against the wall. She couldn't bear it. Great waves of grief seemed to beat in her throbbing head. Behind her eyes there pressed an ocean of tears. For a moment she thought she might be swept away and longed for it: to be obliterated, to be unconscious as she had been after the accident in the car. But no relief of that sort was allowed her. She realized she had no option but to bear it. She was not being offered alternatives.

She blew her nose hard and walked back to the compartment. She sat down and began to read *The Tale of Two Cities*. She read it without looking up all the way to Bragton, except for one interruption when a man brought round cups of tea, and Mrs Blunt's assistant bought one for her and insisted that she ate one of her sandwiches with it. Nell accepted rather than argue, although she was not hungry and did not want to be reminded, even by the act of eating, of her own existence.

They met her at the station, Aunt Liz and Chrissie: the

shock of seeing them again standing there on the platform, looking exactly as they had done when she had set off so joyfully on her journey, almost made her cry. It was still there, the ocean of tears; reading had only kept it at bay, not despatched it for good. It had allowed her to inhabit another world, but now she must return to her own. Fortunately the Newboulds did not press her to talk; it was not their way. Besides, Mrs Blunt's assistant was there.

By the time they were back in the farm kitchen having tea, she had prepared herself a little, set up a few small defences, raised puny barriers against pain. The kitchen was cool and tidy and familiar. London was far, far away. Everything that happened there belonged to a different world. Except that the worlds were divided only by the thinnest of membranes, through which the pain throbbed continually.

She told them about the excitements of London, and the lovely room she had had, and how the cupboard door had banged against her head and her father had rubbed butter on it. She found herself believing it, with one part of her mind. But the membrane would not allow her to tell of anything true, not even of the wonderful things like standing and listening to Big Ben or walking the tree-lined streets, because all of it, the pain and the pleasure, were unbearable and belonged to the other side, to the other world.

When her father wrote, he talked cheerfully of what fun they had had and would have again next time she came. Things were looking up in the property market, he said. All the estate agents were telling him so. Perhaps on her next visit they would look at houses together. She wrote back saying she would like to do that, and sent him drawings and descriptions of each ideal room. They discussed in long letters how many bedrooms they would need and which way the house should face and how the kitchen should be fitted. He asked if she would like to have a shower, and she said she would. And she would like to have a herb garden, too.

It was all done by post. After her visit to London, she did not see him again. He died the following November.

That was all that she was told; just that he was dead. Any knowledge that the Newboulds had of the circumstances of his death, they kept to themselves. That was their custom. And she, who was in part a Newbould, kept her grief to herself. Besides, they did not take her to the funeral, so no permitted ritual was allowed to force open the floodgates of her grief; it was all kept locked up in her small person.

She did not think about the future any more; there was no point now that it held no home with him. She had nothing of his except a small red case with two bundles of letters tied up with blue string and a memory of somebody she loved who, when she had talked to him, had seemed to understand.

Chapter Six

Nobody had expected that there would be any money for Nell. Her father's wish, expressed in the will he had written himself, probably in a moment of alcoholic depression and certainly without benefit of solicitor or witness, that her guardians should send her to a boarding-school called Brackengrove Hall outside London, had not, for that reason, been taken seriously. Furthermore, although he expressed this view of how the guardians should act, he omitted to say who they should be. It seemed quite right and natural, therefore, that Nell should continue to live – as she had always lived – with her Newbould cousins.

The situation was altered, however, by the discovery of a large insurance policy taken out by her father in Nell's favour. The existence of seven thousand pounds, which must clearly be spent on Nell, made the boarding-school proposition a practical possibility. Furthermore, a Thorpe relation, of whom none of them had so much as suspected the existence, suddenly wrote to George Newbould, explaining that she was Nell's late father's aunt and would like to help in the rearing of his child.

'It's an old-fashioned kind of letter,' Liz said after George had read it slowly to her when the children were all in bed.

'Ay,' George said, examining it carefully and then folding it up and putting it back in the envelope. 'None the worse for that,' he added.

'I meant that if she's a very old lady, it's not suitable. Our Nell needs young company.'

'Ay,' George agreed, and they were silent for a while, both of them wondering what kind of an aged aunt Patrick Thorpe had so unexpectedly bequeathed them.

'Of course, she'd get young company if she went to that boarding-school he wanted her at,' George said at last.

'She gets young company here – there's our Derek and Chrissie.'

'Ay.'

There was another long silence as they thought about their two children and Nell.

Then at last George said incontrovertibly, 'At boarding-school there'd be more than just two.'

His wife glanced at him impatiently. Then, recognizing that logic would only lead them round in circles as it always did, she said sharply, 'Well, Nell belongs here with us, that's what I feel about it.'

'I know,' George said slowly, 'but it's not just what *we* feel, is it?'

'Well, that's my opinion,' his wife told him, taking up her darning with finality.

George stayed sitting up at the big kitchen table, his elbows pressing into the thick pile of the cloth which always covered it between meals. Then he took the letter out of its envelope again and spread it out, rereading it slowly. There was no doubt about it, he reflected, the Thorpes did have a claim to Nell. Yet Liz was right: she belonged here where she had been bred up. He read the letter many times, hoping that it might yield up some new meaning, reveal some hitherto neglected vein of decision-helping ore. For it would have to be his decision in the end. She was Liz's flesh and blood, but he was the man of the family and it was his place to decide.

He felt his responsibility gravely, and was made uneasy by his inability to reach a decision. He was not used to having to make choices about such things. Of course all his working life he had made decisions, important ones too, about when to plough and what to sow and if it would be better to rush the hay in a bit soon or shake it out again and risk more rain and maybe never get it in at all. His father had had to make decisions like that, and his father before him, and in their day, George Newbould reflected, it meant the difference between thriving and starving. Whatever people said, it was easier now, but all the same a farmer could still ruin himself by a few wrong decisions. But then in all these matters there were rules to guide you, like the state of the land and what the weather was likely to do and how you felt about it in your bones. Your bones knew a bit about it too, after all these years, and maybe there was something bred into them from the start.

But a decision about whether your wife's sister's child should go to a strange school in the unknown south or if she should be put in touch with a great-aunt none of them had ever seen, that was a decision of a different order altogether. There was no guidance to be had by looking up at the hills or picking up a handful of earth, no knowledge of it in your bones. George sighed deeply and folded up the letter. Come to think of it, he didn't reckon much good could come of a school called Brackengrove. Nasty stuff, bracken. It reminded him of something.

'Eh, Liz,' he said, getting up from the table. 'I must go to the smithy tomorrow and see if he's got that scythe mended yet.'

'You could ask her to stay,' Liz said suddenly the next evening, as she turned the washing-up bowl upside-down in the sink and spread the dishcloth over it, like a fishing net spread out to dry.

'Who?'

'Aunt Thorpe, of course,' Liz said, for that was how they had named her.

George stood for a while thinking, then, 'It wouldn't do any harm,' he said cautiously.

Aunt Thorpe wrote them a long letter when she accepted their invitation. She said she would like to discuss Nell's schooling with them and the possibility of Nell's spending some time during the holidays with her. She explained that she was a headmistress and couldn't easily get away, but would come at half-term if it suited them.

'You can see she's not wanting to take our Nell away,' George said after reading the letter to Liz. 'I mean, she couldn't manage if she works all day. She just wants to be friendly, like.'

'We'll see,' said Liz suspiciously.

'She must be good with children if she's got a school.'

'It's not the same as having children of your own.'

'No, but you'll make her welcome, won't you?'

'As if I wouldn't, George Newbould,' snapped Liz, who had

in fact already been planning what meals to set in front of Aunt Thorpe.

Nell caught her first sight of Aunt Thorpe as the train pulled into the station. She was the only person standing in an otherwise empty corridor, and was bending down, obviously looking out for them, her face close to the window. Nell stared back fascinated, for the large face was compellingly ugly. For a start, it was an unusual colour and texture, being mauve with masses of little purple veins tracing their way all over it like contour lines on a map. Down the centre of this bumpy landscape, the great nose ran like a mountain ridge; it was long and uneven and took a sudden turn half-way down and went wandering off westwards. Her mouth, too, seemed to have carved out a place for itself hurriedly and without regard to symmetry, for it lurched right up on one side and the upper lip, which was very long and mobile, did not seem to match the lower one, which was much tighter and somehow puckered into the beginning of her chin, which was a massive affair that ended in a shiny knob.

Her eyes were astonishingly round, like those in a child's drawing. In fact the whole face might have been drawn by a very young child, or moulded by an apprentice sculptor or by God in experimental mood. You couldn't say if such a face were young or old; it just was. It was impossible to imagine it changing or being subject to those slow and gentle alterations by which time refashions ordinary flesh. Aunt Thorpe's face was made of sterner stuff; nothing short of an earthquake seemed likely to change its contours.

If Nell had only glimpsed Aunt Thorpe's face at the train window for a moment and then never beheld it again, she would have remembered it for the rest of her life. But no sooner had she taken it all in, than the train stopped and Aunt Thorpe jumped down, yanking her case on to the platform after her.

Nell saw that she was very tall and thin. Her angular body was brilliantly clad in orange, yellow, purple and red. She reminded Nell of pictures she had seen of brightly-coloured tropical birds, an impression that was heightened by the shock of grey-black hair that stood up in a quiff, like a coxcomb, on the top of her head, and was the only sombre-coloured thing about her.

Although they were the only people waiting on the platform and had no doubt that this was the guest that they had come to meet, the Newboulds remained standing where they were, cautiously waiting for her to make the first move.

She came briskly towards them, with a swooping kind of walk, and, as she approached, her face broke into an enormous lopsided smile revealing a mouth stuffed full of an unruly array of uneven teeth. A curious change came over her face when she smiled, as if a light had been turned on inside her head. Nell blinked; this ugly great-aunt was astonishingly beautiful.

'You must be the Newboulds,' she said, and her voice provided further cause for astonishment, for it was a lovely, resonant, powerful voice, the like of which Nell had never heard. It was clear but not sharp and it rang with authority although it was not in the least bit bossy. It was a voice that carried you along with it, like a stream that nothing blocks or diverts or muddies.

'So you are Mrs Newbould,' she said, shaking Aunt Liz by the hand. 'How do you do?' She shook hands with Derek and Chrissie too, but Nell she kissed. 'We meet at last,' she said, holding Nell for a moment a little away from her, and looking at her with the incredibly round eyes bright with interest. But Nell was not embarrassed; she stared back at her great-aunt with equal interest.

They crossed the road to the bus station, Derek remembering, after a sharp look from his mother, to carry Aunt Thorpe's case. On the bus the two adults sat together and the three children spread themselves out on the long bench at the back. They would have liked to discuss Aunt Thorpe but were afraid of being overheard by their mother, and anyway none of them knew what to say about her. They had never seen the like of her and did not want to commit themselves to an opinion which might afterwards prove dreadfully wrong.

Since Liz could not get it out of her head that Aunt Thorpe's visit was some kind of military encounter, she launched her campaign with a very impressive high-tea, which they sat down to later than usual, after milking, so that George could get into his best suit.

'What a spread, Mum,' Derek said appreciatively, surveying the table as they sat down.

There was blackberry tart as well as apple pie and custard pie, and four sorts of cake as well as teacake and parkin.

'It's nothing out of the ordinary,' his mother told him sharply.

'But we don't usually . . .'

'That's enough, mind your manners. Pass Miss Thorpe the sugar.'

It was the first time Nell could ever remember an outsider sitting down to a meal with them. She observed that her Aunt Liz was edgy and that her usually calm and placid Uncle George seemed unsure of who he was, sitting there in his best suit although it wasn't Sunday. They began to eat in unnatural silence. It wasn't that they usually talked much, but this was a different kind of silence, made conspicuous by efforts to break it.

Oddly enough, it wasn't the delicacies which impressed Aunt Thorpe, it was the perfectly ordinary home-made bread which they had every day anyway. Slice after slice disappeared into the interesting cavern of her tooth-crammed mouth; she ate it with butter and farm cheese, with redcurrant jelly, with honey, or just plain by itself.

'That bread, Mrs Newbould,' she said afterwards, 'was more than food; it was an *experience*.'

Not only her round eyes, but even her nose and chin shone with appreciation.

'Oh, it's nothing out of the way,' Aunt Liz said modestly. 'Have some teacake, do, and let me give you some more tea.'

It was obvious she was quite won over. As she took Aunt Thorpe's cup, she added, 'And please do call me Liz like everybody else does.'

'That goes for me too, Miss Thorpe,' George said.

'It'll sound daft if she calls *you* Liz, Dad,' Derek put in.

Nell waited for the roof to fall in on this impudence, but into the horrified silence there burst a great gale of laughter from Aunt Thorpe. It was an astonishing sound – torrential and infectious. Soon they were all laughing and Aunt Liz was saying, 'Get along with you, great cheeky thing. You can all three get down and leave us in peace.'

Somehow after that they all stopped being polite and Aunt Liz seemed to forget that she was waging a war. The children didn't get down, but sat on at the table, listening and joining in.

'And what will you call *me*?' Aunt Thorpe suddenly demanded.

'Just Aunt?' Nell suggested.

'But Aunt what? You see I don't like my name at all, a highly unsuitable Victorian effort with floral connotations, which I never use if I can possibly avoid it. What have you called me up till now?' she demanded suddenly.

The children hesitated, thinking it was probably rude to have called her by her surname. Then Derek said, 'Aunt Thorpe,' and again Nell held her breath expecting rebuke, but instead the guest seemed delighted.

'I like that,' she said. 'Just go on calling me Aunt Thorpe.'

'But you're Nell's *great*-aunt,' Derek objected.

'Never mind, we can manage without greatness, can't we, Nell?' Aunt Thorpe said. 'Now what about the washing-up?'

It was a suggestion that finally vanquished Liz. Not only did Aunt Thorpe insist upon washing-up, she made a good job of it, methodically piling up plates at the start and wiping up every drop of water when she had finished. She even turned the tin bowl upside-down in the shallow stone sink and spread the dishcloth over it, as Aunt Liz did.

'I can see you're handy,' Liz said as they returned to the fireside.

It was high praise and Aunt Thorpe accepted it modestly.

'I have to be,' she said. 'You see, I leave the flat early in the morning and I couldn't bear to come back in the evening to find a muddle.'

'Tell me about the school you work at,' Aunt Liz said.

Aunt Thorpe told her and answered all her questions, while George sat trying to hide his astonishment at the way his wife was chatting amicably with the woman she had planned to do battle with. He, who had imagined a weekend filled with skirmishings and verbal exchanges, sat now sucking his pipe with relief.

It was Liz who suggested that Aunt Thorpe should go and see Nell's headmistress.

'She lives near and you can ring her up from the post office first; she's on the telephone.'

Aunt Thorpe hesitated. 'It seems a bit mean on her free day,' she said.

'She won't mind. She gets long enough holidays.'

'You can talk to her better than we can, like,' George put in.

'And don't forget to tell her you're a headmistress too,' Liz advised sharply. 'Then she won't try anything on.'

So Aunt Thorpe spent the next afternoon with Nell's headmistress and in the evening reported back to Liz and George.

'First of all,' she said, 'she thinks Nell is very bright indeed.'

'Ay,' George said proudly. 'We know that.'

'Brains aren't everything, mind,' Liz warned.

'She spoke to me very frankly and fairly. She says she's never yet had a girl to go to university from her school.'

'I should think not, indeed.'

There was silence, then Aunt Thorpe went on, 'So if that is how Nell's future lies, it would mean her either going as a weekly boarder to Horseborough High School, if they can take her, or going away to boarding-school in accordance with her father's wish.'

'Well, what her father wanted should weigh some,' George said.

'I don't know what she's on about, running down her own school,' Liz said. 'It's been good enough for our Chrissie.'

'Yes, Chrissie's lucky, they do seem to have a very good domestic science department and quite a few girls go on to the School of Housecraft in Bragton as Chrissie is doing; but you see, that isn't Nell's strong subject.'

'That's true; if ever a girl had ten thumbs it's our Nell,' Liz reflected.

'So really we're no forwarder,' George said sadly.

'I think our best plan is to consult Nell herself,' Aunt Thorpe said.

'Ask Nell? She's far too young to decide about such things,' Aunt Liz said, and it was obvious from the shocked expression on George's face that he agreed with her.

'You know your Nell best, of course,' Aunt Thorpe said carefully. 'But it's her life we're deciding about and it might be helpful to know how she feels about it, don't you think?'

'We don't want her upset,' Aunt Liz said. 'We've always kept everything from her so she wouldn't be upset.'

Aunt Thorpe looked at her, but said nothing, recognizing that there are times to argue and times to remain silent and this was one of the latter.

When Nell came into the room Aunt Thorpe made way for her to sit with them by the fire.

'How do you like school, Nell?' she asked a few seconds later.

'It's all right,' Nell replied guardedly, not wanting to split on Jenny Shuttleworth's gang, who had replaced the evacuees as her chief tormentors.

'Would it upset you very much to leave if that seemed necessary to your career?'

'Oh, *no*, I'd love to leave,' Nell said, thinking how like heaven it would be never to see any of them again, but especially Jenny Shuttleworth with her great coarse face and fuzzy hair and eyes that had no pity.

They were surprised at her vehemence.

'You've never said you didn't like school,' Liz rebuked.

'I've never thought I might be able to leave.'

There was silence for a while and then George said, 'Well, it's something we've been thinking about, Nell.'

She looked at each of them in turn, not knowing what to make of it. Aunt Liz, Uncle George and her great-aunt Thorpe: they seemed a very united trio to her because they were adults and she was a child. Yet she sensed that it was the Thorpe influence that was pulling her away from Bragton.

'Have you any idea what you want to be when you grow up, Nell?' Aunt Thorpe asked.

Nell hesitated.

'Only to give us some idea how to decide, like,' her uncle said, to help her.

'I want to be independent.'

'Eh? That's a big word for a little girl.'

'Independent of what, Nell?' Aunt Thorpe asked gently.

'Everybody.'

'I see. Well, it's a good thing to want, nothing wrong with it at all. But have you any idea what else you'd like to do?'

Nell shook her head. 'No, I just want to live in my own house by myself.'

'You don't plan on a husband, then?' Liz said in the bantering voice she used on the rare occasions when she wanted to indicate that she wasn't being altogether serious.

Nell shook her head. 'No, just me,' she said.

'It might be lonely,' Aunt Thorpe pointed out.

'Oh, I'd have *friends*, but they'd go away and then I'd shut the door after them and lock it and be on my own.'

'Then what would you do?'

'Decide what to do the next day,' Nell said promptly, getting quite carried away with the new world she was creating for herself.

'I live on my own now,' Aunt Thorpe told her, 'and I should very much like you to come and spend some of your holidays with me, though this would still be your home, of course. Your aunt and uncle are quite happy that you should visit me.'

'That's right,' Uncle George reassured her. 'We've talked about it, Nell.'

'So would you like to come and stay with me sometimes? You've been to London once, so you have some idea of what it is like; very different from Netherby.'

Nell remembered the leafy London square and walking the evening streets holding her father's hand. An unswallowable lump rose in her throat. She felt panic rising in her, but managed to say, 'Yes, please, but not in summer.'

'Very well. And I expect you'd like to have Christmas here with the other children. So perhaps you'll come to me for the Easter holidays?'

Nell nodded, recovering. Then she said good night and went upstairs to bed.

'Well, fancy that,' Aunt Liz said, after she had gone. 'I never thought she'd want to leave school like that. I'd have thought she'd have been afraid to go somewhere strange.'

'We don't know much about what goes on in a child's mind,' Aunt Thorpe said. 'And if we did, we still wouldn't understand.'

'Oh, I don't know about that,' Aunt Liz contradicted. 'We've all been children once, so we know what it's like.'

'We forget,' Aunt Thorpe said simply.

'And fancy her being so definite she wouldn't come to you in the summer!' George said, shaking his head. 'Now I wonder whatever could have made her feel so sure about that?'

'Raspberries,' Aunt Liz pronounced. 'She's very fond of soft fruit is our Nell. She wouldn't want to miss the season.'

Chapter Seven

Of all the forms and papers that arrived once it was settled that Nell was to go away to school, the most important was undoubtedly the clothes list. Over this formidable catalogue of apparel Aunt Liz frowned and clucked disapprovingly, exclaiming at its senseless extravagance. She contrived various economies by means of false hems and inserts, but there still remained a few new garments which had unavoidably to be acquired: the making of these was, to Nell's relief, put into the charge of Chrissie.

So it was Chrissie who took Nell into Bragton to buy yards of material, having first measured her all over. Then she disappeared into Aunt Liz's bedroom and worked away at the old treadle sewing-machine, the ironing-board alongside, transforming yards of boring-looking flat cloth into pretty nighties and blouses. Chrissie's feet worked ceaselessly and the treadle hummed rhythmically up and down, up and down, so swiftly that it made a blurred arc of moving air, like insects' wings. Meanwhile, up above, the machine puffed away like an express train, eating up the material which Chrissie fed gently into it, her fingers deftly manoeuvring the cloth and escaping, by some miracle, the swift jab of the needle as it rushed along puncturing everything within range.

Nell seemed to spend hours that August watching entranced as her cousin worked at the old sewing-machine, with its six little drawers, three a side, each with its brass plate and handle. Sometimes Chrissie gave her small tasks to do, like neatening the ends of threads or oversewing a hem. But then the crisp material immediately turned itself into a crumpled grey mess, which malignantly resisted any attempts to be sewn, knotting the cotton and tangling itself up into puckers and bumps. Chrissie would sigh and say, 'Never mind, our Nell. Give it back here,' and with a few swift stitches, and a dab or two of the iron she would restore everything to order.

Even Chrissie, however, did not attempt to make such things as one dressing-gown (warm), one best frock (for Sundays) and one winter suit (optional). She took Nell into Bragton and after unsuccessfully trying the General Drapers, bravely led her to Clara Mead's. That was brave because Clara Mead's was what Aunt Liz called a Select Little Shop, presumably because it only had one garment on display in the window and nobody was ever seen going in or out.

There were certainly no other customers in the shop when Chrissie and Nell went inside; as they walked across the thick carpet an assistant rose unwillingly from her chair by a table, and, looking at them with contempt, asked if she could help them. Somehow Nell could not imagine herself ever being helped by the superior-looking woman who was hard all over. She had a hard face with a lot of make-up on it, her hair was dyed a hard yellow and her tightly-upholstered body looked as if it would feel hard if you poked it, like an uncomfortable couch. Her eyes were hard and her hard voice seemed to have had its accent covered up by an unnatural one. Even Chrissie looked a bit scared when she asked for a dressing-gown for Nell.

But Nell forgot all about the hard assistant once she had the dressing-gown on. In a little curtained cubicle she stood in front of the long glass wearing this magnificent garment; it reached to the ground and was made of soft woollen material and had buttons all the way down the front. Its colour was something the assistant described as burgundy. Nell looked tall in it and very grown-up; she could hardly believe it was herself standing there.

'It's not so much a dressing-gown, more a housecoat,' the assistant pronounced.

Nell was afraid that Chrissie would think that it was too good for her, but she just said, 'It suits you, Nell. Would you like it?'

Things went less well when she began trying on dresses.

'She hasn't got a waist yet,' the assistant said disdainfully, when Chrissie pointed out that a blue frock didn't fit well. Nell hung her head in shame. It was a relief when Chrissie said knowledgeably, 'It'll crease badly, that linen. No, we won't have it, thank you.'

Thus it was the frock that was rejected, not Nell.

The suits, too, looked dreadful: skirts hung on her stomach, and jackets drooped off her shoulders.

'She's not developed yet,' the hard voice said. 'She's not ready for suits.'

'Well, if you can't show us anything better,' Chrissie retorted, 'we'll just take the dressing-gown, thank you.'

She paid from a bundle of notes that Uncle George had provided, and they left the shop.

'I'll make you a best dress, don't worry,' Chrissie said as they walked away. 'And the suit's only optional. You can get one later, maybe.'

'I'm sorry,' Nell said, 'about my shape.'

'There's nothing wrong with it,' Chrissie said indignantly. 'She can talk! I bet she measures forty-two inches all the way down, silly old thing.'

Nell took her hand gratefully; for her sake Chrissie was breaking her rule of never saying anything unkind about anybody. Chrissie was like that. She set herself very high standards, but never expected anybody else to share them and would drop them, if friendship ever required it, whatever the cost to herself. If ever Chrissie committed a murder, Nell thought, it would be for somebody else's sake.

They seemed to have grown closer during these weeks of preparation. Chrissie was a grown-up now really, but she hadn't gone over to the adults as some people would have done. She was still on Nell's side.

'I'll miss you when you go, Nell,' she said now, as they sat together on the bus home.

'I'll be back for Christmas.'

They sat for a while thinking about next Christmas and how Nell would reappear for it.

'You will write to me at school, won't you, Chrissie? Often, I mean, and tell me what it's like at your domestic science college?'

'Of course I will. They call it a pudding school – at least Derek does.'

'Oh, *him*,' Nell said in disgust. 'You don't want to bother about *him*.'

In the last week of the holidays Aunt Liz spread out all the new clothes on Nell's bed and checked them off against the clothes list, which was now a thin and crumpled piece of paper, worn away at the folds.

'What any girl wants six pairs of knickers for, I can't imagine,' she snapped. 'Don't they know there's been a war on?'

Nell knew better than to argue, so said nothing in defence of her new school, but got on with rolling up socks and squeezing them into the toes of shoes, as she had been told. She tried not to look at the big new trunk which stood alongside, menacing and empty.

The trouble was that she felt so mixed up about going away. It had been lovely to have all these new clothes, she had never imagined herself having so many all at once. Then out of the pleasure in the clothes had come a guilty feeling because the others weren't getting any of this fuss and because she was leaving them behind, especially Chrissie. But as the day of departure drew nearer, guilt was replaced by envy. She would have given anything now to be staying behind with them and passionately wished that nobody had ever mentioned boarding-school. The thought of going away filled her with panic. She took to creeping upstairs and sitting crouched on the window seat in the bedroom, gazing out at the garden and the fields and the hills beyond. She wondered how she would manage without the sight and sound and smell of it all. Sometimes she even wondered how it would exist without her, although she knew that that was nonsense.

Now, with only a few days to go, she felt neither excitement nor guilt nor any other feeling except simple misery. She hated the empty trunk because it foretold homesickness, as a coffin foretells grief. She was very glad when the wretched thing was filled and Uncle George had fastened a strap round it, and then a rope, too, for good measure, and taken it off to the station.

Three days later she followed it.

The four Newboulds stood on the platform after she had gone, not knowing what to say to comfort each other. Then Liz said, 'Well, she's off then.'

'Ay, it's not for long though,' George said, his voice gruff. Then he added without conviction, 'It's best for her, no doubt.'

'Might as well go,' Derek said, and he and his father led the way back to the car.

'Come on, Chrissie,' Liz said, taking her daughter's arm as they followed their menfolk. 'There's work to be done back home.'

Chrissie could not speak, but swallowed miserably and nodded.

'She'll be back at Christmas, love,' her mother said as they caught up with the others by the car.

'No, she won't,' Chrissie said, and she spoke fiercely for her, who was the gentle one of the family. 'Somebody else will come back at Christmas with her name.'

'Don't talk like that,' her mother said sharply. 'It's not right. It's, it's – it's proper *morbid*.'

It was not the sort of word that any of them ever used and it served to depress them all still further. They got into the car in silence and nobody spoke all the way back home to the farm.

Chapter Eight

For as long as she could remember Chrissie had wanted to be a nurse. When she was only two she had enjoyed fetching and carrying for her new baby brother, and four years later she had helped her ailing aunt look after the infant Nell. But if she could not remember a time when she had not wanted to be a nurse, neither could she remember a time when she had not realized that it would never be allowed. By instinct she knew her parents' views on such a matter; it was never discussed between them.

It was a surprise to all of them when it suddenly erupted, on the evening of Nell's departure, like a volcano whose dormant presence has been too long ignored. Tea had been an even quieter meal than usual – they were all conscious of Nell's empty chair at the table. Chrissie looked at it uncertainly now as she began to clear away: to remove it seemed like banishment, yet its presence there was a rebuke. She compromised by pushing it partly back at an angle to the table and putting a cushion on it.

'Everyone's going,' she said disconsolately, giving the cushion a thump. 'Margaret Foster's going away next week, too.'

'Where's she going to, then?' George asked.

'She's going to train for a nurse at Leeds General Infirmary.'

'I don't know what her mother's thinking of,' Liz said sharply. 'Nearly fifty miles away – anything could happen.'

'There are buses, Mum.'

'And some of those nurses aren't all they should be, either. She'll get into bad company, I shouldn't wonder.'

'Nay, she's a nice enough lass,' George put in, trying to soothe them both.

'I don't say she's not nice *now*,' Liz told him darkly. 'She'd be better going to the School of Housecraft at Bragton like our Chrissie.'

'No she would *not*,' Chrissie cried out, with such sudden ferocity that they all stared at her and were silent. For a moment she was embarrassed by the effect she had produced and almost lost her nerve. Then she recovered and added defiantly, 'I only wish I was going with her.'

Shock at her gentle daughter's rebellion prevented Liz from replying; it was George who said at last, 'Nay, Chrissie, how'd we manage without you, eh, love?'

Chrissie did not reply; silence turned his words from kindly to selfish in a few seconds.

'Anyway,' Liz said, recovering her power of speech, 'you'll doubtless be a farmer's wife one day and what you learn at the School of Housecraft will come in handy.'

'It would be handy for a farmer's wife to know a bit about nursing,' Chrissie said obstinately.

'Nursing's just common sense,' Liz said. 'There's no need to go away and learn it.'

'Well, then,' Chrissie threw back at her, 'domestic science is just common sense, too – more so, if you ask me.'

'We're not *asking* you,' Liz told her, 'we're telling you. We know what's best for you, your dad and me.'

'It's got nothing to do with what's best for me, nor even with nursing. It's just that you don't want me going away.'

'Well, what's wrong with that, Chrissie love?'

'Nothing, Dad, except that you shouldn't pretend that it'll be *better* for me in Bragton.'

'They'll teach you what's useful there,' Liz insisted. 'Mazie Lawson only stayed one year and she learned to make her husband's trousers.'

'If our Chrissie stays two years, she'll maybe learn to make t'jacket and all,' Derek put in.

George gave him a warning glare.

'I know what it is,' Liz said, bringing the argument to an end. 'You're upset over our Nell's going away. We all are. We'll say no more about it.'

It showed the state she was in; in normal circumstances emotions were not a subject of remark.

'But it's not just that, Mum,' Chrissie insisted, almost in tears now, but unable to give in. 'I've always wanted to go.'

'You've never said.'

'I've tried, but you'd never listen and I knew what you'd say – you've said it about others often enough.'

'I'll say it again too. There's no harm in a bit of training for a girl, but there's no call to go all that way from home.'

She paused and then went on quietly, 'I can't help but remember your Aunt Madge, going off the way she did.'

'Nay, love,' George put in gently. 'Poor Madge would 'ave took ill and died whether or not.'

'I'm not saying she died because of going away. I'm just saying that she was lost to us, to her own mum and dad and me, when she went off and married that Patrick. She'd never have met him if she'd stayed at home.'

'But, Mum, I'm not intending to go away and get married – '

'Neither was your Aunt Madge when she went on that choir outing to Leeds.'

There was no arguing against that. Besides, Chrissie sensed that it was too painful for her mother to talk of. Derek had no such inhibitions.

'I never knew about that,' he put in eagerly. 'What happened on the choir outing, Mum?'

'It's no concern of yours,' his mother snapped. 'A chance meeting, but it was enough. She set her heart on marrying him and there was no stopping her. She was obstinate for all her tender ways.'

'But, Mum,' Chrissie insisted gently, 'I only want to go nursing. If I promise to stay in the hospital and never go out – '

'A hospital isn't suitable,' Liz told her. 'There are things your dad and me don't want you mixed up in.'

'She means a bit of slap and tickle in the morgue, Chrissie,' Derek put in with a great shout of laughter.

'That's enough of that,' George told him. 'We'll not have that sort of talk in this house.'

'He gets it from that cowhand,' Liz said after her son had ambled out. 'He sees far too much of him now that he's left school.'

'Bert's not a bad lad,' George said.

'And that Betty Herbison's a bad influence on our Derek, too.'

'Ay.'

'Making a laughing-stock of him. I wish she'd gone back with the other evacuees. And him only fifteen!'

'Nay, Liz, Derek's a man, you know – at least he works like one.'

'Oh, he's strong, I grant you that,' Liz said, unable to keep a note of pride out of her voice, despite herself.

They went on talking about Derek, and Chrissie swallowed her tears. It was the first and last time she had rebelled and the subject was never mentioned again. Next week she started at the School of Housecraft in Bragton.

She accepted the situation, as she always did, working hard and competently, but without love. The only joy she took in any of it was in making a dress for Nell for Christmas and planning the most beautiful optional suit ever seen within the walls of Brackengrove School.

They were shy with Nell when she came home at Christmas. She talked a bit differently for a start. There was a strangeness about her which made them treat her like a visitor and at teatime everybody was very polite and there was too much handing about of plates.

It was a relief to Nell when bedtime came; alone in the dark she and Chrissie could talk as they used to. It seemed to her that Chrissie was the only one who had not changed. Aunt Liz was sharper and bonier, her uncle clumsier, Derek rougher, but Chrissie exactly as she remembered her.

'What's it really like at school?' Chrissie asked now, disregarding earlier polite enquiries.

'I've got used to it, I suppose,' Nell answered slowly. 'Honestly, Chrissie, if I'd been allowed home at half-term I don't think I'd ever have gone back. You can't imagine how awful it was at first – so flat and I used to dream about the hills and everything . . .'

'We'll go for a walk tomorrow if it's fine.'

'I don't care if it pours. When it rains at school we have to go for Wet Walks.'

Chrissie laughed. 'Whatever for?' she asked.

'It's for exercise – instead of games. We walk along the streets and it's horrible. I got into trouble once for not going – they said I was lazy.'

'Oh Nell, and you who walk for miles,' Chrissie exclaimed furiously, ready for a moment to kill anyone who had hurt Nell.

'Wet streets are so sad somehow . . .'

'Do you hate it, at school, Nell, honestly?'

'No, not really,' Nell said, trying hard to be honest. 'Some people hate just being a number, a tiny part and all that, but I don't really mind. It's places I miss, more than people. Though I miss you, of course,' she added hastily.

But Chrissie hadn't minded.

'I know,' she said.

Nell lay in silence and felt grateful. She had almost forgotten what a comfortable person Chrissie was.

As they walked together next day, under a crisp blue sky

that seemed more like autumn than winter, it was Nell who did most of the talking. She had more to tell, of course, like a returned traveller. All the same it occurred to her that perhaps Chrissie was changed; she seemed quieter, more passive. Before, she had always seemed much older than Nell; she had made the decisions, done the guiding, known everything. Now she listened almost humbly to her younger cousin. There were unexpected gaps in her knowledge, too.

'Some of the girls are going skiing this Christmas,' Nell remarked as they walked up Winterscale Gyll and saw, between the crags at the top, the outline of snow-crested Cumberside.

'What's that?' Chrissie asked.

Nell stared at her. 'Well, it's, well, you know, *skiing*.'

'I've heard of it, of course,' Chrissie explained apologetically, 'but I don't know exactly what it is.'

'You sort of slide about on things like skates only bigger.'

Chrissie nodded.

'Aunt Thorpe says I can go one Christmas if Auntie and Uncle don't mind.'

'You'd go with her?'

'Goodness, no! She's far too old. I'd go in a school party. It's one of those things you do in a group – I think.'

'Oh. Like hunting, you mean?'

Nell nodded uncertainly.

'Only abroad,' she added.

'We'd better turn back soon,' Chrissie said. 'I promised to help Mum later this morning.'

The village, it seemed to Nell as they walked through it on their way back to the farm, was smaller. She had never noticed before how quiet and still everything was. Even the arrival of the bus from Bragton seemed an intrusion from the outside world.

As they passed the bus stop, Mrs Pertree, the vicar's wife, was getting off, laden with shopping.

'How do you like school, Nell?' she asked.

She was a nervous little woman, ill-at-ease, who tried too hard to please her husband's parishioners.

She hardly waited for Nell to reply before adding, with an apologetic glance at her baskets, 'I go into Bragton now they've got that big new store.' She lowered her voice. 'It's so much cheaper than Drinkwater's shop, and everything's well, *fresher*, you know.'

She had quite a strong Yorkshire accent, Nell thought with surprise; she had never noticed it before.

'He's not well, Mr Drinkwater,' Chrissie said.

'Ah, that's why he's not been at choir for two weeks. I must go and visit him. There's always somebody in need of a helping hand, isn't there?'

She left them and almost ran off towards the vicarage.

'Isn't she funny?' Nell said. 'She always seems to be quoting somebody else.'

'How do you mean, Nell?'

'Oh, I don't know; as if she was playing a part.'

'Well, she is really, isn't she?'

'I suppose so.'

As they walked through the village they met other people who asked her about school. Nell answered mechanically, aware that they were not really interested. At least, they were interested in a way – they would certainly repeat what she had said – but they couldn't really understand. It was a different world she was talking about; it didn't seem very real even to herself now that she was back in the village.

She had looked forward to coming back, yet nothing was quite as she remembered. As the holidays slipped past, all the special things they always did at Christmas like the Carol Service and the Nativity play, and even the house-to-house carol singing on Christmas Eve – seemed less exciting than they had been in other years. Since then she had done similar things with other people, watched other – and better – plays. She found herself comparing.

Only the hills seemed the same; immediately she left the village and walked up the lane she felt the same sudden joy, unexpected, unhoped-for. That was it; it was only the things you hadn't built hopes on that could never let you down. She had forgotten, for example, about the shooting-stars. Yet the very first night she and Chrissie went for a walk after dark they saw at least five blaze right across the sky.

'Oh, I'd *forgotten,*' Nell exclaimed, walking along with her head tipped back. 'Aren't they marvellous?'

'Well, there were a lot in November,' Chrissie said in surprise. 'Don't you go out at night at school?'

'Sometimes, but you don't see them.'

'You mean you don't have shooting-stars in towns?' Chrissie asked.

Nell laughed. 'Oh, *Chrissie,*' she said. 'Of course they're there, but you don't see them for all the lights.'

'Oh yes, of course, I hadn't thought of that. Yes, I suppose they must be there.'

It was awful – she sounded so humble. They walked for a while without talking, Nell guiltily determined to say nothing for fear of hurting Chrissie's feelings. It would be a relief in a way, she thought sadly, to go back to school. She was all of a piece there. Or all of a peace, she thought to herself, and laughed aloud.

'What's funny, Nell?' Chrissie asked.

'Oh, nothing – you wouldn't understand,' Nell answered without thinking.

She could not unsay the words, so she took Chrissie's hand and they walked on in silence, their footsteps resounding in the clear night air.

The trouble was that although she was still so close to Chrissie, still felt just the same towards her really, she couldn't help seeing everything differently now that she had been away. To make matters worse, things now struck her as funny that didn't amuse Chrissie at all.

On the last day of the holidays, for instance, she and Chrissie went along to Drinkwater's shop to do the shopping for Aunt Liz. They had got everything they wanted and were just leaving when Mrs Pertree came in. It was a long narrow shop and the two girls stood politely back, against the sacks of flour and oatmeal, to let her come by. But Mrs Pertree stood in the doorway. She was holding a little bunch of flowers in tissue paper and a small basket of fruit.

'And what can I have the pleasure of doing for you, Mrs Pertree, ma'am?' old Drinkwater asked threateningly, his obsequious manner doing nothing to disguise the smouldering resentment underneath.

'I'm sorry you haven't been well, Mr Drinkwater,' Mrs Pertree began squeakily. She was trying to look confident and solicitous as a vicar's wife should, but was obviously scared stiff of the old man. 'We missed you at Matins and Evensong on Sunday . . .'

Old Drinkwater let her stumble on, watching her balefully. Then suddenly his anger burst its bounds and he roared at her, 'You've not set foot in my shop this past four weeks and you come here wantin' to know why Ah'm not in that choir? Ah've done wi' it. Thirty years Ah've been roaring my bloody guts out in that church to get t'vicarage order, but Ah'll be damned if Ah sets foot in it again.'

Mrs Pertree gave a little gasp and fled. Out of the shop and down the path she ran, clutching the basket and flowers. The tissue paper came loose and fluttered behind her.

The two girls stood not knowing what to do, awaiting Mr Drinkwater's permission to leave, so great was the authority of his anger. Then he stalked back to his tall stool and sat himself on it, gazing at the door, so they murmured their thanks and crept out.

Once out of earshot, Nell burst out laughing.

'I bet she doesn't go taking any more flowers to old Drinkwater,' she said.

Chrissie was shocked. 'Poor Mrs Pertree, oh, poor Mrs Pertree,' she kept saying.

'But *Chrissie,* it was so funny. *Roaring his bloody guts out in church* . . .' She choked with laughter and had to stand still to recover.

'He's been in the choir as long as I can remember,' Chrissie said sadly.

When they told Aunt Liz she was neither amused nor saddened. 'I can't see that she saves much going into Bragton for her shopping,' was all she said. 'The bus fares going up the way they have.'

Nell was glad that they didn't all come to see her off at the station. Other girls from school would be travelling on the train and she wasn't sure what they would think of her Newbould relations. It was a relief that only Chrissie came with her into Bragton, though she did feel an unexpected pang at the sight of the lone figure of her cousin waving on the platform, quickly forgotten however when the others appeared along the corridor, laughing and shouting, and asked, 'Had good hols?'

Chrissie went straight on to work in Bragton and did not return home until the evening. Her father was carrying an early lamb across the farmyard; it hung, a pathetic little grey bundle, looped over his arm.

'Its mother's dead,' he said, handing it to Chrissie. 'But I've got another ewe that'll take it later. She had a dead 'un just now; I've got it in the barn ready for skinning.'

'Shall I give it a bottle?'

'Nay, the ewe'll not take it if it smells of strange milk.'

Chrissie took the lamb into the kitchen, collecting an old

piece of blanket from the scullery on the way. She knelt down by the fire, rubbing the lamb. It snuggled against her and tried to suck her fingers. She arranged the blanket in the big side-oven and gently lifted the lamb on to it.

It would be all right, this one. She thought of the other one, dead in the barn. Soon her father would skin it, slipping the coat from the limbs like peeling off a glove. She made herself concentrate on the living lamb; poor little motherless thing, it would be saved by the skin of the other lamb. The mother ewe would take it, knowing no difference.

Her mother bustled in.

'Supper's ready,' she said. 'Tell your dad and Derek, will you, love?'

Again they were aware of Nell's empty place at the table, but typically did not mention it. Only after the meal was over and cleared away and the four of them sat round the fire drinking cups of tea, did they talk of her.

'Well, they've not spoiled her, I'll say that,' Liz conceded.

'Nothing would spoil our Nell,' Chrissie said loyally.

'You do for a start,' Derek put in.

Chrissie laughed. 'Rubbish,' she said. 'You're jealous.'

'Of *her*! By gum, I've better things to do than be jealous of our Nell,' Derek said sourly, and went out slamming the back door behind him.

'I'll go after him,' Chrissie said. 'I never meant to hurt him.'

'You'll stay where you are,' her mother told her sharply. 'He's been bad-tempered all winter.'

'But . . .'

'It's all on account of that Betty Herbison,' Liz went on. 'Sometimes I'd like to get my hands on that little hussy, really I would.'

'Yes, I should have remembered. Poor Derek.'

'All the same, I'm not having him rude.'

'So we shan't see Nell till summer,' Chrissie said to distract her mother's thoughts from Betty Herbison. 'I hope she'll be all right with Aunt Thorpe at Easter.'

'She'll be all right,' George said. 'Aunt Thorpe'll take her different places, like. Show her round a bit.'

'She'll not miss us,' Liz said. 'Don't you fret.'

'I think she does miss us,' Chrissie said. 'At least I think she misses Netherby and the hills and shooting-stars and things like that.'

'Shooting-stars!' her mother repeated. 'Whatever next?'

'It's like plants,' George said slowly. 'Some don't transplant too good.'

The two women looked at him in surprise.

'On the other hand,' he said uncomfortably, 'cabbages do.'

They waited.

'Others only make roots just the once,' he concluded.

They still waited. He looked from one to the other.

'I'll go and get that lamb skinned,' he said.

Chapter Nine

It was the worst lambing time that George Newbould could remember. The winter started early and, although not excessively cold, it brought sudden, unexpected snowstorms and thick mists. Sometimes when the snow melted he found the pathetic bodies of sheep and lambs huddled up against the dry-stone walls. Until then he had thought that that was something which only happened to neglectful farmers, but this year the treachery of the weather defeated even his watchful care.

But the year redeemed itself; when at last the spring came it was warm and pleasant and there was plenty of sweet young grass in the meadows. George looked at it with satisfaction; it promised to be a record hay harvest.

It was a good spring in other ways too; Betty Herbison went back to rejoin her parents in the town and Derek found himself a more suitable girl-friend in whom Liz, rendered uncritical by relief, could find no fault.

It was the spring when the students arrived. Liz found them on the doorstep one evening as she came in from the dairy; they said they wanted work on the farm.

Liz eyed them suspiciously, then she called George.

'They're students,' she warned.

'I doubt they'll bite all the same,' George said slowly. 'Come in, then, lads, and tell us what you want.'

'Work, any kind of work,' the smaller one explained as they went into the kitchen and introduced themselves. 'We don't mind what we do. We're free until August.'

'I could do with help for hay harvest,' George said. 'It's hard work, mind, not like book-learning.'

'We don't mind. We're quite strong.'

George looked them over carefully, as he would a horse. They were all right, he reckoned.

'I'll give you a trial day tomorrow,' he told them. 'And see how you shape up. If we're both suited, I can give you three pounds a week and your keep. Is that all right?'

'That's very generous, isn't it, Jack?' the smaller one said. He was called Tim and did most of the talking.

'And here's our Chrissie,' George said as his daughter came in from work. 'Just in time to make up two camp beds in the loft, love, for these two lads. Then it'll be supper time.'

Tim looked at her appreciatively as they shook hands. As he said to Jack afterwards, having a pretty farmer's daughter on the spot was an unexpected bonus.

'What do you study, then?' Derek asked at supper that evening.

'Electrical engineering,' Tim said.

Liz's face lit up. For the first time she looked with approval at the students.

'That's *very* handy,' she said. 'Would you mind looking at the plug on my Hoover after tea?'

Both men laughed and Chrissie said, 'Oh *Mum*,' reproachfully.

'What's so wrong with that?' Liz demanded.

'Well, it's not like being an ordinary electrician,' Chrissie said, 'it's more complicated.'

'Well, whatever it is,' Liz said unabashed, 'he'll be no good at it if he can't even mend my Hoover.'

'You're quite right, Mrs Newbould,' Tim said gallantly. 'And I'll be delighted to look at it for you. And Jack here's a civil engineer, so if you want any tunnels building or foundations digging, you just ask him.'

Jack smiled, but said nothing.

He puzzled Chrissie. He was so quiet and Tim seemed to be always jollying him along somehow. Used to caring for others, she sensed that Tim was solicitous of him, but couldn't think why. He was certainly big enough to be fending for himself. He had been in the army too; he and Tim had both done their military service before going to college.

The presence of two young men transformed life on the Newboulds' farm. Tim was perpetually good-humoured. However tired after the day's work, he kept them amused throughout the evening. Mealtimes became noisy, even hilarious, because of his teasing. Liz tried to look disapproving, but her mouth would twitch and he would tell her very solemnly that she really mustn't laugh, which made her laugh even more and then she would scold him and generally treat him like a child. Her own children, who had never dared treat her like this, watched with some amazement to which, in Derek's case, was added ill-disguised resentment. Chrissie did not resent it. Tim was charming and she knew that charm was something to beware of, but he was good-natured with it – you only had to see the inexplicable way he watched over Jack to realize that. Since the students had come she found herself looking forward to coming home in the evenings with an excitement she had never felt before.

It was a lovely summer; warm day followed warm day as they gathered in the hay. It was a season of hot sunshine tempered by a fresh, drying breeze. George Newbould could not remember a better.

Half the village, it seemed to Jack and Tim, came to help with the haymaking. One or two women came along during the day, but it was in the afternoon, after tea, that they rolled up in force. Whole families arrived and George Newbould found a job to suit each of them, even the smallest children helping with raking up the hay while their parents forked it into rows or cocked it up into hubs to dry. The young families left early, but others worked on until late at night. At nine o'clock Liz and Chrissie brought out the supper and the haymakers downed tools and went over to the side of the field where piles of bread and a great Wensleydale cheese, custard pies and all the other baking that Liz had been busy with all day, were laid out ready for them. Tim jumped about handing round cups of tea and plates of food, teasing the womenfolk mercilessly. The villagers watched and listened with amusement, saying little. He was a performer, was Tim, and they recognized him as such and enjoyed the free entertainment he provided.

Afterwards they went back to the haymaking. The twilights were long quiet affairs, night coming slowly. When it was dark, George and Derek brought out lanterns to work by.

It was such a good season that the haymaking was nearly over by the time Nell came home from school. She observed the transformation wrought by Tim and Jack in the Newbould household with interest. Not only was Aunt Liz changed, though that was remarkable enough, but Chrissie too was subtly altered. Physically, Nell decided, she was the same, but there was something about her which you could only call a kind of sophistication. She reacted to Tim's teasing with the nearest her sensible, kindly manner could get to flirtatiousness. Since Christmas, Chrissie had grown up.

Nell thought the change deplorable. Her resentment was increased when she found that the next evening, her very first proper night at home, Chrissie was actually going out. Tim had seen a poster in the shop window about the annual village Flower Show dance, and promptly asked if he could take Chrissie. They did not usually go; the date fell awkwardly in the middle of haymaking, but they were well ahead this year and George had no objections.

Because it was Saturday they didn't have a meal in the hayfield, so the family was assembled in the kitchen when Chrissie came down. Nell stared at her in disbelief: Chrissie was a different being. She was wearing a New Look dress which she had made herself. It was made of pale blue lacy material through which the midnight-blue lining moved like a living night. Her golden hair was turned back into a roll which went right round her head, framing her face. She was wearing a lot of make-up, especially lipstick. She looked, Nell thought, just like a film star.

At the sight of her Tim reeled back, his hand shielding his eyes.

'Radiant!' he exclaimed. 'A goddess!'

Nell thought him extremely silly.

'Back by half past ten, mind,' Liz said.

'Oh, *Mum*.'

'Thank you so much, Mrs Newbould,' Tim put in with excessive gratitude. 'Midnight, did you say? I'll see your daughter is delivered safely back to you on the first stroke.'

'Now, Tim – I said . . .'

'Maybe half past ten *is* a bit early, Mother,' George intervened. 'I think we might say midnight.' He turned to Tim. 'But Mother and me'll be waiting up, mind, and when we say midnight we mean midnight and not five minutes past.'

Tim held out his hand solemnly.

'Agreed,' he said.

Having shaken hands with her father, he turned to Chrissie. 'Come on, Cinderella,' he said, 'there's no end of rats and pumpkins at the door.' They went out laughing and the kitchen seemed very quiet when they had gone.

That night Nell lay awake for a long time alone in the bedroom she shared with Chrissie, missing her. She wondered what they were doing now, Chrissie and Tim. Dancing maybe? Kissing perhaps? She tried to imagine it and couldn't. They were probably only eating supper at the trestle tables in the village hall. Or unromantic bridge rolls with fishpaste. She hoped so, anyway.

She must have fallen asleep for she did not hear Chrissie come in. She examined her cousin carefully next morning for any signs of adult experiences, but could see none. Somebody at school had said that when you lost your virginity the whites of your eyes went cloudy. Nell took a close look next morning at the whites of Chrissie's eyes, and then, as quickly as she could without attracting attention, compared them with her own in the old looking-glass that swung in a wooden frame on top of the dressing-table. They didn't look much different; in fact, if anything her own looked cloudier, but then that might have been because the glass was a bit pitted. She wasn't altogether sure anyway what virginity was, nor how one set about losing it. She didn't even know why its loss mattered, but hadn't liked to ask since all the others seemed to know, and she didn't want them to think that she was just an ignorant country girl.

It seemed very quiet in the Newboulds' kitchen after the students had gone. Chrissie walked home slowly; only because there was no point in hurrying, she told herself, now that there was no work waiting for her in the fields. Liz reverted to her usual self; the teasing and laughing seemed like a temporary aberration – almost an illness.

The students wrote to thank them. Two weeks later Tim wrote asking if they might come back and help with the corn harvest.

'You'll say no, of course,' Liz said sharply.

'Well, I could do with a hand.'

'They said they were only farm-working until they'd got their results. They said in their letters they've both passed, so why aren't they looking for jobs, then? That's what they should be doing, not trailing back here.'

'He's stuck on our Chrissie,' Derek said. 'That's why he wants to come back.'

'That's not true,' Chrissie said, and blushed.

'You're going red, our Chrissie.'

'Little boys of sixteen are thoroughly objectionable,' Chrissie snapped at him, and flounced out.

The three of them stared at the door in amazement.

'By gum,' George said, 'that's not like our Chrissie. You'll go after her, lad, and apologize.'

'Oh, heck, if you say so.'

Derek got up. He also slammed the door after him.

Their parents looked at each other.

'Don't take on,' George said, before Liz could speak. 'They're growing up, that's all there is to it.'

'It's not just that,' Liz said. 'It's true what he said, George.'

'Ay.' He paused for a moment and then said, 'She could do worse.'

'*What?* Our Chrissie marry someone like that and not settle down near us? You must be out of your mind, George Newbould.'

'But . . .'

'Our Chrissie's cut out to be a farmer's wife, if ever a girl was. I've pictured her living near us as long as I can remember.'

There was silence for a while, then George said, 'Mind you, maybe we're worrying about nothing.'

'What does he want coming back here for, then?'

'Maybe,' George said hopefully, 'maybe he's just partial to a bit of harvesting?'

'Maybe pigs can fly,' Liz told him.

They were all surprised when only Jack turned up.

'We were expecting you both,' George explained.

'Tim's very sorry to let you down, Mr Newbould,' Jack apologized. 'But he only got the telegram yesterday. He's been offered the job he wanted, but only on condition that he starts right away.'

'He did right to go, then,' George said, nodding approval. 'And what about yourself?'

'I was offered my job a couple of weeks ago, but I don't start until November.'

'Well, come along in and get that great rucksack off your back,' Liz said. 'Your bed's ready in the loft and I expect you're hungry.'

Jack was surprised at the warmth of her welcome. True, she

had given him her characteristic suspicious upward glance, but seemed much better pleased to see him than he had expected. He had felt quite sure that she would resent his arriving without her favourite, Tim.

'By the way, Tim sends his love,' he said to Chrissie as they sat down to tea.

'Very kind, I'm sure,' Liz cut in. 'Send him ours when you write.'

'I doubt there'll be much letter-writing time,' George said.

The corn harvest was a much more serious business than the hay had been; it was less sociable for a start, since it was not the kind of work which unskilled families could join in and help. Moreover the whole atmosphere was much less light-hearted without Tim. There was no teasing now. Nell had gone, too, back to her aunt to get ready for school.

Jack made an effort to play Tim's role, but the effect was strained. Chrissie listened and watched, sensing that it was for her sake that he was trying to be like Tim. She wished he would just be himself. She wished she understood his underlying sadness. Once, when she casually asked him how he had filled in his time between haymaking and harvest, he had not only answered evasively, but had looked at her with a kind of panic. She talked quickly of something else, but she made up her mind there and then, that one day she would talk to him, share his burden, whatever it was.

'Go and fetch the men in, Chrissie love,' her mother said one evening when she came in from work. 'I'm sure I don't know what's keeping them, and tea's spoiling.'

Chrissie walked up the lane, just as the three men came out of the field. Her father and Jack leant on the gate, looking back with satisfaction at the neat rows of stooks of corn. It struck her, as she watched the two men, that Jack was like her father in his appreciation of a job well done, in the craftsmanlike way in which he had to do everything properly for its own sake. Derek was waiting impatiently in the lane, kicking at the ground like a tethered bull.

'Come on,' he said, as she approached. 'Here's our Chrissie sent to fetch us.'

'Now then, Chrissie love,' her father said, his eyes looking his welcome.

'Good evening,' Jack said stiffly.

'Ay, it's a grand crop,' George went on, continuing the interrupted conversation as they walked back down the lane.

'But t'last. It's grazing land, is this, grazing land intended by nature.'

'Oh, never mind all that!' Derek cut in. 'Tea's waiting.'

He moved ahead, pulling at his father's arm. Jack turned to Chrissie and said, 'It's beautiful, this scenery. I should love – I mean, I wonder if you'd – perhaps we could go for a walk this evening?'

But Derek heard and turned round, laughing loudly.

'Walks! Townsfolk are always on about walks. Don't you get enough of walking, going round and round the dratted fields?'

'Take no notice of him,' Chrissie said, but she knew that Jack had taken notice and been shamed into silence. With that curious boldness that came upon her only when her need to help could not be thwarted, she said, 'Well, *I* like walking – I often go for walks with Nell – and I'll go with you, Jack, if Mum doesn't need any help this evening.'

But Liz did need help that evening, and every other one, too. So the days passed and Chrissie began to be afraid that she would never be able to talk to Jack, not really talk, and that he would go away from the farm with no easing of his burden.

It was Liz who inadvertently gave them an afternoon together.

'These chickens have to go up to Bleathorpe's,' she said to George. 'Chrissie will see to them, but can you drive her up?'

'Nay, I've to get on with cutting Bran Meadow.'

He turned to Jack.

'Can you drive them up?' he asked.

'I'll be glad to, Mr Newbould.'

'Well, I didn't – ' Liz began.

'That's all right,' Jack said quickly. 'Got the keys, Mr Newbould?'

'In t'van, lad. Thanks.'

So it was done, and soon they were driving up the rough lane, Jack at the wheel, Chrissie beside him in the passenger seat and a load of cackling hens squawking away in the back.

'It's nice to have a bit of time off harvesting, isn't it?' Chrissie remarked, smiling up at him.

He nodded. He would have liked to say: only because it was with her; but was afraid it would sound like a commonplace piece of flirtation, so he said nothing and they drove up the lane in silence.

At the farm they were greeted by Mrs Bleathorpe, a talkative lady who cross-examined them on their harvesting, the Newboulds' health, and what had become of Nell. All the while she never took her sharp eyes off them, glancing from one to the other, as if afraid that they might escape before she had finished her questioning.

She and Chrissie saw to the fowls, while Mr Bleathorpe, a fat, monosyllabic little man with a red face, showed Jack round the farm.

'You going to farm?' he asked Jack as the two women reappeared in the yard.

'No, I'm a civil engineer.'

'Pity.'

'Will you stay for a sup of tea?' Mrs Bleathorpe asked.

'No, thank you,' Chrissie said. 'I've brought a flask with me and we'll be needed back home.'

She moved back to the van as she spoke and Mrs Bleathorpe had to accept defeat.

'She's lonely,' Chrissie said, as they drove down the lane. 'You didn't mind not staying, did you? But honestly we'd never have got away. And I have brought a flask of tea.'

Jack stopped the van with a jerk.

'Do you want to picnic here in the lane?' he asked, abruptly.

'Oh, we'll go over the stile into the field.'

They sat on boulders at the foot of the wall, protected by it from the wind, which had been quite sharp in the lane.

'That's Hartshead Fell in the distance,' Chrissie said, pointing. 'It's only from here that you can see it. It's hidden by Westerbirt lower down.'

'It's beautiful,' he said. 'So – so *clean*,' he ended unromantically.

Chrissie smiled at the adjective, but she knew what he meant; by late summer most countryside looks a bit dusty and shop-soiled, but here in the Dales it was still fresh and the grass green and springy.

'Our Nell loves to come up here,' she said. 'It's the first place she comes when she's been away. I'm afraid I hardly notice it; I suppose farming people take it for granted. It's where they work.'

'What a work place!' he said, gazing at the miles of upland pasture whose different shades of green were broken by outcrops of grey rock, and dotted with boulders and sheep. Lower down, the land was patterned with fields cut in squares and rectangles and irregular shapes without name. Some still swayed with crops ripe for cutting, while others were a pale carpet of stubble with a tiny darker speck in the corner where the stack awaited the thresher.

He turned to her as if to say something important.

'What a work place,' was all he managed to repeat.

'Where will your work be – in November, I mean?' she asked, handing him a cup of tea from the flask. 'Biscuit?'

He took one automatically.

'It's up in Northumberland,' he said. 'I should think Newcastle's the nearest town. Or Morpeth. I should need to look it up on a map.'

He sounded pedantic, so much did it matter to him to get it right for her. She smiled encouragingly up at him.

'It's a sewerage scheme,' he added tragically.

Briefly she gave thanks that nobody else was present to hear him – and laugh.

'You'll go home, I suppose, before that? I mean, after you leave here?'

'Well, I don't really have a home,' he said with dreadful forced lightness.

'Oh, but you *must* have a home,' she exclaimed, astonished. 'I mean, everybody has a home somewhere.'

He looked at her wordlessly. She knew that he was trying to find the right light-hearted phrase to please her, as Tim would have done. Instinctively she put up her hand to prevent him, touching his cheek.

'Tell me about it, truly,' she said.

Obediently, he told her about his father, a doctor who had died suddenly last spring. It was the term before finals; he himself had been distracted, he had not given as much time and thought to his bereaved mother as he should have done. But she was always so capable, had seen to everything so calmly. He told her how he had gone home for the weekend, just before his exams, how he had found his mother when he went up with her morning tea, so still in the silent room. She had got the overdose right. Lay people often make mistakes, but his mother was a nurse and never made mistakes about things like that. He told her how Tim had insisted on taking him away to work on a farm after finals, and how Tim had afterwards gone back with him and helped him to clear the house. That was what they had been doing between haytime and harvest.

He talked quickly, as if once started he could not stop. Tears came into his eyes, but he did not seem to notice them. Only when he told her about going back to the empty house which had been his lifetime's home, did his voice break and he could not go on.

Chrissie moved towards him and he reached out for her blindly.

'Oh, Chrissie,' he said, 'Chrissie, I – '

'Well, there you are!' Mrs Bleathorpe's voice cut in behind them. She was standing on the step of the stile, her face bobbing through the gap in the wall. 'I saw the van in the lane and I knew you wouldn't mind giving me a lift down to the village.'

Jack jumped up, guilty and ashamed. Chrissie moved protectively in front of him, shielding him from Mrs Bleathorpe's eyes. 'Of course we don't mind,' she said and her voice, as always, was calm and kindly. 'There's a little tea left in the flask. Would you like some?'

'No, love, thanks. I had a cup before I left. I was intending walking down, you see, and then I saw the van and I thought – are you sure you don't mind?'

'Of course not,' Chrissie said again and they all three got into the van, Chrissie sitting in the back where the hens had been.

That evening the men worked again in the fields and afterwards Jack went to bed early, pleading a headache. Chrissie knew he was avoiding her and she knew why; he was ashamed of breaking down in front of her, of seeming to want her pity. Her father hadn't helped by recounting at teatime at great length the various sick or motherless animals Chrissie had nursed and coaxed back to life. He kept on about how tender-hearted she was, full of pity for anything or anyone in distress. She didn't need to look at Jack to know what he was feeling; he couldn't bear to think she had treated him like a sick calf or orphan lamb. She had made everything worse for him, she thought miserably, and she had only wanted to help.

The weather got hotter and heavier, reaching a peak the day they carried the last field of barley. All day long the men toiled, building up the stooks into a stack at the corner of the field near the yard. Chrissie thought of Nell who always liked to watch a stack being built: it grew like a house as the men carried the sheaves, rattling with corn, up the ladder which ran down its side. Tomorrow it would all be taken down, the corn stored away in sacks and the straw built into a new stack.

'The weather's on the change,' George said gloomily at breakfast the next day.

'When's the thresher coming, Dad?'

'It'll be here by ten.'

'I'm looking forward to this,' Jack said. 'It's new to me.'

Work might save him, Chrissie thought humbly, where I have failed.

'It's worst toil of lot, is threshing,' Derek warned.

'Now don't put t'lad off before he even starts,' George said.

When the thresher arrived, Jack watched fascinated as the tractor manoeuvred itself into position near the stack, backing up to it as closely as it could. George stationed the men, as a general might his troops; Derek and Jack were sent up on top of the stack to throw down the sheaves, another farmer, whose corn was already threshed, cut the bands and fed the sheaves into the thresher, Mr Philby and his friend were stationed at the back of the machine to cope with the straw, Bert was to carry the sacks full of corn, while his ancient father, who always came to help, was put in charge of changing the sacks.

The contractor himself saw to the thresher and his mate carried water for it, as the belt, which was already causing trouble, was in constant need of moistening.

'That danged belt,' George said irritably. 'It was nowt but a trouble last year. Can you stand by, Chrissie? We may need a hand with water, and fetching tools and such like.'

He was anxious and harassed. It wasn't just that he was worried in case the weather broke before the threshing was done; he was ill-at-ease in the presence of the great machine and at being dependent on its good behaviour. He knew what a man could do, but machines he found unpredictable.

Jack soon realized that Derek had not been exaggerating when he said threshing was the worst toil of all. It was laborious work, dusty, and dominated by the machine, but when the first corn rattled out of the funnel he felt a sudden and totally unexpected leap of excitement. It might seem like factory work, but really it was just a modern version of the age-old ways of separating corn from straw, of beating grain out of husks. He stared down at the grain with delight, almost with awe. Chrissie saw the expression on his face and suddenly she wanted to shout to him, to celebrate the harvest, to embrace him because they had all worked for this and she knew how he felt as he looked at the corn. She turned away, shocked at herself; it wasn't pity she felt for him at all.

'Get a move on,' she heard Derek say to him roughly. 'Got to keep the damned thing fed, you know.'

Jack apologized and concentrated on heaving the sheaves down to the ground.

They worked all day, under a sky which every hour grew heavier and more thunderous. In the afternoon Bert's father left and George put Chrissie in charge of changing the sacks. She was soon as dusty as the rest of them.

The stack slowly diminished, the straw one which they built alongside growing steadily. There was now no need to throw down the sheaves; they could be reached from the ground. Jack was moved to humping the full sacks of corn. It was a relief at first to use different muscles, but soon he felt as if a great hole was being dug somewhere in the middle of his spine. He tried taking the weight first on one side and then on the other, but still the pressure concentrated there. Chrissie watched him; she could almost feel the ache in his back.

'Feeling like giving up, are you?' she heard Derek ask, a jeering note in his voice.

She waited anxiously for his reply, knowing, as Derek knew, that Jack was near to exhaustion and less used to this heavy work than the others.

'No, I'm fine, thanks,' she heard him say cheerfully. 'A bit of a thirst on me, that's all.'

She felt proud of him, so proud that she wanted to run to him and tell him so and hug him. Again she checked herself, shocked. Whatever would her mother say?

'Well, here's Mother bringing out something to quench it,' George said, as Liz appeared carrying cans of tea and baskets of food.

They didn't waste energy walking to eat under the trees, but just crouched by the stack, afraid that if they relaxed their limbs would refuse to work again. They drank tea and ate potato pie without pleasure; it was just a necessary refuelling which they got over quickly and returned to their toil.

It was a gentle twilight; the moon did not rise, but rather emerged high in the sky, through the mist. It was a huge moon, pinkish and hazy, and it hung above the stack as if watching over their harvesting. Soft and luxurious, it was a promise of indolence in the world to come.

The last corn clattered out of the funnel and into the last sack. The men stood for a moment like figures in a tableau. There was no rejoicing, no sound, only a grim satisfaction in the red-rimmed eyes with which they looked at the pale rectangle which marked the place where the stack had been.

'Well, thanks all,' George Newbould said. 'It looks like it's done.'

Though the men's throats had been too dry to speak, they somehow raised a cheer.

'There'll be rain by daybreak,' George remarked, glancing up at the sky as he gathered up the tools. He led the way back to the barn and they all followed, trailing forks and rakes because they were suddenly too weary to lift them up on to their shoulders.

Chrissie was collecting together the cans and mugs and plates and putting them into the hamper.

'I'll take that,' Jack said.

'No, you're laden.'

He moved the rakes and forks into one hand and took the hamper from her.

'I can manage,' he said.

He smiled down at the weary face. During the weeks he had spent on the farm he had watched her face and throat and arms deepen from pink to rosy brown and her hair turn a paler honey-colour in the sun. Through the pain and grief of this golden summer he had watched her as he had watched the ripening corn. As life had stirred in him again, he had seen her as part of the living countryside, beautiful and wholesome and good.

Now her face was pinched with exhaustion, her eyes were bloodshot, her hair dull and rough with dust. She had been working since half past five this morning, he knew that. He was filled with pity for her, with a longing to comfort her. He couldn't take his eyes off her work-weary face. His voice when it came was distant, slurred, but the words astonished him.

'Chrissie,' his voice said, 'I love you.'

She didn't move. Just stared back at him. His voice croaked on desperately. 'I mean, will you marry me?'

His surprise was perhaps marginally less than hers as they stood in the empty field by the straw stack, their feet scratched by the stubble, their throats dry with corn dust. They continued to stare at each other in surprise and even when she had said, 'Yes, oh yes,' he just went on looking at her and did not move. His hands of course were laden with forks and rakes and the hamper. It seemed a very long time to Chrissie before he managed to put them all down.

'Marry a civil engineer?' Liz repeated. 'I'd as soon she married a gypsy.'

'Nay, Liz, you don't mean it.'

'I do. I didn't stop her going nursing just so she could marry somebody who would take her off to the other end of England – abroad even.'

'It might have been better if she *had* gone nursing – at least she'd only have been fifty miles away.'

'That's right; blame me.'

'Nay Liz, don't talk of blame.'

'Well, I do blame myself. I wish I'd never let those two students inside my kitchen.'

They were in the kitchen now, Liz and George, sitting by the fire after Sunday dinner. Outside the rain was beating down as it had done ceaselessly since the night of the threshing. They were alone because Chrissie had gone into Bragton to see Jack off on the only Sunday train, and Derek was getting ready to go out with his girl-friend.

They had had the conversation many times before. George was philosophical about it; he had taken the catastrophe with a calmness that incited Liz to greater furies of opposition than she would otherwise have felt.

'I can't understand our Chrissie; she hardly knows him.'

'She will by the time of the wedding. They'll wait a year at least, they've promised that. They've plenty of time to change their minds in a twelvemonth.'

'We knew each other fifteen years before we were married.'

'Ay, but things were different then. There's been changes since.'

'For the worse.'

'Maybe.'

They sat in silence for a while, then George got up. 'I'll put the kettle on, Mother,' he said, going into the scullery.

Derek came downstairs. He was dressed in his best suit ready to go out to tea with his girl-friend's parents. He was carrying a new umbrella which she had given him.

'Chrissie back yet?' he asked.

'No.'

'Don't look so worried, Mum. He's all right, is Jack. I wish I was in his line myself. I'd rather have machines than animals any day.'

'Don't let your dad hear you say that,' Liz told him sharply.

'What's that I'm not to hear, then?' George asked, coming in from the scullery, carrying the kettle.

'Our Derek's on about machinery,' Liz told him.

'There'll be some changes here when this farm's yours, eh, Derek?' George said, pushing the kettle firmly back into the glowing embers of the fire.

'There should be changes *before* that,' Derek said gruffly.

'Not while I'm still master.'

'Give my regards to Mrs Claypole,' Liz called after Derek as he went out. Her voice was unnaturally polite; even to send a message to Mrs Claypole she mentally took off her apron.

'Well, we must be thankful our Derek'll be settled here one day,' she said, reverting to her normal accent as she went over to the dresser to fetch the teapot. 'Moira'll make him a grand wife, too.'

George said nothing.

'Won't she?' Liz insisted.

'I'd sooner Jack and our Chrissie than Moira and our Derek.'

Liz looked for a moment as if she might throw the teapot at him in exasperation. Then she put it down on the hearth to warm, and turned to face him.

'I don't know, George Newbould, really I don't. You bear with Chrissie choosing a real foreigner and yet when our Derek finds a girl who's been born and bred up here you don't think that suitable.'

'It's not a question of location,' George said slowly. 'Sit down.'

They sat in silence until the kettle began to sing. Then Liz reached the caddy down from the mantelshelf and made the tea. They heard the click of the latch as somebody opened the back door.

'There's our Chrissie,' Liz said.

'Now mind what you say,' George warned.

'As if I wouldn't!'

Chrissie came in.

'Bring yourself a cup, love, when you've got your wet things off,' George said. 'We've just made some tea.'

A few minutes later Chrissie brought the cup and sat down quietly between them.

'Got his train all right, then?' Liz asked as she poured the tea.

'Yes, thanks, Mum.'

'You'll miss him, love.'

'Yes, Dad, but term starts next week and I'll be busy enough,' Chrissie said calmly.

Liz made a great effort.

'He's welcome to come at Christmas – if you're still, well, friends by then.'

'Thank you, Mum. I expect we shall be.'

George filled his pipe slowly. 'Your mother and I would like him to think of this as his home,' he said deliberately, 'since he hasn't one of his own, like.'

'Oh thank you, Dad, thank you.'

To the amazement of all three of them, Chrissie got up, hugged her father, burst into tears and ran out of the room.

'Now look what you've done!' Liz said. 'Upsetting her like that.'

'She's all right.'

'I'd best go and . . .'

'Nay, leave her. It'll do her good to cry.'

He lit his pipe and Liz got her mending, both of them thinking of nothing but the girl crying upstairs. But when Chrissie came down a little later she was quite composed.

'We thought we might announce our engagement at Christmas, Jack and I,' she said. 'If that's all right.'

'If that's what you still want by Christmas, it's all right by us, isn't it, Mother?'

Liz nodded, but she couldn't quite bring herself to speak the words of agreement.

'Then we could get married next summer.'

Again her father said, yes, if that was what they still wanted. Again her mother nodded, but couldn't bring herself to speak.

'I'd like just to have Nell for a bridesmaid,' Chrissie went on.

'What about your cousins?' Liz asked. 'You don't want to upset them. Or Moira? Moira might like to be asked.'

'Mm, we can think about that. I'll make the dresses.'

'It's a lot of work.'

'I'll start in good time.'

'You'll have the veil, of course. It's going a bit yellow, but

I'll see what washing it 'll do.'

'The one you had?'

'Yes, and your Grandma Howell. She had to go by pony cart over to Barnston for her wedding. I've got the photograph somewhere. It's a beautiful veil.'

'I'll make the cake, too.'

'Nay, you're not baking your own cake. That's my job. You can see to the icing.'

'Thanks, Mum. What do you think about the reception? Here or in the village hall?'

'The village hall; we've not enough room here. And it's nice to have a bit of dancing after. Peggy Gargrave'll play the piano.'

'What about the meal, d'you think?'

'A proper sit-down do,' Liz said firmly. 'I hate that business of standing up holding plates. I thought it was an awful mess at Mazie Lawson's. Folks want to rest their feet a bit after a wedding.'

'Then we'll need the hall. Auntie Elsie'll help with the cooking, won't she?'

'All of them will; Bertha, Elsie, Marjorie, oh, and Dorothy Ackroyd. There'll be no shortage of helpers.'

George sat and listened to then, puffing at his pipe to hide his amazement. Somehow, once Jack was out of the house, Liz seemed to have quite come round to him, or to the idea of a wedding, anyway.

'You'll make a real nice pair, Chrissie,' he put in injudiciously. 'He's a grand-looking man, is Jack.'

'Handsome is as handsome does,' Liz told him sharply.

Chapter Ten

Nell travelled up by train with Aunt Thorpe to Chrissie's wedding. Since she had spent the previous Easter holidays in London and the previous Christmas skiing with a school party, it was a year since she had been to Netherby; she felt more than ever like a visitor.

Like a visitor, she offered to help.

'You don't think there's anything left to do the day before the wedding?' Aunt Liz dismissed her offer sharply.

'You can come along to the hall and help me finish decorating,' Chrissie said kindly.

'What, are you *painting* the place?' she asked in amazement.

'Oh, Nell, you don't change,' Chrissie said laughing. 'Of course I'm not painting the village hall. Flowers and greenery, you know.'

The village hall was a gaunt Victorian building, high-ceilinged and unwelcoming. Nell hardly recognized it now. From its uncovered rafters hung festoons of leaves and paper flowers. There were real flowers everywhere, too, in vases and urns and hanging baskets. In the side room the trestle tables were spread with white linen and decorated with flowers and table napkins which Chrissie had folded in about six different ways.

'It looks like a very, very grand hotel,' Nell said, awestruck. 'Yet it looks homely, too. You are clever, Chrissie.'

'Oh, I had lots of help,' Chrissie said. 'I didn't do much myself.'

She was busy crossing items off a list.

'We'll need more trays,' she murmured, 'for serving.'

'Golly, how can you think of things like trays, the day before your wedding?'

'What's wrong with trays, then?'

'If I was getting married . . .' She stopped, great dark eyes shining in her pale face. 'I'd . . .'

'Well, what would you do?'

'Oh, I don't know, but I'd be thinking about all sorts of things, not *trays*. You're so *calm*, Chrissie. It's not natural. Honestly, you're different from other people.'

Chrissie laughed. 'Nay, love, it's you that's special, not me.'

'What do you mean?'

'Well, you're different from the rest of us – more interesting, somehow.'

'Of course I'm not.'

But she was, she thought with satisfaction. She was an orphan for a start and that was always interesting. Then she had been lifted out of this ordinary little village and removed to a boarding-school where she had met heaps of different sorts of people. She had broadened her outlook, as Aunt Thorpe would say. And she was going to have a career; one of the post-war generation of freed women, she'd be. Free of all the things that tied Chrissie. And clever, yes, definitely clever.

'Anyway, I shan't get married,' she said suddenly.

Chrissie laughed.

'You say that now, at fourteen.'

'I mean it, honestly.'

'I'll ask you again in five or six years and see what you say.'

'I shan't change.'

Her seriousness was catching. Chrissie stopped teasing and said, 'You mean, you want to have a career after the university – Aunt Thorpe said you'll be going away to college.'

Nell nodded. Almost fiercely, she said, 'I shall make my own living and be quite, quite independent of everyone. It would be jolly silly after years and years of earning my independence to chuck it all away by marrying some chap or other ...'

'Well, if it *was* just some chap or other ... but not if it's a *special* chap – like, say, Jack.'

'No – any chap.'

'Well, I don't feel as if I'm throwing away anything,' Chrissie objected.

'You're not,' Nell told her airily. Then she added, 'I mean, it's different for me – I shall have a career.'

'Yes, I can see it would be different for you,' Chrissie said humbly.

'I didn't mean – I mean you – after all, it's jolly useful what you've done at Bragton and ...'

'It's all right, love,' Chrissie said, taking her arm as they walked down the hall. 'I know what you mean.'

She locked the door behind them, pocketing the enormous key.

'Come on,' she said, 'we'll be late for supper.'

Tim and Jack, who were staying at The Curlew, came for supper, so it was festive, despite Liz's frequent apologies for the deficiencies of the meal. She apologized for Derek, too.

'He's out with his young lady's family. He's promised not to be late, though.'

'Tell me about Derek's girl-friend,' Nell asked Chrissie as they got ready for bed.

'She's all right,' Chrissie said guardedly. 'Mum likes her.'

'I can see that. Why does she call her his young lady?'

'Well, she's a bit – you know.'

'Stuck up?'

Chrissie smiled. 'You could say so, I suppose,' was as far as she would commit herself to criticism.

'I'll see her tomorrow, anyway.'

'No, they can't come. They have to go to Moira's grand-parents' golden-wedding party; it was a previous arrangement.'

'It must have been very previous – you arranged this ages ago,' Nell remarked, following Chrissie along the corridor to the bathroom.

'Do you remember,' she asked later, as she began to clean her teeth at the basin, while Chrissie lay in the bath, 'do you remember how shocked you were when I first came home from boarding-school and told you we had baths together there?'

'Well, it wasn't our way. It didn't seem right, somehow.'

'You were so modest. I think I was until I went away to school – I remember being quite shocked at the way everyone stood about naked at bedtime – even the head girl.'

'Do spit, Nell. I can't hear you properly with that mouthful of toothpaste.'

Nell spat. 'It's been jolly good for you really, having me go to boarding-school. It's broadened your outlook.'

She sat down on the laundry basket and looked down at Chrissie as she lay in the bath. Even with her hair dragged back into the bathcap Chrissie's face still looked lovely; calm, clear-skinned, gentle-eyed. The skin of her body was fair and smooth too. She floated in the water like some pale, forked plant drifting in a stream.

Nell sighed. 'You are a lovely shape, Chrissie,' she said enviously. 'I wish I wasn't so skinny.'

'You'll fill out,' Chrissie said. 'It's better than being all fat and bulgy.'

'I'd like to be just like you. Jack's jolly lucky.'

She is Titian-coloured, Nell thought, gazing down at her cousin, but didn't say so in case Chrissie didn't understand what she meant.

It was interesting, she reflected, that the hair on Chrissie's head was pale gold, but her pubic hair was darker in colour, reddish, really. Somebody at school had said that the hair on your head ended up the same as your pubic hair – presum-ably only in colour.

'You're a terrible one for staring, Nell,' Chrissie said.

They were all up early on the morning of Chrissie's wed-ding. Nell heard the household stirring as she lay in bed unwilling to get up. Through half-closed eyes she watched Chrissie getting dressed. She was putting on an ordinary cotton dress. On the wardrobe behind her hung her wedding dress, covered by a linen bag made out of an old sheet. Alongside was the smaller one which contained Nell's dress. She remembered that these two macabre shapes were the last things she had looked at before going to sleep. No wonder she had dreamed of a hanging.

It would be the last time, she thought miserably, that Chrissie and she would share this room: no more lying in bed in the dark at night talking, or waking in the winter, both snuggled down beneath the bedclothes, chatting in order to postpone getting up and facing the icy run to the bathroom. No more of that, no more waking up together in the morning.

'Oh Chrissie,' she blurted out, 'I wish you weren't getting married.'

Chrissie came and sat on the edge of the bed.

'It makes no difference, Nell love,' she whispered, hugging her.

But it does, it does, Nell thought. Aloud she said, 'No, I suppose not.'

She wondered what would happen if Chrissie and Jack came to stay during the holidays when she was here. With a bit of luck Aunt Liz would put Chrissie and her in this bedroom and Jack up in the loft where he belonged. She giggled.

'That's better,' Chrissie said. 'Come on, up you get. We've a busy day ahead.'

'I'm supposed to look after you, aren't I?' Nell said as she pulled on her clothes. 'I mean, being a bridesmaid and all that?'

'Yes, and you'll do it marvellously. You'll see to the flowers for me and help me get ready and everything.'

'Ah yes,' Nell said. 'And put in the odd stitch here and there and run the iron over the wedding dress – and turn it dark brown in no time like I did Uncle George's best shirt.'

Chrissie laughed. 'Never mind, love. Nobody can be good at *everything*. There are lots of other things you can do.'

Nell hugged her. 'You're so comfy,' she said, thinking how nice and soft Chrissie's bosom was to lean against. Then she sighed; Jack would find it comfy, too.

'Hurry up, you girls,' Liz's voice called upstairs. 'Breakfast's on the table.'

When they went downstairs George and Derek were coming into the kitchen from the scullery.

'Golly, you don't look a bit like a wedding,' Nell exclaimed.

'Nay, lass, you don't expect us to milk cows in our Sunday best,' George said, smiling at her.

'If we had a milking machine it would help,' Derek pointed out.

'It's not worth it,' George said obstinately.

'You've got to keep up with the times, Dad, or go out of business.'

'It'll be yours one day and you can do what you like with it then. While it's mine, it'll be run my way.'

'Will you have done arguing and get on with breakfast,' Liz cut in, 'so that I can get cleared away?'

After breakfast Nell helped Chrissie to carry the last of the provisions along to the village hall, where George's cousin Elsie was already in charge of operations. She was a huge woman, wrapped in a flowered apron with her hair knotted up into a kind of turban made of butter-muslin. She was organizing what seemed to Nell a whole army of other women all similarly clad in flowered aprons and muslin turbans. They filled the kitchen with their noise and bustle. Although it was a big kitchen it was crowded with women and food: great bowlfuls of eggs and tomatoes, buckets of potatoes and cucumbers, loaves of bread and, on a huge baking-board, a whole array of hams and chickens, scotch eggs and sausages. The women were peeling and shelling, carving, slicing, spreading, scrubbing and all the time talking and laughing without pause.

A man appeared with a sackful of lettuces and was positively attacked by a tall angular woman whom Nell did not remember ever seeing before, but who bore such a striking resemblance to Aunt Liz that she knew she must be a relation.

'Whatever 'ave you been doing wi' 'em, Edward Dowbiggins?' she shouted, seizing the sack and shaking its contents out on to the wooden draining-boards between the sinks. Two other women joined her, unasked, and the three of them fell upon the lettuces, tearing them apart, tossing the leaves into water, shaking and patting, chastising the dirt out.

'I'd almost gived up 'ope of getting these lettuces,' the angular woman shouted over her shoulder.

'Nay, think on't,' the man said, lifting his cap to scratch his head. 'You said you wanted 'em fresh.'

'Any fresher and t'guests would've 'ad to eat 'em in t'fields,' she shouted back, as she pounced on an unfortunate caterpillar lurking in a lettuce heart and squashed it between her thumb and forefinger.

The man continued to scratch his head and look bewildered.

'And are you goin' 'ome now or do we 'ave to walk round you for rest o' morning?'

'Ay, 'e'd make a good pillar, would Edward,' somebody said, and they all screamed with laughter.

'Well, I'll be goin', then, if that's all,' the man said and, still scratching his head and looking puzzled, made for the door.

'Don't leave t'sack,' the woman called after him. 'We don't want it cluttering up t'floor.'

He retrieved the sack and ambled out.

'Anything we can do to help?' Chrissie asked.

'Nay, love, you get along home,' her Aunt Elsie said. 'It's no place for a bride, isn't this. Off with you and get yourself ready. Tell your mother we've got everything we need and there's nowt for her to worry over.'

They left the kitchen, walking through the silent dining-room with its rows of linen-covered trestle tables.

'I was sorry for the man who brought the lettuces,' Nell remarked as they made for the door. 'That woman didn't half go for him, poor chap.'

'I suppose he's used to it,' Chrissie said. 'She's his wife.'

Nell burst out laughing.

'What's funny about that, Nell?'

'Oh, but it's *awful* – don't you see? And on your wedding day, too.'

The words sobered them both. They walked in silence through the village.

'I hope Jack's keeping away from the windows,' Chrissie said as they passed The Curlew. 'It's bad luck to see your bride before the wedding.'

'Maybe that's what Edward Dowbiggins did,' Nell said. 'I'll make sure it doesn't happen to Jack,' and with exaggerated care she kept her cousin to the far side as they crept furtively past the inn.

The house seemed unnaturally quiet when they got back; Aunt Thorpe, George, Liz and Derek were upstairs getting ready.

It was so quiet in the kitchen that when a little trickle of soot pattered down on to the paper stuffed up the chimney they both jumped.

'Time's standing still,' Nell whispered. 'I can feel it. It's ever so creepy.'

Chrissie laughed. 'Come on; you'll have Mum after you if she finds you waiting about while time stands still.'

They went upstairs and into the bedroom. It is really happening, Nell thought, it is really happening at last. Chrissie will be married in a few hours and gone away for ever. She won't belong here any more, she won't belong to me.

Up till now it had seemed such fun; important and exciting, of course, but somehow a bit of a joke all the same. Now it was suddenly deadly serious. They got ready in silence. Nell would have liked to talk, but everything that came into her mind seemed either too sad or too frivolous to be uttered an hour before Chrissie's wedding.

Aunt Liz appeared in the doorway; she was almost unrecognizable in the outfit Chrissie had made for her. It was of soft material, in a gentle shade of blue; it made her seem much less hard and bony. But it was the pink hat which transformed her. It framed her face perfectly and she looked beautiful.

'I can't wear this hat, really I can't, Chrissie,' she said. 'I'll just put on my navy.'

She took off the pink creation and laid it on the bed. Going over to the looking-glass she proceeded to ram a sensible blue hat, apparently made of felt and cardboard, firmly on her head.

'No, Mum . . .'

'I'm sorry, Chrissie, I know it was a job to make but it's important to be comfortable at a wedding. It's bad enough these shoes, but not my head and all.'

'All right, Mum. You did say you'd wear a bit of powder, didn't you?'

'Oh, very well,' Liz said, giving way because she had won about the hat. 'Just a little, mind.'

Chrissie sat her mother down on a stool and reached for a jar.

'Just powder,' Liz said sharply. 'Nothing else.'

'Just a bit of cream, Mum, to make it stick on.'

'When I was a girl nobody wore make-up except . . .' She glanced at Nell and then said meaningfully to Chrissie, 'women who weren't *nice*.'

She sat with her face screwed up, eyes puckered, while Chrissie gently applied the powder puff.

Suddenly Nell felt sorry for her aunt. Aunt Liz was usually so much in charge of everything, but sitting there with her sharp little face screwed up against the onslaught of a powder puff she seemed suddenly vulnerable, out of her element.

'Aunt Liz,' she said impulsively. 'Do wear that lovely hat. It really does suit you. Chrissie and I both want you to.'

Liz looked at her for a moment. Her face softened. She removed the felt-and-cardboard hat and, still sitting on the stool, allowed Chrissie to arrange the pink creation on her head, tucking her hair under the brim. She even let her daughter lead her over to the glass.

Liz stared back at her reflection in the long glass in Chrissie's wardrobe: the elegant hat framed a face which was still clear-skinned and youthful, the figure in the soft blue suit was slender, the legs slim, the delicate ankles flattered by the new court shoes.

'You ought to dress up more often, Mum,' Chrissie said.

'Once is enough,' Liz said sharply. 'And speaking of dressing, what about you two? Look at you both in your dressing-gowns and less than an hour to go.'

'Don't worry, Mum, we're all ready underneath. I'll get Nell into her dress first and then she'll help me into mine, won't you, love?'

'Er, Nell,' Liz said. 'Go down and see if your Uncle George is ready.'

Surprised, Nell went to do as she was told. Liz turned to her daughter. 'Well, good luck, love,' she said. 'And don't be upset by anything that happens tonight. Men have funny ways but they don't mean any harm.'

She went out quickly, her cheeks red under the newly applied powder. It was the only allusion to sex she had ever made in her life and it took all her courage to make it. Nothing but her love of her daughter, deep and unspoken, could have made her do it.

Chrissie was still standing in front of the glass looking surprised when Nell came back into the room.

She jumped when she saw Nell, then said, 'We'll get you ready first,' and took down the bridesmaid's dress.

Despite innumerable fittings, it still came as a shock to Nell to see herself; very grown-up she looked in the long pink frock with the little satin shoes carefully dyed to match. The dress made her look slim rather than the usual skinny; it was ruched to emphasize her non-existent hips and Chrissie had contrived some quite unnecessary darts in the bodice to imply the presence of breasts.

But if her dress made her look older, Chrissie's transformed her into a different being. Once inside what seemed to Nell to be acres of lace and net and satin, the circle of orange blossom in place on her head, she was a creature of such mystery and power that it was astonishing to hear Chrissie's calm and placid voice issuing from her.

'That's Aunt Thorpe and Mum and Derek gone,' she said, as a car drew away. 'We'll go downstairs now, Nell, there's just Dad left.'

She had insisted that Nell should drive with her to church, in the same car.

Nell picked up the train and together they manoeuvred the full skirt through the narrow doorway and down the uneven passage, fearful of every nail or splinter of wood. The smell of furniture polish and mignonette and old wood seemed to Nell almost overwhelming as they made their way slowly down the stairs.

'By gum,' Uncle George said when he saw his daughter. 'You look like a queen.'

Nell wished her uncle looked a bit more regal; he never looked right somehow in his best suit. He seemed to discard his manliness with his work clothes. His face was red with too much scrubbing, not its usual healthy ruddy colour, but pink and pig-like.

'Your collar's too tight, Dad,' Chrissie said.

That was it; poor Uncle was being strangled.

'Sit down and let me see,' Chrissie said, and her long fingers moved deftly about shifting studs, tugging at celluloid, until the collar was less hostile and her father's face a better colour.

Nell watched them, thinking how typical it was that Chrissie, who ought to be playing the bride, waited on by everyone, was busy looking after somebody else's comfort, even a few minutes before her own wedding. I hope Jack looks after her, she thought with sudden fierceness – he jolly well ought to.

A car slid to a halt outside.

'Ready, are you, love?' George asked gruffly. 'You don't want to be late.'

'I promised Jack not more than five minutes late,' Chrissie said, arranging the veil over her face.

How remote she seemed now, Nell thought, mysterious behind her veil. Now she really was special. 'Don't talk any more,' she said. 'I'll see to everything.'

'Thanks, Nell.'

At the door she hesitated.

'Nell, love . . .'

'It's all right, everything's all right. You look lovely.'

'But, Nell . . .'

'Yes?'

'The flowers, Nell,' she whispered.

'Oh, my goodness, wherever are they?'

'In the scullery. On the marble slab.'

'Oh, Chrissie, how awful, I'd have forgotten. We'd have got to the church without them, and it would've been all my fault.'

'Never mind,' Chrissie said cheerfully. 'We didn't.'

Very subdued, Nell followed her uncle and cousin, carefully lifting the train of the wedding dress as they crossed the damp cobbles to the waiting car. There had been a brief shower, but now it was fine and the air smelled sweet for the rain had brought out the scent of the flowers and grass.

It seemed very strange to ride like this through the village, Nell thought, as she sat in her long dress next to Jim Boothby, the village taxi driver. She could not think of anything to say to him. Behind her, Uncle George and Chrissie sat also without saying a word.

Immediately Chrissie arrived Mrs Peters at the organ burst forth with a great explosion of 'Here Comes the Bride'. Slowly, mysterious under her veil, Chrissie walked up the aisle on her father's arm. Nell followed, careful not to tread on the train.

It seemed a very long walk to Nell, all the way up that aisle. She was trembling with excitement and tension. Somewhere in the distance Mr Pertree was standing, white-robed, waiting for them; his solicitous smile made him look very much like his wife. She saw Jack and Tim standing alone at the front on the right. On the left she saw Aunt Liz and Derek and Aunt Thorpe. How strange they all seemed, how special, as they acted their parts in the drama of Chrissie's marriage.

She had never been to a wedding before. It was much more impressive than she had imagined. The solemn majesty of its binding promises overawed her. Suddenly Chrissie and Jack seemed too frail to be repeating such everlasting vows. In the intense silence their voices seemed so small, the words so terrifying in their grandeur. This had nothing to do with the play-acting and dressing up. It was as real and naked as death.

In the vestry everything swung back to normal. People joked and congratulated, the vicar looked benign, Liz fiddled nervously with her hat, Uncle George tugged at his collar. Jack and Chrissie were ordinary mortals once again.

Mistakes were made; Liz signed her maiden name in the register. 'I can't think in this hat,' she said, all flustered.

A strange man crossed the vestry towards Nell, right arm outstretched. She proffered her own, expecting introductions, but he walked past her. 'Congratulations, Jack,' he said, and shook hands with his nephew. For a moment she saw her own hand still sticking out, an absurd object, and felt dreadfully ashamed. Later, the thing she always remembered most clearly about Chrissie's wedding was that tiny unimportant moment of rejection.

After the signing, they formed up in twos, lining up for the walk down the aisle. 'Come to the ark with me, Nell,' Tim said, grinning down at her.

The moment they reappeared Mrs Peters let fly with the wedding march. They positively paraded down the aisle, Nell thought, contrasting how it had been as they had walked up a few minutes earlier. As they approached each pew the people in it turned towards them and smiled, so it seemed as if the whole congregation was swaying. It was like cutting your way through a cornfield, she thought suddenly, remembering how it looked when the first swathes fell.

Nell walked the short distance to the village hall with an usher called Bertrand. He was a sophisticated-looking young man, a neighbour of Jack's.

'I must warn you, he's clever,' Tim said when he introduced them. 'He's landed a job lecturing undergraduates next term.'

Bertrand stayed with Nell throughout the reception; she was immensely flattered. It was the first time any young man had taken the slightest notice of her.

The whole village came from the church to the reception, as well as several who didn't get to the church because they were too busy with jobs on the farm, or just didn't fancy it. The Newboulds welcomed them all and everyone drank champagne, a gift from Jack's Uncle Charles. It was the first time Nell had tasted it and it was better than she feared. She said as much to Bertrand, as they sat down at one of the trestle tables in the dining-room.

'It's almost as nice as cider,' she said, and wondered why he laughed.

It was easy to make him laugh; he was very funny himself, too. She enjoyed herself, flirting for the first time.

'Now,' he said, as they sat down. 'Tell me all about you.'

'For what we are about to receive, Oh Lord make us truly thankful,' George prayed.

Bertrand winked at her and they both giggled.

'Nothing much to tell,' she said.

'But there must be. Tell me where you fit into the family for a start. Obviously you don't belong with the farm lot.'

'I'm Chrissie's cousin,' she said, angered by his condescending reference to the farm lot, yet flattered in a way at being distinguished from them.

'I'm sorry,' he said humbly. 'I didn't mean to be rude about your relations. Truly, I wasn't casting nasturtiums.'

He looked so solemn and penitent, like a rebuked sheep dog, that she found herself laughing.

'They're obviously splendid, anyone can see that,' he went on, 'but it's just that you don't belong to the same species.'

Part of her wanted to tell him that it was only money which had sent her away to school and removed her accent and given her a different manner, but she couldn't do it. It wasn't just that it would be rude. It would be too serious for the occasion and that was worse. She had learned not to speak the truth if the setting were unsuitable.

'It's lovely grub,' Bertrand was saying cheerfully. 'Not like your town weddings. Do you always eat like this?'

'No, it's been dry bread and water for six weeks beforehand.'

'It's kept you in good shape,' he remarked, glancing down at the pink dress approvingly.

'Potatoes, love?' Aunt Elsie asked him.

She had put down a plateful of ham and chicken in front of him and now proffered a bowlful of new potatoes afloat with butter and parsley.

'Yes, please,' he said. 'Lots.'

Aunt Elsie smiled benignly down at him, doled out a huge helping and moved her massive floral bulk down to the next table.

'Now that's what I call a waitress,' Bertrand remarked. 'None of your skinny misses.'

'I'm skinny.'

'Nonsense. You're very elegantly contrived.'

He took out a monocle and stuck it in his eye, and leaning back in his chair, surveyed her judiciously. 'The bone structure is very fine,' he drawled. 'You should be an artist's model.'

'Excuse me,' Aunt Bertha said, pushing between them, offering more champagne. They hadn't been able to get wine glasses locally so Uncle Charles's champagne was being poured into tumblers.

Nell took a long drink.

'It's so lovely and cool and fizzy,' she said, laughing as the bubbles went up her nose. 'And I thought it would be foul, like wine!'

'I say,' he counselled, 'I'd go a bit easy with the stuff. You won't half feel awful tomorrow.'

'Really?' she asked, taking another long drink.

'Well, it can make you feel depressed, but then one never knows if it's the after-effect of the champagne or the wedding.'

The ladies in floral aprons appeared en masse to remove the plates and replace them with bowls of trifle and fruit salad and cream, custard pies and tarts.

'What a spread,' Bertrand murmured. 'I do think Jack is sensible to marry into all this food.'

Nell shrieked with laughter.

'I'm quite serious, young Nell. I haven't seen a spread like this since before the war. I suppose up here in the country you were never short of anything.'

'I can't remember, really. I was only one when the war started so I didn't take much interest in the housekeeping.'

He dropped the spoon with which he had been about to ladle cream on to his plate of fruit salad and stared at her with what seemed to be genuine astonishment, though it was hard to tell with Bertrand.

'Do you mean to tell me that you are only . . .' he did some calculations with his right index finger on the palm of his left hand '. . . only fourteen?'

She nodded, not sure how to take it.

'Forgive me, I thought you were a contemporary of my aged self.'

He took out the monocle and scrutinized her again.

'It's only the dress,' she said. 'I look much younger in school uniform.'

She wished she hadn't said it; it sounded so childish and simple somehow, blurting out the truth like that.

'Then I shan't come and see you at school,' he reassured her. 'I shall wait and look you up when you leave. Five years' time, perhaps?' he asked, as if it were days.

'Five years would suit me nicely,' she said, imitating his tone.

'Where shall I look for you?'

'At the university,' she said firmly.

'Ah, an academic lady. Any particular university?'

'There aren't many. You can look around them all.'

He laughed. 'There'll be more by then. They're going to shoot up like mushrooms in the next few years.'

'Really?'

'Yes,' he said, rubbing his hands. 'Lovely for chaps like me hunting for jobs. Chairs will soon be two a penny.'

She sat in silence, puzzled by his reference to furniture. 'Are you staying up for the rest of the school holidays?' he asked.

'No, it's a shame, but I've got to go back with Aunt Thorpe tomorrow. She's taking a party of school-children from London to Paris and I'm going too.'

'A shame indeed! What a blasé young woman you are! Most people would be wild with excitement at the thought of going to Paris.'

'I shall be, but the wedding has blotted out everything up till now.'

'Of course.'

'When are *you* going?'

'I'm driving off tonight. I've to be at a conference in Cambridge tomorrow at ten.'

For a moment he sounded very serious and grand and she felt in awe of him. Then suddenly he whipped out his monocle again, pressed it into his eye and looked with exaggerated astonishment at what the floral-aproned women were bringing out of the kitchen.

'Pudding *and* cheese,' he exclaimed. 'I didn't know such a state of affairs existed in the British Isles.'

Great cheeses were being carried to the tables – Lancashires and Caerphillys and home-made Wensleydales. They were being carved up into great slices, like cake.

He helped himself liberally.

'A piece of apple pie would go well with that, love,' one of the floral ladies said, cutting him a piece and putting it on his plate.

'What an absolutely splendid mixture,' he said.

'You know what we say up here,' Aunt Elsie said. 'Apple pie without cheese is a kiss without a squeeze.'

She gave him a poke in the back and roared with laughter, her great stomach, spread with the flowered apron, heaving with mirth.

'Oh, this is a marvellous wedding,' Bertrand said to Nell. 'Actually, I'm fond of weddings. I know a lot of people can't bear them – I mean, other people's, not just their own – but I think, you know, it's so nice to have a *real* reason for a party.'

Chairs were being pushed back from the table a little, plates were emptying.

'I'll tell you something,' Bertrand said, 'the speeches will be good for a laugh.'

He means Uncle George, she thought resentfully.

'Old Tim's a good speech-maker,' Bertrand said. 'More cheese, Nell?'

She shook her head and sat back, sipping champagne, enjoying the grown-up feel of it all, listening to Bertrand who had launched himself into a monologue. As he talked she found herself seeing everything through his eyes; the kind and helpful neighbours in their flowered aprons were funny old girls, lesser beings to be teased, treated pleasantly, of course, but somehow not quite like equals, not to be afforded the seriousness due to equals. In a way, too, what had seemed like generous hospitality now seemed vulgar overfeeding, to be thoroughly enjoyed, but mocked at all the same. As if this was simply a splendid excuse for a bit of amusing self-indulgence. Part of her joined him in this feeling, but part of her bitterly resented it and part of her was ashamed.

The moment for speeches came. She saw Uncle George stand up. A few other people noticed and stopped talking. Uncle George stood there, ill-at-ease. Nell regarded him. He had been her childhood protector, all-powerful, all-knowing. But at this moment she could see him as a figure of fun in his tight blue suit. No, she could not bear him to be mocked. She longed for him to sit down. She didn't want to view him as an outsider, she didn't want to be obliged to recognize the comic in him.

More people had noticed he was standing up. Silence spread among the guests, who were now looking up at him expectantly. Uncle George lifted his hand, as if in acknowledgment. He left it in the air, not sure what to do with it next. The silence seemed to worry him. He cleared his throat noisily. At the same time he described a circle with his great strong hand, so that he seemed to be stirring the air like a pudding.

He took a deep breath and then, inexplicably, emitted a piercing whistle between his teeth, as if calling the sheep dog on the hills.

Nell saw Chrissie look up at him, her eyes mildly surprised, but full of affection and trust.

Nell looked down, her cheeks burning. Next to her she could feel Bertrand's shoulders shaking. She hated him.

George Newbould stood there, isolated, surrounded for the first time in his life by a sea of faces all turned towards him, waiting for him to speak. He was bewildered. How could he speak of his Chrissie whom he loved? One did not speak of such things. She was leaving home, where she had been born, and the house would not be the same again. It was right, though, and natural, like death, but too hurtful to speak of.

But they were expecting him to speak of it, even joke of it, George Newbould realized in his moment of agony.

'It's not to be spoke of,' he burst out accusingly.

Liz nodded agreement, the pink hat slipping a little.

Chrissie smiled up at him. 'Thank them for coming, Dad,' she said.

'Chrissie says to thank you all for coming,' he repeated. Then added, on his own account, 'And I do sincerely hope you've had enough to eat. And if not, please be remedied.'

He sat down, exhausted.

Tim jumped up and began to talk. Oh, dear Tim, thank God for Tim, Nell thought. He introduced Jack who spoke briefly and seriously, thanking Chrissie's parents, for all the world as if he believed they had brought her up with the express purpose of creating the ideal wife for him. Then Tim was on his feet again, telling funny stories about Jack, praising the bridesmaid, reading telegrams, all of which came from Jack's relations and friends. He gave a polished performance and when he had finished there was no need, of course, to refer to the dreadful business of Uncle George's speech ever again.

'I suppose people will start to drift away now?' Bertrand asked.

'Oh no, they dance.'

'Dance?'

'Yes, dance. Mrs Gargrave plays the piano.'

They did dance, too. Jack and Chrissie led off alone while everyone stood around admiring them. Round and round they circled and Nell watched them, wide-eyed with amazement at their beauty and grace. Never had Chrissie looked like this before, sparkling, radiant like the stars. And Jack looked at her as if she was the only precious thing in the whole world and he could only gaze in wonder at her for being his.

'Come on, Nell,' Bertrand said. 'Even if we can't beat 'em, let's join 'em.'

It was a waltz; Bertrand danced well, whirling her round and round. She was glad that Aunt Thorpe had paid extra for her to have ballroom-dancing lessons at school.

The others joined in: Tim led on Aunt Liz and Uncle George steered Aunt Thorpe round with great dignity. She was surprised at how well the old ones could dance. Aunt Thorpe was resplendent in purple. She had been proud of Aunt Thorpe today, Nell thought. She had diligently gone the rounds of all Jack's friends and relations, talking to them with great warmth and vivacity, obviously genuinely interested in each and every one of them. They all took to her, you could see that. She made clear, too, her delight in the match, whereas Aunt Liz made no effort to disguise the fact that her delight was a bit less than total.

Once all the family were on the floor, everybody else joined in, though the young village lads, she observed, sat as usual on a bench at one end and watched, biding their time. She was dismayed to see some of the girls dancing together. It was ill-bred, she knew, and hoped that Bertrand wouldn't notice.

But he did. He rolled his eyes expressively and said, 'What, such decadence even up here in this innocent little village?'

She smiled vaguely, not sure what he was on about.

Dance followed dance. Sometimes she danced with other people, but mostly with Bertrand. The hall began to get warm and dusty. It was a friendly atmosphere, she thought, sniffing. Everyone was dancing now, even the village lads had deserted the bench. Mrs Gargrave sat at the piano, playing without pause, beating out all the old familiar tunes.

'What's your favourite tune, Nell?' Bertrand asked.

'"These Foolish Things",' she said without thinking.

Before she could stop him, he had slipped away through the dancers and was standing behind Mrs Gargrave, whispering something in her ear.

He came back looking pleased with himself.

He looked less pleased when, after about half an hour, his request had still not been played.

'She's not very co-operative, is she?' he complained.

'She's stone-deaf,' Nell said.

Bertrand laughed. 'I thought she wasn't very responsive.'

'You have to write her a note,' Nell explained, 'but even then she doesn't always take much notice. She just goes into a kind of trance and goes on and on playing.'

She had no sooner said that than Mrs Gargrave stopped playing and supper was announced.

'More lovely food,' Bertrand said, taking her by the hand. 'Come on.'

In the dining-room the trestle tables were laid out again with ham and salad, puddings and cakes. The ladies in flowered aprons bustled between them, pouring out tea, beer and champagne with equal generosity, replenishing plates of sandwiches, doling out trifle.

'Eat up, Nell,' Bertrand said, helping himself to a chicken leg. 'Tim says there's more dancing afterwards. Golly, but you take your celebrating seriously up here.'

Chrissie came up to her, drawing her aside.

'Jack and I are going away now,' she whispered, 'but we don't want everything to break up, so we're just slipping off quietly.'

Nell could only gasp, so great was her misery, compounded of a sudden overwhelming sense of loss and the effects of the champagne.

'Good-bye, Nell.'

'Oh, but shouldn't I be helping you? I mean, isn't the bridesmaid supposed to help you get ready for going away, or something?'

'I'll manage,' Chrissie said.

She kissed her quickly and she and Jack vanished. Nell nearly ran after her, wanting to point out that she'd need somebody to help her with all the hooks and press-studs and the long zip down the back. Then she remembered Jack. Jack would see to all that now. Nell stood desolate among the wedding guests.

'Poor Jenny sits a-weeping,' Bertrand said, coming up behind her. 'What's wrong, Nell?'

She knew better than to try to explain.

'You're right about the champagne,' she said flippantly. 'It *is* depressing.'

'Then I'll get you a nice cup of tea,' he said cheerfully, putting down the champagne he had brought for her and going in search of tea. By the time he returned she had recovered.

The dancing continued afterwards, but Jack's friends and relations soon began to drift away. Some of them had long journeys ahead. The older ones were obviously exhausted by the day's entertainment. The younger ones and most of the Newboulds' relations stayed on, dancing well into the next morning. Mrs Gargrave, oblivious of time, sat on unwearied at the piano.

Liz and George sat it out, too, though at one stage Nell noticed that they were both asleep on the hard-backed chairs at the far end of the hall and had to be woken by departing guests proffering thanks.

'Looks like closing time,' Bertrand said, when only a handful of people remained. He glanced at his watch. 'Nearly two o'clock! By jingo, it's been quite some wedding.'

'I'm not tired,' Nell said brightly.

'Ah, what it is to be fourteen,' he said sadly. 'How I envy you.'

She laughed. 'You know you don't,' she said. 'It's horrible. You're not one thing or another. People treat you like a child and then expect you to behave like an adult.'

'Poor Nell. Never mind, you're looking very well on it. And it *does* get better. I was quite awful at fourteen and look how nice I am now.'

'Nice, but definitely tired,' she said, laughing. 'You can go if you like.'

'Thanks ma'am, but I'll restore you to the bosom of your family first,' he said, and led her over to where Aunt Liz and Uncle George were sitting by the door saying good night to the last of the guests.

He thanked them, said good-bye to Nell, looked for a moment as if he might kiss her, thought better of it, and left the hall.

Derek and Aunt Thorpe had already gone home; there was

nobody left now except Nell, her aunt and uncle and old Ernest Booth, who had stayed on because he was custodian of the village hall and in charge of the key.

The hall looked to Nell unbearably sad, with its great empty expanse of floor, its deserted chairs and even the piano abandoned by Mrs Gargrave.

'Shall we sweep up tonight?' Liz asked.

'Nay, we'll leave it while tomorrow,' George told her.

'I'll give thee a hand with it in t'morning,' old Ernest said.

'Thanks. We'd best just make sure it's all right in the other rooms.'

In the dining-room everything was cleared away. The kitchen was spotless, scrubbed clean, wiped dry. A note on the draining-board explained that all the remaining food had been taken round to the Newboulds' farm.

'They've been grand,' Liz said. 'We've got some good friends.'

'You do the same for them,' George pointed out.

He took her hand and together, Nell following, they walked back into the empty hall, their footsteps echoing on the boards.

'They made a grand pair, your Chrissie and that Jack,' Nell heard old Ernest Booth say to Uncle George, as they went out of the door.

'Ay, they match up well.'

'Ah liked tha' speech, lad,' Ernest went on. 'It were a grand speech, it were that.'

'Nay, I'm no speechifier,' George told him.

'Ah reckoned nowt o' young man as followed thee,' Ernest went on, locking the door and putting the key in his pocket. 'Ah couldn't fathom 'im at all.'

He paused for a moment as they stood outside the hall, letting their eyes get used to the darkness, then he said kindly, ''E's nobbut young, mind. 'E'll learn, maybe.'

They said good night to him, then walked home in silence through the sleeping village.

Chapter Eleven

Nell sat in the corner of the compartment and stared out of the window. Aunt Thorpe sat opposite; they had the compartment to themselves.

Nell was too tired and miserable to speak. She had scarcely slept the night before; the music had swirled in her head, her thoughts had raced. She missed the sound of Chrissie's quiet breathing, hated the outline of Chrissie's deserted bed, with its pile of folded blankets sticking up awkwardly under the counterpane.

It had been awful getting up, too, without Chrissie, dressing in silence, hurrying downstairs. The household was astonishingly normal. The only reference Aunt Liz made to the wedding was when she insisted upon making them sandwiches to eat on the train, because she had so much food left from yesterday. Everyone said that it was a pity that she and Aunt Thorpe had to rush away, but she was glad now. At least she was spared another night alone in that bedroom. She knew she wouldn't miss Chrissie so much once she got away from the place where Chrissie belonged.

She had not expected it to be such a miserable journey, she thought, as she watched the green and grey countryside slip by; she hadn't expected to have this dreadful feeling that she was leaving it for ever. She should be excited, now that the wedding was over, by the prospect of the trip to Paris. But she wasn't. All she felt was profound misery as she gazed out at the hills with their patterns of dry-stone walls and at the sheep who stared up uncompromisingly at them as the train rushed by. Every familiar landmark seemed a sad farewell.

She remembered the first time she had travelled on this route to see her father in London. How excited she had been! She had had no sense of leaving then, even though she had been hoping soon to go and live with him in London. She belonged to him; home was where he was. It had seemed quite all right to leave that village, those hills; they would always be there to come back to.

But now – her eyes filled with tears. She dabbed them away surreptitiously. Out of the corner of one eye she saw with relief that Aunt Thorpe was absorbed in a book. She told herself that she was overtired. Maybe it hadn't been a joke about champagne making you depressed; maybe that's all it was. Suddenly a memory which she had kept suppressed for years presented itself clearly to her mind: her father lying on a couch apparently dead, surrounded by empty bottles. It was so clear and fresh that once again she felt a scream rise in her throat, felt her eyes dilate with horror.

Aunt Thorpe's voice said quietly, matter-of-factly, 'Will it help to talk?'

Nell casually flicked away another tear, coughing to hide the gesture.

'It's nothing,' she said. 'I was just looking out of the window and thinking.'

'Thinking of what?' Aunt Thorpe persisted.

'Nothing much. I suppose the first time I came on this train, when I went to London . . .'

'To see your father?'

Nell nodded.

Aunt Thorpe hesitated. Then she said, 'I don't expect your Newbould relations have ever spoken much about him to you, have they?'

'No.'

'I thought not. It was hard for them, and besides, they don't talk about such things.'

'I wish they had,' Nell said.

'You can't blame them, Nell. Certainly I have no right to blame anybody.' She paused and then went on bitterly, 'I acted foolishly enough myself.'

Nell was surprised, and yet it was like Aunt Thorpe, she reflected, as she waited for her to go on: she always treated her as an equal. Most adults wouldn't dream of blaming themselves in front of a mere child.

'I acted very stupidly when a favourite nephew married in a silly hurry because he thought there might be a war coming.'

A curious rush of excitement filled Nell when she realized that Aunt Thorpe was going to talk about him. Never mind what was said; it didn't matter. Good or bad, it gave him life.

'I was his closest relative after my parents died, and I let him down, Nell.' She paused, the round eyes for once less than bird-bright. 'I was against his engagement to your mother,' she went on. 'And I said so. I got what I deserved. They married quickly and he didn't even tell me. It was a young man's pique. He saw himself as choosing between his young bride and his carping old relation. Naturally he thought he was proving his manhood and independence by administering a gentle slap in the face to the elderly relation.'

She smiled a funny, twisted smile. 'It's happened before and it will happen again. And the less the real manhood and real independence, the greater the need to prove its feeble existence. But I was too stupid and too hurt to see that – I took it as some kind of personal affront. He was all the family I had.'

It was strange to see this other Aunt Thorpe, hurt and dependent. She was always so wise and strong; trying to imagine her different was like imagining the back of the moon.

'So naturally,' she went on, 'when he went away to the war, he turned to the Newboulds for help and took you and your mother up there.'

She paused, looking at Nell, as if the words were too painful to be uttered. Then she went on firmly, 'I never met her and I didn't know when she died.'

Outside the hills were slipping into the distance, soon drystone walls would give way to hedgerows as they moved south. Aunt Thorpe had not even known when Nell's mother died. For both of them, Aunt Thorpe and Nell, her mother was an unknown being. They had been given no picture of her – nothing.

Painfully Aunt Thorpe continued, 'It was, of course, impossible for him later, in his bereavement, to turn to me of all people. I understand that. It was my punishment, well deserved.'

'If he had . . .' it was awful to ask, but she couldn't help herself '. . . if he had, do you think he might have – been – all right?'

'Lived, you mean? I don't know, Nell, I don't know. He was a man upon whom life laid too heavy a burden when he was too young.'

She spoke the words like an obituary, as if she had thought them many times before.

Suddenly she smiled her strange, luminous smile. 'He was a delightful person, Nell, so loving and full of life. He was a real Thorpe – his father had this quality too. Charm, perhaps, that much misused word. I am quite sure that if your mother had lived, he would have been a marvellous husband and father. But you see, when he was still too weak, this unbearable thing happened to him and he couldn't get over it. So he started to drink and that was a very poor kind of support.'

'Was that why he died?'

She was surprised at how easy it was to ask. He was real again, she could talk about him as if he were still a flesh-and-blood father.

'Yes, I don't know much, but what I do know, I'll tell you. It seems that he lost his first job, with an insurance company. Then he had a series of others, but he couldn't hold them down.'

'Yes, I know – at least, I realize now.'

'He *did* want you with him, Nell, I'm sure of that. He loved you, but he couldn't take the responsibility of that love. It was easier for him to let the Newboulds manage – too easy.'

'I expect I made it worse for him, always wanting a home.'

It was partly her fault, she had loved him too much, put too heavy a burden of love upon him.

Aunt Thorpe shook her head slowly. 'No. I'm sure that you were the one thing that made him try to keep going at all. The end, as far as I could piece it together, was a muddle. It seems that he caught 'flu and a doctor gave him drugs and told him not to drink at the same time, but of course he did.'

'The doctor should have made sure – should have known that . . .'

'But you see, Nell, people who live alone, like your father, are the ones that don't have a doctor who knows their problems. They're the very ones, without family or real friends, struggling along somehow or other, who don't get professional help either.'

'It's all or nothing, isn't it?'

'It seems so, sometimes. But there, it's over, it's in the past.'

'But it isn't really, is it?'

'No, I know. Of course these things live on and are never over. They mark the future. We have to accept that. But having done so, we must try not to dwell too much upon what cannot be changed.'

They sat in silence for a while. The countryside was getting flatter; soon the hills would disappear out of sight.

'We'll have a treat,' Aunt Thorpe said suddenly. 'Lunch on the train.'

'But the *sandwiches?*' Nell was quite shocked. 'Aunt Liz's sandwiches?'

'They'll be just right for supper,' Aunt Thorpe said. 'What we both need now is a good hot meal to cheer us up.'

She led the way out of the compartment and into the corridor, her angular figure swaying from side to side with the rhythm of the train. Nell stood in the corridor for a moment, looking out, and watched the hills of her childhood receding. Then she followed her aunt down the corridor.

Part Two

Chapter Twelve

Above the black diagonal line of fir trees, the peaks of the Alps rose, pink in the brilliant midday sun, to thrust themselves like conicals of glass into the ice-blue sky. Far below, where the sun never reached, a tiny crescent-shaped lake lay frozen in the valley.

There was no movement in this vast winter stillness until a train appeared through a cutting and threaded its way between foothills down to the shore of the lake. It skirted the edge of the frozen water, following the curve of the lake so closely that it seemed to bend right back on itself as it snaked its way along the bank.

Nell Thorpe, sitting in a front carriage, could see the rear end of the train as it looped along behind. She watched it with satisfaction; its movement, contrasting with the surrounding stillness, gave a final touch of perfection to the scene. She had almost forgotten, after a year in England, how beautiful these mountains were, how blue the sky, how clear the air. Soon the lake was out of sight and the mountains closed in. The train hurtled itself into a cutting and then a tunnel, becoming suddenly noisier, bigger, more important. Darkness engulfed them, then they shot out into the bright sunshine. The valley broadened out, and the train moved quietly along again, a tiny, man-made thing at the foot of great mountains.

She settled herself into the corner of the empty compartment, wrapping her cloak about her. She was glad she had come by train, she reflected, although there were easier ways of getting oneself to a skiing holiday, as plenty of people had pointed out; it was simpler and cheaper nowadays to fly on a package to Zurich or Munich and have the coach waiting at the airport to take you to your chosen resort. But she liked trains, loved poring over international timetables, working out routes and connections. Besides, there was something very precious about having the right to change your mind, being able to stop off anywhere for a few hours if you wanted to: independence mattered to her more than convenience.

She liked the sound of Gauberg, too. Giles Barclay, whom she had known and briefly loved while she was having a sabbatical year at Geneva University, and he was working at the Embassy there, had told her about it. It was a quiet, unspoilt little village, he said, which he had come across by chance. Devoid of night-life, it had nothing to attract the crowds, it wasn't the kind of place which package operators would patronize. Not that she had anything against night-life, actually, but there was plenty of that at home and she didn't want it interfering with her skiing.

She glanced up at her skis on the rack opposite, lying behind her label-smothered cases. She had a string bag of books up there, too; if the weather was poor, she intended to spend hours reading Dickens and George Eliot in the simple but pleasant room which the Gasthof Benderwirt, also recommended by Giles, no doubt provided. It was, he assured her, one of those old inns that prided itself on unpretentious comfort. Her room at college was pleasant too, of course, but there she was always at everyone's beck and call. This quiet holiday would, as the Principal would certainly have said if consulted, recharge the batteries.

In fact she felt recharged already. She had slept and breakfasted well, and now her sense of animal well-being was crowned by delight in the pure awe-inspiring beauty of the world outside.

Even meeting Bertrand in the dining-car had not shaken her composure. She had felt nothing except perhaps a little pity; he had aged and had a lonely look. He stooped a bit and his hair was thinning. Soon his amusing affectations would become the eccentricities of the elderly.

He must be well over forty, her first lover.

She had known, of course, that he had lost all power to hurt her, but she had been agreeably surprised that even his sudden appearance unheralded had not disturbed her in the least. It might have been expected to, just a little. He was, after all, the same man who had created such excitement a decade and a half ago, by seeking her out in her first term at college, romantically fulfilling a childhood promise. She remembered how amazed she had been, how intensely flattered. Probably he had nothing better to do that weekend. It had amused him to come and find her; he had never intended that visit to be the start of the serious affair it had been for her.

She understood his attitude because that was how she herself would behave now, taking pleasure where she could, enjoying the moment. For this lesson she was grateful to him; he had helped her to grow up in exactly the way her career required. In a sense she owed her success to him as much as she did to Aunt Thorpe. If, at that vulnerable age when all experience seems uniquely personal, she had fallen in love with a monogamous man she might easily have married and thrown away everything.

People did. She thought of her contemporaries cheerfully saying they could manage a home and a career, like Mary Snaith always in chaos with laundry lists among her lecture notes, harassed by au pairs, looking middle-aged with the worry of it all even when she was still in her twenties. By the time she was forty she would have wrecked both her careers. Others said they'd have their families and come back to work in ten years' time when the children were off their hands. That didn't work, either. It wasn't any old ten years they were losing; it was the vital ten, the ten in which the kind of men who know how to put work first established themselves firmly on the upper rungs of the ladder of any profession. Their wives, when they went back to work, did not join them at the top; they went back to the bottom rung and stayed there. Sometimes it seemed to her that even if they had the chance they were no longer able to take it: a habit of dependence seemed to have crept up on them in consequence of matrimony. Presumably the strain of having children always dependent on them made them emotionally dependent on their husbands. It fatally weakened them.

It was obvious, really, she thought, beginning to take down her luggage as the train approached Innsbruck: to be successful at anything you had to concentrate on it, put it first. For a woman that meant postponing getting married and having children until her career was secure. It meant being emotionally independent; that was the lesson she owed to Bertrand, bless him. She could even remember with gratitude the awful day when he had told her on the eve of her final examinations that he preferred one of his men students to her. After that she had ceased to be vulnerable, her course was set. She enjoyed all subsequent affairs without any sense of dependence or guilt, or regret when they ended. Love was not for her the whole of existence, as it is supposed to be for women. It was a thing apart, and a very good thing, too.

Nell was surprised, when she went to look for her bus in the square, to find a party of English skiers waiting for a coach. They had evidently come from Munich and had been told that a coach would take them from Innsbruck and drop them off at various ski resorts in the area. She went to enquire about her own bus and, finding it did not exist, decided to go back and see if the skiers' coach went to Gauberg.

There were about thirty of them standing waiting; they were grumbling and stamping their feet, for the sun had abandoned the square long ago and now brightened only the tops of the mountains.

'Are you by any chance our courier?' a middle-aged blonde with an aggressive voice asked her as she walked across to join them.

'Sorry,' Nell said. 'I'm on my own. I'm going to try and cadge a lift, that's all.'

'I've never known anything so badly organized. We've always gone to Switzerland in the past – Verbier or Davos. This year we thought we'd try Kitzbuhel for a change. Where are you going?'

'It's a little village called Gauberg.'

'Never heard of it,' the woman said, her voice implying that the fault lay with Gauberg.

At last the coach appeared, its long body negotiating with difficulty the corners of the little square.

'You're late,' the blonde woman told the driver as he jumped down. He shrugged and went to open the back of the coach and stow away the luggage, while the passengers climbed aboard.

Nell followed him.

'I wonder if you could take me, too?' she asked. 'I want to go to Gauberg and . . .'

'We go to Gauberg,' he told her. 'It is our last stop.'

'Then can I come?'

'Of course.'

He took her skis and cases and began stowing them away in the back of the coach.

'We have tourists for Gasthof Benderwirt,' he added, to her dismay. Evidently things at the Gasthof had changed in the three years since Giles' visit.

She went and sat by herself in an empty seat at the front of the bus, wrapping her cloak around her.

It was a long drive with frequent stops to drop off passengers or transfer them to other coaches. Darkness was falling by the time they had made the last of these stops and set off for Gauberg. The road now climbed steadily in great hairpin-bends, the snow getting thicker as they gained height, grinding their way through the night up snow-padded roads between dark forests of pine trees. Inside the bus it was very quiet; there were only about six or seven people left sitting behind her.

'It's been like the ten little nigger boys, hasn't it?' a girl said, coming forward and sitting down beside her. She was a friendly-looking girl, red-cheeked. 'Do you mind if I join you?' she asked rhetorically. 'I'm Ros, by the way. Are you with our party for the Benderwirt? You weren't on the plane, were you?'

'No. I'm on my own; I'm just having a lift up, that's all.'

'It's a shame, you're all by yourself.'

'Not at all; I like it.'

'Well, you must just chum along with us any time. There's me and Graham – that's my husband – and then there's Sal and Nick. We're all Australians.'

'Oh yes?' Nell said vaguely, not sure if the girl expected congratulations or condolence.

'We're settled in the UK, Graham and me, but Sal and Nick are on vacation. They've never seen snow so we thought we should try a bit of skiing. You been before?'

'Yes, quite often.'

'Then you must be good at it. Then there's another bloke, Mr Nansen. Graham says that's a Swedish kind of a name, so I bet he skis well, too. He didn't say his christian name. What did you say your name was?'

'I didn't, but it's Nell Thorpe.'

'Nice to know you, Nell.'

Their headlights lit up a little snow-hooded house by the wayside, isolated, lonely.

'How do they manage?' Ros asked. 'I mean, they're so cut off in the winter. Whatever do they do for transport?'

'They ski.'

'Really? I thought it was just a sport. But isn't it terrible to think what would happen if they had an accident? Doesn't it make you just want to do something to help such people?' She paused and then added, 'I'm a chiropodist.'

Nell could think of no suitable reply. It seemed churlish to point out that in the event of a skiing accident, the services of a chiropodist were not exactly the most urgent requirement.

The bus had slowed almost to a halt. Ahead of them lay the sharpest bend they had yet seen. The bus edged its way forward like a nervous animal, its head at one side of the abyss, tail at the other. It seemed that it must stay there for ever straddling the chasm, or risk crashing into it, impaling itself on a fir tree. Then, incredibly, it had crept slowly round the corner and they were safely on the other side. They saw lights ahead.

'This must be Gauberg,' Nell said.

'I'd best get back and tell the others. See you, Nell.'

They stopped in front of an old inn, with the name Gasthof Benderwirt carved on the gable. Angles of dark wood stood out clear against the white background and welcoming lights shone forth from leaded windows. Nell observed it with relief; it didn't look as if much had changed at the Gasthof Benderwirt in three years, or even three hundred.

'Oh, isn't that just too picturesque?' she heard Ros exclaim. 'I love these historical places.'

'It looks like a giant cuckoo clock,' a man remarked as they climbed out of the heated bus into the cold night air. While their luggage was being unloaded they hurried up a flight of steps, swept clear of snow, and into a warm hall which smelled of wood fires and food.

Frau Bender herself greeted them in the hall. She was a big, powerfully built woman. Nell guessed that she had come up from the kitchen, for her face was flushed and the plump forearms which bulged out of the short sleeves of her light blouse were pink and mottled. Her eyes were shrewd and watchful: little black currants pressed into the dough of her fleshy face. She welcomed them warmly in fractured English. Then she summoned a little boy who led away the two Australian couples.

Then, 'Ah, Miss Thorrup,' she said, turning to Nell. 'I expected you not so soon to be.'

'I was lucky: I got a lift up. May I go in?'

'Is good. But you are not in hotel. You must in annex go. It lies on the other side of the square. Ursula will show you.'

'But I asked for a room in the hotel when I booked, I . . .'

'Is no difference, same good rooms, same price, I distinguish not.'

Nell felt suddenly too tired to argue. Tomorrow, when her German came back more easily, she would have it out with Frau Bender.

'Ah, Mr Nansen,' Frau Bender was saying. 'You also is not in hotel, but in annex.'

'All right.'

He didn't seem to mind. Obviously he wasn't going to be much use as an ally tomorrow.

Ursula was summoned. She was a fair, bony girl, who grimaced cheerfully at them and said, 'Please?'

It turned out to be her only word, but she could make it mean anything. This time it was an order. Nell followed her obediently down the steps, across the road and up the slope to the annex, a sharp rise evidently formed from snow compacted on unswept steps. Grimly she made a note to point out to Frau Bender that the steps to the annex and the gasthof did not enjoy equal treatment, whatever else. Meanwhile, the three of them walked as carefully as cats, stepping delicately in each other's footprints.

Inside, the annex was better than she had feared. There was a fresh strawy smell of pine-wood and rush matting. Skis were propped up in the corner of the hall. Through an open door she saw a large, comfortable room furnished with pine-wood and bright linen.

Ursula grimaced again, pointed to a flight of stairs and said, 'Please?'

They climbed up, one behind the other, not speaking, leaving nuggets of snow on the stair carpet.

The rooms on the next floor, she observed through open doors, were smaller, but still pleasant.

'Please,' Ursula said again, injecting a note of apology into the word as she led the way up stairs covered this time in rather threadbare matting.

At least, Nell thought when they reached the next landing, they couldn't go up any further. She was wrong. Ursula made her way into a dark corner, said 'Please?' almost in a whisper and led them up a narrow flight of steep wooden stairs to what seemed to be a little loft. Three doors faced them on a tiny landing.

Ursula took a key out of her apron pocket and opened the first one for Nell.

'Where is the bathroom?' Nell asked, standing in the doorway.

'Please,' Ursula said, pointing down the stairs. She held up two fingers. For a moment Nell thought she was making rude signs at her for wanting a bath, then realized that she was indicating that the bathroom was two floors down. She thanked her, went into her room and shut the door behind her.

It was a tiny room with a sloping roof. She could scarcely stand upright without cracking her head on the ceiling which sloped steeply in front of the door. It was gloomy, too; there was no light apart from a single bulb, shaped like a candle, which wobbled in its socket above the basin.

What a fool she had been, she thought wearily. So much for lying reading in a simple but cheerful room on dull afternoons. It was a depressing room, no getting away from it. She'd have done better going on a package to a luxury hotel in a big resort. She unpacked impatiently. She should have got something in writing about being in the hotel itself; it was going to be a wretched nuisance having to dress up for the snow just to get to the dining-room. Of course it was the usual thing, they didn't like letting single rooms; it was less profitable for them. No bathroom, either; she would have to paddle downstairs in her dressing-gown, clutching towel and sponge bag, meeting that silent Nansen man on the stairs, all embarrassment. Oh hell and blast. Tears of anger pricked her eyes. Stop it. She went over to the basin and washed quickly. The light was not only dim, it was also intermittent. It went out when she trod on certain floorboards.

She dressed quickly, choosing a long skirt and blouse. She was half-way downstairs before she remembered that she would need a coat. She went back for it, but forgot, until she was outside the front door, that she should have brought boots to cross the snow-covered square. Her light shoes were sodden before she had even slithered down the slope from the annex into the road.

In the dining-room, Ursula led her to a large table where the two Australian couples, another older couple and the man called Nansen were already sitting.

'We were talking about the beds here,' Ross said, after she had introduced Nell to everybody. 'Does yours have a funny kind of big pillow-thing on top?'

'Yes – it's called a *federbett*. They're old-fashioned, but very warm once you get used to them.'

'You mean you get *under* it?'

'That's right. It balances on top of you, better than you'd expect.'

'We were going to *lie* on ours,' Sue said and they all laughed. 'Truly we were. What did you say they called it?'

'*Federbett* – it's really just a very plump kind of eiderdown.'

'Feather bed; but it's not a feather bed at all, is it? I mean, you sleep *on* a feather bed, not *under* it.'

'You are translating the actual words,' Mr Nansen said slowly, 'but of course they don't necessarily refer to the same object in different countries.'

He spoke carefully, his voice was scholarly, slightly pedantic. His round eyes gave him an owlish look. He had a fair, clear skin which made him seem, at first sight, younger than he was. It was deceptive, he was probably in his late thirties.

'Come to that,' he went on, 'an English feather bed isn't a bed either. It's a species of mattress.'

'Well, I'm just glad we've got twin beds here,' Ros said. 'I can't imagine us keeping one of those things on top of us in a double bed.'

There was a moment of small embarrassment which her husband disposed of by saying, 'Well, are we all joining ski classes tomorrow? The four of us are. What about you, Mr Nansen?'

'*Gregory*, please,' the careful voice corrected. 'Yes, I shall join the beginners.'

'And so shall I,' Mrs Morley, the middle-aged woman said. 'My husband joins something more advanced.'

'But you've both skied before?'

'She's a cheat,' Mr Morley said. 'She always joins the beginners and doesn't let on she's skied before, so they all think she's amazingly good – at first.'

She laughed, not in the least put out. 'I enjoy my shining hour,' she agreed. 'Then after about three days, they all catch up with me, then they get better and I end up at the bottom of the class. But I don't mind, I'll still outshine all the new ones next year, and it saves me having to make any effort.'

'She's bone idle, my wife. What about you, Miss Thorpe, will you join a class?'

'*Nell*, please,' she said, although the saying of it embarrassed her. 'No, I think I shall go to Suderau and take the chair lift up the plateau and spend the day skiing down. You can get a snack at an inn up there, I'm told.'

'Nell's a real expert,' Ros announced solemnly.

Nell laughed. 'I'm not at all,' she said, 'but I have been quite a few times and I do love going off on my own.'

They were silent for a while as dinner was being served, then Ros, who was sitting next to her, said, 'What's it like in the annex, Nell?'

'Awful.'

'It's a shame. Never mind, we'll look after you, won't we, Graham?'

'Sure.'

They insisted upon buying her wine, which she accepted guiltily, knowing it was kindly meant but also that she could probably afford it better than they could. To spare them further concern, she pleaded exhaustion and went early to bed.

Chapter Thirteen

She awoke early the next morning. It was very still, there was no sound either from outside or within the building. It was exciting to arrive, a stranger at night, and have no idea what you would see from your bedroom window by daylight. She lay for a while, her body warm under the massive *federbett*, the air sharp against her face, savouring the strangeness of it. Then she reached out for her dressing-gown, contriving to slip it on as she slid out of bed, and crossed to the window.

The mountains were nearer than she had expected; they seemed to tower over the village. The sun was already topping the peaks, turning them a soft, rosy pink against the grey-blue of the early morning sky. Everything else was still in deep shadow. Her room was evidently at the back of the annex, overlooking the ski slopes, for from her window she could see the drag lift with its little wooden house at the bottom, its wires scratching parallel lines against the white hillside. The hooks which hung from them were blood-red sickles against the snow.

Nothing moved. It was hard to imagine that anyone stirred in the little houses which crouched under snow-laden roofs in hollows around the village. To the left was a great cliff of snow which must be the side of the church whose porch she had just made out, fronting the square on its third side, as she had crossed over from the gasthof last night.

She sat on the floor, her legs tucked under her, her elbows resting on the window ledge, and gazed out at the great expanse of white, the quiet buildings below her, the soaring mountains in the distance. All her irritation and disappointment of the night before had left her. She was filled with peace, as she had been when, as a child, she had looked out from her bedroom at the smaller whiteness of snow-covered Netherby.

She was cold, too. She got up and washed and dressed quickly, putting on layers of skiing clothes. Nobody was stirring as she made her way down the annex stairs. Somehow, having to negotiate the slope outside the front door and cross the square mattered much less in the morning when you were dressed for it, she thought as she scrunched through the snow.

She had the dining-room to herself. None of the others was down yet; perhaps they were exhausted after a sleepless night, struggling with the *federbetts*. She chose the place which gave her the best view of the mountains as she sat eating her rolls and honey and drinking coffee which Ursula, who seemed to be on duty everywhere and at all times, brought for her.

As she left the dining-room she met Frau Bender in the hall.

'You are early, Fräulein,' Frau Bender said.

'Yes, I like to start early. About my room in the annex . . .'

Frau Bender shrugged.

'All is the same. Some people prefer in the annex to be, because it is more modern, built only two years ago, but I make no extra charge.' She shrugged generously and walked away before Nell could say any more. She hesitated, decided that the morning was too beautiful to spoil with argument and went outside instead.

She saw that the drag lift had started working. The hooks were moving steadily up and down the hillside with nobody on them. It seemed a waste; she decided to warm up by having a few runs on the nursery slopes before going to Suderau.

The snow in the field at the bottom of the drag lift was thick and untrodden; she had to push herself along. As she approached the hut there appeared at the window first a bright red cap and then, peering from under it, the gnarled and tanned face of the old man in charge.

'*Das Fräulein ist früh,*' he said, the voice coming out suitably guttural from the leathery old lips. 'Early lady,' he added in English.

She offered him money, but he grinned at her and said there was no charge for early ladies. She thanked him, took up her position on the drag lift and was soon sliding gently uphill, her skis bouncing quietly over the bumps. It was very cold. She did several runs to warm herself up before returning to the village.

Her skis were sticking slightly; she would call in at the ski shop for wax before going to Suderau. It was only an excuse, really; she loved the atmosphere of a ski shop, the sense of being at the working centre of the village. There was something about the bustle and craftsmanship, the smell of leather and metal that carried her back instantly to the blacksmith's shop in Netherby where she used to go and watch the horses being shod when she was a little girl.

Whatever the reason, she never felt she had really settled into a skiing village until she had explored the ski shop. I suppose it's the way some people feel about pubs, she thought as she pushed the door open.

Inside there was the usual array of skis and boots and implements, and the usual expert fitter and harassed boy trying to learn the trade. She waited while the man, broad-shouldered and thickset, fitted skis on to a lanky German. He had hold of his foot, as a smithy takes hold of a horse's hoof, and was knocking at it with a hammer. Meanwhile the boy was having difficulties finding boots for an Austrian woman.

Gregory Nansen came in. He looked at her in surprise. 'I thought everyone at the Benderwirt was in bed except me,' he said. 'I've come to hire skis.'

'You're wise – there'll be a rush later and it often takes time.'

They stood for a moment watching the big German being shod. The boy, who was wearing a leather apron which was too long for him, tripped up as he fetched yet another pair of boots to try on the Austrian lady.

'If they meet round the ankles they are too big for the foot,' he mumbled to the boss.

'I have no ankles,' the woman said sadly, leaning back in her chair and holding up the two sausage-shaped appendages which were her legs, to show what she meant.

The boy scratched his head.

'Perhaps Fräulein might go tobogganing?' he said.

Nell caught Gregory Nansen's eye and they smiled at each other. He had a nice smile; it softened the lines of a face which in repose seemed hard – it was something about the set of the mouth and chin, combined with the beakiness of the nose.

The owner, having despatched the German with a final slap on the calf, made clucking sounds of disapproval at the boy and told him to serve Nell while he dealt with the Austrian.

'So you are off to Suderau?' Gregory Nansen asked her as she paid for the wax.

'Yes, there's a bus shortly, and then I'll take the chair lift from there up to the plateau.'

'The bus isn't running today,' the owner said. 'It's Thursday.'

He pushed the Austrian's foot into the boot he had chosen for her, shovelled the fleshy ankle in after it, pulled hard on the straps, lifting her foot up to his shoulder to get extra leverage, then turned to Nell and said, 'Sebastien will take you down.'

He went to the back of the shop and shouted, 'Sebastien!' through into a back room. Nell couldn't follow the rapid conversation that followed, but found herself being led outside, put into a car, her skis on the roof, and driving to Suderau. Sebastien was a man of few words. When she tried to thank him he said he was going anyway, and that was the sum of their conversation.

Thanks to Sebastien it was still early when she reached the chair lift. Scarcely anybody was about: Suderau was still at breakfast.

The man at the chair lift also said, *'Das Fräulein ist früh,'* as he locked her into the chair. Then she was up and away, swinging high above the snow. The air was ice-cold against her. She tucked the mackintosh cape over her knees, pulled her fur cap down over her ears and put up her anorak hood. The whole mountainside was still in the shade, the trees dark and cold against the slate-blue snow. At one point the chair lift stopped and she hung there, suspended above the trees. Looking back she could see nobody: empty chairs were swinging ahead and behind her. It could have been a moment of panic. She savoured the tension of it. A few minutes later the apparatus jerked and started up again.

She was swinging above the tree line now, she could see the next range of mountains appearing, and the next. The chair lift levelled out, appeared to be making straight for the side of the mountain, and then she was sliding on to the landing-stage, stiff and awkward with cold.

It was only a short climb up steps out in the snow to the plateau. She stood at the top; it was the moment she had been waiting for, yet it took her by surprise. Mile upon mile of snow and ice surrounded her. Wherever she looked nothing was to be seen except snow and mountains. She stood for a while gazing about her. She was in the sunshine up here: everything sparkled and glowed in the morning sun. Yet it still had the intense silence of winter, the season when there is no sound of insects moving, of earth settling, even of grass growing; no sound at all.

She fastened on her skis and set off. She alone was creating sound, the gentle glissing of skis on hard snow, her own breathing. But she seemed not to disturb the silence, just moved quietly through it, taking with her her own world of tiny sounds.

She followed a track across the plateau, marked by signposts. Now and then she caught a glimpse of the chair lift in the distance, saw people get off, stand for a while in a little group and then go their various ways, to be lost in the vastness of the mountain plateau.

That was what she loved about it, she thought; the sense of space and of solitude. She felt herself growing stronger; it was almost a physical thing, this need for solitude. Yet some people didn't seem to need it. Impossible to think of Chrissie wanting to isolate herself from her loved ones. People like Chrissie somehow managed to derive strength from other people, not be drained by them.

She felt hungry and, glancing at her watch, saw it was past one o'clock. She turned and headed for the mountain chalet above the chair lift. She would have a snack there, and then ski down to Suderau and drink coffee until a bus appeared to take her back to Gauberg.

The chalet was a disappointingly modern building with a patio where skiers were lazing in the sun. It was well placed, though, she realized as she lay back in a deck-chair, very sheltered and hot.

The woman who brought out the sandwiches was fair and very pretty. She was also pregnant. Nell watched her idly, wondering how she managed to get about in the snow and ice, fit into a chair lift. Perhaps they lived up here. She was extraordinarily like Chrissie.

She watched the woman clearing the little table, and remembered the pregnant Chrissie. They had come to see her at school, Chrissie and Jack, when they got back from their first tour abroad for Jack's firm. She had been embarrassed at Chrissie appearing like that, so hugely pregnant, at school. Then she had taken them to her study out of sight of her friends' censorious eyes, and she had realized suddenly how lovely Chrissie looked, so soft and rounded. It had been a surprise, when she hugged her, to discover how hard the bump was.

Next time she had seen her, in hospital, she had looked surprisingly frail and, if not exactly disillusioned, somehow chastened, almost shocked. Presumably that was what childbirth did to you. All the same she had gazed with adoration at the baby, which was odd, really, because the baby was not much to look at, being purple and mauve and screwed-up looking.

Chrissie had a special way of looking at her children, a kind of probing look, as if she needed to be sure that all was well within their innermost souls. At the least sign of anything amiss, there were Chrissie's eyes, raking, raking. She herself had not cared much for baby Sarah, or for Claire who arrived a year later. But when they had turned into proper small children she had adored them. She remembered particularly spending a holiday with them when the children were aged about three and four. Jack and Chrissie were living in Devon for a year, while Jack was in charge of building a reservoir or a dam or something. She hardly saw him the whole time, for it was summer and work always went on until nightfall. Chrissie didn't seem to mind. 'I suppose it helps, being a farmer's daughter,' she said. 'I'm used to the idea that work's a way of life.'

Nell was surprised, sometimes, at the way Chrissie knew instinctively things which she herself had to work hard to discover. She was studying sociology at the time, and having read all kinds of theories about work and the satisfaction thereof, had reached conclusions which had evidently been obvious facts of life to Chrissie for years.

They had been sitting in the overgrown garden of the Devonshire cottage one afternoon when Claire had run up to them, crying. In her distress she rushed up to the wrong adult, burying her head in Nell's skirt. The child's hair smelled unbelievably sweet. One of the few things she had liked about them when they were babies was the smell of their heads after Chrissie had bathed them, a smell compounded of powder and cleanliness. But this was more than that, this smell of the child's head with her hair burnt by the sun.

Claire looked up, said, 'Oh, it's *you,*' in surprise, and ran across to Chrissie, who gave the scratch on her knee her characteristic probing glance and said, 'It's nothing; it'll kiss better.'

'Smell her head,' Nell said. 'I can't think what it is.'

Chrissie lifted the child up on to her knee, snuffling the fair hair. Then she laughed.

'It's rosemary,' she said. 'They've been playing houses in that rosemary bush by the fence.'

It was true; the fair hair was scattered with tiny olive-green spines of rosemary. It was strange to remember that warm summer smell up here in the snow. It was a different world, that Devon garden, from these cold, scentless mountains. As different as Chrissie's world was from her own.

'*Das Fräulein ist allein?*' a voice asked her.

It was a young man, red of face and lascivious of smile, who had drawn up a deck-chair beside hers.

'Yes, I prefer to be,' she said, the firmness of her tone making her meaning clear. It was one of the many bonuses of being over thirty, she reflected, that one didn't agonize about what to do about prowling men. Once, fearing to seem young, she would have left being rude until too late, and been saddled with him for the rest of the day.

'I'll get you a drink,' he offered, getting up. 'I'm going to the bar for one.'

'No, thank you. I've finished.'

He strutted rather than walked to the bar. He had a jutting little bottom over which his black ski pants stretched so tightly that they seemed likely to burst apart at any moment. When he returned with his drink he grinned at her, pulling off his ski cap in greeting. His hair, black and oily, sprang forth. It was an extraordinarily luxuriant growth, as if nourished on compost.

'A pity you have to go; we might have lunched together.'

'I'm just off to Suderau,' she told him, gathering up mittens and ski sticks.

'To Suderau? You are staying in Suderau, like me?'

'No, I'm staying at Gauberg.'

He wrinkled up his little snub nose in disgust. 'It's dead there. That village hasn't changed since my grandmother was a virgin.'

'That's what I like about it,' she said, enjoying the phrase.

'You don't need to go by Suderau,' he said. 'You can ski direct to Gauberg from here, along the Spitzen trail. If you wait I'll show you.'

She forgave him his prowling ways, his jutting buttocks and his compost-grown hair. It was a very useful piece of information he had given her.

'That's very kind, but I must go now,' she said, getting up. 'I'd forgotten about that route, but I'll certainly take it.'

It was a very quiet, unfrequented track, mainly through the forest, running fairly level for a great deal of the way and therefore heavy going. Distinctly less easy than skiing straight downhill to Suderau. But it saved her having to hang around waiting for the bus and she always preferred to get back under her own steam if she could; it gave her a feeling of being independent of everybody.

By the time she came within sight of Gauberg the sun had gone off the valley and the skiers were beginning to leave the slopes. She stood at the top, looking down, watching them. There were still plenty of people about, brilliant specks of colour moving across the snow. Several classes were lining up for their last descent of the day; she watched them zigzagging their way down the nursery slopes. First the ski instructor would set off slowly, calling back instructions over his shoulder, demonstrating snowploughs, parallel skiing, slow turns, everything beautifully under control. Then, in a kind of parody of him, the class followed one by one, starting equally slowly and carefully, but then going too fast, getting out of control at the corners, falling in a heap. How patient the instructors were, she thought, how tireless in their advice to lean away, change the weight, edge forward. It was understandable that their environment should make natural skiers of them, but what quality of the air produced such natural teachers?

She could make out the Benderwirt group of beginners; their class was disbanding at the bottom of the slope. The Australian couples were hobbling away together, Mrs Morley was taking off her skis by the church, waiting presumably for her husband to join her. Only Gregory Nansen was not giving up; she saw him set off again, edging his skis into the hillside as he plodded slowly and painfully up the slope. She could imagine the look of scowling concentration on his face. He turned to face downhill, paused, and then pushed himself forward. He did quite well, turning three times, then moved too fast into the straight and ended up in a heap at the bottom. She watched him struggling to get up, and then setting off up the slope to try yet again. She remembered how it felt when you were a beginner, how everything ached. He would manage it, though; she could see determination in every movement of his body even from here. Not that he would ever be really good; he'd started too late. It was like everything else; you had to start young. Not sex, maybe. Or maybe.

She skied slowly down. He waved to her.

'You're doing well,' she said.

'For a beginner.'

'No, really. I've been watching you from up there.'

'It's this climbing up sideways kills me. That sadist of an instructor won't let us go up on the drag lift yet.'

She laughed. 'It's easier, of course, but you need the climbing up, you know, when you're learning. It makes a lot of difference to how you come down.'

'Mostly I come down on my bottom.'

'You'd have been all right that last time if you'd just slowed yourself after turning. You must make yourself lean on that lower ski, however dangerous it feels.'

'I say, would you mind . . .' he asked hesitantly, as if it were a great favour '. . . just doing one more run down and telling me where I go wrong?'

'Of course not. I'm naturally bossy. I love telling people how they should do things.'

They set off together up the slope, then turned, and she preceded him, calling back instructions. At the bottom she waited, watching him as he skied down under perfect control.

'I did it,' he shouted to her. 'That's the first time I've done it without falling over.'

He was as pleased as a child with his success.

'Shall we go up again?' he asked.

'No, I shouldn't. It's much better to end on a good note like that.'

'All right, then come and have a drink with me instead. There's a restaurant at the other end of the village which has marvellous cream cakes. They were talking about it at lunchtime.'

'Thanks. I'd like that.'

'You're very good at explaining,' he said as they took off their skis. 'Better than our instructor chap, actually. You've missed your vocation.'

She laughed. 'Once a teacher always a teacher, alas.'

'Ah, you teach. I wondered what you did for a living. What do you teach?'

'Sociology.'

'University students?'

'Yes. Wincleriton University, the new one in Hampshire. Do you know it?'

'By reputation. It's a lovely part of the world to work. I envy you that.'

'Yes, I'm very lucky.'

He glanced at her. 'It's refreshing,' he said, 'to meet someone who's so contented with her lot.'

They left their skis at the annex and set off for the restaurant. Gauberg lay in a very steep valley; the sun had deserted it long ago. Ice-topped snow scrunched under their boots, the air was freezing, their breath puffed out in little grey clouds as they talked.

'It's such a tiny village,' Gregory Nansen said. 'I can't think where all the people come from. The ski slopes were quite crowded this afternoon. They can't all be staying at the Benderwirt.'

'There are more houses than you realize scattered around outside the village; you just don't notice them under the snow.'

He stopped and looked about him. It was true; the white hillsides were dotted with buildings almost hidden under great domes of snow.

'It must be very different in the summer,' he remarked. 'Green and full of flowers and all the glamorous skiing instructors forking dung.'

She laughed. 'Not a bad description. Do you resent the ski instructors? Men are said to.'

'No, I just envy them,' he said humbly, opening the door of the restaurant for her.

It was warm, steamy and pleasantly crowded inside the little restaurant. On the counter was a vast array of cakes and pastries; apfeltorte, käsekuchen, streuselkuchen, florentiner, mohrenkopf.

'I'll have cheesecake,' Nell said. 'What about you?'

'I can't make decisions,' he said simply. 'You decide.'

'I think you'd like schwarzwälder kirschtorte – it's the richest and is stuffed full of cherries and cherry brandy and cream. No, you don't take it now, just order and they bring it to the table later.'

They found a corner table and sat down.

'How do you know,' he asked as they sat down, 'how the system works? And how do you come to be so good at skiing?'

'The skiing was just a matter of starting young; I came with school parties every year from the age of about twelve, then with university parties, you know how it is. Then I skied a lot in Switzerland when I had a year in Geneva.'

'Why did you choose Austria this time?'

'I like it the best. I love these quiet little villages. I used to come simply because it was the cheapest country to ski, but I still come now even though it's no longer cheap and anyway I could afford more expensive places.'

'That's nice.'

'What is?'

'Not pretending to be poor – most people carry on about it.'

'Well, a single woman on a good salary. I'm just lucky. And I don't have particularly expensive tastes, other than holidays.'

'I, by contrast, don't have a good salary but have very expensive tastes in buns. Are you having another?'

'Yes, please. But they'll throw you out if you call them buns.'

He laughed and ordered again. His German wasn't bad, she noticed, better than his skiing, anyway.

'Are you going to go off skiing by yourself every day?' he asked.

'It depends on the weather. It's silly to go up there if it's misty or likely to snow. I'm very cautious, you know.'

He gave her his long, scowling stare.

'Yes, I imagine you keep within your limits, but then they are pretty wide limits, aren't they?'

Aware that he was finding out more than he was giving away, she asked brusquely, 'What do you do for a living?'

'I've done all sorts of things. The last one was teaching English to Asian dentists.'

'Ah, a fellow teacher.'

'You wouldn't have thought so if you'd heard their English when I'd finished with it.'

'And now?'

'I'm enjoying a kind of premature retirement.'

'I don't believe it.'

He didn't reply, just stared back at her.

'You mean, you're resting – like an actor?' she persisted, stirring dark brown sugar delicately into the pale brown foam.

'Not exactly.'

It occurred to her suddenly that he might be ill and she shouldn't ask questions. People are usually shy about speaking of their illnesses until they really get launched.

'Since you are going to find out anyway, I'll confess,' he said. 'Thanks to a recent windfall of a few thousand pounds, I'm spending a year writing full-time instead of doing it now and then.'

He paused and looked at her defensively, as if expecting adverse criticism.

'It wouldn't be embarrassing,' she pointed out gently, 'if you didn't make it seem so.'

'All creative activity is embarrassing,' he said, 'to talk of.'

She thought about this; remembered the awfulness of being shown friends' paintings and asked to comment, or manuscripts other than non-fictional ones, if it came to that. Or sex other than jokey or fantastical. All embarrassing to speak of. Why? Because of the gap between reality and words. Once, once upon a time, there must have been other ways.

'When I say *windfall*,' the careful, pedantic voice was saying, 'I mean money received in consequence of the death, slow and unpleasant, of my father.'

'It matters to you, doesn't it, to get everything right, however painful?'

'You find it a self-indulgent masochism?'

'No, I don't. I quite understand that in creative writing the only lodestar is honesty.'

'You've written, too?'

'Only papers and articles, mostly on economic history. Nothing fictional, nothing creative. I keep to the lower slopes, which I can manage.'

He laughed; it was extraordinary how it transformed a face which seemed to know no middle way between scowling darkness and a look of bright and childish delight.

'You're going to have to live more economically than this,' she said, 'if you want those few thousand pounds to last a whole booktime – however long that is.'

He groaned. 'About three years,' he said. 'I'm living in his flat. It's very much grander than I need. I could sell it and go into digs. But I like being there. Still, it's always a possibility.'

She nodded and said nothing.

'You're surprising,' he said suddenly.

'Why?'

'Most women are such busybodies – they'd have rushed in with advice to sell the flat or get a part-time job or something. They regard such things as how one lives as their speciality. I quite expected you to offer advice.'

'Do I seem so nasty?'

He smiled suddenly and touched her hand. 'No. The nastiness was all in my mind.'

The little room was packed now, and very warm. After the day out in the snow and the sharp air, the warmth brought the blood tingling to her cheeks. She could feel them burning as she sat back, smiling contentedly.

'You look marvellous,' he said. 'Full of fresh air and cheesecake.'

She laughed.

'No, truly; pale people go a wonderful colour, kind of glowing. Not red, you understand, like pink-cheeked people.'

'Writers should make good spies,' she said.

'Why?'

'It matters to them so much to get trivialities right.'

'What barmy deductions you make from your observations. I suppose it comes from being a sociologist. Besides, the colour of your face isn't a triviality.'

Through the pleasant, contented haze, a needle of resentment pricked. 'I happen to think,' she said, 'that it's useful to study societies and how they work.'

'Useful to whom? Sociologists looking for employment?'

'Useful to society if it can learn from past societies, useful to individuals if they can see their lives in relation to contemporary society, instead of adjusting it to the past, as most people do.'

'Rubbish. What do all your statistics and studies tell you except a lot of external facts?'

'Aren't we talking about external facts?'

'Ah.'

'By which you mean, I suppose, that what really matters are the unseen, unaccountable things, felt and imagined, best left to the novelist and poet?'

'Couldn't have put it better meself, ma'am.'

'But why should you attack my approach when I don't attack yours? They're different, they're complementary. One leads to the other.'

'On the contrary, they're mutually exclusive and one destroys the other.'

'What are you so afraid of? It's only common sense to start from the outside and work in. There are whole areas of problems that can be resolved if you use the right methods and work systematically.'

'Rubbish. Have some more cheesecake.'

'Saying rubbish and offering cheesecake is no substitute for argument.'

'All right. I am just trying to say that the notion that you can apply rational exploratory methods to anything other than objects is nonsense. Human beings don't behave rationally, and to try to apply that kind of method isn't just irrelevant, it's damaging.'

'Not in my experience.'

'Really? You mean to tell me that you have no areas of pain, nothing the mind shies away from? You can really examine and speak of every aspect of your life and resolve all your problems in that commonsensical manner you put on when you defend your profession?'

'Yes. And by the way, you're not managing to annoy me,' she added, although it was not true.

'I don't believe it.'

'Go on then, try me. Ask me anything you like,' she challenged.

'Right.' He paused, scowling at her. 'You are unmarried and must be over thirty. Yes?'

'Yes. Thirty-four to be precise.'

'Do you mind?'

'No, why should I?'

'I think part of you must mind being thirty-four and unmarried.'

'Not nowadays. This is what I meant when I said people must live their lives in terms of contemporary society. You are thinking in terms of the past. Of course, if I'd lived a few decades ago I should have been scratching frantically around looking for a breadwinner, but we live in a different society now. I can support myself without any props.'

'Emotionally?'

'That too. That's what I mean when I say the two approaches overlap. Society hasn't just changed in the external things, but in emotional attitudes and assumptions, and these *do* affect individual lives. You no longer have to have a husband to prove that you're feminine, as you did then. You don't have to choose between being a woman, or having a career like a man, as people like my Aunt Thorpe did.'

'Who's Aunt Thorpe? Tell me about her.'

It was clear from his voice that he would rather hear about her relations than her theories.

'She brought me up, practically. She was a headmistress of a school in London when she took me over. She's retired now. But my point was that in her day, before the war, she had to choose. If a woman teacher married, she had to stop teaching. That was the law. She loved her work and was marvellous at it. A natural. So she chose never to marry, which in those days, for someone of her background, meant no sex either, no relationships of any kind, really, with men – it would have been too dangerous to risk getting involved. Plenty of scope *there* for your areas of pain. But explore the facts, look at the statistics and you find the situation has changed, and so should your assumptions.'

'You really believe, don't you, that it's all tidily resolved now?'

'I wouldn't go quite so far as that, but I do think that my generation of women are incredibly lucky. Of course we still have to make choices, but we don't have that kind of destructive "career" or "life" choice any more. We don't have to say half of us can't be fulfilled and then decide which half to kill.'

'And do you make the other common liberated woman's mistake of thinking it's all so easy for men?'

'No,' she said, just managing to keep anger out of her voice. 'Men often have to cope with mortgages and children just when work is most demanding. But they can at least postpone all that until their career has taken shape. And so can women, now, without anyone casting doubts on them as people. I shan't marry until my late thirties, at least. And if I never do, it doesn't really bother me.'

He had been scowling at her over the brim of his cocoa mug. But the scowl had become no more than a thoughtful stare.

'It's dangerous, Nell,' he said softly. 'I tell you, it's dangerous.'

'That's right. When you lack argument, fall back on warnings.'

He didn't rise to the bait, but continued to look at her with something approaching pity. 'All these reasons, deductions, have nothing to do with human feelings, Nell. All misleading. No help when the shock comes.'

She looked at him in surprise. His concern was genuine. So was his pity.

'Maybe,' he said, changing his tone, 'I just find it hard to believe because it's so unusual. You are so refreshing after all the lady grumblers. I mean actually to say you're *incredibly lucky*. It's heresy, Nell, when everybody else is crying woe.'

She laughed, reassured.

'Of course,' he said suddenly, 'all your arguments only apply to you because you're beautiful. It wouldn't do if you'd been ugly.'

'Why ever not?'

'You wouldn't have dared. It's easy for you: nobody will ever look at you and say, "She's on the shelf, nobody wanted her, poor old thing." '

'As if I'd care! It's hopeless trying to make you understand we no longer think in these terms. Plain or pretty, what does it matter?'

'Oh Nell, all that logic and reason and you can't even see the simple fact that ugliness is a terrible, undermining thing for a woman, a mere incidental to a man. And age, too, Nell. What about age? Women are vulnerable to it, not men. Like everything else. When women attack men for inequalities, they're picking the wrong enemy: it isn't men who have it in for women – it's nature.'

She thought suddenly of Chrissie's pale, chastened face, which had shocked her when she went to visit her and the new baby in hospital. Jack hadn't looked exhausted, tortured. But then Jack didn't have the same joy in the children, either. His eyes didn't rake their innermost souls as Chrissie's did.

'If women pay a heavier price for their joys, perhaps it is because their joys are greater?' she said.

'Ah, you say that because you are thinking of a real flesh

and blood person, not some theory. No?'

She smiled. 'You're right. I was thinking of my cousin Chrissie.'

'Tell me about your cousin Chrissie.'

He was like a child, the way he wanted to be told. Deliberately she chose not to describe Chrissie, except as an example of her theory.

'She is another woman who's incredibly lucky. She can choose. We're through the stage of thinking that women must have a career or they've failed. It so happens that she is the kind of woman for whom home and family *are* a career; she has never wanted anything else.'

'Are you sure?' he asked, determined, evidently, to be awkward. 'How do we know what other people really want?'

'She'd have said so. She's a simple kind of person.'

'Even simple people have their areas of pain, of the unspeakable.'

'Not Chrissie,' she said definitely. 'She's direct and very straightforward and, oh, just good.'

'Now you really are talking nonsense. Nobody is just good.'

'Chrissie is.'

'You mean you need to feel that she is.'

'You've never even met her,' she said sharply.

'There, you see, it worries you.'

'Of course it doesn't worry me.'

He leant forward suddenly and took both her hands.

'For all your theories, Nell, for all your confidence, for all your insisting that you're an incredibly lucky liberated woman, for all that, I tell you that even you have areas not to be probed, inaccessible to reason. We all do: parents, childhood.'

He was silent for a moment and then asked suddenly, 'What about your parents?'

She thought of her father, of walking with him in the snow, of sitting in the square in London on a summer evening long ago.

'Dead,' she said quickly. 'Both dead.'

The crowd was thinning, they were surrounded by empty tables. The windows were black rectangles. Night had fallen.

'Time we were off,' she said brightly.

'All right.' He relaxed his hold of her hands. 'End of cross-examination.'

'It was rather cross, in parts,' she acknowledged.

Chapter Fourteen

It was perfect skiing weather with plenty of crisp snow and sunshine. All day long the slopes which surrounded Gauberg were bright with skiers performing what looked from a distance like a ritual if haphazard dance of interlacing patterns. In the evening the dining-room of the Gasthof Benderwirt was loud with conversations about parallel turns and snowploughs, accounts of near disasters, eulogies of ski instructors.

In the morning they were more subdued, quietly describing bruises over cups of coffee, exchanging recipes for keeping *federbetts* from falling on the floor. Ros had remedies for both, offering homoeopathic cream for the former and lengths of tape for the latter. Her husband had given up skiing after spraining his ankle on a toboggan ride, and now spent the day walking the forests with the help of an elaborately decorated alpenstock bought at the tourist shop in Suderau.

Nell left early each morning to go up on the plateau, returning when the sun went in, joining Gregory Nansen for cream cakes at the restaurant, talking, arguing. Sometimes in the evening they danced a little in the Benderwirt's tiny bar, but mostly she went to bed early, afraid of spoiling the next day's skiing. Gregory Nansen also took his skiing with immense seriousness, scowling with concentration as he listened to her advice or tried to carry it out. In the middle of dinner he would suddenly ask where his weight should be at the start of a parallel turn and which way he should be facing at the end of it, disrupting the table by using knives for skis and plates for slopes to demonstrate his problems.

'You don't seem to mind,' she remarked one evening, 'relying on reason and deduction when it comes to skiing.'

'Such methods are eminently suited to *things*,' he said. 'I've never denied it. Treat a ski in a certain way and it will react in a certain way. People don't happen to be planks of wood.'

'Actually, skis don't either.'

'Don't quibble, woman. You know what I mean.'

Only the two of them were left in the dining-room, sitting

over their coffee. The others had gone to Suderau in search of night-life.

'Have a brandy with your coffee?' he offered.

'What about glühwein? It's a kind of punch. Do you know it?'

'Yes, I do actually. I got drunk on it with an Austrian lion tamer when my first book came out.'

'Don't say you worked in a zoo as well as everywhere else?'

'No, the lion tamer happened to be my landlord.'

She hadn't realized that any of his books had been published. She reflected, as he ordered the glühwein, that despite the fact that she was supposed to be the one who believed in systematic exploration, she had in fact found out much less about him than she had given away about herself. She decided to reverse the process.

'How many books have you had published?' she asked as Ursula set down the glühwein in front of them.

'Two.'

'What were they called?'

He told her; she hadn't heard of either of them.

'It's all right,' he said. 'Don't be embarrassed. I'm not one of your famous writers.'

'I'll read them when I get back home,' she promised.

'Oh, don't do that,' he said anxiously. 'There's really no need to feel obliged to read them. Just buy them.'

She laughed.

'I mean it,' he said. 'Writers don't want to be read. Just bought.'

Not sure if he were serious, and wanting to avoid either hurting his feelings or inviting his mockery, she played safe and said, 'I'll do both.'

'It's a disadvantage for you,' he observed, 'having this nice sensitive nature when intellectually you believe in the direct questioning method.'

'Funny you should say that. I was thinking just now that you in fact resist questioning more than I do.'

He sat for a moment sipping the glühwein and scowling at her. 'Writers give away enough in their books,' he said at last. 'I don't care to give away any more than I need outside them.'

'But they're separate things, surely, your books and yourself; creator and created.'

'Oh Nell, nothing's *separate*.'

'*I* can separate work and life. Plenty of people do.'

'They think they do.'

'Who do you write for?'

'Myself, of course.'

'I can't understand that. I mean if I settle down to write a paper on, say, "Capitalism in the mediaeval wool trade", or whatever, I do the research for its own sake and because of my own need, but I write it down to communicate. Surely you do, too, otherwise why bother writing it down at all?'

'You're wrong. It sounds reasonable, but you're wrong. I'm not sure why. I write to explore, I suppose. And the exploring is bound up in the writing. *Ergo* I must write.'

'But not necessarily publish?'

'Clever old thing, there you have me. Let's drink to you. I suppose it's a feeling that once the thing is done, once it's been made into an object, it's a pity not to use it somehow or other. Writers are people with strong economical instincts.'

'Messy.'

He laughed. 'You're right, of course,' he said. 'My way of looking at things *is* messy, not cut-and-dried like yours. But tidiness isn't everything, Nell. Your methodology approach may keep your ideas about people nice and tidy, but it won't tell you anything about them that really matters. The whole process is shallow. It has no strength.'

'And yours is a strengthening process, despite its evident tendency to make you vulnerable?'

'I believe so.'

'You mean, for example, you'd be more immune to cross-examination than I am?'

'Try me if you like.'

'Were you ever married?'

'Once.'

'Go on.'

'I was twenty-two. It lasted six and a half months. Fifteen years later Cynthia asked me for a divorce because she wanted to remarry, and it's just got itself settled.'

'I'm sorry,' she said automatically, wishing she hadn't asked.

'Oh, don't be,' he said, sounding surprised. 'It's much better to be a divorcee than a bachelor. People get odd ideas about bachelors of forty.'

'And about spinsters of thirty-four, now that lesbianism is the "in" thing. It's quite unimportant.'

'It's nice the way you say your age,' he said. 'Unusual.'

'I can't get it into your head, can I? I consider myself

lucky. I often think how it would have been for me thirty or forty years ago: frustrated, terrified of getting pregnant. I'd have been half-way to having a nervous breakdown.'

Come to think of it, she had been half-way to having a nervous breakdown at the end of an affair two years ago.

'Or rather *all* the way to having one,' she corrected herself, to keep the record straight.

'Don't over-estimate your own strength, Nell,' he said unexpectedly.

'I don't,' she said, getting up. 'In fact I'm going to leave you to your glühwein now and get to bed ready for tomorrow's rigours. How's that for conserving strength?'

'I didn't mean that,' he said, looking up at her.

'What did you mean?'

'Oh, I don't know. I don't know. Perhaps I just meant that people like you should beware of people like me.'

'That's a lovely Victorian phrase to end an evening on. I don't happen to view you as a threat.'

'I didn't mean it in that sense. Never mind. Are you really going off early again tomorrow? Are you going to keep this up the whole holiday?'

'Yes, so long as the weather holds, and it shows no sign of breaking.'

She was wrong about the weather; she could feel the difference in the atmosphere when she went up in the chair lift from Suderau the next morning. Although it was still sunny, it was no longer calm and settled. Small clouds moved restlessly across the sky, the pine trees looked more forbidding, the slopes less friendly. It grew steadily colder and mistier as the day went by. She was glad to go inside the restaurant for lunch, and noticed that nobody was coming up the chair lift now. The mist was lying on the plateau, hiding the peaks, beginning to obscure the mountain slopes. Soon it would be creeping down into the valleys. She watched as yesterday's beautiful, welcoming landscape turned sinister and threatening in front of her eyes, and it seemed a kind of treachery. She ate her lunch quickly and skied straight back to the safety of Gauberg.

She saw that the ski classes were stopping early. They were already dispersing as she came down the slope towards the church, handing in their tickets to the instructors, making for home. Gregory Nansen showed no signs of giving up;

he was walking towards the drag lift, but saw her and waited.

'I'd like to go on a bit if you don't mind,' he called to her. 'It's such a good chance to use the lifts when there's no queue.'

'Right. I'll join you.'

They walked together to the lift.

'We've only been promoted to this one today,' he said, as they waited. 'I warn you I'm not very good at it; I hope I don't pull you off if I fall.'

'Don't worry; I'll hang on. Here it comes.'

The hook swung towards them. She snatched hold of it and they both jumped on and were jerked forward. He lost his balance for a moment but managed to right himself.

'Don't sit too much on it,' she said. 'Just lean back slightly and watch your skis.'

He leant back, relaxing. Together they were drawn up the slope, side by side, their skis hissing on the compacted snow.

'Are you going down first?' he asked when they got off at the top. 'Then I'll follow and try to imitate.'

She looked at the hillside below them, assessing it.

'I'll stop half-way, just at the top of the steep drop, and wait. That'll make you stop, then you must turn and go sideways to the slope. After that it's an easy run down.'

'Yes, ma'am. Off you go.'

She pushed herself lightly forward and went slowly and carefully down, calling back instructions at each turn. He followed; doing everything exactly as he was bidden.

'I'm learning more from you in a few minutes than I did in an hour's lesson,' he said when he caught her up at the top of the steep drop.

'Don't speak too soon. This is the most difficult bit.'

She showed him how to place his skis, which way to lean, and set off as slowly as she could. Over the final run she accelerated and waited for him at the bottom.

He negotiated the steep slope perfectly, slowly and under control. She saw him glance towards her triumphantly, wave a ski stick in greeting, misjudge the easy slope ahead and fall in a tangled heap of skis and limbs.

She waited for him until he had disentangled himself, sure that he would have had enough.

'That must have given you an appetite for apfelstrudel,' she said when he came up.

'I hate stopping on a bad note,' he said petulantly, obviously cross with himself, like a child. 'You go on to the restaurant. I'm having one more go.'

'I'll stay for another run. I don't mind,' she said, although she was in fact feeling very cold.

'It's just that I've made up my mind I'm not stopping until I've come down that damned slope without falling over.'

'All right. You'd have been fine last time – it was just that touch of bravado at the end did it.'

'I know – I lost my concentration; your fault, actually.'

'Naturally. A woman's place is in the wrong.'

Nobody else was using the ski lift. Empty hooks swung in front of them all the way as they were drawn up the slope. Fine snow was falling now, driving cold against their faces. Beyond the top of the ski lift the mist was a grey wall.

'I'm grateful, you know,' he said apologetically. 'I know it's a bore for you, this kid's stuff.'

'Nonsense. I wouldn't come if I didn't enjoy it. And actually it isn't kid's stuff. It's very steep for a beginner's slope, especially now that it's freezing hard. Do watch it – if you find yourself going too fast, do a snowplough and get back under control. Don't wait until it's too late.'

When they got off at the top the ski lift stopped.

'They reckon we're the last customers,' he said.

'What, only two fools left in Gauberg?'

They stood on the ridge looking down. Behind them the mist engulfed everything in swirling grey cloud. Below them the slopes were deserted. At the bottom they could see the last of the ski classes dispersing, tiny figures moving about like little people on a painting. The ski lift was still and silent, its empty hooks swinging on the wires like a broken mechanical toy. The old man who sold the tickets emerged, ant-like, from his box at the bottom of the lift, a tip of scarlet, and disappeared.

'I'll go first, shall I?' she asked. 'If I follow it might make you want to rush to keep ahead.'

He smiled down at her. 'It wouldn't. Really, I don't feel competitive about it.'

'Good. Then I'll go. Don't forget to stop at the top of the steep drop. I'll wait there.'

She glanced up at him. It was one of those moments; she recognized it: very still, electricity tingling in the air, a conspiracy of eyes, sudden understanding, his mouth on hers.

She forgot that she was standing facing him, with her back

to the slope. As their mouths met, she felt herself slipping away from him backwards down the hill. She managed to wrench herself round, skidded sharply sideways and collapsed in the piles of snow thrown up at the side of the ski lift. She lay, laughing helplessly with surprise, unable to get up, floundering about in the deep snow.

'So sorry,' he called, but he too was slipping down the slope.

'At least you're facing the right way,' she shouted back. 'I'll join you at the bottom.'

'Can't stop,' she heard him say grimly as he sped past.

He was gathering speed, making no attempt to stop himself. With his skis parallel and close together, he was tearing straight down towards the steep drop, approaching it head on.

She struggled up.

'Fall down,' she shouted after him. 'Make yourself fall!'

If he heard, he couldn't obey. She watched in horror as he hurtled towards the drop, bounced down it, and, to her amazement, still did not fall. There was a succession of terraces after that, which he shot down, bumping and bouncing on his skis but not falling, going faster and faster.

Horrified, she set off after him.

He was heading directly towards a group of skiers standing near the bottom of the ski lift. No doubt they would think that anyone going at that speed was an expert, they wouldn't bother to move away. My God, she thought, he could kill somebody at that speed. He tore through the middle of the group, incredibly hitting nobody.

He was now hurtling towards the bottom of the run where the ski schools gathered in the morning. It was marked by a long wire suspended between two poles, with class numbers hanging from it. The wire, she remembered, hung not far above her head. Just about at his neck-level. He was quite out of control: he wouldn't duck. He couldn't do anything except keep going straight on until something stopped him.

She was only a few yards behind him now.

Decapitation. She wanted to scream to warn him, but no sound came. He swept towards the wire. Something red whirled towards her. The wire had sliced off his ski cap.

A few yards further on was the church. In front of it were piles of snow which the snow-plough dumped there when it cleared the slope. He would go straight into it. He would break both his legs as his skis cut into the snow while his body stopped with the impact. She had seen it happen before. No, it was going to be worse, for the surface of the snow was so hard that his skis didn't plunge in, they slipped over the top. He was going so fast that he skied uphill towards the church. There was nothing now between him and its granite wall, even if he tried to turn there was no other way. The whole length of the side of the church was in front of him, not even a wooden door to make the impact softer.

He was doing nothing to help himself, not trying to snow-plough or fall, just standing straight upright, letting the skis take him where they would. But as she watched, the rise began to slow him down, more than she would have thought possible. More and more slowly he went. She came up behind him as he stopped, the points of his skis not more than six inches away from the wall.

She didn't say anything.

Slowly, as if not sure if he really was alive or not, he turned his head towards her. His face was deathly white, almost green.

'Well, I didn't fall, did I?' he said, his voice a croak.

'I think,' she said, 'we need a drink.'

They didn't talk as they took off their skis and walked to the annex.

In the hall he said suddenly, 'I could have killed somebody.'

'I know.'

'They didn't move. You see, they thought I was doing it on purpose.'

'You can't blame them. It didn't look like the kind of thing you do by mistake. It had a professional look.'

'Professional suicide,' he said, propping their skis up against the wall.

'Don't.'

'Look, there won't be any alcohol in the restaurant. I'll go and get a bottle of brandy at the shop.'

'It's what we need. I'll come with you.'

'It's odd how guilty you feel when you've nearly had a fatal accident,' he remarked, as they crossed the square to the village shop on the corner.

'I know. I feel guilty, too.'

'And a voice from the past whispers, "Thank goodness the adults don't know".'

'It's all right; nobody knows except us.'

Almost secretively, like children breaking the rules, they bought the brandy and carried it back to the annex.

'Medicine in my room,' he said, leading the way upstairs. 'You can have the glass, I'll take the shaving mug.'

As she followed him up the wooden stairs she reflected that a half-kiss established a very unsatisfactory relationship. They were no longer the mere friends they had been, but their swift and accidental parting had prevented them from becoming anything else.

His room was similar to hers, but even smaller. She ducked just in time to avoid cracking her head on the slope of the ceiling. He filled her glass and she sat down on the bed. He removed a case from the only chair and sat opposite to her. She watched him as he sat there; she had thought he would be killed. She shivered and drank some brandy. She could feel it branching out inside her, warm and comforting.

'You're looking better,' he remarked, filling her glass again.

'I didn't know I looked ill.'

'You looked awful when you came up to me.'

'Well, it made pretty horrific viewing, you know, that descent of yours.'

He came over and sat beside her.

'I'm truly sorry, Nell. I was just so scared I couldn't do anything to help myself.'

'Has it put you off skiing for ever, do you think?'

'Oh, no, I'll go back to it tomorrow. But I'll go carefully.'

'You'd better; you've reached the dangerous stage. Really, it's after five or six days that people who've got on well start hurting themselves.'

'Let's forget about it,' he said, turning her towards him. 'We have some unfinished business,' he said.

It was a long kiss; he kissed pleasantly. She relaxed, enjoying the feel of him and of the brandy.

He laid her head gently back in the crook of his arm, against the pillow, stroking her hair back from her face.

'I shan't let you slip away this time,' he said, holding her tightly. 'Besides, the terra is firmer.'

'Not if your bed's anything like mine, it isn't.'

Later he remarked, 'You're wearing an incredible amount of clothes.'

'No, I'm not. One anorak, one sweater, one blouse, one pair ski pants, one pair wool tights, one pair thick oiled socks, one bra and pants. Nobody could call that excessive for skiing.'

'Actually, it wasn't skiing that I had in mind.'

She laughed, rubbing her cheek against his. Then she got up and stood by the bed, looking down at him. 'For anything else, I agree, it *is* excessive.'

She took off the anorak and hung it up beside his, on a hook behind the door. Then she pulled the sweater over her head and unbuttoned her blouse. She folded both garments neatly and put them on the chair. He watched her as she bent over and removed the thick grey oiled socks and unzipped the ski pants. The single candle bulb flickered as she moved. Her body as she bent down threw grotesque shadows across the sloping walls. She had some difficulty peeling off the tight ski trousers, but she did not hurry. She undressed calmly, methodically. She had reached her bra now and red woollen tights.

'The storm window isn't shut,' she said, crossing over to the window and closing it. Flecks of snow were drifting past the blackness of the window, like the milky way. She stood staring out, saying nothing. Then she drew the curtains.

When she turned round he was already undressed and in bed.

She crossed slowly back to him and stood by the bed. Her tights made little electric sounds as she pulled them off. She took her time, folding them neatly and placing them on the pile of clothes on the chair, like a well-trained child.

'Shall I take off the rest?' he offered, his voice not altogether under control.

'No, thank you,' she said, smiling down at him. 'I can manage.' And she proceeded, slowly and calmly, to do so.

He lay looking at her as she stood there naked: the white skin glowing strange in the dim light, the way pale flowers do in an evening garden.

She had long legs, tapering to tiny, sharp ankles. Her hips were narrow, boyish, her waist not sharply defined, just a gentle curve between the small hips and breasts. They were funny little breasts, high and pointed. It was a childish, appealing kind of a body. But the face was not childish; he had always thought it compellingly beautiful, pale and intense, an expressive face, now sad now humorous, vibrantly alive, reflecting experience.

Yet as the great brown eyes looked down at him he thought that perhaps there was something naïve in the honesty of that gaze which belied the calm, controlled manner. He held out his arms to her and she slipped into them.

'Minnow,' he said, drawing the *federbett* over her. They lay flesh to flesh for a while without speaking, scarcely moving. It was quiet in the tiny room under the eaves. The strawy smell of rush matting and pine-wood was warm, comforting, homely. The dim light flickered. The wind moaned gently around the shutters. In the distance it would be sweeping across the mountains, whipping up snow, tearing at the tops of the pine trees. Their little world seemed the safer for it.

The plump eiderdown began to rock as body spoke to body, the pine-wood bedhead creaked in rhythmic protest, the light came and went. She moaned, at one with the elements. The quilt shifted, hung perilously for a moment on the edge of the bed and finally slipped to the floor. The *federbett* has many advantages, but it is not a satisfactory covering for lovers.

Chapter Fifteen

Frau Bender met her in the hall as she crossed over to breakfast with Gregory Nansen the next morning.

'Ah, Miss Thorrup,' she said, 'I can now offer you a room in the main buildings, as you wished.'

'That's very kind, Frau Bender,' Nell said carefully. 'But I don't think I really want to bother moving all my things now.'

'Ursula will see to all.'

'No, thank you, really. I've grown quite fond of my room.'

Frau Bender gave her a long, hard stare, and evidently decided that she meant what she said.

'Perhaps, Mr Nansen, you would like to come over?' she asked. 'Your room is small, is it not so?'

'Small but beautiful,' Gregory Nansen assured her. 'Do you know, Frau Bender, I have loved my room in the annex from the moment I saw it.'

Her eyes flickered from one to the other.

'Very well,' she said at last. 'Thank you.'

The dining-room was crowded: there had been new arrivals the night before. Their usual table was full; they called out greetings to Ros and the others as Ursula led them to a little table for two by the window.

'I'll tell you something about Frau Bender,' Gregory said as he pulled back Nell's chair for her.

'What about Frau Bender?'

'She knows, you know.'

Nell laughed. 'She guessed, half-way through; I saw comprehension dawn.'

'No, she's a witch and knew already,' he said, pouring out her coffee. 'She was just confirming suspicions.'

'How could she? Not that it matters.'

'For a moment I thought she'd *make* you go,' he said, looking genuinely alarmed. 'It was a terrible moment of panic. I could see her carting you off by one foot like the wicked fairy in a ballet. And you fluttering your arms and slipping away from me again.'

'It's much more likely,' she said, buttering a hot roll, 'that you'll do the slipping. How do you feel about skiing today?'

'All right. Do you know, I loosened one of the bindings yesterday? I shall have to take it to the ski shop for mending before I can use it.'

'Well, I can't say I'm surprised. You're jolly lucky to have got off with one broken ski binding. In fact I think you're probably the luckiest person alive in Gauberg this morning.'

'I'm sure I am,' he said, looking at her with meaning. There was silence, and then he asked quietly, 'Are you going off for the day again?'

'Do you want me to?'

'No, but it's your holiday and you must do as you wish.'

'Thank you. Then I will go. I'll go every day as long as the weather holds. Oh, isn't it glorious this morning? What a sky!'

'So we'll meet on the slope as usual, at about four?'

'Right.'

'Shall we go to the restaurant – or stay at the annex?'

'We'll wait and see what we feel like, shall we?'

'I know what I'll feel like.'

'Me too. The annex.'

He laughed and, leaning forward, whispered, 'Oh, Nell, you're lovely – and so refreshing. Do you know, you don't make me feel at all as if I'd seduced you.'

'But you haven't!' she said, surprised. 'Why should I make you feel guilty about it? It's ridiculous.'

'Maybe, but women do.'

'Not nowadays. Women are free now; they make their own

choices, like men, and shouldn't pretend otherwise.'

'Oh Nell, you do shape the world to match your own pattern, don't you? I tell you most women still want to have their cake and eat it, or rather lose their virtue and keep it.'

'But the whole idea of feminine virtue was imposed on women by men. It helped men to keep them in their place.'

'That's a point. If they're up there on a pedestal at least you know where they are, don't you?'

'Quite. And I suppose the thought of stolen fruit was always fun, too.'

She glanced at her watch.

'Nearly quarter past nine,' she said. 'You must go and get that ski mended or you'll be late. Do you want me to come?'

'No, you sit over breakfast. I suppose I'd better go or I'll hold the class up. Ugh, but it's hard work, this ski class routine,' he added, stretching as he stood up.

'You'll be careful, won't you?'

'I promise. There's been quite a lot more snow in the night, so that should make the going slower.'

He touched her hand lightly by way of farewell. She was glad he did not kiss her. She liked to observe the conventions, had a horror of people who flouted them for the sake of flouting. She watched him go, affectionately. She really liked him very much. She was lucky, she reflected as she poured out another cup of coffee, to have met Gregory Nansen on this holiday.

Ursula brought more hot rolls. Normally she would have resisted the temptation, she thought as she took another, but there was nothing like love-making for inducing this state of lazy self-indulgence. Quite right, too, within limits, on holiday. And she still had another week to go, seven days of skiing on the plateau in the sun all day and coming home at night to Gregory Nansen and the little room in the eaves. It was important, on a skiing holiday, to get the balance between skiing and love-making just right. That was an idea, she thought, smiling to herself, calculated to annoy Gregory; she would threaten him with a thesis on it.

It's odd, she reflected, how soon in a love-affair you adjust your mind to include the lover even in the silliest little thoughts and ideas, and somehow persuade your subconscious to drop all such references to the last one. At least, she did.

There was a sudden explosion of sound outside the window. A band was making its way through the village. Craning her neck she could just see it winding its way into the square, then stopping and forming up outside the church.

A child left the table and ran up to the window.

'Oh look, Mummy, it's a band! It's a procession, too.'

'It must be a feast day,' Nell heard Ros say. 'What is the feast day for, Ursula?'

Frau Bender appeared. There was some subdued talk at the big table.

'Oh, dear, a funeral! How sad! Come away from the window, Kathy.'

'But Mummy, it's *such* fun – do look. All the little old ladies are wearing black with funny little hats.'

'Come away, Kathy. I shan't tell you again.'

'But they're such funny little hats. Like boxes – oh, and there are so many *people*. Where have they all come from?'

'I've said I won't tell you again. Come down from that window,' the mother said firmly but illogically.

'But Mummy . . .'

There was the sound of a chair being pushed back.

'Did you hear what I said, Kathy? Goodness, they *are* funny hats.'

The mother stood for a moment by the window, and then returned to the table almost as reluctantly as the child.

'Well, we can't very well go out skiing yet,' Nell heard Ros saying. 'It wouldn't be tactful. What do you think, Nell?' she called across.

'I should think wait until they've gone inside the church.'

'It must be strange for them to have their village taken over by skiers,' she heard Mrs Morley say. 'I wonder if they resent it, especially the old people.'

'All the ladies were old,' Kathy said. 'Very old.'

'After all, they don't get any benefit from the skiers – not like the younger ones with jobs as ski instructors, or hotel work. For the rest, it's just a disruption.'

The band was playing quietly outside the church, a large silent crowd of people dressed in black was assembling in the square. The drag lift had stopped, Nell noticed. There wasn't a skier to be seen. The real village was reasserting itself.

'It used to be like this in England years ago,' she heard Mr Morley say. 'I remember when I was a lad how the whole village went to weddings and funerals.'

Nell sat at her table by the window, listening to the quiet sad music, watching the villagers assemble. She remembered

Uncle George's funeral. Everyone in the village had come. Work had stopped, the farmers had left their fields to follow the horse-pulled bier through the village. She had walked behind it with Chrissie and Jack and Aunt Liz. It had been a clear spring day, with young lambs calling, new grass growing, the day that George Newbould had returned to the soil which had given him being.

He was only sixty. It was young to die. It was so unfair, she had thought bitterly as they walked slowly up to the cemetery. After a lifetime's toil he had just retired, given the farm over to Derek and gone to live up at Fairbents with Aunt Liz.

She kept her bitterness to herself, knowing they did not, would not, share it. 'He didn't linger,' his friends said, as if that was all that mattered. Perhaps it was because they had always accepted him for what he was, a good, kind man, with a rare sweetness and simplicity. Only she had ever wished him different. Perhaps it was guilt that made her feel bitter as she followed his body through the village.

How matter-of-factly they had taken his death. There was no sense of outrage, only of the fitness of things. 'He'd not have cared to be ill,' Aunt Liz had said quietly as she and Chrissie had helped her change the sheets on the double bed in which he had died. 'He hated to be a bother.'

Even now, years later, she felt the pangs of bitterness again. She couldn't accept his death as part of the order of things, as they did, seeing it like the seasons, which come early or late but always and inevitably. You don't argue about it. No more sense in resenting death than in resenting winter, they'd have said.

He would have understood their attitude, not hers. Of all the people at his funeral, she reflected, she was probably the only one whose life he would not have understood, much less approved of. Yet she wanted his approval, she had always wanted it. Even as a little girl she had wanted to appear well in his eyes. What would he think of her and her way of life now, he who never thought of rights, only duties? What sort of sense would talk of personal liberty make to a man who did not think that being bound to till the soil and care for animals, year in year out with never a break, was any kind of slavery, and for whom faithfulness was as much a part of his being as his blood and his bones?

What would such a man make of her career and her affairs,

of her and Gregory Nansen now? she asked herself as the church bell tolled.

'Was it somebody very important in the village?' she heard Ros ask as the bell ceased to toll. 'I mean was it a *personage?*'

'It was a ski instructor's grandmother,' Frau Bender said.

'I tell you you've missed your vocation as a ski instructor,' Gregory Nansen said, pouring out her brandy. 'I've been trying all day to make out what Hans was on about, and hey presto it's quite easy when you explain it.'

'You've come on a lot today,' she said. 'I don't think you'll go hurtling down the slope again, somehow.'

'Oh Nell, it was a terrible moment when I felt you slipping away from me yesterday. I shall always have nightmares about it.'

He put his glass down on the dresser and took hold of her tightly. 'To touch you at last and then have you melt away. And I'd just worked out what was happening when I felt myself sliding away, too.'

He released her, took a long drink of brandy and then added thoughtfully, 'What a film sequence it would have made!'

'Do you always do that? I mean, consider how things would look from outside – in a film sequence, for example?'

He hesitated. 'In a way, yes. Not a film, though. More often I find myself wondering if this incident, this situation, this character would "do" for fiction, testing reality, really, to see if it's fictionable.'

'You mean, like an artist looking at a view and making a frame with his hands and saying, would this do for a picture?'

'Exactly. Only of course it's more difficult for a writer because you can't see it as a whole, in a frame. It's a more subtle kind of assessing, a weighing up of something that isn't there yet.'

'Doesn't any creative person always think another art form *must* be easier?' she asked.

He laughed. 'Yes, I suppose so. It's like other people's jobs – you just see the interesting bits that you wouldn't mind having a shot at yourself. Oh, let's forget about work.'

'You started it with that talk about slipping away being a nice film sequence,' she said, beginning to undress.

Later, when they were in bed, he said, 'Oh Nell, I've waited so long for you.'

'What, five whole days? Poor old thing!'

'Years and years, don't mock. I have been looking for you, Nell, you lovely, free, proud, independent spirit, you.'

With each syllable he kissed her hard on her face and breasts and stomach. She took his head in her hands; his hair was soft for a man's hair and very thick. Gently she laid his head on her breast and stroked his hair while his hands explored, caressed. As the familiar longing grew in her, persistent, demanding, with its inexplicable aches and stabs of yearning, she felt an unexpected delight that she was so totally his, exclusively his. And he mine, her mind added, just in time.

The pine-wood creaked, the light flickered and the *federbett* began its slow descent to the floor.

Later, after they had dozed a little, they heard Ursula's voice saying, 'Please?' at the foot of the stairs.

'Ye gods, she's coming to turn the beds back,' Nell said.

They waited; to their relief Ursula did not come up the stairs. They heard her descending to the floor below. 'I suppose you can't really turn back a *federbett*, anyway,' Gregory pointed out, pulling it up over them.

'And anyway it wouldn't have mattered. She's probably quite used to skiing holiday romances.'

He turned her towards him. 'But it isn't just a ski holiday romance, is it?' he said.

She didn't reply.

'Is it, Nell?' he persisted.

'I don't know.'

'I do.'

His next words astonished her.

'Will you marry me, Nell?'

'Whatever for?'

'Because I want you with me, for sure, for the rest of my life.'

'But you don't even approve of me. When you said all that about being free and independent – dammit, that's what we've been arguing about. You're always laughing at the liberated-woman theme.'

'No, Nell, I'm not. You're right about the spirit of it; I respect it, I love it in you. I just don't think that the theories are worth the paper they're written on. It frightens me that you rely on them in any way.' He paused and then said almost apologetically, 'It's one of the reasons I want to marry you, Nell; you need someone to protect you from your theories.'

She propped herself up on one elbow and looked down at

him. She shook her head, genuinely bewildered. 'I've no words,' she said. 'You astonish me, that's all.'

'Let's talk about it. Look, you'll get cold. Here, put my sweater round you and have a drink.'

He got up and arranged his sweater round her shoulders, knotting the sleeves under the tiny little breasts. Then he filled up a glass and handed it to her. He filled his own and squeezed back into the narrow bed beside her.

'There now,' he said in a no-nonsense kind of voice. 'We'll talk about it.'

There was silence.

'It's no good,' she said. 'I can't think of anything to say. It seems to me we're perfectly happy as we are. I can't think why you should want to start upsetting everything.'

'You mean, you view marriage as an upset?'

'In our case, yes. You've just settled down to your three-year stint on that book. You need to concentrate everything on it – all you've got. You'll probably never get such an opportunity ever again. You decided to do this thing and you must go ahead and do it.'

'Hm. I somehow don't see myself concentrating on it with you miles away surrounded by lovely clever men.'

She laughed. 'Don't waste your time being jealous of my harassed, moth-eaten colleagues,' she said. 'Do you know, you are saying what students often come to me and say; "I'd like to get married," they say, "I'll work so much better for finals next year if I'm married". The poor silly things tie themselves up with cooking and messing about being domestic and it's so sad when most of them have so few years in which they might be free just to be themselves. They've got a lifetime of domesticity ahead. But they won't listen.'

'I won't, either. And by the way,' he added sarcastically, 'I'm not a female student of twenty, so perhaps you're starting from the wrong premiss.'

She sighed, drank some more brandy, stared about the room. Behind the door on two hooks hung his anorak and hers. Side by side; they had a married look. There was something agreeable, companionable, about it. She remembered the cluttered hall at Chrissie's house; the miniature anoraks, the little wellington boots alongside the big ones. A very unsavoury muddle, she had always thought it; if it did have any appeal it was of the false kind, the kind that makes you smile indulgently at the sight of children playing in a garden, at a distance, and preferably on the other side of a window.

'It isn't as if we worked *very* far apart; it's not more than an hour and a half or so by car.'

'Two hours.'

'Don't quibble,' she said, leaning over to kiss him to show that it was kindly meant.

He took the ends of the sleeves of his sweater and stroked her breasts with them.

'Don't you think, Nell, it would be nice to be able to lie like this always, only in a nice sensible double bed?'

She laughed aloud.

'Do you really believe that respectable married couples spend their time sitting up in bed, naked except for one sweater between the two of them, drinking brandy? What very unrealistic novels you must write.'

It riled him more than she had intended. 'The only people who are allowed to criticize books they haven't even read,' he said, 'are professional reviewers.'

'Sorry. Really *very* sorry.'

She undid the sweater and pressed up close to him, creeping into him like an animal. He gave her all his attention. Over his shoulder she saw the two anoraks side by side and they had a familiar, agreeable look. More than agreeable. *Homely*. Then she saw no more, her eyes tightly closed in concentration.

Later, as he was retrieving the *federbett* and replacing the sweater she said, 'Perhaps we could rent a flat half-way between your work and mine and both commute in opposite directions?'

'Do you mean married quarters?'

'No, just something temporary until we could see how it worked out.'

'I don't believe in seeing how things work out,' he said. 'Nobody would ever marry anybody if they saw how it would work out.'

'And you think *I'm* cynical!'

'Oh no, I don't,' he contradicted. 'It would be better for you if you were. Then you would be less vulnerable to your theories.'

'Let's talk about it another time. Look, it's nearly half past seven. I must go and get my bath.'

She jumped out of bed and made for her pile of clothes on the chair.

'Don't wrestle with that lot,' he said. 'Take my dressing-gown.'

It was quiet in the annex as she made her way downstairs, his dressing-gown trailing behind her on the ground, the sleeves covering her hands, making it difficult to get a grip on the sponge bag and towel.

The narrow little bathroom filled rapidly with steam. It was like a Turkish bath, she thought, as she climbed into the hot water.

She lay relaxing, her body floating luxuriously in the water. She noticed that she had quite a considerable bruise on her thigh and wondered idly if it had been caused by that fall at the chair lift or by Gregory. He was a marvellous lover, no doubt about it. He concentrated so. That was it; he had the gift of exclusive concentration. Whatever he was doing he did it to the exclusion of all else, whether it was skiing or arguing or her.

All the same, the idea of anything permanent like marriage was quite out of the question. How unpractical he was not to realize that it would put his career at risk. And what about her own career? With the Chair at Keele a possibility in six months' time, it was certainly not the moment to be committing matrimony. A splendid time for an affair, she thought, when you still had no idea how it would work out; it might be just a few weeks' wonder or something precious for months, years even. It didn't matter at all either way with an affair, she thought as she fingered the bruise gently; it wasn't as if anybody was going to get hurt.

Chapter Sixteen

It was a raw, misty morning, the day she settled down to read Gregory Nansen's first book. Outside the big picture-window of her college room the bare boughs did not move against the grey sky, even the upper branches remaining still and unblurred. The sparse lines of winter might have been an extension of her room, which was likewise still and uncluttered.

It was not a gloomy room, for all its charcoal curtains,

dull grey carpet and papered stripes of pale and dark grey. Its sombreness was alleviated not by garish blobs of colour but by a lightness of texture, an underlying blending of tones, a peaceful symmetry. Nell looked around her, as she often did when she came in, pleased that it was her own creation, made in her own image, matching herself.

It was in this self-consciously created orderliness that she opened the first of the two books which she had collected from the bookshop the day before, for Gregory Nansen was one of those worst-selling writers whose books are never in stock, but always have to be specially ordered. She scarcely moved until she had read the last page. Then, forgetting lunch, she immediately started the second book.

Afterwards she remembered it only as a light being suddenly turned on. It was so totally unexpected. She had assumed that he would have something interesting to say, and from the way he used the spoken word she had taken for granted a lucidity of style. She had also expected him to be a responsible writer who understands that having persuaded someone to open the book, he owes it to the reader not to let him down with unlikely plots and unbelievable characters. Unconsciously she had assessed his books, as she would have done a student's future work from an interview.

What she had not expected was greatness. There was no other word for it. She read both books and at the end of the day felt stunned, curiously appalled by her own failure to foresee, her own silly assessments. She remembered by what puny standards she had been prepared to judge him and felt ashamed. This man did not need to pander to likelihood, to statistical probability or to some guessed-at credulity on the part of his readers. He could dispense with such rules; as he had written it, so it must be: the story unfolded with the inevitability of all great writing. Or so it seemed to Nell.

She sat staring out at the bare branches of the tree and wondered what it was, this greatness which was so hard to define and so impossible not to recognize. A kind of authority, perhaps, which gives the reader a sense of security, a readiness to take risks. But then any good writer does that. It was more than that; the reason that his voice carried conviction was because, as you read, you heard in it the rhythm of time. It had nothing to do with style; it was an unconscious beat and it was always there behind the words.

It so altered her view of him that when he arrived the next

day she felt shy and awkward.

He was coming to see the furnished flat that she had seen advertised at Hilsborough. During their last week in Austria and first week back in England they had talked a lot about getting a flat together, so that when, by chance, she had seen this one advertised it had seemed dishonest not to tell him about it. It was to let for a year and in exactly the right place, only a few miles from the university. There was nothing against it really except that she was unwilling to give up this room, disturb her settled routine. She had made an appointment for them to go and view it, in the confident belief that it would turn out to be ghastly.

Reading his books changed all that. Giving up her room in college now seemed a trifling sacrifice to live with such a man. It was suddenly very simple to move out, to store furniture and become a commuter. The flat seemed likely to be ideal.

When he walked into the room, the ordinary mortal she had met skiing, she couldn't relate him to the man whose books she had read yesterday, and reread this morning. He held her tightly to him and said he loved her. She couldn't speak.

'What's wrong?' he asked, and she could only reply, 'I've read them, your books I mean,' which sounded absurd.

He laughed and insisted that they went straight to bed although it was only four o'clock and not a ski resort.

Afterwards, as she made tea and set it out on a table in front of the gas fire, he said rather defiantly, 'Well, go on then.'

'What?'

'You were saying – about the books.'

Incredibly, he seemed to be expecting some kind of criticism, a bit of well, what-did-you-mean-by, and wouldn't-it-have-been-better-if kind of nonsense.

She stared up at him; her pale face flushed by gas fire and sex.

'They're great,' she managed to say. Then, hearing her own voice sound misleadingly as if it were uttering an Americanism, corrected it to, 'I mean, they are great books.'

'Oh Nell, perfect, perfect Nell,' he said, drawing her up to him. 'I'll tell you something about writers, Nell; they never want criticism however much they pretend to ask for it. All they want is lots of lovely praise.'

'But I mean it – don't mock.'

He waited for her to go on, but it was no good, she couldn't put it into words; it would immediately become sycophantic, silly, belittling, like trying to describe sunsets or mountains, conveying the smallness of the viewer, not the greatness of the scene.

'I don't understand,' she said, resigning herself to the lower slopes, 'why you're not famous.'

He looked at her, startled.

'I mean, I'd expect your books to be in paperbacks and be written about everywhere. I can't ever remember seeing a review of either of them.'

'Well, you've answered yourself about paperbacks. No paperbacks without big sales in hardbacks, and you don't get those without reviews.'

'But when you think of all the quite ordinary books that get attention and all the space that goes on criticism of books by well-known people – I mean, it just seems so unfair.'

'Tell you something, Nell,' he said, taking her head in his hands and looking solemnly down at her. 'For a very intelligent woman you are sometimes remarkably stupid.'

'Why, particularly?'

'You like my books, you think they're great, *ergo* I should be famous.'

'That's right. I don't see why it's stupid.'

'Because fame has nothing to do with it.'

'But it *has*. You're better than anything I've read by, let's see – ' She reeled off a list of well-known writers, starting with a bevy of women novelists. 'Why should they hog all the reviewing space? Any reviewer who reads either of yours can perfectly well see it's better.'

'But Nell, you must have noticed, surely, that books aren't reviewed? It's authors who get reviewed, and publishers.'

She was genuinely shocked.

'But if a student applies here, we judge him for himself. We may get him wrong – just as a review may be wrong about a book – but at least we judge him on his own merits and not on the parents who produced him or the school that sent him to us. It should be the same for a book.'

'In an ideal world it would be. A college in a way is an ideal world. Books are judged quite differently: maybe they should land on the reviewer's desk without the writer's name or the publisher's imprint, just with a number like an examination paper. Then it really would depend on nothing except the value of the book, but until the millennium comes it must depend on other things.'

'What does it depend on, then?'

'Well, it helps if the author is related to or acquainted with the reviewer. Ideally, of course, he should himself be a writer of signed reviews. Failing that, he has to be famous in a different sphere. Can you imagine a film star or well known TV personality writing a book and nobody reviewing it? Unthinkable, Nell. Notoriety is just as good. If I'd been a sadistic murderer, or a lesbian of international repute, or even one of the many relations of Lord Simonsbath, I shouldn't have lacked reviews, Nell.'

'But just one or two, surely?'

'No, it's all or nothing. A big notice in one paper, and the rest follows. You see, they're not bothered about ignoring a book that everyone else is ignoring, but they are scared of being caught out, not noticing something that the other chaps are on to – it's the newshound instinct.'

'But it shouldn't be *news* – it's literature they're supposed to be concerned with.'

'You're incurable, Nell, an incurable idealist for all your realism.'

'Well, next time it isn't going to be like that,' she said defiantly. 'I'll get you in the news somehow or other.'

'A scandal wouldn't do *you* much good, Nell.'

'Then I'll just have to confine the publicity to you.'

'But if it's a rotten system, shouldn't you be breaking it, not joining it? You're like those eighteenth-century Whigs and Tories, always on about corruption when the other lot were enjoying it.'

She laughed. 'Or modern politicians objecting to minority government unless it happens to be their own.'

She poured out some more tea and made herself ask him about the book he was working on now, although it embarrassed her to do so.

He pulled a face. 'So-so; it's not moving along the way it should. It's going odgedy-plodgedy not very fast. Tedious really.'

She waited for him to go on, but instead he said, 'When are we going to see the flat?'

'Seven o'clock, Mrs Rawlinson said.'

He yawned and stretched. 'Will college mind if you move out?'

'No, not a bit. They'll be glad to have this room. I'll keep my study, of course, and I'll be here just as much. It's been unusual living in as I have. Most of the other staff are married.'

'You still don't see marriage as a part of your scheme of things?'

She shook her head, though, somehow, since reading the books, she had felt less definite about it, she didn't know why.

'I want,' she said, 'to work here just as I used to. I think you should have hours and hours alone to write without my being there to distract you.'

'If you say so.'

'I think I'll work in college during the vacs, too.'

He nodded owlishly.

'How sad. I was rather looking forward to the long vacation. But I suppose you're right; otherwise it'll be all bed and no book.'

He picked her up. 'Speaking of which . . .' he began.

'No, we've got to get there by seven.'

'Just a quickie.'

'I hate quickies.'

'Ah, but you don't know *my* quickies.'

'I was expecting you two hours ago,' Mrs Rawlinson said when they finally reached the flat at nine o'clock.

She had a veiled Yorkshire accent and her voice was accusing. She reminded Nell of Derek's wife.

'Traffic, you know,' Gregory lied vaguely.

'My husband's out on business,' Mrs Rawlinson went on, 'so I'll show you myself.'

'Sounds like a promise of exhibitionism,' Gregory whispered to Nell as they waited for her to get the key. Maybe it was the afternoon's sex or the awful gentility of Mrs Rawlinson's voice, but they followed her round the upstairs flat suppressing giggles like adolescents, having to avoid each other's eye at each *double entendre*.

All the same, it was the ideal flat: clean and orderly and ready for immediate occupation. Nell pictured herself managing everything while Gregory wrote his masterpiece on Mrs Rawlinson's dining-room table. There was only one snag; the thought of Mrs Rawlinson in residence down below.

'My husband and I,' Mrs Rawlinson said as she led them downstairs, round the side of the house and in her own front door, 'are going on our cruise next month, and so I am afraid that we shall not be in residence while you are in the flat.'

They both made sounds of regret which echoed hollowly in the hall.

'My mother-in-law will be in residence,' Mrs Rawlinson said. 'But as she is hard of hearing and partially sighted you must deal with the agent if the need arises.'

'I'm sure it won't,' Nell said, to drown the audible sigh of relief from Gregory.

'The flat is for you, Mr Nansen, I believe?'

'That's right. I'm very grateful to Miss Thorpe here for spotting the advertisement for me,' he said blandly.

'Quite.'

A car door slammed and Mr Rawlinson came in noisily. He was a big, red-faced man and carried in with him a strong smell of beer. He shook hands with Gregory, leered at Nell, insisted that they all move into the lounge and have a drink.

'It's a very convenient flat and all newly decorated,' Mrs Rawlinson said, 'in the best of taste.'

'They've said they're taking it, Mother,' Mr Rawlinson said, coming in with a tray full of bottles. 'You don't 'ave to go on selling it.'

'It's ideal,' Gregory said politely. 'I'm sure we'll find it very convenient.'

'*We*, Mr Nansen?'

'Royal plural,' Gregory lied. 'Legal formality.'

'There, I'll get some cashew nuts,' Mrs Rawlinson said.

'Don't mind Mother,' her husband said, looking at them knowingly. 'We've never had tenants. We did the conversion for an investment when we came into the money. It's nowt to do with us, so long as you pay the rent.'

'I'll do that,' Gregory said.

'Then we'll say nine o'clock at the agent's tomorrow, and get it all signed and sealed. Cheers.'

'Cheers.'

'I prefer my tenants not to use the garden,' Mrs Rawlinson said, returning with the cashew nuts. 'Unless they are partial to a bit of weeding.'

Gregory assured her that he would not disturb the garden.

'It is small but very attractive, the garden is,' she continued.

'Come off it, Ruby, you can see nowt o' garden from upstairs lounge, except t'compost 'eap and incinerator.'

'Pardon me, but you can catch a very nice glimpse of the

herbaceous border.'

'The best view of flowerbed is from t'bog,' Mr Rawlinson said and shouted with laughter. They joined in and more drinks were slopped into glasses.

'This time next week,' Mrs Rawlinson said, smoothing her short tweed skirt over her thighs, 'we shall no doubt be in the West Indies.'

'Well, we mustn't interrupt your packing,' Gregory replied, to Nell's relief because Mrs Rawlinson's remarks had an unanswerable quality that reminded her once again of Derek's wife.

'I have cancelled the cleaning woman,' Mrs Rawlinson stated as she led the way to her front door.

'Ah, yes.'

She opened the door and shook hands with Nell and Gregory.

'It's daft shaking hands when I'm seeing t'bugger tomorrow,' Mr Rawlinson said, keeping his behind his back.

'The gardener,' his wife continued unperturbed, 'will continue to come on Saturday mornings even in winter, to see to the vegetable plot.'

''Night all,' Mr Rawlinson interrupted. 'Excuse me, but nature calls.'

He disappeared noisily down the corridor.

'I like to grow a few vegetables,' Mrs Rawlinson continued as she stood in the doorway bidding them farewell. 'I am partial to a nice garden pea.'

Chapter Seventeen

'I'm worried about our Nell,' Chrissie said, putting down her hairbrush, having finished giving her hair its regular hundred strokes.

'Anything particular?' Jack asked, fastening his pyjama jacket and beginning to hang up his clothes, having taken the change out of his trouser pockets and arranged it in two neat piles of copper and silver on the chest of drawers. 'She looked well enough when we saw her after that skiing holiday.'

Chrissie removed the hairs carefully from the brush, rolled up the combings and put them into the waste-paper basket. Slowly and methodically she turned back the bedspread, took off her dressing-gown, hung it up next to his on the hook behind the door and climbed into bed.

She glanced round the room, as she always did before settling down, to make sure everything was tidy. It was easily the most beautiful bedroom they had ever had. She loved all the rooms in this lovely old Georgian house, their first real home, but this was her favourite. She lay looking up at the ceiling. It had taken months to put that ceiling to rights; its mouldings had been damaged and the plaster rose in the centre had been removed by the previous owners. Even Jack hadn't been able to cope with that; they had had to find a real craftsman to see to it before they had begun on the decorating.

'It's not her health that worries me,' she said.

Jack finished putting his clothes away and said gently, 'We can't all live alike, you know.'

'It's not that,' she said, thinking slowly and carefully, wanting to get it right. 'It's up to her how she lives and if she wants to live with a man she's not married to that's her own affair.'

'The nice thing about you,' Jack said, getting into bed and putting his arms around her, 'is that all your puns are unintentional.'

'You mean I'm stupid,' she said placidly.

She removed his hands from her breasts, but kept them in her own to show that it was not a rebuff, only a postponement. 'What worries me is that I don't see her being happy in the end – just don't see it leading to happiness for her.'

'Well, you know Nell, always wanted to be free and independent.'

'But she *isn't* free, is she? Don't you see that, Jack?'

'I can see you're worried,' he said, 'and it won't help. You've enough to worry about with me and the kids. Nell's got to lead her own life.'

'It's funny, isn't it? When I was young, if people didn't settle down and marry, but always had to be going with different people, we thought it was a weakness and were sorry for them – you know, they couldn't commit themselves to one person. Now it's called freedom when people are weak like that.'

'It's a bigger commitment now; people live longer.'

'Oh, Jack, I wish you'd be serious. You still try and laugh me out of things as if I was a child.'

'Sorry, love. It's just that I don't like to see you worrying. Actually, I agree with you. But then it's her choice – and it seems to suit her.'

'Ye-es. I must say she looked well. She's hardly changed in the last ten years.'

'Neither have you.'

'Oh, may you be forgiven! Wrinkles and grey hair.'

He kissed her hair; soft still, and thick, but the gold was duller and streaked with faint lines of grey. He ran his finger along her forehead. 'You wouldn't get wrinkles,' he told her, 'if you didn't worry about everyone so.'

'What about you?'

His brow was deeply furrowed now, his hair thinning and grey.

'It's different for me,' he said. 'I have to worry. I'm paid by Lomacks to do their worrying for them.'

'Oh Jack, I'm sorry – I'd forgotten all about the meeting.'

He had got home from Cardiff just before eleven: they had had no time to talk.

'I was going to keep it until tomorrow morning,' he said. He hesitated. Then he cleared his throat, propping himself up against the pillows, clasped his hands behind his head. She sensed that a lecture was about to begin. It pleased her that he always used her as an audience when he sorted out his ideas by thinking aloud. It was a compliment in a way, and she didn't have to listen.

'You see,' he began, 'the theory under the last government was that industry should expand gradually and concentrate on those areas where things were slack, so that we could have some growth without overheating the whole economy and risk galloping inflation. It made sense, in that context, for Lomacks to send us up here to a development area like the north-east.'

It was remarkable how he had adapted himself, she thought, as his job had changed. Once his talk had been all about subsidence and cranes, then of site management and contracts, and now of overheated economies. She couldn't imagine herself growing like that, changing with a job. She hadn't changed at all, really, since they were married nearly twenty years ago, except for the wrinkles and grey hairs. Well, changed maybe, but not grown, not developed as Jack had done.

'But that's all gone by the board now,' Jack was saying. 'We've got a Chancellor who says he'll go for expansion at any price. I think it's very unwise; I don't think industry can cope with it. I mean, slow expansion is one thing, but a mad dash for growth is another. There are going to be huge shortages of materials and labour, prices will go through the ceiling, foreign firms will rush in. But there it is, we've got to go along with it.'

'Why? Why not just go on as you were?'

'You can't, Chrissie. All industry is affected by government and ours more than any other. They're pumping money into the economy, Chrissie, you've no idea. And it's not just government schemes, either; money's to be had for the asking, so there are any number of private schemes out for tender as well as all the others from the government and we can't but be affected by it. Anyway, Delders is mad keen that we get our share of the boom and . . .'

'Oh, *him* . . .'

Her voice showed she hadn't much faith in any decision reached by Lomacks' latest whizz-kid. It wasn't a reasoned opinion; she had instinctively distrusted the mixture of arrogance and weakness in his face and manner the only time she had met him, at the firm's annual dance. His appointment wasn't exactly on merit, either; the chairman had lately acquired a new wife and Delders was her brother.

'He wants to open up a new regional office in the Southampton area. It makes sense as we've just landed the big Clinton contract down there, so . . .'

Realization dawned.

'Oh Jack, not *us*.'

'Sorry, love, but they want me to go down there as soon as possible to set up a new regional office as well as organizing the Clinton contract.'

'But they said we'd be here for at least five years, maybe for ever. I mean, we'd never have had all those alterations done if . . .'

'Oh, we've always done things to houses, Chrissie, you know that.'

'But not as much as here.'

'We'll get it back in the price.'

They wouldn't; they never did. And it wasn't the money, anyway. She loved this house as she had never loved any other.

'It's not Lomacks' fault, Chrissie; they weren't to know. You can't blame them.'

She could, actually, but knew better than to do so aloud. Jack always defended his firm against all comers. Sometimes it seemed to her that it was a one-way loyalty.

She thought of all the toil of the past three years – the longest they had ever spent anywhere – the earth-shifting, the building, the levelling of lawns, the planting of trees, the wall-making, with Jack's few precious free hours spent always in toil. It was always like that; they could never afford paid help with the decorating and altering. But this time she had really believed that it was permanent. Permanence had been one of the persuasions used by Lomacks to get them to come up here in the first place. Unfortunately Lomacks' promises were never put on paper, and Jack was so trusting. So was she; she really had believed it would be their permanent home. She thought with sudden anguish of the garden. She shut her eyes, partly because they had filled with tears and partly because she could not bear to look at the bedroom now that it was soon to be handed over to strangers.

'Anything wrong?' Jack asked.

She shook her head. 'Nothing, love. It's just that we've put so much into it, so much of ourselves, I mean, and now . . .'

'Bricks and mortar,' he said cheerfully. 'Never let bricks and mortar stand in the way.'

'Of what?'

'Work, of course.'

'Oh. Perhaps,' she said, with sudden hope, 'nobody will buy this house. Perhaps we could keep it and just rent something down there?'

'Couldn't afford it, love, and anyway, you can't live like that, looking back. If we go, we go. No, if the house doesn't sell quickly the best thing is for me to go down there and you stay on here. The agents always say a house sells better if it's occupied.'

She hated the thought of being left behind as a mere occupant.

'And I suppose we shall have to go and look for a house near Southampton soon?'

'I'll leave that to you, Chrissie. Can you go next week? You've nothing special on next week, have you?'

She thought of the jumble sale for the NSPCC, the outing to Wexford to see the Old Vic she'd promised Claire, Sarah's trunk to be got off, the Peters who were coming for the day on Thursday.

'Nothing special,' she said.

'It's much easier now that the girls are practically grown-up,' he said. 'Some of those removals when they were little were pretty awful, weren't they? It's amazing how quickly you forget.'

Odd that he thought so; she would never forget. Once, after five removals in three years, Claire, always the less secure of the two children, had taken to vomiting day and night. After a week it had seemed that she might die. She had been taken almost unconscious into hospital, where a smug doctor had said, 'In my opinion parents should not move about in view of the harm it does their children.' As if they *chose* to move, she had thought as she sat in silence watching him sit there in his white coat and condemn her, this self-righteous, State-trained, State-employed man with his good salary and safe job with its nice pension at the end of it, all paid for by people like Jack who had no security and never grumbled.

But Claire hadn't died.

'Children are amazingly resilient,' Jack had said cheerfully, the day they brought her out of hospital. Claire had been fourteen before she stopped wetting the bed and biting her nails.

'Well, I suggest you go Monday to Friday,' he was saying now. 'That'll give you three clear days there. And don't come back without a house, whatever you do, will you, Chrissie?'

'I'll try not to.'

'I'll get an idea tomorrow from the estate agent about what this house will fetch and then you can get something in the same price bracket down there. They'll transfer the mortgage all right. Just get something you like. If it suits you, it'll suit me.'

'Thanks.'

'Well, you're the one who's in it most of the time.'

That was true; work didn't allow him much time at home.

'Don't look so doleful, love,' he said. 'I expect it's the sort of area where there are heaps of dilapidated old Georgian houses going cheap. We'll find something every bit as good as this and we'll work on it; we've done it once, we can do it again.'

She did not reply; his groundless optimism was unanswerable.

Then she remembered something else; they hadn't even finished altering this house yet.

'Oh Jack, what about the courtyard – I mean, all those slabs?'

'I'll get it finished. Don't worry.'

'Couldn't you get a builder to help you?'

'No, I'll manage. You know how it always is when we move – no money to spare.'

For three years he had toiled, taking down old outbuildings, cleaning each stone and using it to build an extension on to the house. He had done it beautifully; it blended in exactly as if it were part of the original building. He was a perfectionist, was Jack. When it came to paving the enclosed courtyard, which the extension had made, he had decided not to do it with concrete squares, but to wait until he could get hold of real old slate slabs. He had managed only last month to buy up the kitchen floor of an old house that was being demolished. The irregular slates were more expensive and more difficult to lay than the concrete squares would have been, but they looked lovely; at least, the part which he had finished looked lovely. There was still three-quarters of it left to do. Her heart sank as she thought of the piles of slate blocking the drive, the mounds of sand, the bags of cement.

'You'll be able to see more of Nell when we move down there,' Jack said encouragingly. 'You'll like that.'

'Yes,' she said, trying hard to be cheerful, not to let Jack down. 'She'll be able to come and stay sometimes for a weekend, with her Gregory.'

'You'd never ask them *both*?'

His voice was shocked.

'Why not? If it's all right to live together at the flat it's no different if they do it anywhere else.'

'Well, but, Chrissie, really – *in our house*? And what about the children? They'll know they're not married.'

'The children aren't going to be at home much now, are they? Besides, you always say they've got to know about life in the outside world and mustn't be over-protected.'

'I know, but all the same . . .'

'Just as you like. I'll only ask Nell, if you'd rather. It's just that I'm not sure she'd come without him. I think she's really in love with this one.'

She spoke apologetically; the last thing she wanted was to put extra anxiety on to Jack when he had so much else to worry about just now. It was her own fault; she should have remembered that men can afford to have theories about these things because they don't have to deal with practicalities. She shouldn't have taken him literally; she was too simple, too much inclined to accept things people said at their face value.

'I wish you could come with me to Southampton. We could choose the house together, Jack,' she said, suddenly mistrusting her own judgment.

'Not a hope. I'll be terribly busy here, handing over. I'll leave it to you. I'm not fussy, you know that.'

It was true; houses didn't matter much to Jack. He wouldn't really miss this one, despite the loving care with which he had altered it, doing everything perfectly as if they were going to live in it for ever. He always said that you must treat every house as if it was your permanent home, even if you knew you'd be away again within a year. It was all right in theory, she supposed, but she had taken it literally and now the leaving would be a heartbreak for her. Not for him; it didn't really matter to him as it did to her. Work was what mattered to Jack.

'I was up to the eyes already,' he said, 'with the Garforth job. And Tim Corbett couldn't have chosen a worse time to get himself killed. Then the Whizz-Kid's coming up with an idea that I might fly back to Mombasa for a few days to see if we could do another scheme there like the Piera one.'

'We wouldn't have to go and live out there again?'

'Oh no. They'd send somebody else out if they decided to go ahead. This would just be a feasibility survey to see if the same system would work. I don't see why it shouldn't, really.'

His voice trailed off and she knew that he was thinking of soil investigations and offshore piling and floating foundations.

'Poor Jack,' she said.

He turned to her in surprise.

'I'm not grumbling,' he said.

'I know. All the same, I'm glad I'm not a man.'

'So am I,' he said solemnly, rolling her over towards him.

Chapter Eighteen

It was a slower drive from college home now that summer had come. It took at least twenty minutes longer, Nell reckoned, glancing at her watch as the traffic came to a halt at the crossroads. The holiday cars were streaming down to the coast, the day trippers were beginning to return. It was hard on the regulars; she found it tiring. Not that she minded. She had always said she would travel in just the same during the long vacation, and she had kept to it. Gregory worked exactly as he did in term time, and that was all that mattered.

It had been an idyllic six months in Mrs Rawlinson's flat. Perfect. No snags at all. From the moment she had seen the advertisement in the paper, everything had gone smoothly. Gregory had let his father's flat easily and profitably and had used the money to pay his share in the flat. They halved every expense between them with scrupulous fairness, as they would have done if they had been friends, not lovers. That was the secret of success for this kind of relationship, Nell theorized as she drove slowly in a queue of cars: never to take advantage, never to trade on passion.

Gregory, of course, had mocked at the methodical way she had set up house with him. Love flourishes or withers, he had said, for reasons of its own which have nothing to do with sharing rents and allotting tasks. But it had worked, it had worked in fact better than she had hoped. He was writing better, he told her, than he ever had before. The book was going to be finished much sooner than he had expected. Sometimes, he said in awestruck tones, he typed up whole chunks without having to alter a word. It was coming through straight, unmuddied. She knew better than to ask him to explain the process.

About once a week he read aloud to her what he had written. At first she did not dare venture any comments other than tiny points of syntax, then she began to risk remarking on any passage that seemed to her awkward or untrue to the rest. Her pleasure when he actually said he found this helpful was almost unbearable.

'It's funny, Nell,' he said to her one evening, 'but you know sometimes I write something and when I read it through I just know it's wrong, but I can't see why, so I cheat and leave it. But when I read to you, you'll frown when I get to that piece and say, "Could you read that again?" always.'

She beamed at him.

'It isn't that I alter anything just because you say so, but you make me recognize what I knew before, but ignored. You are a kind of literary conscience.'

The words stayed with her. They were in her mind now as she took the detour round Four Lanes, following the old road which came out at the other side of the crossroads. Most people didn't know of it, but it was a quicker way if there was much traffic on the main road.

It was a leafy, pretty, winding road. She relaxed, enjoying the countryside and the relief of being out of the line of cars. She slowed as she approached the cottage they had named The Lonely House, because it looked so forlorn in winter, standing by itself among a few bare trees. It was quite hidden from sight now by leafy branches. It was ideally placed, they had often agreed, facing due south and near the main road, yet cut off from it by the chance decision of highway planners.

She went very slowly, peering through the trees to see if she could catch a glimpse of the house. She could see nothing of it. What she did see was a large 'For Sale' notice.

She stopped. The gates of the drive were open. The notice was a licence to pry. She drove up the drive.

She saw at once, even before she got out of the car, that the house was empty. The grass was long and there were no curtains at the bedroom windows. The downstairs shutters were closed. She walked quietly round the side of the house; the side gate hung open on broken hinges. The back garden was full of evening sunshine. The cobbles were warm and there was a smell of mignonette. She leant against the wall of the house. It was solid, as all old houses are. Its walls must be two feet thick at least. There were no shutters on the kitchen windows; she could see a window-seat inside, and a dresser. It was a battered dusty old dresser; but she could imagine it, cleaned and polished, arranged with china. There were stone flags on the floor. By some miracle the cottage had not been modernized, tarted up, fitted out with Formica and chrome.

In a dream she walked across the long grass, disturbing

smells of thyme and another herb she couldn't put a name to. A path led to a gate in a tiny walled garden. She went and stood among the riot of cabbage and sprouts long gone to seed, bearing masses of bright yellow flowers on their branching candelabra stems. The flowerbeds were overgrown and the fruit trees unpruned for many a year. Like the house, the little garden seemed to have been in the care of the same uninterfering hands for a long long time.

She lay back against the wall, her face turned towards the evening sun, and breathed in the stuffy smell of warm bricks, mingled with the scent of that elusive herb. She wandered back into the garden. Of course, that was it; it was rosemary. Once it had edged the herb garden, been trained up the wall at the back. Now it was lying prostrate, thick-stemmed, in banks of grey-blue spines scattered with misty blue flowers. She looped her fingers around one of the soft stems, let it slip through her hand. Then she put her hand up to her face and the smell of her flesh reminded her of the smell of Chrissie's child years ago, its hair warmed by the sun, smelling of rosemary.

As Nell stood in the overgrown garden, it came to her like a revelation that she wanted to live in this house and marry Gregory Nansen and have his child.

She knew immediately she went into the flat that he had had a bad day. Papers were strewn over the floor as well as the dining-room table, and he had evidently worked himself into a state of nervous irritability.

She hesitated, decided not to tell him about the house yet.

'Thought you were never coming, Nell,' he said.

'Hungry?' she asked.

He shook his head.

'My unhealthy way of life fails to stimulate the appetite,' he said.

She laughed. 'It hasn't been noticeable in the past,' she remarked, going into the kitchen and putting on the kettle.

'Now happens to be the present,' he said coldly.

The kitchen, which she had left clean and wiped this morning, was strewn with dirty cups and crumby breadboards, buttery knives and a chunk of cheese which had been untidily hacked about and left lying on the outside of its plastic bag. Gregory never put anything away.

She felt suddenly tired as she set about tidying up and

preparing a meal.

'Feel like a drink?' she called through to him.

He groaned.

She went back into the dining-room.

'You'll feel better for a drink,' she said, going across to the cupboard for glasses.

'Must you be so bloody cheerful, Nell?'

She stopped, stared at him.

'Yes,' she said reflecting. 'If one of a pair is grumpy the other one instinctively compensates by being cheerful. At least, that's what I've observed.'

'Oh, for God's sake, Nell!'

She filled the glasses and set them down.

'Would it help to talk?' she asked calmly.

'No.'

His voice was petulant. He scowled at her like an injured child. She handed him the glass.

'Well, have a drink instead.'

'Look, Nell, I've had an unspeakable day. Everything I've written deceives me.'

She didn't understand him. With sudden resentment she turned on him and said, 'Well, I've had a pretty exhausting day, too. Long drives both ways, a ridiculous meeting to discuss entrance procedures wasted over two hours, that idiot Venables woman on to me about getting her moronic daughter into college next year. In the end I only had about an hour to get on with my own work. If I'd had the amount of time *you*'ve had, I'd have got that paper finished by now.'

He looked at her; he put his face in his hands.

'It's no good for you, Nell,' he said. 'You're absolutely right. You're doing all the giving.'

In a panic she ran to him, took his head in her arms, pressed it against her, saying over and over again, 'I'm sorry, I'm sorry. I didn't mean it. I *do* understand, truly.'

'It's no good, Nell, I tell you it's no good. The sooner you get shot of me the better.'

'No, no,' she put her hand on his mouth.

She thought of the evening she had planned, telling him about the house, re-negotiating their future together. What evil force had taken over?

'Reality,' he said, 'has set in.'

His voice was cold, sarcastic, but so quiet that it might have been inside her own head. She could not bear it. She turned away from him and went out into the back garden.

The gardener had been; the lawn was cut and even, its edges sharply clipped. Its little beds were edged with neat bunches of lobelia and filled with rows of bedding-out plants. She observed Mrs Rawlinson's mother-in-law making her way along the path to the other door, holding the sink-tidy in her hand. She was plump, deaf, almost blind. She walked with alarming casualness down the path, narrowly missing a tub of geraniums, and zigzagged her way across the lawn. There she stood and hurled the contents of the sink-tidy in the direction of Mrs Rawlinson's compost heap, now rich in bottle tops and plastic bags. Then she turned and made her way back to the house.

She did not see Nell, who watched her uneasily, for to observe the blind is to become a spy. She made herself walk quietly round the garden. She must get control over herself. They must talk it over sensibly. She walked by the neat rows of vegetables. They had both had unsuccessful days, they must expect that. They mustn't tear each other apart, like married people did. The gardener had been busy planting peasticks. Mrs Rawlinson was partial to a nice garden pea. She smiled despite herself. They laughed at the same things, Gregory and she. It wasn't the end of the world, a little quarrel. It was her fault, really, because she had expected the evening to be so special, telling him about the house being for sale. She walked slowly past the incinerator, empty except for a few grey ashes hanging on the bars at the bottom. Her eyes filled with tears as she remembered how the evening should have been. What was she doing walking miserably round this horrible garden, anyway? She forced herself to go back into the flat; she had nowhere else to go.

The dining-room was empty; he had cleared all his papers off the table. Everything was neat and tidy.

For a moment she thought he had gone. Then she heard a sound from the kitchen. She hesitated. Perhaps he had packed and was preparing to leave. She went into the bedroom, but nothing was changed. She sat down on the bed to think. She didn't know him, that was the trouble, not really know him as a person. At Gauberg they had been holidaymakers; it had all been unreal. Then the writing had intervened; it had distorted her vision of him. She must try to see him clearly, sitting here now, detached, without him. Now was the time to see him as an outsider and to see her own life clearly, as she used to do.

She heard the door handle move. She sat rigid, expecting further argument. He stood in the doorway. He was ridiculous in a pinafore. On his head he wore a long white lampshade as a chef's hat.

'Dinner is served, madam,' he said.

Afterwards they sat by the gas fire because the evening had turned cool. He had not let her do anything to help. He had waited on her, washed up, brought her coffee.

'You do know, don't you,' he said, 'that really I'm not wearing these clothes, but sackcloth and ashes?'

She kissed him.

'I want you to forget everything I said, Nell. Promise?'

'Of course.' There was nothing, nothing in the whole world that she wanted more than to forget.

'I know it isn't an excuse, Nell, but you know, when my sort of writing goes wrong, it's *me* that goes wrong.'

'I know. It's easier for me. If I get stuck with a paper I can go back next day, it's all there, it's outside me. I do understand, truly.'

'Sometimes I'm afraid of working too hard, in case I bend the book instead of finding it.'

'You mean, like a sculptor chipping away at the stone to uncover the statue inside?'

He nodded. 'And yet, the more I write the more I'm aware of being able to change it. I mean, I used to think the book was fixed once I'd written it. Now I know I can reshape it, alter, not be scared of it. It's all very contradictory. I'm sorry, Nell, to go on so. I've never been able to talk to anybody else about it.'

Proud, humble, grateful, what did she feel? Too much to speak.

'Yet at the end, if it's any good, it must seem inevitable.'

'Is the end inevitable?'

'It explains the beginning, as death explains life.'

'Humph.'

'Don't humph at me, beloved. Let's go to bed. The nights are so short nowadays.'

She laughed; he was always grumbling about spring and summer. Autumn, he said, was the writer's season, the time to turn in on yourself. Spring pulled you apart, he said.

She awoke early, the birds singing at the window. It was

only five o'clock. She lay, listening to the dawn chorus, her face towards Gregory, watching him as he slept.

He opened one eye.

'Bloody birds,' he said.

She smiled at him, contented.

'Do you think you could borrow some of that expensive recording equipment your college no doubt possesses, Nell?' he asked suddenly.

'Why?'

'We could record this racket and play it back at the wretched birds in the afternoon when *they're* trying to sleep.'

'Lunatic. It's a lovely sound.'

'No sound is lovely at five o'clock in the morning. Oh well, since we *are* awake . . .'

He drew her to him and the night ended as it had started, with love.

At breakfast she told him about the house.

'What do we use for money, Nell?' he asked.

'Mine,' she said firmly. 'It makes sense. I've quite a lot saved and a house is a better investment than most.'

He agreed surprisingly easily. Guilt, still lingering from yesterday evening, no doubt played its part.

She went to see the estate agent on her way to college next day and the whole transaction went smoothly thereafter; the house would be theirs before the lease of the flat was up. Day followed idyllic summer day and Gregory's book progressed well. Every evening he read her what he had written and she ventured comments. Helping in an activity she did not understand gave a new dimension to her life, a touch of mystery. She couldn't explain it, except that she felt privileged, blessed. And every day, of course, she fell more deeply in love with Gregory Nansen.

Chapter Nineteen

'Where are the sandwiches, Mum?'

'In the green grip. They're on top, so be careful not to squash them.'

Sarah laughed. 'Last time you did that I sat on them all the way from Paris to Milan,' she said.

They were standing in the hall waiting for Jack, who was to take his daughter to the station on the way to work.

Chrissie looked at her younger daughter, taller now than she was herself, fair, pretty. 'Just like you were at her age,' Jack used to say. She smiled when he said it, not contradicting, just wondering if he could really think that she had in any way resembled this confident young woman with her casual ways and pert expression. Paris to Milan! She hadn't even been allowed to go fifty miles to Leeds Infirmary when she was seventeen.

Jack came clattering downstairs; they still had no carpets.

'I'm driving straight up to Cardiff from the office tonight,' he said. 'Then it's London the next day, to interview staff. So I should be back some time on Wednesday night – don't stay up. I'm bound to be late. I shan't want anything to eat.'

She worried about the way he was always missing meals and was past hunger by the time he got home, but she knew it was no good saying so.

'All right,' she said, as he kissed her briefly. 'Got everything?'

He nodded, picked up the small travel bag and briefcase and opened the front door.

'Well, looks like we're off, Mum,' Sarah said, giving her mother a kiss.

For a moment Chrissie clung to her. 'Take care, love,' she said, almost in a whisper.

Sarah laughed. 'I always do,' she said. 'Don't you worry.'

'We'll miss you, your dad and me.'

'You won't know what to do with yourself now, Mum, with both your daughters off your hands!'

'Don't worry; I'll keep her busy,' Jack promised.

'If Claire marries that Peter you'll be a grandmother in no time,' Sarah said.

'God forbid,' Jack exclaimed.

'I can't imagine our Claire looking after her own kids,' Sarah said cheerfully as she picked up the green grip and parcel of books. 'It'll be Granny or the abortionist when she conceives.'

They were gone. Into the car, down the drive.

Chrissie stood waving. She only says such things to shock me, she told herself. She doesn't really mean it. People don't mean what they say any more. It's all cleverness.

The house was empty, hollow. Her footsteps echoed as she walked across the bare boards. They'd have to stay bare for a few weeks longer, Jack had said. Although this house was smaller than their last one, it somehow needed more carpets. None of the curtains fitted, either.

She glanced in at the dining-room on her way back to the kitchen. It was half filled with rolls of dusty old underfelt which they had been measuring up last night. Today, when she had finished altering curtains for the bedroom, she had promised to try to work out how much new carpeting they'd need. 'We'll be able to afford it in a month or two,' Jack had said cheerfully. 'We're always poor when we've just removed, but we catch up, don't we? Not that rolling stones like us ever gather much moss.'

It had been a typical move. Houses were few and therefore expensive when they wanted to buy, but other rules seemed to apply when it came to selling their own. A Georgian house in the country, the estate agent had said of it, isn't everybody's cup of tea; it was a question of finding just the right purchaser, and that took time. So she had had to stay on there after Jack had gone on ahead; in the end they dropped the price sharply just to get it sold, for the purchase of the Southampton house had gone through quickly and they couldn't afford two mortgages.

Contrary to Jack's expectations, there had been no dilapidated Georgian houses going cheap down here. In fact there had been very few houses on the market, cheap or otherwise. She had disliked this house on sight, but on the last day of her house-hunting week she had no option but to buy it. She had promised Jack not to go back without a house, and it was at least habitable. It was just that she hated it. She said as much to the estate agent.

'Being on a main road,' he had told her with adenoidal persuasiveness, 'it is eminently negotiable. Later you can always look around for something else at your leisure.'

She did not bother to tell him that an unnecessary move was unthinkable to people like themselves, always making necessary ones. They moved when it suited Lomacks, not when it suited themselves. And gathered no moss in the process. For incredibly they had had to pay much more for this suburban villa covered in pebble-dash, with a strip of garden back and front, than they got for their lovely old Georgian home in an acre of garden.

She thought of their old house now as she cleared the breakfast dishes into the sink. From the kitchen she used to look out at distant hills, and a line of poplars on a ridge against the skyline. There was a viaduct, too, across the valley. Long views are calming; she hadn't realized how much she would miss them until now, when she found herself staring out of the kitchen window into the pebble-dashed wall of the neighbouring house whose owner, the milkman had told her, was away for three months. To her dismay she felt tears pricking her eyes.

She turned on the transistor radio to cheer herself up. It was the start of a phone-in programme about abortion. As she listened, pushing dishes around in the sink, fishing them out with the mop, standing them on the draining-board, as she had done thousands of times, it seemed to Chrissie that the outside world was as black and confused as her own. Nothing was clear, as it used to be. Of course it was right that women should have control over their own bodies, shouldn't have to produce babies they couldn't care for. She agreed with this pleasant-voiced woman who was phoning in. Nell would have agreed, too. It was all much more sensible and hygienic than back-street abortions and shame and infection. Of course. Yet, yet it frightened her all the same, the casualness of it all, the callousness of remarks like Sarah's this morning. Not that she meant it, of course. It alarmed her that in her own lifetime, in ten years even, that which had been unthinkable had become commonplace.

It must have been the same for Mum, she thought suddenly, it must always have been the same. It was just that you didn't realize until you got older that changes which seemed right for individuals became terrifying when generalized. Besides, people meant different things by the same words, so you didn't know whose side you were on. True equality, a caller was saying, meant doing the same things as men and getting away with it the way they do. Chrissie snatched angrily at the tea-towel and began to dry up. What sort of equality was it, this equality of selfishness and irresponsibility and callousness? It wasn't true all men were like that, anyway. Why choose to be equal with the worst? She turned off the radio, realizing, in a moment of self-preservation, that if the outside world made her feel worse, she'd do better to exclude it.

She heard the post arrive: two circulars addressed to the occupier and a letter from Shirley Barnes. Her heart sank. About ten years older than Jack, William Barnes had worked with Lomacks all his life, moving as they had done from job to job. He had died suddenly in his early fifties, about three years ago. They happened to be living near at the time and Shirley Barnes had turned to Chrissie in her despair. She had had to remove her son from boarding-school, sell the car and the house and find a tiny flat. Once the funeral was over, she had told Chrissie, Lomacks just hadn't wanted to know about her. When Chrissie had removed, Shirley Barnes pursued her with letters. Bitterly she complained of the treatment she had received from the firm. She began to issue warnings. *Your Jack reminds me of my William*, she wrote. *He lived for work too – and look where it got him. Don't let Jack do the same.*

She is bitter, Chrissie thought; it is understandable. She always wrote back kindly and promptly, offering invitations to stay which were never accepted.

She made herself some coffee before she read the letter, knowing it would be depressing. It was worse than usual. *Don't let Jack go the way of my William*, Shirley Barnes wrote, *it's not worth it. There are some in Lomacks who give and some who take. The ones who take get all the profits, and ones like Jack and William who do all the giving get no thanks. They're taken for granted.*

For the first time, Chrissie didn't think, She's bitter, naturally, poor soul. She thought, She's right.

What was the sense of working as Jack did for Lomacks, always putting them first? What would they have to show for it at the end of the day? And the end of the day was getting nearer.

The letter was blurred. She realized, to her dismay, that she was crying over Shirley Barnes' letter.

She got up briskly. This was nonsense. She must snap out of it. She must keep going, as she always had. She went upstairs and collected some curtains from a trunk. It was a good drying day, she'd get them washed and ironed and start altering them. With Jack away she wouldn't have to stop to cook; it was a chance to get everything in order in the house. She carried the curtains down to the kitchen and then remembered that the washing-machine wasn't working yet. Jack had started on it, but the pipes were the wrong size or something. She'd have to wash the curtains by hand.

She went upstairs again, dumped them in the bath and turned on both taps.

Bending over the bath, washing curtains, made her feel sick and dizzy. She stood up, steadying herself against the basin. It wasn't the first time she had felt this kind of nausea recently. I'm tired, she thought, that's all it is; naturally I'm tired; it's been a rotten removal. It had been a nightmare getting the alterations to the old house finished before selling it. All the joy had gone out of it; it had just been a matter of toiling away to hand it all over to somebody else. Jack had still been laying the last of the slabs in the courtyard the evening before the removal. The wholesale butcher who had bought the house at a knockdown price came and watched him, an expression of immense satisfaction on his big red face.

How she had hated that man! But she mustn't get bitter like Shirley Barnes; bitterness is destructive. Anyway, it was all over now, the old house, the removal, all over. It was just that it had left her tired. She must stop moping and get on with life. She must go downstairs and hang up the clothes-line in the garden ready for the curtains.

On the way down she stopped to examine the woodworm holes in the stairs. The surveyors had warned them that the house had woodworm, but the owner had denied it and Jack had been too busy, too eager to get settled into work down here, to argue. She remembered the awful day she and Jack had spent here prior to coming down, with the surveyor shaking his head over the woodworm holes and the owner – a nasty little orthopaedic surgeon with a wife who looked like a pig – shouting abusive denial. Jack, large and tolerant, made soothing sounds and said it didn't matter. Yet this same Jack would fight for Lomacks' rights as if his life depended on it, she thought as she went in search of the clothes-line.

She found it in a basket of bits and pieces in the spare bedroom, which was filled with furniture. She looked with dislike at the cheap veneer coffee-tables and four chairs bought as a job lot at a sale. It was pathetic the way they carted their shabby furniture around the country, never acquiring anything good, anything you could look at with pleasure. They always spent everything on doing up houses and then moved in a hurry and sold them at a loss. Jack was wrong; they shouldn't pretend each home was permanent, they should spend as little as possible on it and instead buy belongings which they could take with them. She turned away, shocked at the bitterness, the meanness of her thoughts, and at the way she had for the first time in her life doubted Jack's judgment, even in the silence of her mind. She snatched up the clothes-line and ran down into the garden.

It was a silly little garden, all chopped up with tiny flower-beds edged with stones which Jack said had been put there by somebody with shares in lawnmower blades. He was going to take it all up and reorganize it – when he had time. She couldn't raise any interest in it herself. She gave herself up to the indulgence of remembering the garden they had left. It was still much more real to her than this one. They had made it out of a piece of waste land, gently scaping it into the surrounding scenery. Scarcely a day had passed without her walking slowly round it, planning how it would be in years to come. She loved to walk quietly in it in the evening after a hard day's gardening, or early on a summer morning when rain had fallen on the previous day's plantings. Somewhere in that northern garden her ghost was walking now.

She sat down on the back doorstep and sobbed. If only, if only she was still there in that house she loved with its thick walls and peaceful garden, instead of being exiled in this unfriendly suburban street.

She pulled herself together with an immense effort. It was just that she was tired; perhaps she was anaemic. She would go to the doctor; she ought to register the family with one, anyway; it was one of the many things to see to when you removed. More people had breakdowns when they moved than at any other time, she had read somewhere. Not, of course, that she was having a breakdown. Besides, she argued with herself, suddenly terrified that she was, she had had to cope with removals before and never been like this. Of course the children had always been there before; she had made friends through them. And she had been younger, had more energy. Her age. Perhaps it was her age; some kind of menopausal depression. It happened to women, it had happened to some of her friends; their children grew up and didn't need them, their husbands were absorbed in work.

She was a bit young for that, surely. But no, Claire and Sarah were moving towards the age at which a mother ceases to be a necessity and becomes a burden. But where had they *gone*, she thought in sudden desolation, those little children she had loved so simply? She herself had helped them grow into strangers, independent of her, mocking, irritated by her concern for them. It is a hopeless kind of love, love of one's own children, she realized. It leads nowhere, has no fulfilment, belongs to memory.

It can't be what nature intended, she argued back at herself. Nature meant women to be busy having children throughout all their childbearing years and yet here many of them now were, still in their thirties, with no children to care for. It was all very sensible and modern, but perhaps part of them resented it, perhaps nature sometimes lashed back. She would have liked to have more children; it was just that she didn't have any more after the two girls. Jack would have liked a boy to teach things to, like cricket and engineering. But perhaps he would have been an unathletic, non-scientific little boy. She began to shed more tears as she thought of the son she had not had.

She must try to cheer herself up, as she had often cheered other people. She knew she was always regarded as a calm, sensible, cheerful sort of person, her house always full of other people's children, her shoulder always available for friends to cry on. Now she needed a friend, that was all. She'd go and ring up Janet, she thought suddenly, wondering why she hadn't thought of it before. She'd go and ring her up and ask her round for a cup of coffee.

She stopped in horror, staring at her hand on the back door-knob. She must be going mad. Janet was a friend in the north, at least three hundred miles away. She knew nobody down here. Nobody had called since she arrived, except the tradesmen and a woman collecting money. And two Mormons.

She made herself go indoors. The state of the rooms brought home to her how low she had sunk. She hadn't even been capable of getting the place straightened up, she thought dully as she looked about her. They had been here a month and it still looked as if they had just moved in the day before. In the past she had always made a home quickly. But then she had had to get on with it for the children's sake. There had always been deadlines. Now the days stretched endlessly before her, postponement didn't matter. She ought to have got a job, made a life for herself. That was the trouble, she had never had a job, had just gone on existing as Jack's wife, as the children's mother. And now she wasn't needed, and there was nothing else. I should have put myself first when I was young and had the energy, she thought, like Nell did, but I didn't know then. I didn't understand.

It had crept up on her unawares. One minute she was rushed off her feet, looking after the children, the centre of family life, and the next she was a lonely, depressed woman approaching middle-age with nothing, nothing to show for her life. Stop it, stop it. What would she have said to a friend who spoke like that? That she had two daughters, strong and healthy, and a loving husband and a home. It was dreadful of her not to like this house, when others were homeless. She could not even count her blessings, she thought guiltily. Besides, if she had been a person of any value in the past it was only because she had done useful things. Dimly she perceived that she only existed in her actions and if she could now achieve nothing, she was nothing.

She heard a strange sound. Water dripping. It came from the dining-room. She ran in and saw water descending from the ceiling on to the dining-room table. Amid all the underfelt and carpets there was the sewing-machine on the dining-room table, and water drip, drip, dripping on to the pile of curtains beside it.

She ran upstairs to the bathroom. Water met her in the doorway. She managed to turn off the taps and stood staring hopelessly at the water. I am no good, she thought. If I died nobody would be any the poorer.

Stop it, stop it. She clenched her fists. Stop it, think, be sensible; don't look into the abyss.

She took towels and began to mop up the water. She squeezed out the curtains as best she could, hung them on the line, put on her coat and went down town in search of a doctor.

'I'll put you on Dr Striding's list,' the receptionist said.

'Would it be possible to see him now?'

'Have you an appointment?'

'No.'

'Then you can't see him.'

There was a murmuring behind her.

'Apparently he's just had a cancellation,' the receptionist said grudgingly, 'so you can go along in a few minutes.'

Chrissie looked around the waiting-room; it was as different from the one up north as it could possibly be. It was empty for a start, and then it was decorated with notices saying how precious was the general practitioner's time and he must not be disturbed, and how to get prescriptions without bothering your doctor. In the northern surgery, always crowded with coughing patients, the notices had been all about injecting your children against diphtheria and how to claim pregnancy benefits.

She planned what she would say; she would tell him about the dizziness and then try to find the courage to tell him about the depression, but the thought of doing so shamed her. It seemed so feeble, a kind of self-indulgence. One ought to be able to cope. Perhaps there was a physical cause. *Please* let it be a physical cause.

Occasionally people came in and were brusquely dealt with by the fierce receptionist, who seemed to be employed not so much to receive as to keep at bay.

A woman came in carrying a baby. She was holding a toddler by one hand, almost dragging him along, so reluctant was he to walk. An older child, of about four, held on to the hem of her coat. They made their way up to the counter and rang the bell. The receptionist appeared.

'Could I wait and see one of the doctors?' the woman said. 'It's for the middle one, Timothy.'

'Name, please.'

'Mrs Cobb.'

'Have you an appointment, Mrs Cobb?'

'No, he only started it last night. It's his tonsils, I think, and the sooner he gets the medicine, the . . .'

'Who is your doctor?'

'Dr Striding.'

The receptionist looked at the book.

'He can see you on Friday,' she said, 'at ten fifteen.'

'But he's ill *now*,' the woman said.

'That's the earliest he can do,' the receptionist said. 'It's only the day after tomorrow.'

The woman seemed near to tears. She shifted the baby on to her other arm, so that she could get a firmer grip on the toddler. 'You see, it's two buses,' she said, 'to get here, and the baby's had a cold as well and . . .'

'Do you want me to book the appointment on Friday or not?' the receptionist cut in.

Suddenly Chrissie could bear it no longer.

'You can have my appointment,' she said. 'Mine isn't urgent. I could come on Friday instead.'

The receptionist turned on her angrily. 'Your card's gone in,' she said. 'Where should we be if patients kept interfering in the appointments system?'

Chrissie murmured an apology and the woman said she would take the Friday appointment.

The receptionist banged the hatch down, but not before giving them a final look of disapproval.

The woman came and sat next to Chrissie, or rather collapsed on the chair, and let the children fold on top of her. 'Thanks,' she said, 'for trying to help. I'll sit a bit. It's twenty minutes till the bus comes.'

'Let me take the baby,' Chrissie said.

The woman handed the baby over without hesitation, as if it were a parcel. She picked up the little boy who lay against her, eyes closed.

'His brother was just the same with his tonsils,' she said, 'but he grew out of it. The old doctor used to visit, though. Used to pop in. But it's all modern now, so they've no time.'

The hatch was raised. Chrissie was summoned.

'It makes you wonder how they used to manage,' the woman concluded with a wan smile.

Dr Striding was a big man, still young. He sat sprawled in his chair, tilting it back and biting on his pipe, which he removed from his mouth as Chrissie went into the room and waved in the direction of a chair. She sat down.

'Well, so you're Mrs Er – ' he began. 'What's the trouble?'

She hesitated, suddenly aware that just expressing her fear, just putting the thing into words might make her break down. She fell back on talk of sickness and dizzy spells.

The telephone rang when she was in the middle of explaining. He seized it with a dramatic gesture. 'Yes, yes, yes,' he intoned, consciously moving his voice down the scale. 'Splendid, right you are, decision taken.'

He banged down the receiver and turned back to her.

'In view of your age,' he said, 'I think an internal examination is called for.'

He picked up the telephone, which made little coughing sounds. Then he took an instrument from an assortment in a dish and used it on the telephone as a screwdriver, a function for which it had not been designed. It slipped, inflicting a minor injury on his thumb. He went over to the door, sucking his hand. 'Joanna,' he called, 'Joanna, I'm sending a patient down to room ten. Tell nurse, will you?'

As she walked down to room ten she heard him striding off in the direction of the reception room, making unintelligible roaring sounds. She waited in the empty room. It was very cold. After a few minutes, a nurse put her head round the door.

'Tights and pants off,' she said, and vanished.

Chrissie looked down at her trousers. If she'd thought this was going to happen she'd have worn a skirt. In the end she took off everything except her bra and sat, shivering, on the edge of the couch. An unlit gas fire adorned a far wall.

The nurse reappeared.

'Doctor not here yet?' she enquired.

'No.'

The nurse looked at Chrissie with disapproval. 'Can't you cover yourself up a bit more?' she asked. 'I mean, it's not very nice, is it?'

She went out without waiting for a reply.

Chrissie folded her trousers and laid them across her knees. She sat there for what seemed a very long time. She shut her eyes, let her mind drift away. Everything was unreal; she so completely forgot where she was that when she opened her eyes she stared about her looking for something she could recognize in this unfamiliar room. She pulled herself up sharply, consciously retrieving her mind, drawing herself back into time and space. Perhaps, she told herself, this doctor really was on to something; hadn't she once heard that illnesses connected with ovaries could make you depressed? She yearned for some physical affliction that wasn't her fault or responsibility, that somebody else could put right.

The nurse put her head round the door. 'Doctor's coming,' she said. 'It's cold in here. Too cold by half. And he's pinched the matches again for that damned pipe.'

She went in search of matches.

'Seen Dr Striding?' Chrissie heard her ask of somebody in the corridor.

'In reception. Talking to Dr Runt; they're having coffee, I think.'

The nurse reappeared with matches and lit the fire. 'That's better,' she said, standing in front of it. Chrissie could just make out the orange glow to one side of the navy skirt.

A few minutes later the door flew open and Dr Striding burst in.

'Splendid, splendid,' he said, rubbing his hands. 'Now that's what I call excellent organization. Patient, nurse and doctor all assembled. No time loss.'

He turned to the nurse. 'Gloves,' he said.

'Gloves?' the nurse repeated. 'Oh, gloves. They're in the dispensary drawer. Back in a sec.'

She went to get them. Dr Striding did not talk to Chrissie, but stared at his watch and paced the room impatiently.

The nurse returned. Dr Striding seized the gloves and pulled them on.

Chrissie had her face to the wall, so heard but did not see what it was that Dr Striding dropped with a clatter. He swore quietly and there was a bit of a scuffle.

He was ham-handed, but blessedly brief. In no time at all he was hurling the gloves in the direction of the litter bin.

'Back in my room for discussion,' he called back to Chrissie as he strode out of the room.

Against her better judgment she found herself hoping, as she walked back down the corridor to his room, that he had discovered the cause of it all. She had been brought up to believe in doctors.

The door was open, the room empty. She hesitated. Loud laughter was coming from the reception room. Dr Striding then appeared with another doctor, a little man. Although tiny, he had the same swagger, the same expression of being delighted with himself as his bigger, bouncier colleague. He went into the room marked Dr Runt.

'In you go,' Dr Striding shouted at Chrissie.

'You will be delighted to know,' he said, tossing himself into his chair and leaning back importantly, 'that there was nothing sinister to be seen.'

He might have been a renowned surgeon reporting on a very long and difficult operation. She smiled gratefully, humouring him.

'Now the question you will so rightly ask is: what next?'

She waited, hoping that he would ask questions which would enable her to talk; if she could just start to tell somebody; just start.

'Are you insured?' he asked.

She looked at him in astonishment. Did he think that the surgery ceiling might fall down and maim her?

'Insured?' she repeated.

'Yes, medically insured. You know, BUPA and that sort of thing.'

'No.'

'A mistake,' he reprimanded. 'Everyone who can possibly

afford it should be privately insured. Your health is worth more than a penny a week, you know.'

He drummed his fingers on the desk. He picked up a small hammer of the kind used for testing reflexes. Absent-mindedly he tapped his knee. His foot, predictably, jerked up.

He sighed and pulled a pad towards him.

'Let me see now,' he said. 'Faintness, sickness. I think we'll try something to help the digestion. And if that doesn't work, come back in a couple of weeks and we'll think again.'

He wrote out the prescription and handed it to her, adding, 'If there's any problem, I can always send you to my friend and colleague, Pip Snodgrass. He's not everyone's cup of tea, isn't Pip, but I reckon he's the best guts doctor we've got.'

He paused and then added gloomily, 'Lord knows how long you'd have to wait for an appointment, of course. Unless you went privately. So don't forget what I said about insurance. Very worthwhile. Talk it over with hubby tonight, eh?'

She was dismissed.

For a moment she hesitated, glancing back tentatively at him as she walked to the door, in the forlorn hope that even now, at this eleventh hour, he might say something, ask a question that would enable her to talk. But no help came. Dr Striding had already picked up the telephone and seemed oblivious of her existence. So she left the surgery clutching her flimsy little slip of a prescription as one clutches at a straw.

'I don't think you've paid for the vitamins, have you?' the assistant said.

Chrissie stared at her, not understanding.

'What vitamins?' she asked.

'The ones you picked up and put in the bag with your prescription,' the woman said knowingly.

She opened her bag; it was true. Inside, with the prescription, was a packet of vitamin tablets. She had no recollection of putting it in. She tried to think; yes, she did remember looking at them and thinking they might do her good. But she didn't remember picking them up.

'Just give me the fifty-five pence,' the woman said, 'and we'll say no more about it. But it's lucky it's me what saw and not the store detective.'

She paid the money, thanked the assistant and went out. She was trembling. If it had been the store detective, if she had got outside before being challenged, there would have been no hope for her. She leant against the shop window shaking with relief. She thought of the publicity there would have been. The local paper would have been full of it. She was a newcomer without friends, they would all have believed that she was a thief. And Jack – poor Jack in his new job, everyone talking behind his back. He must never know. And the children, the shame for them of having a mother who was guilty of shop-lifting.

It was all right, it hadn't happened, she told herself firmly. All the same she did not dare to do the shopping she had planned. The thought of going inside another shop terrified her. She must just get herself home quickly, before she did any more harm.

At home, she walked round the garden, trying to get a grip on herself. It was a piece of absent-mindedness, that was all. Anyone could do it, plenty had. They said it was a cry for help. She began to think more calmly. It was true that she had felt let down that the doctor had not been like their old one, someone you could talk to. Feeling let down, she had unconsciously cried out for help. That is what the psychiatrists would say. That is what she herself would say on behalf of anyone else. Of course it was easy to talk like that about other people, she would never blame anyone else, but it was different when it was herself. There was no excuse for her. None.

The door bell rang. It wouldn't be a friend. It couldn't be. It must be a tradesman or someone collecting money.

It was the latter. A snowy-haired lady stood on the door-step proffering a tin.

'Good morning,' she said. 'Would you care to give something for the hospital? The last people did.'

Ah, the orthopaedic surgeon with woodworm. She wondered what the snowy-haired lady would have thought had she heard him bawling and swearing at the surveyor in this very hall. It had been a frightening exhibition, adding to her dislike of the house.

'Of course I will,' she heard herself say. 'Do come in while I find my bag.'

'How nice to have somebody who gives willingly,' the woman said as she took the money.

'Well, I've collected enough myself to know it isn't much fun,' Chrissie said. How normal she sounded, she thought; what a hypocrite she was. How many other thieves and depressives were going round disguised as pleasant, middle-aged ladies?

'Have you? Perhaps you could help me with it, then? When you've settled in, I mean,' she added, glancing at the bare boards. 'Moving's awful, isn't it?'

On an impulse, Chrissie asked her if she'd like coffee, although it was nearly lunchtime.

Together they sat in the drawingroom, the one room they had finished decorating; the new paint outclassed their shabby old furniture.

'I was matron at the hospital for twenty years,' the woman said, biting healthily into fruit cake.

'Were you really?' She was feeling so much better, it was ridiculous. 'I've always wanted to be a nurse,' she confided. It was the first time she had spoken of it for twenty years.

'Well, it's never too late.'

Chrissie laughed. 'Oh, I'd never do it now,' she said.

'Why not? We have plenty of mature students about nowadays.'

'No, really?'

'We have retraining schemes . . .'

'But it wouldn't be retraining,' Chrissie interrupted gently. 'The only training I ever had was a two-year domestic science course.'

'That would be invaluable,' the ex-matron said airily. 'And what about years of experience as a housewife, and I bet you've nursed your family very capably.'

She smiled at Chrissie. 'I think you'd make a splendid nurse,' she said.

She really meant it, there was no question. A stranger had come into her empty, hollow house and filled it with hope.

'You get quite well paid nowadays while you train,' the stranger was saying, unaware of the significance of what she had done. 'I should think the timing would work out just right, too; you'd just have enough time to settle in before starting if you joined the August set.'

'We do have to move quite often. I might not finish a three-year course,' Chrissie said, raising obstacles for the sheer pleasure of having them demolished.

'I daresay you could transfer. And of course you might settle for a two-year course. Look, I'll get my collecting finished and then I'll call back this evening with the brochures and so on.'

When she had gone, Chrissie set about putting the house

to rights. She could hardly believe it; this sensible, friendly, rather bossy woman had really thought that she was capable, worth having, that a hospital would actually be willing to train her, even pay for her being trained. She was smiling as she undid the hairy string that bound a great roll of under-felt and set about measuring it up to fit the hall.

By the time Jack came home later in the week she had not only got the house organized, she had arranged her nursing career as well.

He was less delighted for her than she had expected. He was more puzzled than anything else.

'I'd no idea you wanted to nurse,' he said. 'Why ever didn't you say so before?'

'Well, it wouldn't have been possible before, would it?'

'No, I suppose not.'

'And then there wasn't the *need* before.'

'Need? Look, Chrissie, we're not rich, but there's no need for you to go out to work.'

'I don't mean that sort of need. You see, Claire and Sarah are both away now and you're away a lot, too, and so none of you need me as much . . .'

He got up and kissed her. 'We need you just the same,' he said. 'Maybe we're not here much, but I like to think that when I do come home, you'll be here waiting for me, and I'm sure the kids feel just the same.'

'Well, I may not always be here waiting in future,' she said with unexpected feeling.

He hesitated, at a loss to know why his kindly reassurance had been misinterpreted. He thought of something else.

'Will you have to work at nights?'

'I don't know,' she said, as if it didn't matter. 'Maybe.'

'You mustn't overdo it,' he said. 'You've been looking a bit peaky lately.'

'Thank you.'

'By the way,' he went on cautiously, 'I'd been thinking we might do a bit of entertaining. In view of this nursing idea perhaps we'd better get on with it as soon as possible.'

'You mean a party?'

'Well, a series of dinner parties really. It's better, I think, for talking. There are quite a few local contacts I'd like to get to know better, and then, of course, the new staff as they come along. Of course I could take them out, but it's always pleasanter at home, more relaxed, and besides I must keep the expenses down or there'll be grumbles from Head Office.'

She nodded, reflecting that it wouldn't be the first time the housekeeping had been sacrificed to the interests of Lomacks' shareholders.

'You see, we're not actually paying our way down here yet. Mind you, they understand that. You don't set up a regional office and get it making money in anything under two years.'

'Well, let's get on with it quickly,' she said. 'I start work in two weeks' time. Besides, we might as well do it while we still have the excuse that we've just moved in, in case everything's in a muddle.'

'I'm sure it won't be,' he said diplomatically.

It irritated her, the way he talked to her soothingly, like a child. She was a person in her own right now, not to be condescended to.

'I must ask Nell for a weekend,' she said. 'And Gregory too, if he wants to come.'

Chapter Twenty

'You see, Mrs Venables,' Nell explained. 'It really isn't in my hands. Your daughter's application will be considered in the usual way and . . .'

'But that's the point, Dr Thorpe, I feel she needs *special* consideration. She is one of those unfortunate few, you see, who has great potential, but alas hasn't the knack of showing it. Particularly in examinations.'

The rubbery pink lips never stopped, words writhed endlessly out of them. Nell tried to look with friendly interest at the heavily made-up face, the expanse of powdery mauve cheeks, while avoiding the cunning little brown eyes.

'Well, to talk of other things, Dr Thorpe. We were wondering, the family and I, if you would care to have dinner with us tonight? We are staying at The Golden Chimes.'

Other things, indeed! As if the implication wasn't obvious enough. Did the Honourable Mrs Venables really think she was totally bereft of perception about her fellow human beings, just because she was an academic?

'Well, I'm afraid . . .'

'Of course, my daughter Julie and I are only too well aware that we could not provide the intellectual conversation you are used to,' Mrs Venables went on in dreadful self-abasement against which every complacent, powdered pore seemed to cry out denial, 'but my son will be with us and I think that you will find *him* interesting. You may have heard of my son Ian; the name may be familiar, perhaps?'

Ian Venables. It rang a bell. Good heavens, yes, she saw his name every week when she read the book reviews.

Mrs Venables' little eyes were watching her, gratified.

'He's done extremely well,' she said. 'He is the youngest Literary Editor in the land, I'm told.'

Nell looked suitably impressed.

'Of course, he is twelve years older than Julie.'

'Ah yes, Julie,' Nell said brightly. 'I look forward so much to meeting Julie. I have heard so much about her from you during the past year.'

'Then you'll come tonight?'

'It's very kind of you – I'd love to.'

'Well, shall we say seven thirty in the residents' bar?'

'That would be lovely.'

Mrs Venables heaved her massive bulk out of the delicate chair and Nell opened the door for her. After her guest had departed, she returned, smiling, to her desk and worked steadily for two hours.

At five o'clock she rang The Golden Chimes and asked for Mrs Venables.

'I am so sorry, Mrs Venables,' she began when she was put through.

'Oh, don't say you can't come!'

The disappointment was genuine and profound. Evidently there was no hope for Julie of entering the university through the door marked examinations.

'Well, I've just remembered that I was going out to dinner with a friend tonight – a Mr Nansen. You may have heard of him: he's quite a well known novelist. It was so stupid of me, because we had thought of going to The Golden Chimes ourselves, actually. I can't think how I forgot.'

'In that case, perhaps you'll *both* join us? If it wouldn't upset your plans?'

'How very kind.'

'I mean, being a writer and my son being a reviewer, it

would be nice for them, wouldn't it?'

'Lovely,' Nell said.

It was a balmy, still evening, as Nell drove home smiling to herself, pleased with her plotting. It had been a marvellous term and now even the bugbear of Mrs Venables, who had plagued her for over a year with letters and telephone calls and visits, had been turned to advantage.

It seemed to be one of those rare periods of life when everything goes smoothly. At the end of January, when the lease of the flat ran out, they had moved into the new house, which they still absurdly called The Lonely House, not because it was in the least bit lonely, but because Gregory admired a Lowry painting of that name. They had bought it just before house prices shot up, so it was a good investment, not that that mattered to her in the least, but it is always pleasant to find sound economic reasons for doing something you want to do anyway. She loved the house. Whenever she went in she felt as she used to in her college room: that it was her own creation, composed in her own image. But it was more, far more, than that. It carried deeper feelings, reaching back to forgotten stores of memory. It was the home she had been seeking all her life, the home she had not had with her father.

It would not have been a practical proposition without Mr Odgers. Mr Odgers was a carpenter who lived in the nearby village of Spermsby. At least he was a carpenter by trade, but could turn his hand to anything. During the week he worked in a factory because there was more money in it, but he filled the weekends with odd jobs in the neighbourhood. It was an ideal arrangement, Nell reflected. A lot of the work on the house she did herself; Mr Odgers saw to the jobs which Gregory might have done had he had any talent for practical work, which he had not. She wouldn't have wanted everything done at once, anyway; she enjoyed working slowly on the house, so that change seemed a natural process. Besides, Gregory would have hated to have men disturbing him during the week and she herself would have resented having hordes of workmen around the place, taking it over. She did not want her home invaded, any more than her life.

But they both enjoyed Mr Odgers. He was a nutty little man, short and compact. Nothing ruffled him, he worked steadily at everything he did, talking quietly to himself. There seemed to be nothing he did not know how to tackle. This neat little man was possessed of a huge wife, nervous as a mouse, whose wobbly pink flesh positively shook with apprehension even at a knocking on the door. Somehow Mr Odgers managed to get this mass of nervous flesh into the tiny side-car on his motor-bike and together they would ride around the countryside on warm evenings obviously blissfully contented with each other. Nell and Gregory did not know her real name; Mr Odgers always referred to her by the pet name of Blossom.

Gregory had finished his book more quickly than he had expected and sent it off to the publishers soon after Christmas. He was expecting the proofs any time. Meanwhile he had started on the next and it was going well. Nell typed up the chapters for him as he finished them. It helped him, he said, to have her type the final copy, for he himself was always tempted to make alterations as he typed. She was a poor typist and had to work hard to make her typing worthy of him, but she did it gladly. She loved him so much that she could hardly bear him to be grateful to her, which he always was. She had resolved, however, not to say anything to him about getting married until the book came out. He had been very good about not pestering her to marry him, ever since those early days in Austria. And now, to crown all, she was going to make him famous, going to see that his latest book would get the recognition it deserved, not go unnoticed like the other two. It was a gift she would give him, like a dowry.

In college that afternoon she had longed to ring him up, cursed the fact that the telephone hadn't been installed yet. Now she was glad; it was much more exciting to tell him in person. Her heart was thumping as she jumped out of the car and ran into the house.

'Enter a cat with two tails,' she said as she went into the study. She instantly regretted the joke. He was clearly not in a joking mood. The galley proofs of *The Spindle Tree* had arrived. They were strewn about the room, like toilet rolls unleashed, and amidst all the confusion he sat, with his head in his hands, the personification of wretchedness. He looked up as she came in and scowled at her.

'It's awful, Nell, it's awful,' he said.

'Nonsense, I've read it,' she said briskly, 'and it's the best yet.'

'You're prejudiced, Nell.'

'It wouldn't have been accepted if it had been dreadful.'

'I sometimes think that nobody but little Mr Kaufman would have taken it. Probably they were just a bit short of their quota of novels this summer.'

She poured out a drink for him.

'Do you always get like this when the proofs come?'

He nodded sheepishly.

'It's seeing it *printed*, Nell. It looks so different *printed*.'

She breathed deeply with relief. It wasn't serious.

'What are you so pleased about?' he asked.

'Well,' she hesitated. Somehow it didn't seem quite the great break-through she had thought.

'We are invited out to dinner tonight.'

'Oh, Nell, no!'

'Hush, don't swear until you hear all. A fairly terrible woman called the Honourable Mrs Venables has asked me out to dinner in order to induce me to wangle a place for her daughter in college next October.'

'Oh, then you won't want me there.'

'But I do – that's the point.'

'Won't it be embarrassing enough being corrupted without having me as a witness?'

She put her hand over his mouth. 'Will you let me explain?' she asked.

He bit her fingers gently. 'Oh, Nell, lovely Nell, must we go on about Venables and things? Wouldn't it be a better idea to go to bed?'

'No. Does the name Ian Venables ring a bell?'

'Well, there's an appalling chap called Ian Venables who writes unbelievably pretentious reviews about books he doesn't understand . . .'

'That's it! He's her son – and he's coming tonight.'

It fell very flat, her wonderful news.

'Oh. Well. Nell, you can't really think he'd be an inducement to go out tonight? I mean, he's enough to spoil anyone's dinner, he is. A real destroyer of the appetite if ever there was one.'

'But don't you see? It's your chance. You'll make a great impression on him and he'll *bother* to read *The Spindle Tree* and it'll get a rave review. Then all the others will follow suit, because they won't like to think they've missed something.'

'It's not his sort of book,' Gregory said slowly.

'Oh, *honestly*!' She shook his shoulders. 'You've said yourself it's not books that get reviewed, but authors.'

'I grant you he may read it if he's met me, which he wouldn't do otherwise. But Nell, you don't know this chap. I mean, you'd admit you just glance at review pages, don't you? You don't chew them over like I do.'

'True.'

'Well, the one thing he can't bear is a straight book, a tale, you know, with believable people with feelings and thoughts. It scares him stiff. Anything which produces any kind of gut reaction makes him run a mile, screaming with terror.'

'Ye-es, I can imagine that having a childhood dominated by Mrs Venables might have that sort of effect.'

'He only feels safe with the incomprehensible.'

She laughed.

'But it's *true,* Nell. Do you remember that microbiologist in, I think, *The Lost World,* who couldn't take seriously anything that could be seen with the naked eye? Ian Venables is the literary equivalent.'

Nell sat down, suddenly tired.

'I wouldn't dream of pandering to Ian Venables to get a review,' he went on, not noticing. 'I'd as soon ask to be shot out of a cannon. It's not just the pandering, it's the thought of being written about by him. He's deadly, Nell, absolutely deadly.'

She said nothing.

'And I'll tell you another horrible thing about him,' Gregory went on, beginning to pace the room as he warmed to his theme, 'he goes in for pickings. He picks about among the bones of dead writers, finding little titbits. And he's so *boring,* Nell. He writes the most incredibly boring pieces of literary criticism ever published and . . .'

'But isn't that part of his job?' she interrupted, feeling called upon to defend the one who was to have been their *deus ex machina.* 'I mean, I suppose he sometimes has to write about authors he isn't particularly interested in and that must be boring for him, too.'

'Ian Venables is boring beyond the call of duty,' Gregory pronounced.

The disappointment was too much. She leant forward, her head in her hands. 'I wanted to help,' she said miserably.

He stopped pacing and turned round. 'Sorry, sorry, sorry,' he said, coming over to her. 'Of course I'll come. It's a splendid idea. Oh Nell, I'm ungrateful and beastly to you of all people, you who *enabled* me to write the book.'

'But it's not enough to have written it . . .'

'Yes, it is. I don't mind as much as you think about reviews and so on, Nell. Honestly, I don't care what they say or don't say.'

'But I do.'

He looked at her stricken face, realized at last the depth of her disappointment.

'Oh Nell, I haven't understood, I'm no good to you, Nell.'

'Don't, I can't bear it,' she said and, as if to prove it, burst into tears.

He picked her up and sat her on his knee. He did not make love to her, but kissed her like a child, rocking her in his arms, soothing. He let her sob until she was exhausted, and then wiped her blotchy face carefully, gently dabbing round her eyes.

'That,' he pronounced, 'was a lovely cry.'

'Idiot.'

'Better. Abuse is always a good sign. Now listen, darling Nell, we are going out, you and I, for a splendid evening with Ian Venables and I shall be a credit to you. Mrs Venables will sell Julie to you and you will sell me to her admirable son Ian.'

She laughed despite herself.

'And you, my lovely Nell,' he went on, 'will now go and get ready and put on your new black and purple dress which would make anybody else look like a bruised banana. But first of all I'll get you a drink. I don't deserve one, and anyway I must be sober to impress Mr Venables.'

'No, we'll share it,' she said, reaching for the glass and holding it to his lips.

'I bet Mr Venables looks all rabbity,' he said, 'and squeaks.'

'Stop it,' she warned.

They drank from the same glass, like a loving-cup. Then she went and did as he had asked, putting on the purple and black dress, making-up carefully. The evening was dusky, sweet-smelling. Never had she loved him more. She did not attempt to disguise it now; they walked hand in hand into The Golden Chimes.

Ian Venables was so absurdly like Gregory's picture of him that at first she found it hard not to laugh. He had anxious, protuberant eyes like a rabbit, set in a pale bony face which disappeared at one end into an expanse of bald head and at the other into a tiny pointed beard. His thin pink lips twitched as he talked which he did most of the time in a high-pitched, clever voice. Like most clever but uncreative people he talked easily and destructively.

It was hard to believe that Julie Venables was his sister. She was stunningly beautiful. It was a classic, madonna-like beauty, calm and placid. Out of the perfect symmetry of her features her eyes gazed with an expression which was either very composed or very stupid. From Mrs Venables' attempts to by-pass the examination system, Nell presumed that it must be the latter. But beauty confused the issue.

Mrs Venables also wore purple and black. She was such a different shape from herself that it was a few seconds before Nell realized that their dresses were identical. Furthermore they were both wearing a double row of pearls; Nell's lay slack against the blue and black material, while Mrs Venables' stretched taut across the doughy no-man's-land where her chins merged with her neck. Nell considered, as they finished their drinks and went to their table in the dining-room, remarking upon the coincidence and so disposing of the matter for good, but she was too nervous, and so it remained as a kind of unspoken rebuke.

Mrs Venables placed her son at one end of the table and Gregory at the other, with Julie on one side and Nell and herself opposite. At first, over the soup, she did most of the talking herself, trying to draw out Julie for Nell's benefit, but doing it with such obvious purpose that the beautiful girl was reduced to monosyllables of agreement.

'She is very shy,' her mother said to Nell. 'Aren't you, poppet?'

'It's a nice change,' Nell said. 'Overconfident youth is very trying. I often wonder why some public schools pride themselves on producing it.'

They spoke of schools for a while and then, as the fish was being served, the talk turned to writing.

'I gather from my mother, Mr Nansen,' Ian Venables said, nibbling at his bread roll, 'that you are a practitioner of the craft.'

Nell saw Gregory's face take on a wary look. Please God make him be *sensible*, she prayed, tugging nervously at her pearls.

Before Gregory could reply there was a little tinkling sound as the pearls fell and rolled. Both men jumped up and began scrabbling under the table. Nell said, 'Please don't worry,' and a waiter came over and joined the men on the floor. Julie asked, 'Are they poisonous?' and daintily picked a pearl out of her parsley sauce, wiped it on her table napkin and offered it to Nell, like a child proffering a gift.

Order was eventually restored, a waiter provided an envelope into which the pearls were poured and put for safe keeping in Gregory's pocket. Duckling replaced fish on the table.

'We were talking, were we not, about the art of writing?' Ian Venables squeaked.

'*You* were,' Gregory corrected, but he said it nicely; he was wanting to make up to Nell for the pearls, she realized. Perhaps it had been a happy small accident.

'I have a big review coming out tomorrow,' Venables went on, 'of Bartholomew Snyde's latest book. In fact we are doing a whole feature on his work. *Fascinating* man, that.'

'He is my godson, Barty is,' Mrs Venables put in. 'Not, of course, that that would affect the reviews at all.'

'As I said to him the other day,' her son went on, 'he gets his characters so exactly right, such precision, such ice-cold precision.'

He popped some crackling into his mouth and crunched it up methodically, his jaw rotating in little nervous circles.

'He captures his characters like dead butterflies,' he went on, 'impaled upon a pin.'

There was silence, impressed silence. Then Gregory's appalled voice cut in, 'And you think he *means* to do that?'

'But of course!' The protuberant eyes stared out of their bony sockets, astonished at the question.

'He actually means to *impale his characters like dead butterflies on a pin?*'

'It is hardly the effect that a great writer achieves by mistake, my dear Gregory,' Venables said with a little giggle.

'How do you know?'

'How do I know what?'

'How do you know that he didn't intend to create real people, warm, living, breathing, funny people? But his own limitations turned them into these dead butterflies?'

'Oh come, Gregory, my dear fellow, Snyde is a writer proclaimed by every critic of standing in the land. His publisher is the most prestigious in the business.'

Nell's heart sank; she knew what the use of words like

prestigious did to Gregory.

'I'm always amazed,' he said angrily, 'at the way you critics assume intention in the achievement. In fact there is a great abyss, you know, dividing them.'

'Ah, you speak of lesser writers – '

'I speak of *all* writers, Mr Venables.'

'Do you do much writing on your own account?' Nell cut in desperately. 'I mean, other than reviewing?'

'Ah, how interesting that you should ask that,' Ian Venables said, turning to her, gratified. 'I am at the moment launching myself on a memoir about the minor men of letters of the first quarter of the eighteenth century.'

As he spoke he picked about among the litter of tiny bones on his plate, poking, prying, for little rewards of meat.

Mrs Venables smiled at Nell.

'So nice,' she whispered, as the plates were cleared away, 'to hear them talk. I always enjoy a literary conversation.'

Nell was spared the need to reply by the arrival of the dessert trolley and the necessity of choosing between great gateaux of chocolate and pears, wobbly cream caramels, drifts of lemon meringue pie. Please God don't let Gregory offend Ian Venables, she prayed, making a choice at random.

The trolley was pushed round the table. Venables blinked at it. 'Puddings displayed like beauty queens for selection,' he said, and giggled. 'I'll have cream caramel.'

Gregory requested cheese.

'Very wise, my dear fellow,' Venables said. 'These confections delight the eye and appal the stomach.'

For a few minutes Nell could not hear the conversation between the two men because Mrs Venables was talking to her in a low confidential voice about her son. 'He's reached the very top of his profession so young,' she said. Nell nodded, straining her ears to hear what Gregory was saying, ready to interrupt if necessary. 'All on his own merit, too. His father being a newspaper proprietor scarcely entered into it. Well, perhaps a tiny bit. Connections shouldn't matter, but they do, don't they?'

Of course, even Ian Venables can't harm the *book*. It's there, finished, safe; but he could damage the man, the writing man, who needs encouragement to keep on trying, always encouragement.

'I'm so glad it's my son that's clever,' Mrs Venables said, as the last of the lemon meringue pie disappeared between the rubbery pink lips.

'I mean, it doesn't matter nearly so much for a girl.'

She put the lipstick-smeared fork down on her plate, wiped her mouth and sat back relaxed. Then, as if her words had reached her own ears, her expression changed and she added hastily, 'Though of course Julie is very clever too; it's just that it's not *showing* yet.'

Nell nodded, smiled vaguely across at Julie and turned her attention back to Ian Venables.

'What I find fascinating in my job,' he was saying as he dipped the point of his teaspoon into the cream caramel and drew it down the side, leaving a clear, shiny groove, 'is the opportunity it gives me to study the different methods of creative writing, something which has always interested me. I mean, how it is actually *done*.'

He had made tiny grooves right round the little caramel dome and looked for a moment with pleasure at the consequent convolutions.

'Now some writers,' he went on, 'clearly start with the plot and you soon sense that the characters are forced to fit the requirements of the same. Others start with a situation, a problem. Others, the best I think . . .' he paused to chew ruminatively, for he could even chew ruminatively on cream caramel, this literary gentleman, 'start with their *theme* and from there they work outwards, building up plot, characters and scenes.'

Gregory was not drunk. It might have been better if he had been. But he had downed enough alcohol to remove the inhibitions which usually so pressed down his anger that it could only express itself in writing.

'You critics,' he said, jabbing at the air in Venables' direction, 'are always in on the end of the act, aren't you?'

Venables stared back at him, rabbity.

'You don't *understand* anything about creation. You can't.'

Even Mrs Venables noticed that something was amiss. She turned her attention away from the coffee tray which had just been put in front of her, and directed it towards Gregory.

'I always say,' she remarked soothingly, 'that the pen is mightier than the sword. And *so* much more lethal.'

'You are like a paediatrician,' Gregory went on regardless, 'who looks at a newborn baby and says, "Now here we have an interesting specimen of creation . . ." '

It was awful; he was even imitating Ian Venables' voice. ' "Its parents made it by starting with the extremities and then worked inwards to create the body ..." '

'Oh, I say, my dear fellow ...'

'And another says, "Oh, no, they started at the feet and worked straight up to the head." And another paediatrician comes along and says, "I think they started with the navel problem and worked outwards in all directions. And so this marvellous living child was created." '

He paused, glared at Venables for what seemed to Nell a very long time and then concluded, 'But the sweating parent knows it wasn't like that at all.'

'Ah,' Mrs Venables said, handing him some coffee, 'I see you understand women, Mr Nansen.'

Her son rallied. 'What you are saying, I think, is that there is a great and – er – necessary difference between the viewpoint of the critic and the creative writer?'

'Oh, well *done*,' Gregory said rudely.

'Though I say it myself,' Mrs Venables said, smiling and fingering her pearls, 'my son has the gift of understanding.' She gave a little gasp as her pearls tinkled to the ground just as Nell's had done.

'Oh,' Julie exclaimed, uttering her second sentence of the evening, 'and Mummy's are real!'

Chapter Twenty-One

'I don't think we ought to rely on that dinner party really,' Gregory said at breakfast the next morning, 'to do me much good, I mean.'

'That's the understatement of the year.'

'All right, I know. It was a disaster. I'm sorry.'

Nell laughed. 'Never mind. It was a crazy idea, anyway. At least it's let me off the hook as far as poor Julie Venables is concerned.'

'Why *poor*? A rich and beautiful girl like that?'

'She has academic ambitions.'

'She's no need of them – not with her face and figure.'

Irritated by this view of women, Nell began to object, and then checked herself. It was not typical of his usual attitude.

Besides, she didn't want to upset him with arguments.

'Anything in the post?' he asked.

'Just a map from Chrissie,' she told him, handing it over. 'To help us get there on Saturday. Do you know, they've been there a whole year and we haven't been to see them once?'

'Now I wouldn't have thought your cousin Chrissie was a map-drawing sort of person,' he said, scowling at the piece of paper.

'Go on. You've never even met her.'

'I have a picture of her as domesticated, thoroughly dependent on Jack for such things as maps . . .'

'And once you have a picture of somebody in your mind, they have to conform to it, don't they?'

'That's right. Otherwise it undermines my confidence in my own judgment.'

She laughed. 'All right. Actually it *was* Jack who drew the map for her.'

He got up and stood beside her chair.

'I'm always right about women, you see,' he said, leaning over her, running his hands down her breast and on to her lap. 'Who'd like to be late for work this morning?'

'Not me. Stop it. Actually you *are* wrong about Chrissie. Her letter is surprising; I hadn't realized how seriously she was taking this nursing course. Her attitude really is quite professional. She plans her life around her work. She has set hours, everything. I never had the remotest idea she wanted to. She's always seemed so contented with her lot.'

'Perhaps,' Gregory said thoughtfully, playing now with her hair, 'her lot changed? Children grew up and all that?'

'Mm. But she'd expect that, wouldn't she, plan for it? Perhaps it's Chrissie who has changed.'

'Maybe she never was quite as you imagined.'

She shook her head. 'No, Chrissie is Chrissie. She isn't a person one imagines things about. As you'll see on Saturday.'

She removed his hands, slipped out of her chair before he could prevent her, and began to clear the table.

It was a lovely run down to the coast on Saturday morning in clear sunshine, everything fresh and the light thin, pared down.

'I feel curiously nervous,' Gregory remarked. 'It's the nearest thing to being inspected by the in-laws.'

She glanced at him. Should she tell him that she had changed her mind, now on this June morning? No, she would wait until the book came out. She longed to tell him, she realized as she watched his hands on the steering-wheel, but something held her back, some half-conscious fear of abandoning all the assumptions and safeguards which had stood her in good stead for so many years. It occurred to her that she was just as trammelled by the conventions of her own life-style as any Victorian maiden who couldn't bring herself to have an affair, even though her whole being demanded it. She, Nell, had found it perfectly simple to have an affair, but dithered when it came to committing herself to the kind of respectable old-fashioned marriage pairing that she had for so long ignored, even mocked. We women get rid of one set of chains, she thought, and forge ourselves new ones.

She was unreasonably glad to see that Chrissie liked Gregory, who was at his sunniest and most charming all day. She did not even stop to remind herself that her cousin always liked everyone, as she would once have done. Love seemed to have diminished her critical faculties. Maybe she had been over-critical in the past. Now she felt nothing but admiration for Chrissie, so full of life and energy, such a home-maker, so ready to make the best of things. For the first time in her life she wanted to be more like her.

'Tell me about the nursing, Chrissie,' she said as they prepared the dinner together in the kitchen that evening.

'I love it, Nell, every minute. This last year has just flown.'

There was no doubting the sincerity in her voice. 'I was scared at the beginning, and the others seemed so young. It was like being back at school with my own girls, but I don't mind now, not a bit.'

'Isn't it exhausting? I mean, you can't just go home and study the way they can. I've realized recently how much there is to do in a house.'

'I'd love to come and see your house, Nell.'

'Oh, *do*. I'd love to show it to you. There's still a lot to do, but you won't mind that?'

'I shall be terribly jealous. It sounds a lovely old place.'

'*You* jealous?' Nell laughed at the very idea. 'I'll take these rolls in, shall I?'

'Yes, please. Then I think you could call the men now.'

'Call the men', it had an old-fashioned sound. It might have been Aunt Liz speaking.

'Do you know,' Nell remarked as they were eating their

soup later, 'in all the twenty years you've been married, I don't think I've visited you twice in the same house? They're terrible nomads, Gregory, the sort of people who wreck one's address book.'

'But you're wrong, Nell,' Jack said, laughing. 'You came twice to see us in the Sheerness house. Remember? The furnished one. The one with the mice.'

'I'd forgotten that. Yes, and the china in the piano.'

'Tell me about it,' Gregory said, always childishly eager for a story.

'It was all we could get, our first winter back from abroad,' Jack told him. 'It was furnished with broken bits of chairs and tables and there was this old piano which made extraordinary noises when Chrissie tried to play it, so we opened the back and found it was full of broken china which the last tenants had dumped there.'

'And do you remember the bed, Jack? It had a darts-board over the hole in the springs.'

'And the water froze every night and I had to thaw it out with a blowlamp.'

'One morning he wouldn't tell me where he'd got water for the morning tea,' Chrissie said, 'and after I'd drunk it he said he'd got it out of the lavatory cistern.'

'Ugh!'

'Perfectly pure,' Jack said. 'It came direct off the mains, actually.'

'It's the thought,' Nell said. 'Poor Chrissie! Being married to a civil engineer is distinctly more dangerous than being married to a writer.'

It slipped out. For a moment she was embarrassed, but nobody seemed to have noticed and anyway, she thought, she didn't really care. They'd know soon enough, anyway.

'Yes, poor Chrissie,' Jack was saying. 'You've lived in some awful places, haven't you?'

'Oh but I *loved* it there.' She turned to Gregory. 'Jack was demolishing a pier and there were piles of wooden sleepers to be got rid of and we used to burn a huge fire of these lovely oily logs. It was so cold we hardly ever went out, and it's the only place I didn't bother to get to know a soul. It wasn't worth it when we were only there for such a short time anyway. And I didn't mind a bit. There were just the three of us: Jack and me and the baby.'

Nell pictured it. Once she'd have thought it laughable; impossible to live without the society of friends and colleagues, without talk and college life. Now it seemed idyllic: herself and Gregory and a baby and a hearth. She wanted nothing more. And nothing less.

They sat over the meal reminiscing, Gregory demanding stories about the houses Jack and Chrissie had lived in, what it was like working abroad. It was all lovely, relaxed, trusting, Nell thought, and her mind went back to the Venables' dinner last week and she smiled at the contrast.

Chrissie caught the look.

'Penny for them,' she said.

So they gave her a blow-by-blow account, she and Gregory in turn, of the evening at The Golden Chimes, exaggerating their hopes as well as the subsequent disasters. They fell about laughing, and it hardly seemed possible that she had once taken it seriously, really had imagined that she might snatch success for Gregory's latest book with such a silly ploy.

'Poor Julie Venables,' Chrissie said. 'I'm sorry for children who are pushed into doing things by their parents. We wouldn't have made our girls go to college if they hadn't wanted to, would we, Jack?'

'We wouldn't have been able to, love, we never had that sort of control over them. But no, I agree with you; it *is* hard on poor Julie.'

'You wouldn't be sorry for her, Jack, if you could *see* her,' Gregory put in. 'She's the most gorgeous, stupid, lovely thing that any man could hope for.'

'That's dreadful,' Chrissie exclaimed. 'I should hate anyone to think of our girls like that, wouldn't you, Jack?'

'It's all right,' Nell said. 'He doesn't mean it.'

'Yes, I do,' Gregory contradicted. 'I can't think of anyone I've ever seen who combines such beauty and such undemanding stupidity as Julie Venables.'

'The key word is undemanding, isn't it?'

'Right, my clever one.'

'I still think it's dreadful . . .' Chrissie began.

'Of course it's dreadful,' Gregory agreed. 'Men *are* dreadful, Chrissie. And there's a bit of them, whatever they pretend, that still thinks it would be absolutely marvellous to have a nice little helpmeet running to greet them when they come in from work, bringing their slippers and gazing up at them like a lovely uncritical well-trained spaniel.'

'I *love* that,' Nell exclaimed. 'Particularly from a man who doesn't go to work, never wears slippers, and hates dogs.'

They all laughed.

'Come and have coffee,' Chrissie said, getting up. 'I'll bring it into the other room.'

'Can't we help you to clear this lot away?' Nell volunteered.

'Oh no, I'll do it when you have gone. Jack always helps me and it doesn't take long.'

'How's work going?' Nell asked Jack as they went into the drawingroom. 'I gather from Chrissie that you're setting up a whole new department down here. That's a new venture for you, isn't it?'

He sat down next to her on the shabby old couch.

'Well, the theory is that we catch the boom . . .'

Nell pulled a face. 'I don't like it, Jack. I don't think this crazy rush to inflate is at all what we need, and I don't see it lasting, either.'

Jack looked at her.

'I know,' he said. 'I'm interested that you feel that too. I mean, you know the theory of what I have to deal with in practice. But I can't get anyone in Lomacks to see it. You see, all we'll get is shortages of everything – steel, cement, labour, and then prices going sky high. What industry needed was a slow build-up, not this crazy boom and bust approach.'

'But if we gloomy old economists say a word against consumer-led inflation we're told that you people in industry love it.'

'Some do. Obviously, if they're out for a quick profit, it's much easier to get one nowadays by selling at home than bothering to export. But it's the road to bankruptcy for a trading nation.'

'They're always like this,' Chrissie said to Gregory as she poured out the coffee. 'On about economics and politics.'

'It's a bit boring,' Gregory agreed.

'Oh, I didn't mean – I mean, I'm glad for Jack to have somebody to talk to who understands what he's on about.'

'Don't worry, Chrissie,' Nell put in. 'Gregory thinks all my work's boring. I'm quite used to it. We always talk his shop, never mine, at home.'

At home. How casually it came out now. They were an established couple, like Chrissie and Jack.

'Besides, Chrissie,' Jack was saying, 'it may seem remote,

but really it affects every one of us. If you think of it as the nation's housekeeping . . .'

The way he looked at Chrissie, his patent desire to help her to understand, took the ring of condescension out of the words. Once, Nell thought, she would not have noticed the look, only winced at the words.

'Well, it still seems remote to me,' Chrissie said, shaking her head. 'Men's talk.'

'Oh, Chrissie, you're *incorrigible,*' Nell said, laughing. 'Men's talk indeed!'

But her tone was affectionate all the same. It suited Chrissie and Jack, this kind of relationship, it was a kind of conspiracy between them. It was what they needed and it was founded on honesty. Never mind how it struck the outsider. They didn't.

'When the consequences begin to show in everyday things like high prices, Chrissie,' Jack was saying, 'and firms are closing down because of the competition from all the foreign goods that are rushing in now, then you'll want something to be done about it, but it'll be too late.'

'You make it seem,' Gregory said owlishly, 'as if it's all Chrissie's fault.'

They laughed, but Gregory persisted. 'If it's not Chrissie's fault,' he asked, 'then whose is it?'

'Politicians',' Jack told him. 'Because they always think in the short term.'

'Which is only another way of saying that it's all our faults since they only do what they think we want.'

'Ah, so it's the system that's failed.'

'Then clever people like Nell must get together and draw up another constitution and everything will be mended,' Gregory said cheerfully.

'Truer than you think,' Nell said. 'If this expansion policy results in the kind of inflation I think it will, then we shall end up with an extreme political right and an extreme left, if we keep to the present arrangements, and heaven help us all. It's a civil war situation.'

'Oh, Nell, no,' Chrissie put in. 'You don't *mean* that?'

'Yes, I do. It can happen. It did in France before the war. People felt they had to choose between one extreme or the other. There was no middle way. I think we are moving into such a situation and I'm quite sure that the present economic policies will bring it about more quickly. You can't separate out economics and politics.'

'Don't you get very depressed,' Chrissie said, pouring out more coffee as if to bring comfort, 'knowing all this?'

'No, it doesn't depress me. It's interesting to observe and . . .'

'You see, Chrissie,' Gregory explained gently, 'it's all *theoretical* to Nell.'

'Well, I agree with Nell,' Jack said. 'Only it does depress me, particularly as we've done it at least three times since the war. Then we have a change of government, put everything into reverse, import controls, the lot. It'll be just the same this time, you'll see.'

'And all so unnecessary,' Nell said. 'If we'd only expanded gradually . . .'

They were off again. Chrissie listened dully. She wondered if she could slip out and get on with the washing-up. She had to be up early tomorrow; she was due on the ward by eight. A blur of white sheets, beds, pillows, corridors, passed in front of her eyes. She wanted to get to bed. She could hear Nell and Jack, wide awake and talkative, going on about inflation and over-heating the economy. It was remote. Not like getting bedpans. Anyway, what could anyone *do* about it? Even Jack and Nell who understood such things couldn't actually do anything. Only talk.

Chrissie sat wishing they'd stop putting the world to rights. Or at least, if they must, do the washing-up at the same time.

Chapter Twenty-Two

On the day in early September when Gregory's book came out Nell went into town and bought all the papers, periodicals and weeklies that might possibly mention it. She had so little hope of reviews that she did not even look at them, but took them back unopened to the house and presented them in a bundle to Gregory.

'Shall we try Mr Venables' ah – prestigious, ah – publication first?' Gregory squeaked in imitation of Ian Venables' pedantic speech, as he unfolded the pages and spread the paper out on the kitchen table.

There it was. Not just a few lines, or even a column alongside other books. But a whole article all to itself. Almost half a page was given over to the book. There was a photograph of Gregory, too.

They stared at the print, awestruck. Then, without saying a word, they began to read, both standing leaning over the table. At the end they straightened up, looked at each other, baffled.

'I suppose it *is* the same book?' Nell asked.

Gregory nodded. 'You're stuck with Julie Venables now,' he said.

None of the other papers so much as acknowledged the existence of *The Spindle Tree*.

'You'd think one of them might at least have given it a few lines,' Nell said, still hunting hopefully in the books-received columns.

'They will,' Gregory told her. 'You'll see, next week and after. They'll read this and they'll go scuttling back to look among the books they'd tossed out because they weren't produced by – er – prestigious writers and – er – publishers.'

'Do stop talking like that. But will *they* be able to make out what he's on about?'

'No, but that doesn't matter a bit. He's drawn attention to it, so they won't want to miss out. They'll review it honestly enough – I've never thought otherwise. It's the way books get chosen for review that's wrong, not what they write about them. All I wanted was that they should do them the justice of *reading* them and they will now – thanks to you.'

'Isn't it extraordinary? You know, I really thought the whole unfortunate episode was over after I'd written and thanked her for the dinner.'

Gregory laughed. 'What was it she said when she replied?'

'After commending Julie to my notice, as always, she said how much her son had enjoyed meeting that nice Mr Nansen.'

'Ah, what discernment. Come here and give nice Mr Nansen a kiss.'

'I was going to make some coffee. Then let's read that review again.'

'Darling Nell, a whole plantation of coffee wouldn't enable you to make sense of Ian Venables' review.'

'Actually, a cup of instant was all I had in mind,' she said, putting on the kettle.

He came and stood behind her.

'I have something in mind, too, Nell,' he said, pressing against her.

'I don't doubt that for one moment. And it doesn't feel as if it's entirely in the mind, either.'

She slipped away from him to make the coffee.

'Do you know it's only eleven o'clock?' she asked in surprise as she put the cups down on the table. 'It seems weeks and weeks since we saw that review.'

'It's very odd, isn't it?'

In a dream they sat looking at each other across the table, the papers strewn about the floor.

'What shall we do with the rest of the day?' she asked. 'You can't work now, can you?'

He put down his empty cup.

'Give you three guesses?' he said, crossing over to her.

She couldn't answer; his mouth was on hers.

Then he held her away from him for a moment, looked down at her and squeaked, 'I'm going to devote my day to expressing – ah – gratitude to my beloved, and showing – ah – appreciation of all her – ah – talents.'

She lay against him laughing. 'Oh, I wish you wouldn't. It *hurts*, it's so like him. Oh well, so long as you've finished appreciating by the time Mr Odgers comes this evening at six.'

'Have you ever seen Mr Odgers on a bike?' Gregory asked suddenly. 'The push bike, I mean, not the contraption he takes Blossom about in.'

'Yes, it's a marvellous sight, isn't it? I don't know why exactly.'

'I was walking down the road the other evening when he was coming here, and I realized what it was. His knees stick out so far that he looks as if he's rowing himself along.'

'Yes, *that's* it.'

'He's a very good example of the adaptation of the species, is Mr Odgers. He's developed bow legs so he can straddle his lovely big Blossom.'

'Gregory, sh!'

'Prude!'

'I'm not, but poor Mr Odgers, really!'

'Haven't you ever noticed the gleam in his eye when he so much as says her name? I tell you his Blossom is his obsession.'

'Rubbish!'

'Why? Why shouldn't poor Mr Odgers have an obsession?

I'm obsessed with writing, you're obsessed with this house.'

'I'm not obsessed with this house.'

'Of course you are – haven't you realized? You're quite boring about it sometimes. But today we shall just be obsessed with each other. Come on.'

He snatched at her suddenly, and made for the door, carrying her in a fireman's lift over his shoulder. So the last thing she saw was a curious upside-down view of the kitchen, with its dirty coffee cups, its newspapers strewn everywhere, and Ian Venables' review spread out on the table.

He had sounded so confident when he said that all the papers would now review *The Spindle Tree*, that Nell felt frightened that he would be disappointed. She need not have worried; the following week practically every review column placed his book first, and it was universally acclaimed. Most of them seemed to think it was a first book, which annoyed him. Then copies of notices in provincial papers began to arrive, sent on by his publishers.

'At least the provincial ones all seem to know about the earlier books,' Nell pointed out one morning as they sat looking through the cuttings after breakfast, which they had had outside on an improvised table on the cobbles beneath the kitchen window.

'Ah yes, they reviewed them at the time, you know. They don't seem to work on the same principles as Fleet Street, if principles is the right word.'

'Well, you've nothing to complain of now.'

'It doesn't make the system any better, Nell, just because it's suddenly worked for me.'

'If we had a telephone,' Nell said suddenly, 'I bet it would be ringing now. I do wish they would hurry up and get it installed.'

'Yes, it's one of the disadvantages of being stuck out here,' he said.

'Oh.'

'Why "oh"?'

'Just the way you said that. I've never thought there were any disadvantages. I thought the house was perfect.'

'Some of it's perfectly awful,' he said, picking at old putty round the window, a large lump of which fell out on to the flaking paint of the window ledge.

'It won't be long now until it's finished. Mr Odgers is busy repairing the old brick wall in the walled garden, it makes sense to get on with it while the weather's so good. It isn't as if there was much structurally wrong with the house.'

'What about those bloody rattling windows in our bedroom? Honestly, Nell, I don't know how you sleep through it. If there's any wind at all it sounds as if the room is full of maniacs rattling their false teeth.'

'Stretched sash-cords, Mr Odgers says.'

'But what is he going to *do* about your stretched cords, Nell?'

'*Our* stretched cords. He's going to bring new ones, and if they still rattle he'll have to take the windows out and weigh them to make sure that the weights are right.'

'He's very talented,' Gregory said humbly.

'And then there's really not much left to do. I thought you and I might have a go at painting the outside of the house, the woodwork, I mean, before next term.'

'Have you ever seen me handle a paint brush, Nell?'

'You'll learn. And if not, I don't mind. I'll do it.'

'Poor Nell. You've saddled yourself with quite something, haven't you?'

'Do you mean you or the house?'

He didn't reply. Then he said awkwardly, as if he had been postponing it, 'Nell, you know my father's flat is empty until the new tenant comes in next month?'

'Yes.'

'Would you mind very much if I went up there for a few days? I've been thinking – I really ought to go and see the publishers and I know they'd like me to be a bit more available than I am down here.'

'Do you really think you're so much in demand?'

'It seems so. And, well, you were right about how the phone would be ringing – if we had one. It makes sense to stay in the flat where there *is* a phone.'

'Mm, I suppose so. It's a pity, though; you've been writing so well this week.'

It was true, though extraordinary. Instead of distracting him, all the fuss about *The Spindle Tree* seemed to have given him a great surge of confidence and energy to get on with his present book. It was almost finished.

'Well, I'll leave what I've done for you to type, and I'll get on with writing up there, but it's just that I'll be handy if the phone rings.'

'I thought,' she said, aware that she was being difficult, 'that you hated being interrupted by the telephone when you're writing?'

'I do, but it's different at the moment,' he said patiently. 'I might miss some chance or other.'

'Yes, of course. I'm sorry. I know I'm being stupid. It's just that I can't possibly come with you now. I've got so much to get ready for next term – I've quite a few appointments next week.'

'I wish you could, Nell. I shall be lonely up there in London.'

He paused, looking down at her, and then said resignedly, 'But never mind, that's the way our lives are.'

'I'll miss you,' she said.

'It's not for long, and you'll be busy with students and paint brushes. You don't need me.'

Oh but I do, I do, she thought, but somehow could not bring herself to say the words aloud.

'Anyway, it's your fault really,' Gregory went on. 'You're the one who caused all this success.'

'Nonsense. The books would have made their own way in the end. Good books do.'

'Some do. Others make their way unread to the second-hand book shop in Fleet Street,' he told her.

She made the most of the time that Gregory was away. She filled every empty minute with decorating or getting ahead with work so that she would be able to give more time to him when he came back. Because it was going to be a new way of life then. It was obvious from what he had told her when she rang him up from the call-box on the corner every evening, that he was now at last going to be able to make his living by writing. The snowball effect of Ian Venables' review had been almost unbelievable. It had already led to a television interview, to two radio interviews and an invitation to share in a broadcast discussion. Gregory Nansen had become news and no cultural programme felt itself to be quite up-to-date without him. Furthermore, *The Spindle Tree* was to come out in paperback almost immediately and the American rights had been sold.

It had all worked out wonderfully, she thought, as she scraped away at the old paint on the outside of the windows, the day before Chrissie's visit. Gregory need no longer feel that if he married her he would be living on her earnings. She had always feared that if they had married, as he had wanted them to do, they would have drifted into a situation in which he would have felt obliged to give up writing to take a money-making job in order to support her. Now he was quite able to provide for a wife and children. She would give up work at the end of this academic year, she thought; she was so well established now that she could easily go back to it in a few years' time. She would be coming up thirty-eight, she reckoned, by the time she had a baby. There was no time to waste.

She looked at her watch. Nearly six o'clock. She went indoors, cleaned the brush and herself at the kitchen sink, and walked along to the phone box, well armed with small change since she was too independent to reverse the charges.

'The Venables syndrome works backwards, too, Nell,' Gregory squeaked at her after they had talked for a little while.

'How?'

'The first two books are coming out in paperback next year. And there's talk of television plays being made out of them. When I go out to lunch tomorrow with this man . . .'

'Which man?'

'The one I told you about from ITV.'

He had, but she'd forgotten. There was so much happening and he always assumed she knew everyone's name and who had rung him the day before. She couldn't keep up with him at this distance, she thought uneasily.

'I'm loving the new book,' she said. 'I can't think how it is going to end.'

'Neither can I,' he admitted. 'How's the typing going?'

'I've almost finished what you left me to do.'

'Nell, that's marvellous.' He sounded surprised. 'I never thought you'd get it done so quickly. Kaufman was asking about it. I could show him what's typed up so far.'

'I've just one more chapter. I'll get it finished tonight.'

'Could I collect it on Sunday? Shall I come then?'

'Oh darling, that would be lovely.'

She hadn't liked to ask when he was coming back, not wanting to press demands upon him when he was so busy.

'Are you sure it'll suit your ladyship and Mr Odgers?'

'Idiot! Idiot!'

'All news then.'

'Lovely. Oh, by the way, Chrissie's coming for the day tomorrow, for lunch anyway.'

'That'll be nice for you. Give her my love.'

'I will.'

On the way back to the house, Mr Odgers overtook her, riding in his curious water-boatman style. He got off his bike when he realized who she was, and they walked up the drive together.

'You won't be too long with the sash-cords, will you, Mr Odgers?' she asked, her mind full of Gregory. 'The windows rattle so.'

'Ah've 'ad trouble getting new cord, Miss. Ah've 'ad to put an order in.'

'Oh, never mind. I'll stick more bits of cardboard round the windows, and jam them up that way.'

'I'll get on in t' walled garden, then,' he said, leaning his bike up against the back wall. He removed his cycle clips and hung them on the handlebars. 'Ay, it's a grand evening, a grand evening.'

He went off, talking to himself.

'Oh, and Mr Odgers,' she called after him, 'could you look at the fence if you've time?'

He shook his head as he turned back to her. 'It'll not stand up to a storm, that fence won't,' he said. 'You'd do better to plant a hedge.'

She nodded.

'What sort?'

She had come to take his advice on everything to do with the house and garden.

'Not privet,' he said. 'Nasty old stuff, is privet.' He scratched his head thoughtfully. ''Olly makes a good 'edge, but it's terrible slow. You plant 'olly for your children, you do.'

She smiled at him.

'Thorn's as good as anything,' he went on ruminatively. 'Ay, thorn makes a good 'edge. My neighbour planted a thorn 'edge last year. It's comin' on nicely.'

'Where did he get the plants?' she asked.

'Off the A32,' he said.

She looked puzzled, trying to think of a nursery off the A32.

'Where they widened it,' he explained, going back to repairing the wall. ''E just took every other one. T' Council always plant 'em too close anyway.'

She watched him for a moment, puzzled, then it dawned on her that his neighbour's hedge was obtained free from the Highways Department, and she almost laughed out loud. Mr

Odgers was full of surprises. She went back into the house, shaking her head and making a mental note to tell Gregory.

She was up early, the day of Chrissie's visit. As always, the first thing she did when she got downstairs was to open the back door wide and let in the day. A slight mistiness hung in the air, promising heat. Chrissie would see everything at its best. A heavy dew sparkled on the grass. She stood for a while on the cobbles, entranced with it all. Then she went inside. The kitchen smelled warm and aromatic. She touched the bunches of herbs she had hung up in one corner last week. They were drying nicely.

She prepared for Chrissie in a leisurely way, enjoying all the domestic tasks, dawdling over them. Even so she had finished everything by eleven o'clock. She went and leaned against the back door; only three days now, she whispered to herself, and he'll be back. Every minute away from him had hurt; she couldn't live without him. She was like a girl with her first lover, not like a woman in her mid-thirties.

How lucky she had been, she thought, as she stood leaning against the door post, watching the sun shaft in through the flecked air, just reaching the polished dresser and the blue and white china on it. How incredibly lucky. She'd had her career, interesting and successful, she'd made a home, she had the man she loved. She'd planned it, of course, but then plans don't always work out. People have to make do with second-best, she might have had to settle for companionship and motherhood with some nice enough chap, loved in a middle-aged kind of way; but to have this kind of passionate marriage, to have Gregory as well as a career; it seemed almost too much for one woman to be blessed with.

If only next weekend would come, she thought impatiently, walking back into the kitchen and beginning to prowl round it. She wanted to get on with the next stage of her life *now*. She wished she had talked to him before he went, but the book business had been so distracting, she owed it to him to give it absolute first place. He deserved to have it all by itself, not confused by other issues. Besides, it was less easy to talk than she had expected. Presumably, if one played one role for a long time it was hard to discuss another. It was easy to think about it, dream about it, but not talk about it, discuss it, actually put it into words.

She heard a car draw up in front of the house and ran out

to welcome Chrissie. Her joy seemed to overflow at the sight of her cousin; they hugged each other as they used to do when they were children and she came back to Netherby from boarding-school.

Chrissie was looking radiant. Her hair was loose and she had on a blue garment that she'd had for years, but it suited her, straight, simple, smock-like.

'Oh Nell,' she exclaimed, looking at the house, 'it's *lovely*. It really is a perfect house. I never imagined anything so – oh!'

She stopped as they rounded the side of the house and saw the back of the cottage and the garden beyond.

'It reminds me of the farm,' she said quietly. 'Oh, look, even mignonette. And all the old-fashioned flowers.'

They walked slowly round the garden and then through the gate into the little walled garden, its wall now so well patched by Mr Odgers that the new bricks blended perfectly in with the old ones. He had fixed nails and supports as he worked on the wall and had tied in all the climbing plants which had trailed across the ground.

'Isn't that summer jasmine a picture?' Chrissie remarked. 'Everything's late this year. Have you noticed?'

Nell laughed. 'Not really. You forget I've only just taken to gardening, so I've nothing to compare this year with.'

'Spring was late, that did it. And this garden is even later than ours. Our roses were finished ages ago and all the herbaceous plants are going over. Yours are still beautiful.'

She relished every word of appreciation from her cousin, who examined each plant and found something kind to say about every one.

'Do you know,' Nell said in surprise as she glanced at her watch, 'we've been out here nearly an hour? Come inside and look at the house. And you must be getting hungry. We'll have lunch outside.'

She led the way into the kitchen. Chrissie stood in the doorway. She sniffed. 'It's rosemary,' she said. 'You must be drying rosemary.'

Nell laughed and pointed to the bunches of it hanging from the ceiling.

'Do you remember the time when it was in the children's hair in that wild garden you had in Devon?'

Chrissie looked surprised. 'Fancy you remembering that,' she exclaimed. 'And I never thought you cared for babies much.'

They toured the house, Chrissie delighting in every nook and cranny, Nell glowing with pride at the praise which was being lavished on her home. Then they arranged a wide plank of wood across two stones to make a table, which wobbled a bit on the cobbles, and sat outside eating a picnic lunch.

'And what about Gregory?' Chrissie asked, a trifle awkwardly. 'He likes the house, too, does he?'

'Oh, he loves it,' Nell said, though she was suddenly aware of how little appreciation he had in fact shown, compared with Chrissie's instant love of the place. 'Of course, he's awfully busy just now with all this fuss over his book.'

'Oh yes, we *saw*. And all that in the colour supplement, too. You must be thrilled, Nell.'

'He deserves it. He's a truly great writer, Chrissie,' Nell said solemnly.

'Yes, I'm sure.'

There was a pause and then Chrissie said hesitantly, 'Do you think you, I mean . . .'

'Go on.'

'I mean, will you get married?'

She blurted the words out, blushed crimson, then added, 'Not that it's got anything to do with me, of course.'

'But it has.'

She meant it, too. They would always be bound together, she and Chrissie, and now more than ever, for she was moving into Chrissie's world.

'I hope we'll be married soon,' she said. 'In the Christmas vac, perhaps, or early next year. Gregory comes back next weekend, thank goodness, so we'll get everything worked out then.'

'Oh, I'm so glad!' Chrissie's relief was unmistakable.

'You'll be pleased to have a respectable married woman for a cousin?'

She spoke without sharpness, and Chrissie smiled.

'You know it's not just that, Nell love,' she said. 'But I think it'll be better for you. It's simpler being married, really,' she added vaguely.

'In some cases, yes. In ours it was better this way. When we first met two years ago Gregory was in the middle of writing *The Spindle Tree*, you know. He needed freedom.'

'Oh well, men always like their freedom, don't they? It was *you* I was bothered about.'

'Oh, I was the one who didn't want to get married,' Nell

said quickly, a bit riled at the old-fashioned view that Chrissie took of her situation.

'Oh.'

'An affair seemed to suit my life-style better than matrimony,' she went on, but she could tell that Chrissie didn't understand. Come to think of it, she wasn't quite sure herself now why it had seemed so very important at the time.

'You've always been very tolerant, Chrissie,' she said with sudden warmth. 'And I have appreciated it. I know it must have been difficult for you to understand sometimes – our ways have been, well, different, haven't they?'

Chrissie shrugged. 'It takes all sorts,' she said. She hesitated, and then went on, 'I often think about my two girls. All this sex education they've had. Do you know, I didn't even know the facts of life when I got married? Jack had to tell me on our marriage night.'

It was funny, and moving, and belonged to the world of twenty years ago. Never had Nell felt closer to her cousin.

'Isn't it odd,' she said, 'to think that just as I'm moving towards domesticity, you are taking up your career in nursing? We're changing roles, aren't we?'

Chrissie looked at her. She hesitated. She looked sheepish.

'I'm going to have to give it up,' she said.

Nell stared at her blankly.

'Whatever for?'

'Don't look so horrified.' She reached across and touched Nell, as if in apology. 'Don't be cross.'

'Of course I won't be. Whatever is it? You're not ill?'

'I wasn't going to tell you yet,' Chrissie said slowly. 'I'm having another baby.'

She obviously had to force herself to say it, she expected disapproval.

'Oh Chrissie, my love, it's marvellous.'

Nell got up and kissed her with undisguised joy. It was awful that Chrissie should have expected disapproval at such wonderful news. It added pathos where there should be none. 'I couldn't be more delighted,' she said. 'Truly.'

She knew that part of her delight was because Chrissie pregnant at forty-two somehow raised the statistical probability of herself being pregnant at, say, thirty-eight.

'What about Jack? Is he pleased?'

'I haven't told him yet. He's in Cardiff at the moment. He'll be back in time for dinner tonight. I'll tell him then.'

'He's probably guessed.'

'I don't think so. I've been to the doctor because I felt ill and he diagnosed indigestion again – I'd had a bit of trouble a year ago when we moved. But then I fainted at work and Sister looked after me and suggested a pregnancy test. I just laughed, I mean, after all these years! Anyway, it was positive. Jack will be thrilled. Perhaps it will be a boy this time. He's always wanted a boy, has Jack, though he's never said so.'

They beamed at each other, Chrissie anticipating the joy of telling Jack tonight, Nell wondering if Gregory would prefer her to have a girl or a boy. She couldn't see that it mattered; just a baby, that was all she wanted.

'Will you mind about giving up nursing?' she asked, rousing herself.

Chrissie shook her head.

'I think I only needed the nursing because I really needed another baby, if you see what I mean. I was depressed, you know, after we moved.'

'Depressed, *you*?'

Nell was astonished. Her cousin had never struck her as being a likely candidate for depressive illness. She lacked the necessary introspection.

'Looking back, I realize that it wasn't just moving that got me down. The children didn't need me any more and life seemed so empty, so I filled the gap with nursing.'

'But wouldn't most women feel they'd fulfilled themselves by having two children, and be rather fed up if they got pregnant at forty-two?'

'I suppose so, but it seems right, as if that's what nature meant for me.'

Not long ago she would have argued, at least pointed out that what Chrissie mistook for nature's intentions was in fact only social indoctrination. But now she found herself, if not agreeing, at least understanding. If women had had children throughout their childbearing years since time immemorial, then it must surely be traumatic for some of them not to do so. Chrissie had had both her children in her early twenties. She was one for whom it would have been right to go on having children, deeply right, in harmony. Nell understood the yearning now.

So she did not reply, but sat in contented silence looking across the warm grass at the phlox and hollyhocks and

Michaelmas daisies and enjoying the occasional scent of jasmine and mignonette, as it stirred on the light breeze. How closely the pattern of their lives had come together, she thought as she smiled across at her cousin. Later perhaps they would drift apart again. Meanwhile it was peaceful to sit here with Chrissie, sharing the joys of a late-flowering garden.

Chapter Twenty-Three

Chrissie got home in good time; she wanted to have a meal ready for Jack without having to rush. She wanted to have time to rest and prepare herself. She wanted not to look tired and haggard when she told him that she was expecting their third child. She wanted not to look like a forty-two-year-old expectant mother of a mistake. She wanted him to share her joy and have no fear for her.

Feeling ridiculously excited and young, she laid the dining-room table for the two of them as she used to do years ago, with love and daintiness, polished silver and candles and carefully folded napkins. In the kitchen everything was ready keeping warm; losing vitamins maybe, but saving last minute bother.

She sat in the drawingroom, her feet up on a stool, wearing her new long skirt because she wanted to get some use out of it before she was too fat. She poured herself out a sherry, found she couldn't face alcohol after all, and lay back sipping soda water instead, the newspaper neglected on her knee.

She heard the car in the drive, the garage door being closed. What a time Jack was taking to come into the house; but then he often did. She imagined him sorting something out on the work-bench in the garage. Then she heard him coming in the back door, into the kitchen. She heard him go into the hall, but he didn't call out. She heard him going slowly upstairs. She sat back contentedly, hearing him moving about. He must have glimpsed the celebration dinner table and gone upstairs to wash and change first. Dear Jack, he would; he would want to please her, as he always did. She poured out a drink for him and stayed standing up, wanting him so much that she felt too tense to sit down again and even pretend to relax. It's ridiculous, she told herself, to feel like this when you've been married twenty years. She heard him come downstairs, cross the hall. She heard his hand on the door. She couldn't bear it any longer. She pulled at the door handle from the inside, and without looking up at him, threw herself into his arms, and hugged him there in the doorway.

He felt sticky. She pulled away from him. There was blood on his face. He was deathly white.

'Jack! What's happened?'

'Nothing. Really. Just a bit of a bump in the car – only a few minutes ago.'

'Was anyone . . .?'

'Nobody else involved. Don't worry. It's nothing. I must have dropped off for a minute. Anyway, I came up hard against the side window, of all the stupid things.'

He sat down heavily.

'I'll get a cloth – it's all over your face. That bit of plaster's no good.'

He tried to laugh. 'You undid it when you hugged me.'

'Oh Jack, I'm sorry. I never looked, I didn't think . . .'

'Never mind. It was a lovely hug. Worth every drop of blood.'

He laughed again, shakily. He was making a tremendous effort.

'I'm sorry,' she said again. 'It was just that I had such news. I'll get some plaster.'

'I have news, too,' he said, and there was something in his voice which made her turn back, alarmed.

'Then I'll see to the cuts first,' she said quickly, 'and bring you some brandy and then you can tell me.'

He did not reply. She brought plaster and bandages and patched up the scratches on his hands and face. He sat, sipping the brandy, while she tidied everything methodically away and then sat down beside him.

'Your news first,' she said.

He couldn't speak.

She realized that something else was wrong, something far worse than the scratch in the car. In sudden panic she said, 'You're not ill? It's not the children? Jack, something's happened to the children?'

'No, nothing like that. It's not as bad as that,' he said firmly, as if trying to convince himself as well as her. Then he took a deep breath.

'You know we had a meeting in Cardiff yesterday? It went well, everyone seemed pleased with progress down here. Afterwards the chairman asked me to go and see him next morning – that's today.'

'Yes?'

He looked at her, unable to go on, then he said quietly, 'He told me that Lomacks is being taken over.'

She didn't speak; just stared at him in disbelief.

'It's a Belgo-American firm. Called Ferro-Masters Inc. They are taking over the whole concern. But they're planning to close down the civil engineering section.'

'No,' she whispered. 'They can't.'

'Yes. It's partly for the usual asset-stripping reasons and partly because they don't see it being profitable in the short run now the slump's beginning. And the short run is all they care about. A multi-national doesn't have any interest in employees here. It just has to please the shareholders back home and make an immediate profit.'

His voice was bitter. Everything he had built up, shattered.

'So I'm redundant.'

'But Jack,' her voice was still a whisper. 'They can't. After all these years. After all you've done. I mean, they wouldn't have had a profitable company to sell if it hadn't been for people like you.'

'Oh, they're sorry, of course, but as they say that's the way it goes in the private enterprise system. One of the hazards.' He was silent for a moment and then said with a little laugh, 'You know, I never thought it would happen to me.'

Her mind was whirring. Not long ago they had been sitting in this very room and Nell and Jack had talked about the boom, and the slump which would certainly follow it. But it had all seemed so theoretical. This was the reality of it.

Even so, it was hard to believe. 'But surely, Jack,' she said, 'it couldn't be arranged so quickly. I mean, it must have been discussed for a year or two. Why did they get us to rush down here when . . .'

'Oh, they knew all right. That's what really hurts, Chrissie. I'm quite sure they knew then. But Ferro-Masters wanted a branch down here, wanted it to be a going concern, ready made, and it was part of the agreement that Lomacks would provide it. Hence they got us to come.'

'With promises of permanence. I can't believe it of them.'

'Well, I don't expect the chairman knew what Manders promised, to be fair to him. Overall strategy is his concern.'

'And leave the dirty work to brother-in-law?'

A sudden thought struck her.

'But Jack, *they'll* all be redundant, too, won't they?'

He laughed. 'Not them! There are places for all of them on the new board. That's their reward for getting the take-over to go through smoothly. But I don't see it lasting. In a year or two I should think they'll get a nice golden handshake and part company. But they'll have got it all worked out, you needn't spare any tears for them, Chrissie.'

'What,' she began awkwardly, for she found it hard to ask, 'about us? I mean, what will they pay you?'

'A year's salary. I spent the afternoon arguing with Manders trying to get the same treatment for the rest of the staff, but they won't go above six months even for the ones who've been with us for years. Of course our pensions aren't transferable, so that's another headache for us.'

He put his head in his hands suddenly.

'Oh Chrissie, I'm sorry. I've failed you, now, just when things should have been easier.'

'Failed?' She ran over to him, took him in her arms. 'Jack, you've never failed me. It's that rotten lot of Lomacks that have failed both of us.'

'I've been too trusting, so keen just to get on and work for them. I should have got something in writing before we came here, when Manders was all over me with his promises.'

'Sh, my love. We'll just start again and you'll find something else. I know it'll be strange not to be working for Lomacks after all these years, but . . .'

'It won't be so easy now, Chrissie. And there's not so much in this area as there was up there where we were before.'

She remembered the offers he had turned down. Always loyal to Lomacks, he had never taken any such overtures seriously. This was his reward.

'And it couldn't be a worse time,' he went on gloomily. 'Everyone's cutting back. We're paying now for that frantic boom of the early seventies.'

'Yes, I was thinking just now about how you and Nell were talking about it when they came that day.'

'Oh yes, we saw what was wrong. But somehow you don't

relate these things to yourself. I didn't think it would happen to me,' he said again. 'Like death, you know, something which happens to other people.'

'No, Jack, don't talk like that. We'll manage somehow.'

They sat together in silence for a while, then he roused himself. 'It could be worse, Chrissie. At least the children are off our hands. We've no dependents.'

She could not answer. Could not look at him.

'It's going to be worse for people like Frank Hynde – he's still got a boy at school. Fortunately his wife's teaching, so that will help to tide them over.'

'Don't worry about us,' she said. 'We'll manage, we always have, haven't we?'

'Bless you. We'll be glad of your little salary, too.'

'It's not much,' she said in a whisper.

'Oh, Chrissie,' he said, suddenly taking her in his arms. 'Thank God for you.'

His voice ended in a sob. Then he went on, 'Imagine what it must be like for men who scarcely dare tell their wives, who even pretend to go on working while they're hunting for a job.'

He took her face in his hands and gazed down at her.

'You've always helped and supported me, haven't you, love? And I've never been grateful enough.'

'Don't, Jack, don't. I can't bear it. You've always come first, of course you have. It's only natural. And you always will.' Her voice broke. 'Before anything, or anyone else.'

He kissed her and they clung together. Then he said, 'Let's forget about it for this evening, shall we? I saw you had a special meal ready; let's enjoy it.'

The very thought of the celebration table, of pale candle-light flickering over silver and carefully folded linen seemed to mock her grief. She made herself get up and smile.

'Didn't you say *you* had some news?' he asked as they went into the dining-room.

'No, it was nothing important,' she said. 'Could you light the candles for me?'

Chapter Twenty-Four

It was rotten of the weather, Nell thought, to change like this on the day Gregory was coming home. After seemingly endless bright and sunny days, it was now humid and oppressive. It might rain, she thought as she stood at the back door. Lunch had better be indoors after all.

She had just begun to lay the table in the tiny dining-room, when she heard his car in the drive. She dropped the cloth and dashed to the front door. It was a difficult door; she wrestled for a moment with the bolts and then tugged it open. She could have cried out aloud with disappointment when she saw a car with Mrs Venables in the driver's seat, with Julie alongside.

She made a great effort to pull herself together and welcome them, as Mrs Venables, massively feminine in pink chiffon, walked across the drive towards her.

'I do hope, Dr Thorpe,' she said, 'that you don't mind Julie and me dropping in like this?'

'Of course not. Do come in.'

She fought back tears of disappointment and led the way into the sitting-room.

'What a *dear* house,' Mrs Venables said. 'May I say how absolutely charming you have made everything?'

'Thank you. You'd like a drink, wouldn't you?'

'Well, that's very kind, but we haven't come to stay. Sherry for both of us, please.'

She went on talking as Nell saw to the drinks. At least, Nell reflected, I can leave the conversation to her. I don't need to make any effort.

'You see, I did so want to have a word with you and so when the college kindly gave me your address and I realized that we were literally passing your door . . .'

Untrue, Nell thought to herself; you had to do quite a detour.

'I think you are so wise to live out,' Mrs Venables said. 'The way you work; I am sure you need a change of scene, Dr

Thorpe. Well, as I was saying, I was so wanting a word with you about Julie, so I was sure, *in the circumstances*, that you wouldn't mind if we just popped in. But first, tell me, how is your friend Mr Nansen?'

Nell took a deep breath and wondered why it is always so difficult to thank somebody who obviously wants thanks. 'Mr Nansen was very grateful to your son for the review he gave him,' she said. It sounded awful, positively indecent. 'I mean, of course, he deserved every word, but all the same, it was very kind to go to such lengths . . .'

'Yes, he did, didn't he?' said Mrs Venables, who was not one to deny a kindness done by her son. 'I thought it was a perfectly splendid piece. So did Julie, didn't you, dear?'

Julie lifted a long pale hand with green fingernails to push her hair gently off her brow. Her big brown eyes gazed at Nell, beautiful orbs which seemed to open on to endless nothingness.

'But after all,' Mrs Venables went on remorselessly, 'it is nothing to the help that you are giving us with Julie, is it?'

Nell shook her head, speechless.

'I would so like to bring her to college so that you can show her round, if I may, Dr Thorpe. Any time that suits *you*, of course. I'd like her to get the academic atmosphere, you see. Atmosphere is so important, I always think. You'd be so grateful, wouldn't you, Julie dear?'

Julie looked at her mother, her eyes expressing neither gratitude nor any other emotion.

'She is so sensitive to atmosphere,' her mother went on. 'We all are, on my side of the family. It would be such a help if you would let her spend a day with you in college and soak it up a bit.'

To her relief, Nell heard a car coming up the drive.

She made herself say calmly, 'I think that may be Mr Nansen; he said he would be dropping in.'

She heard him open the front door and call out to her. Evidently he had seen a strange car at the door because he was tactful enough not to bring his case in with him. It took a great effort of will not to throw herself into his arms; she did not dare to look directly at him.

'Mr Nansen,' Mrs Venables said, holding out her hand. 'Many, many congratulations on the success of your book.'

She shook his hand vigorously, the chiffon ballooning out over the heavy, marbled flesh.

'Thank you very much,' he said. 'Your son's article set the ball rolling, of course.'

He smiled and turned to her daughter.

'And Julie, how delightful to see you again,' he exclaimed. 'I never expected to walk in here and have such an unexpected treat.'

The brown eyes gazed up at him, little lights flickering in them.

'I was just saying to Mrs Venables,' Nell said, 'how very grateful you were.'

'Yes, it's led to all sorts of things,' Gregory said, turning his attention back to the mother. 'I've just had an invitation to go to the States. My publishers are keen I should accept because I can meet the American publishers at the same time.'

'Oh!' Nell gasped not so much at the news, but with surprise that he should blurt it out in front of the Venables instead of keeping it for when they were alone. It was news which would both delight and hurt her more than anyone else in the world. Surely he must have realized that?

'America,' Julie said, speaking for the first time. 'I've always wanted to go to America. I think it must be heavenly. I suppose you don't want a secretary?'

'Really, Julie,' her mother said sharply. Nell thought she was rebuking the girl for being so forward but it turned out that Mrs Venables had different anxieties. 'She has this silly notion, Dr Thorpe, that she'd rather be a secretary than go to college and take a degree.'

'Well, perhaps. . .' Nell began, seeing a way out of the dilemma, 'if that is what she would prefer . . .'

'Oh, but it's *not*. It's only what she thinks she'd prefer. It's a fashion. And as I say, where will it lead compared to a degree? Young people nowadays don't think ahead.'

'But I *am* thinking ahead,' Julie began.

'Of course, I blame her school,' her mother interrupted. 'In the sixth form, you know, they let some of the girls attend a typing course, without so much as consulting their parents. When I found out I soon put a stop to it, but by then she'd acquired a taste for it.'

'I liked typing,' Julie said. 'I was good at it.'

'I'm *sure* you were,' Gregory cut in. 'It's jolly useful, too. I'll be glad of your help with manuscripts at any time.'

'Now Mr Nansen, don't be naughty,' Mrs Venables said. 'He doesn't mean it, dear. Writers are always teasing.'

She stood up and drew on her long mauve gloves.

'We must be going,' she said. 'And leave these good people to have their lunch.'

On the way to the car she took Nell's bare arm in her gloved fingers and said confidentially, 'May I say, Dr Thorpe, how very much the idea of my Julie working under you appeals to me? So many of these clever academic women are so hard, don't you think? You seem to me to be so womanly with it, so understanding.'

Once she would have smiled, dismissed it as clumsy sycophancy, but now she recognized an element of truth in it. She knew that since she had been living with Gregory she had mellowed. Physically she had softened. She looked her age at last, having previously been frozen at any age between twenty and thirty. She was glad of it; it brought her nearer to Gregory who nowadays looked all of his forty-odd years.

It's because he scowls so much, she thought affectionately, glancing at him as they stood around the car, wanting at least a visual embrace since any other was being so cruelly postponed. But he was looking at Julie Venables.

'Well,' Mrs Venables said as she prepared to lower herself into the driving seat, 'thank you once again for being so sweet to us.'

'Remember me to Ian,' Gregory said politely.

'I will indeed. And if either or both of you are in London, please do not hesitate to call.'

She opened a commodious mauve bag which she had left on the seat and fished about in it. More delay, Nell groaned inwardly. At last Mrs Venables produced a tiny card which she handed to Gregory.

'That's not far from my flat,' Gregory said in surprise.

'Really? Well, I'm sure Ian will be very interested to know you are so close at hand. Perhaps you would be so very kind as to jot down your address for me?'

She handed him another card on which he wrote his address and telephone number.

Then, at last, she got herself settled into the car and they drove off. Nell and Gregory stood side by side waving politely until they were out of sight and then she collapsed into his arms.

'I'm sorry about them,' she said after a while. 'They weren't invited; they just happened.'

'Never mind, think what we owe them! Or rather *I* do.'

'We,' she corrected. 'Well, it's safe to bring your case in now.'

'What case?'

'Yours – your things.' She shook his arm gently.

'Oh, I didn't bring things. I thought I was going back to the flat tonight.'

'Going back?'

She stared at him, she could feel the blood leaving her cheeks, her eyes distending.

'But what's happened?'

'Nothing's happened. The tenants don't want to move in for another month so I thought I might as well stay up there while I'm packing up for the great US trip.' He affected a strong American accent, presumably to hide his embarrassment.

'You mean, you've only come home to collect the typing?'

'Yes.' Then he added awkwardly, 'You have finished it, haven't you?'

'I'm sorry, Nell,' he said again over lunch. 'It was a misunderstanding, that's all.'

'Yes,' she agreed bleakly.

'I honestly had no idea you were expecting me to stay. You didn't say so.'

'I didn't realize I had to spell it out.'

'How can I know what you want if you don't say? I'm a normal human male, for God's sake, not a mind reader.'

She wondered, in sudden terror, how much else he hadn't understood.

'You've no idea what it's been like up there, Nell. A real mad-house at times. And success is very lonely; I *needed* someone to share it.'

She hadn't gone with him. It was her fault.

'Down here you can't possibly know what it is like,' he went on. 'Contracts to be signed and telephone calls from America and arrangements. You see, I've worked alone for years now and I'd forgotten what it's like in that sort of world.'

'You'll adjust, people do.'

He shrugged, as if it was no use trying to get her to understand. Then he tried again. 'You see, Nell,' he said gently, 'it's the contrast. I mean, the books were conceived in silence and loneliness and now suddenly all this hulabaloo. If it was about something else, it would be different, but it's about my quiet, private books. It's a kind of invasion. Can't you see why it gets me all mixed up?'

She thought about it, wanting to be fair and helpful.

'No. You wanted reviews. If you remember, you didn't get very far when you were ignored, did you? I seem to remember you minded.'

He sighed. 'I minded for the books, Nell, not for me. It seemed to me that, once created, they had a right to be judged alongside all the others. I admit I did resent the fact that they weren't. That they were dismissed, their existence wasn't even acknowledged. But I didn't mind for *my* sake. And I don't like the fuss now being about *me*.'

'Well, I should have thought that they've made up for past neglect and you ought to be happy about it.'

'Don't think I'm ungrateful. I'm just saying my world's a bit confused at the moment. And your being so bloody argumentative doesn't help.'

'I am *not* being argumentative,' she said angrily. 'You are just being illogical. You don't know what you want.'

'And that's the ultimate sin, isn't it? All right, I'm illogical. Human beings are. Haven't I told you often enough? For God's sake, grow up and don't natter on at the human race for being illogical.'

She felt her anger breaking bounds. Afterwards she thought: if at that point I had raged and wept, it might all have been different.

Instead she controlled herself. Reason, it seemed to her, ought to be able to work out what was wrong. 'Yes, I do see that it creates tensions,' she said. 'And I suppose it will make the writing of the next one more difficult, knowing that they'll be looking out for it. It might make you self-conscious.'

'I know. I've found that already,' he said. 'Looking back, it was very agreeable to be able to work quietly away knowing that nobody was going to give a tinker's cuss what I wrote. A kind of privilege.'

She laughed, relieved to be back on safe, civilized terrain, no longer in danger of being swept away on currents of hatred and resentment and unknown storms that might shipwreck them.

But for all that, the day passed uneasily. He seemed like a visitor to the house. They went through the typing together, she mentioned a few passages that seemed to her not to work well, he accepted her criticism politely, making little pencil marks on the script. They walked together round the garden. The rain held off. Everything was heavy, the air humid, the skies leaden. She showed him where Mr Odgers had patched the wall.

'Where did he get old bricks to match?' he asked, showing a polite interest.

'He seems to have his sources.'

'There's probably a great hole in somebody else's nice walled garden,' he said, and she laughed more than necessary to show that everything was back to normal.

In the evening they drove out to a pub for a drink, but when they came home the house seemed strange and quiet. She was aware of their voices in it, breaking the silence. She had prepared in advance what she had thought was a good meal, but it was tasteless and even the wine did nothing to help. They both remained uncompromisingly sober. They talked politely to each other about his plans for America, hers for the house.

By the time they had reached the cheese, conversation had run out. She was conscious of little sounds, of knives buttering, of biscuits crumbling and splintering.

'I'll get the coffee,' she said.

He got up suddenly. 'For God's sake, Nell, stop looking so reproachful.'

She gasped at the unfairness of it.

He strode over to her. 'Come on upstairs,' he said. 'Leave all this mess.'

It was the first time that sex had been proposed as a reconciler. She looked at him warily.

'I suppose I'm to be punished now,' he said.

She had hesitated only because she knew it was dangerous to trade on passion. And now he was attacking her. Men always attack when they feel guilty. Why, why did he have to feel guilty? She let him take her upstairs.

In bed they lay trying to talk. In a kind of panic she tried to think of some way of getting near him.

'Chrissie told me a marvellous thing,' she said suddenly, hoping to amuse him, make him laugh. If they could laugh together again, everything would come right.

'Mm?'

'She said that on her wedding night, Jack had to tell her the facts of life. Imagine the scene!'

She was ashamed; it was treachery. But to win back some

warmth from him, she was willing to laugh, even at the innocence of Chrissie.

'Lucky old Jack!' Gregory said drily.

She lay still, stricken, punished. He would have preferred a clinging innocent. So much for his supposed admiration of maturity, of independence.

The words still rang in her ears even as he kissed her. She felt nothing except a kind of detached resentment at the pretence. He was going through the motions, self-consciously, dutifully, without frenzied concentration, without surrender, without love.

It was the first time that their love-making had failed. She was glad in a way: it deserved to.

Chapter Twenty-Five

Nell rang Gregory on the eve of his departure for America. He sounded pleased to hear from her.

'I'll miss you,' he said. 'It seems so mean that you won't be there to share the excitement.'

'I know. But with term in full swing . . .'

'I know. I just want company, I suppose. It's such a big place . . .'

She laughed. How like a little boy he sounded. Perhaps it would be all right when he came back. Perhaps they would just take up where they had left off before all the fuss over the book.

'Have they given you a schedule?'

'Skedule, ma'am. Yes. And I tell you what's a bit alarming. I've been told to take the manuscript of *The Spindle Tree*: Kaufman rang today and said he'd put it in the post to me and I'm to take it. Goodness knows why. He didn't seem to know either. Do you think they're going to auction it?'

'And you too, probably.'

He laughed. 'I can't believe I'm really going tomorrow.'

'When?'

'Not till the evening. Just as well. I haven't packed yet.'

She thought of his clothes. She couldn't speak.

'I'll be in touch when I get back,' he said.
'Yes.'
'All right?'
'Fine, thanks. I may have a telephone by then. They've promised it in ten days' time, so who knows?'
'I'll ring you straight away.'
'Perhaps you'll christen the line, or launch it or whatever the word is.'
'And Nell, I do know that I owe it all to you. I know that.'
'Nonsense.'
But it was true; he did owe it all to her. She was the creator of this situation.
'I just wanted you to know,' he insisted, 'that I'll always be grateful.'
He did, he sounded truly grateful. But, oh, it had a valedictory sound.

She awoke next morning to heavy rain and high wind. It lashed against the bedroom window and the loose panes rattled and shook. It was Saturday.
Suddenly she thought, I have nothing to get up for; it wouldn't matter to anyone if I lay in bed all day.
She heard the post arrive. She made herself get up.
There was an envelope from the bank for herself and a bulky package for Gregory.
She looked at the bank statement as she made her breakfast. She was surprised to find that she had a thousand pounds in her account, and then remembered that she had had it paid in to cover more work on the house. She had been thinking that if they needed Gregory's study for a nursery, they might convert the attic into a study. She put the statement aside.
The parcel for Gregory looked as if it might be the original manuscript of *The Spindle Tree* being returned. No doubt some secretary at Kaufman's had been told to send it to him and had posted it to this address instead of the flat in London. She wondered how urgent it was that he should take it to America. She could ring him. Suddenly it occurred to her that if he did need it, she could dash up to London with it. She saw herself joining him at the airport. Even going with him, throwing up everything here and going off with him on the plane. She had that thousand pounds in the bank. She had a current passport. She thought of tutorials and lectures and people to be seen and told herself not to be ridiculous.

All the same, she had better let him know about the manuscript. She finished her breakfast quickly, put on her raincoat, jingling the coins in her pocket, giving herself up again to the fantasy of flying with him to America. She decided to walk to the telephone; there was plenty of time, and the weather was almost too wild for driving. She stood outside the front door; the wind tore at her hair. An umbrella would be blown inside out. She took a sou'wester from the peg behind the door and set off, head down, into the storm.

The stuffy, smelly little kiosk seemed a refuge from the gale outside. Enclosed in the quietness of it, she had a sudden presentiment that everything was going to be all right. She would tell him she was sorry, she would explain. She longed to hear his voice; in her excitement she was clumsy with the money, and coins rolled on to the floor.

She picked them up and arranged them in a row ready to feed the box in case they talked for a long time. The number rang out. As the receiver was picked up, she pressed the money in eagerly. A woman's voice spoke.

'Oh, I'm sorry,' Nell said. 'I must have dialled the wrong number.'

'Did you want Mr Nansen?' the voice asked.

'Yes, but . . .'

'I'm afraid he's just gone out, but he'll be back in about an hour's time. He had some shopping to do. Is it the publishers? He can ring back. Hello?'

Nell moved the receiver away from her face as if it had been a serpent. Then she put it down slowly. Click. She threw herself against the heavy door of the telephone kiosk and stumbled out into the rain, desperate to get away from the voice. But the voice seemed to pursue her; it rang in her head. Suddenly she raised her hand and struck her ear hard, as if to banish the sound, but still she heard it. Julie Venables' voice.

The house, it seemed to Nell, was lying in wait for her. She dreaded seeing it again, as one dreads seeing a person for whom one has bad news. She pushed the front door open, as she had done so many times, and stood in the silent hall.

She did not take off her coat but began to wander from room to room. She paused in doorways, staring, seeing rooms as if for the first time. It came to her that there was nothing of Gregory in this house. Even his papers were cleared from the study and, as for the rest, there had never been anything of his in it. He had never really belonged. This house had been her illusion. Its empty rooms were her barren life.

She came back into the kitchen. She seemed to see everything more clearly now. The promise of this house and her life's promise had come to nothing and it was all her own fault. What a fool she had been. Lovingly and with pride, with independence of spirit, with thoroughness, with intelligence, with application, with every gift she possessed, she had prepared her own destruction. No outside force had smashed Nell Thorpe's life; it was all her own doing.

She must close up this house, she thought dully, and go away from it. But what could she do with the rest of her unused life? She couldn't close that up and leave it. Automatically she began clearing up the kitchen. She saw her feet walking about, saw her hands tidying things. Her body did not understand what had happened to her, it was going on doing the everyday things. It was picking up the sink-tidy now, full of vegetable peelings, and carrying it outside in the direction of the compost heap.

She pushed her way through the wind and rain, tipped the rubbish on top of the grass cuttings and turned back towards the house. The pain of seeing it, the back of the house, the cobbles, the door, the little window, all unchanged, stabbed at her. She couldn't go back. She heard herself groan. Then she staggered towards the little walled garden, zigzagging across the grass in her blind despair as old blind Mrs Rawlinson had done. She stopped. She could see nothing, had no idea where the gate was. Tears burned her eyes, she threw back her head and let the rain fall on it. Oh kind elements, if only I could die and be with you.

The distant sound of a car made her suddenly aware of herself. She saw herself as a separate being standing there, arms outstretched, head tipped back, eyes closed; a mad, pathetic thing, not fit to be seen by other human creatures. She dropped her arms, assembled herself.

Around the side of the house, raincoat flapping, a headsquare half off her head, came Chrissie. Nell watched her, stupefied, sure she was seeing things. Then she saw her cousin knock at the door, pause, open it and step inside the kitchen. Chrissie was probably calling out to her, but she couldn't face her, she couldn't face her pregnant cousin Chrissie. She must hide. No, that was nonsense, she must face her. No need to tell her. She would pretend. It came to Nell that if nobody knew that she was broken and humiliated, then perhaps she was not. She took a deep breath and walked towards the house.

Chrissie was just coming out into the garden.

'Hello, Nell,' she said, 'I was getting quite worried. I thought you must be out.'

She looked worried, too. Her face was strained, her hair drawn back severely, in a way which did not suit her.

'I'm so sorry,' Nell heard her normal voice say. 'I was just dumping the vegetable bits on the compost heap. How are you, Chrissie?'

'Well, I'm just going to see the doctor in London so I thought I'd call in.'

'Can you face coffee? Or does tea suit you better now?'

'Coffee will do,' Chrissie said indifferently, taking off her mac and head-square.

Nell looked at her. Chrissie was being deliberately offhand. Furthermore, having her hair dragged back like that gave her a hard look.

'I suppose Gregory is writing his book in the study?' Chrissie remarked as Nell put the coffee down in front of her.

'No.'

'I thought he was busy with a new one?'

'Yes. He's nearly finished the first draft. But he's gone to America. He flies today actually.'

'Oh, Nell, love, I *am* sorry. I thought you were looking a bit peaky. Will he be away long?'

'He's not sure. He may do an improvised lecture tour while he's there, but he may just stay to make arrangements with the American publishers. But never mind that. Tell me about you.'

She forced herself to move from one painful subject to another.

'What did Jack say about the babe?'

Chrissie put down her cup very carefully. She took a handkerchief from her bag and wiped her mouth.

'I'm afraid we've had some bad news, Jack and I. He's lost his job.'

'*Jack?*'

Chrissie nodded. She had spoken firmly, but now her voice cracked. 'Redundant, Nell. Lomacks has been taken over by one of those multi-national companies.'

'Oh Chrissie, I'm so sorry.'

What could she say? And work was everything to Jack. 'Oh, it's very hard, Chrissie, but it's happening to a lot of very good people.' How ridiculous that sounded; some of my best friends are redundant!

'I mean,' she faltered, 'it's not his fault, in any way.'

'Of course it's not his fault,' Chrissie said, and there was a note of impatience in her voice.

'I'm sorry, I only meant . . .'

Chrissie reached out and touched her. 'Yes, I know. I'm sorry. I'm a bit edgy. But you know, if people say it's not his fault it implies that it might be.'

Nell smiled, a little surprised, as she always was, when Chrissie showed that kind of perception.

'After all,' Chrissie pointed out, 'it's no more than you and Jack were saying would happen to people, that day you and Gregory came to see us.'

That day, she and Gregory. Don't think about it. Concentrate on Jack and Chrissie.

'At least he's so well qualified and capable he'll get another job easily enough,' she said. 'But it's a terrible blow, and people like me with safe jobs have no right even to offer consolation.'

'Thanks, Nell,' Chrissie said quietly. 'At least you realize it. Some don't.'

They sat together quietly, drinking coffee, not talking much. When Nell judged that Chrissie was calmer, ready for a happier topic, she asked, 'And what did he say about the babe?'

'I haven't told him,' Chrissie said.

She paused, and looked straight into Nell's eyes. 'That's what I came to see you for, really,' she said. 'There isn't going to be a baby. I wanted to be sure you wouldn't say anything about it to Jack.'

'Isn't going to be a baby? What's happened? Weren't you pregnant after all?'

'Yes, but I can't have the baby now, not with Jack's job going.'

'But you *must*. I don't understand. You can't just *not* have it.'

'Oh Nell, how innocent you are! Of course I don't have to have the baby. I'm arranging an abortion for next week.'

Nell stared at her in horror. Everything that had gone

before became trivial; Jack's job, Gregory's betrayal, everything.

'You *can't*, Chrissie. You *can't*.'

'And why not?'

'*Because it would be wrong*.'

The words came out unsolicited, in an impassioned judgment. If Chrissie, saviour of the weak, the damaged, the unprotected, could kill her own child, the world would scream and shatter. Not just Chrissie would be destroyed, everything would be swept away.

'Well, I'm surprised, I must say, that you feel like that,' Chrissie said. 'You of all people. I thought you at least would understand.'

'Oh God.'

'You've always said that women should have control over their own bodies, you've always said abortion was a woman's right.'

'I know, I know. And I still think so, if that's what they need and want. But not for *you*, Chrissie, *now*.'

'So it's all right for everyone else, but not me?'

'Maybe.'

'Why should I have to have different standards from everyone else? Why should abortions be all right for people like you and not people like me?'

Something in Nell's stricken face stopped her. She went on more rationally. 'You see, we'll need my job and money now, Nell. We've no choice.'

'You could go on nursing. There are maternity allowances.'

Chrissie shook her head. 'I'm always ill, Nell, it's no use. I was sick the whole time with the other two.'

'If you could just get through the next, what, seven or eight months . . .'

'No. It's not possible. I can't do both. Even in my twenties it was difficult enough. I've got to make a choice and I need to be well and earning. I can't put an extra burden on Jack now, not on top of everything else.'

'I can give you money. I can sell this house.'

'Nell.' Chrissie put her hand on Nell's which was trembling. 'Nell, sh. It's settled.'

'At least tell Jack. Talk it over with him.'

Chrissie shook her head. 'No,' she said. 'I won't, it's not fair. It's got to be my decision. I don't want him to know about it. If only I'd never told you, nobody else would have known.'

It seemed to Nell that chance had made her the baby's only friend. She began to organize its defences.

'You're in a muddle, Chrissie,' she began.

'Oh, Nell, really!'

'No, please listen. If you didn't want that baby, if you'd been horrified when you found you were pregnant, if you didn't love Jack and hated the idea of bearing his child; if anything like that, it would be right to have an abortion. But it isn't like that. You love Jack, you want to have this baby of his *I know* you *do.*'

The hard mask seemed to slip from Chrissie's face. She said nothing, but sat very still listening attentively to her cousin.

'If you kill that baby,' Nell went on remorselessly, 'you're letting Lomacks and Company kill it. Why should an institution like that, which seems to be managed by a pretty rotten bunch of hard and selfish men, destroy something good of yours? Fight back at them.'

'Oh, Nell, don't,' Chrissie's voice was imploring. 'I've been through so much to reach this decision. You'll never know. Please don't make me have to decide all over again.'

'Oh Chrissie, and I thought you'd decided too easily!'

'What do you take me for? It's for Jack's sake.'

Nell remembered thinking years ago that if ever Chrissie committed murder it would be for somebody else's sake.

'At least *tell* him,' she begged. 'There should be more honesty, more telling.'

Again the words came unsolicited. If only she had told Gregory, not been so independent. Told him that she had changed her mind, that she wanted to marry him, told him how much she wanted a baby. She had been too confident, too proud, too full of her theories. And too afraid. Yes – something in her had been too afraid of change. He had thought she really was the façade she had acted. He took characters at their face value; he was more honest than she. And so the moment had passed.

'I can't, Nell,' Chrissie was saying. 'You see, in the past it was so special telling him when I was pregnant. I suppose he'd probably guessed, but you know, just to say it and then sit afterwards in a state of – oh, I don't know, wonder, I suppose.'

Wonder, yes, she could imagine that. An unknown being, yours and his, growing inside you. There are so few moments of wonder in this life. Committing yourself to another person, realizing you can give up your life to them and none other, that is a moment of wonder. And conceiving is a moment of wonder, too. They are sacred, these few moments of wonder in a lifetime.

'And to tell him I'm pregnant now and see him look horrified and then pretending to be pleased and then having to talk about – about, you know. It would somehow destroy those wonderful times in the past.'

Yes, it would be a macabre parody. Like their last love-making, hers and Gregory's. A mockery. But there are greater evils than parody.

'I can't,' Chrissie was saying. 'I can't tell him and then sit and discuss killing it.'

'Is that so much worse,' Nell asked brutally, 'than killing it without discussion?'

Chrissie was crying now. 'Yes,' she managed to say, 'because then I only hurt myself, but if I tell Jack I hurt him too, and the past and all of us.'

'Please tell him, Chrissie, please,' was all Nell could manage to say.

Chrissie turned her blotchy face towards her. Her red eyes were suddenly angry. 'It's all right for you,' she said. 'It's always been easy for you. You've always got what you wanted . . .'

Nell stared at her aghast.

'When we were little,' Chrissie went on, as if having loosed her anger she couldn't restrain it. 'You were always the special one, the little orphan girl. You were the one who went to boarding-school, Bragton was good enough for me. You had your career, I wasn't even allowed to go nursing. I just had to hang about until I got married.'

'But Chrissie, it was what you wanted.'

'No, it wasn't. I didn't really know what I was doing. I never had any choice, I just had to get on and make the best of things. If I'd been allowed to train, I'd have had it there, ready to go back to. It would have been so much easier. It's been harder than you think, working with all those young girls and me forty-two. It was bad enough then, but think of being forty-two plus a baby. They would *mock* me.'

'Chrissie,' Nell said gently. 'Forget about the past. Just remember it's your baby, yours and Jack's. You were so happy about it last week . . .'

Last week, we were both so happy, and now our lives are in ruins.

'That was when I thought I could have it,' Chrissie said defensively. 'Now I can't, and that's all there is to it. And don't you lecture me as if I was one of your students because I'm not.'

The hard mask was in place again.

'I should have known,' Chrissie went on, evidently giving herself strength with a kind of cheap vulgarity, 'that it wouldn't work out for me. You've always done everything just as you planned, haven't you? Everything's always gone right for you. You've had your career and now you'll settle down with Gregory. And he's a success, too. You'll be one of those brilliant successful couples you read about in the papers. Jack and I aren't like that. We're different. We're failures.'

I am going to have to tell her, Nell thought with great weariness. Like a wounded animal she needed to hide her hurts until they had healed a little. She didn't know how she was going to mend herself, only by instinct that she needed privacy and time. And now she must surrender all secrecy. There was no alternative. She must sacrifice her last shred of dignity, she must tell her cousin.

Chrissie watched her. For once, she thought, she had silenced her clever cousin. This strange first victory gave her an ignoble sense of triumph.

'So there,' she added childishly.

'Gregory has gone,' Nell said. 'And I don't expect he'll come back.'

'You mean, you've quarrelled?'

'No, it was his choice. He is a success now and he's gone.'

'But Nell, love, what about you?'

Instant compassion. Any damaged thing, any poor wounded creature and there was Chrissie's sympathy.

Nell would not give in to it.

'I don't know yet,' she said matter-of-factly. 'I think I shall probably sell this house. It is too big for me alone. I expect they'll have me back in college.'

'Oh Nell, I'm so sorry.'

She came over to Nell and put her arms round her as she had done when she was a little girl. The years vanished. The feel of Chrissie's arms round her shoulders, of Chrissie's breast against her face was as comforting as it had always been.

'I never did care for him,' Chrissie said with sudden anger. 'Charming, but selfish through and through, I'd say.'

It might have been Aunt Liz speaking. Nell had never slapped her Aunt Liz's face, but she slapped Chrissie's now.

'You don't understand anything,' she shouted. 'You stupid, smug thing,' and burst into tears.

There was an appalled silence in the kitchen. Nell sat with her head down, Chrissie began gathering up her things. She was very white, except for the red mark. The wreckage, Nell thought dumbly, is now complete.

Chrissie stood in the doorway. 'I'd best go, Nell,' she said quietly, and without a trace of false dignity. 'We can't help each other, you and I, can we?'

Yet she did not go. Something deep in her nature prevented her from leaving anyone in distress. Recognizing this, Nell made a great effort to control herself.

'I'm sorry, Chrissie,' she said, 'but you see, the last thing I want is for anyone to attack him. The past is all I have now, and I prefer it intact.'

She knew Chrissie couldn't understand. She was talking to herself.

But Chrissie did understand. 'I know,' she said. 'It was stupid of me, especially when I'd just told you how I wanted not to spoil our past, mine and Jack's. But I couldn't bear that he should hurt you, Nell.'

She had come back from the door and sat down again. She looked dreadfully ill, Nell noticed.

'Let's forget it,' she said. 'We'll have another cup of coffee before you go. I'll say no more. Your baby is no more my business than Gregory is yours.'

Chrissie shook her head. 'We can't help it, Nell,' she said with that intuitive wisdom which always surprised her cousin. 'We've grown up together, we can't be separate, you and I.'

It was true. However little they could help each other, however little they had in common, there would always be something between them that did not exist with anyone else, however close, however understanding. It was nothing to do with common interests or ways of thought. It came of being of the same stock, growing up in the same soil.

'Chrissie,' she said suddenly, 'I shall sell this house. You shall have the money and use it for the baby and anything else you need.'

'I can't. Anyway, Jack wouldn't hear of it.'

'Don't hide behind Jack. You said yourself it's your decision. I've no need of money now. Nobody depends upon me. I shall have to get rid of the house.'

'I'll think about it.'

Then in sudden anguish, she burst out, 'Oh Nell, the appointment's at half past two.'

'Cancel it.'

Chrissie's face lightened. Days ago she had closed her mind, she had shut out the light and now suddenly in the darkness there was a glimmer of hope. 'Oh Nell,' she whispered. 'If I could.'

Nell did not reply. There was no need. Forces stronger than argument were working on her cousin Chrissie.

At last she said, 'Thank you, Nell. I hope it won't be necessary, but if it is I will borrow from you. I'll cancel the appointment and I'll tell Jack tonight.'

Once again she gathered up her belongings. Nell watched her with the calmness of exhaustion. Then together they went outside. The wind had dropped, the rain ceased. The garden was ravaged. Broken branches lay on the ground, bedraggled flowers hung from broken stems.

Together the two women walked through the dreary, spent garden. Water dripped on them from every branch and twig, for the rain lay on everything as tears lie on a face when the storm of weeping is over.

'Go carefully,' Nell said, as Chrissie got into the car and prepared to drive away. Then she added to herself, as the car disappeared round the corner, 'Because it's my baby you're carrying.'

Then she returned to the quiet, lonely house, which seemed grief-stricken in its silent emptiness. She locked the door behind her, not wanting to be disturbed. Then quietly and methodically, she swallowed a bottleful of sleeping tablets and went to bed.

Chapter Twenty-Six

All over England people were assessing the storm damage. Roads were blocked with fallen trees, houses flooded, gardens flattened. In the towns basement-dwellers were sweeping water out of kitchens while in the country villagers were dragging carpets out to dry in cottage gardens. Motoring organizations towed away cars that had been abandoned on flooded roads and contractors looked at damaged sites and wondered about the insurance. In Netherby a few smallholders who had not managed to get their crops in surveyed the wreckage of their fields, mocked by the golden evening sun. In a suburb of Southampton Chrissie returned home to a garden strewn with branches and debris, and glanced at it with light-hearted indifference.

In Spermsby Mr Odgers surveyed the outside world from his front porch. He had a good view of the surrounding countryside, dotted with houses and gardens all of which showed signs of damage.

'My, but there'll be some patchin' up and mendin' to do after this lot,' he remarked to the front gate. 'Nowt wrong 'ere, mind you, though I sez it as shouldn't.' He touched his strong low fence as he walked round the side of his dwelling-place. 'A bit to clear up in t'garden maybe, but vegs is all safely 'arvested. Nowt left outside to spoil, like.'

He looked in his shed: the onions were hanging, neatly strung, from the roof, three sacks of potatoes rested on slats of wood at one end, and next to them a tea-chest full of carrots stored in sand. 'All is safely gathered in like it says in church,' Mr Odgers observed to himself,' except for parsnips, and nobody but a fool would gather them in yet.'

He went across to his workshop and picked up a brown paper parcel from his work-bench. This he put into his saddle-bag which already contained a selection of tools. Then he put on his cycle clips and pushed his bike round to the front of the house.

He waved towards the front window where he could make out the pink bulk of Blossom, wearing her best because it was

Saturday. When he got back he would take her for an evening run in the sidecar and enjoy a look at the storm damage. Then take her for a drink at the pub, maybe.

He rode steadily, frequently swerving to avoid the branches and twigs which littered the road. Occasionally a car passed, the drivers looking with amusement at the funny little man who pedalled in such a curious way with his knees sticking out sharply from the bike. But Mr Odgers was blissfully unaware of this as he rode steadily along, humming and whistling to himself as he contemplated the joys of Saturday night.

When he reached the house he dismounted, pushed his bike up the short drive and round the side of the house. He propped it up near the back door, and knocked. There was no answer.

Mr Odgers paused, scratched his head. 'You'll not mind me if I fix them while you're out?' he asked, and went to find the ladder which he had left in the usual place behind the garage.

He placed it against the wall and began to climb up to the bedroom window. 'T'spout's keeping up well,' he observed with satisfaction on his way up, for he had fixed the guttering on the back of the house before the storm. He nodded a greeting to the down-pipe junction as he passed it. That was holding up well, too. Then he reached the bedroom window.

'Well, I'm danged, beg pardon, Miss,' he said, nearly falling off the ladder. It was seeing her there, so unexpected, did it, as he told Blossom afterwards. 'By gum, I came down that ladder quicker than what I'd went up,' he said.

He stood irresolute by the back door. 'No sense in goin' 'ome,' he said at last. 'Best get on wi' some tasks. 'Er'll wake up shortly, like as not.'

He left the brown paper parcel with the window sash-cord in it by the back door and went round to the front. The fence was down, as he had predicted. He set about repairing it. 'It's only a temporary job, mind,' he explained in case anyone should criticize his workmanship. 'But it'll do until she gets that 'edge planted.'

Afterwards he did a tour of the outside of the house, checking everything. On the far side some of the guttering was loose, and the gate to the walled garden was swinging on one hinge. He got busy with hammer and nails. When he had finished he returned to the back of the house and tidied up the broken bits and pieces on the cobbles. Lastly he fetched the stakes he had prepared last week and drove them into the ground where she wanted a trellis fixed. He made as much noise as he could, but she didn't come down.

'Well, I can't make it out at all,' he said to the back door. 'For one as can't sleep at night just for a bit of window-rattling, she's 'ard at it in broad daylight and me making enough noise to waken the dead.'

Something about the phrase, or perhaps the silence in the garden now that he had stopped banging, made him pause. Then he suddenly seized hold of the heavy old-fashioned knocker shaped like a lion's head and thundered against the back door. The sound echoed and reverberated, but nobody stirred in the house.

'I don't like it, Blossom,' Mr Odgers said. 'I don't like it at all.'

He removed the ladder and replaced it behind the garage, then he put on his cycle clips and pedalled off home to consult his wife.

'I'd best come,' she said when he told her. 'I'll just comb my hair.'

He brought the motor-bike round to the front door and shortly afterwards, with Blossom installed in the little shoe-like sidecar beside him, he set off.

The house was just as he had left it.

'Best knock first,' he said, thundering again with the lion's head.

'You'll have to climb in,' his wife told him.

'I don't like to,' he said. 'What if she wakes?'

'Then you must just excuse yourself.'

He brought the ladder and climbed up once again to look in the window.

'She's not stirred,' he called down in a hoarse whisper.

The window was not fastened. He pushed the bottom section up.

He cleared his throat noisily. 'Excuse me, Miss,' he said. 'I've brought the window cords.'

There was no reply.

He hesitated, then he climbed down the ladder again.

'If she wakes up and finds me climbing in,' he said, 'she could die of fright. It's not unknown, people dying of fright.'

'You did right,' his wife told him. 'We'd best just tell someone else.'

'Nay,' he said, 'we don't know who. What I had in mind,' he added persuasively, 'was for *you* to climb in.' Then, seeing the horrified look on her face, he went on quickly, 'She'd not mind waking up and seeing *you*. I mean, it would be different seeing a lady climbing in the bedroom window. She probably has quite a lot of lady visitors.'

'But I can't climb ladders,' she objected. 'It'd not 'old me.'

'It's steel. It'd take a rhinoceros, that ladder would.'

'What'll I do when I get in?'

'Take a look and see if she's all right. If she's not, then you just walk downstairs and let me in. If she's all right, just come down again and we'll not mention it to nobody.'

She put one nervous foot on the bottom rung.

'You'd do better without your bag, Blossom,' he said.

She lowered herself from the bottom rung, deposited her bag on the ground, and climbed on again. He stood behind her, ready to encourage.

She took a step up.

'Don't look up, Blossom,' he advised.

She took another step.

'And don't look down, neither.'

She took another two steps.

'Just keep looking straight ahead and keep going, Blossom.'

'I'm scared,' she said. 'I feel sick.'

He climbed up behind her.

'There,' he said, 'if you slip I'll catch you.'

She climbed two more steps and stuck again.

'It's 'orrible,' she said.

'I'm right behind you, Blossom,' he said encouragingly into her buttocks.

And so they made the perilous journey, Mr Odgers full of admiration for his wife's courage and also for her splendid backside. He had always loved the sheer bigness of it, but never before had he seen it displayed to such advantage and at such an angle. And there was the new sensation of observing the way the great white wobbly thighs disappeared into the tops of her stockings, for she was too fat to wear tights, and he was glad of it. He had an eye-level view, too, of the backs of her massive knees, two great rubbery expanses which in other circumstances he might have tickled. In the excitement of it all he nearly forgot his anxiety for the woman in the bedroom.

Suddenly she stopped. 'I can't,' she said. 'It's no use.'

'You're more than three-quarters the way there, Blossom,' he told her. Then he added, by way of encouragement, 'Going down is much worse. You'll never get down again.'

'I can't go no further,' she insisted.

She was peering down at the narrow strip of ground far below her between the bottom of the ladder and the wall. If the ladder fell outwards, she would fall backwards. She gripped the rung in a panic.

'Just think,' Mr Odgers said persuasively, 'just think, Blossom, a few more steps and you're through that window. It's a nice big window and you'll slip through it easy as easy. Then you can walk down the stairs like a Christian.'

'Can't,' she said in a sob. 'I'm stuck.'

It called for dire remedies. Mr Odgers braced himself against the ladder, ready to take her weight, grasped the down-pipe junction with his right hand, and reached up with his left. Then he shouted, 'Gerrup,' and pinched her bottom hard.

She was so angry that she almost ran to the top of the ladder. Once there she gripped the window ledge and turned her outraged face towards him. 'You, you,' she began, and then she saw all the empty space behind and around him. 'Oh, my gawd,' she shrieked, and hurled herself through the open window.

Fortunately for Mr Odgers they were so busy after that, trying to rouse Miss Thorpe, getting the ambulance, closing up the house after she was safely in hospital, and then telling their neighbours in Spermsby all about it, that his Blossom didn't really have time to vent her anger on him until they got to bed that night. And then he was able to give as good as he got. Better even.

Chapter Twenty-Seven

Thick cloud obscured the hills which surrounded Netherby and a mist lay over the dale. It drifted across the fields blurring outlines and dampening sounds. Sheep peered at each other through the greyness and their bleating did not carry, any more than did the subdued winter murmuring of the beck as it flowed between mist-laden banks down to the village.

It was raw and damp in Netherby; cold enough to snow,

people were saying as they hurried along the village street, muffled against the weather, not stopping to gossip.

At the far end of the village, at the house they still called the Newboulds' farm, Derek's wife, Moira, was preparing for visitors. Her parents were coming to stay for Christmas. Derek's side of the family were coming to Netherby too, but they were staying at The Curlew. After all, as she had not failed to point out to Derek, she herself would have enough on her hands with both children home from boarding-school. Besides, Chrissie would probably find it more convenient to be in a hotel with the baby. Moira found the idea of her rather elderly sister-in-law having a baby very embarrassing and she presumed that Chrissie and Jack did too.

The house where Liz and George Newbould had brought up their family had been extensively altered. The dairy and farmhouse had been knocked into one. The cobbles outside had been ripped up and replaced by a patio, which in the summer was graced with two little pretence wheelbarrows full of geraniums and petunias. Now, since it was nearly Christmas, the red and grey concrete slabs were unadorned. The little panes of glass which had once looked out over the cobbles had been replaced by a big picture-window. To preserve privacy and sunlessness it was covered with Venetian blinds which Derek's wife dusted regularly with a special spatula-like implement. She was very house-proud, was Moira: rarely without her rubber gloves.

She had to peel them off now as she heard the chimes of the front door. Through the ribbed glass she could see the fuzzy outlines of Jack and Chrissie. She was put out. She was expecting her in-laws for tea, but not as early as this.

'We know we are early,' Chrissie said apologetically, as soon as Moira opened the door. 'We made better time than we expected coming down from Scotland. The roads were very quiet.'

'Everyone's economizing on petrol, shouldn't wonder,' Moira said. 'Derek says the price is shocking.'

'We thought we'd just call in to let you know we'd arrived,' Chrissie went on, wishing that they hadn't. 'Before we book in at The Curlew.'

Moira looked at them uncertainly. She always worked hard preparing for visitors, but never knew what to do with them when they arrived.

'You'd better come in, then,' she said. 'Tea won't take a

moment. I'd put it all ready.'

'Well, if you're sure it's not too soon . . .'

'Of course it's not, is it, Moira,' Jack said impatiently, pushing Chrissie gently forward.

'And how's the – er, baby?' Moira enquired.

'Oh, lovely,' Chrissie said. 'Sound asleep, in the carry-cot on the back seat.'

'Oh I shouldn't – I mean, you'd better bring it in. All this baby-snatching there is about.'

'What? In Netherby?'

'Well, it's always in the papers.'

'All right,' Jack said, and went out to the car. They heard doors slamming and then he returned holding the carry-cot.

Moira took a peep out of politeness. The baby slept gently; long lashes over delicately flushed cheeks. 'Very nice, I'm sure,' she said.

'Sleeps like a log,' Jack told her. 'We're ever so lucky. Is it all right if we put the carry-cot upstairs?'

'Yes, in the spare room would be best.'

Jack took the sleeping baby upstairs. They were just about to put the carry-cot down on one of the twin beds when Moira hurried in.

'I'd best give you something to go on the bed in case the bottom of the carry-cot's dirty,' she said, holding out a dust-sheet.

'She's not fair like the others, then,' she remarked, looking down at the baby almost despite herself. 'More like Nell.'

'Yes,' Chrissie said quietly. 'I sometimes think that.'

'Well, you had the same grandparents, you and Nell, so it wouldn't be so surprising,' Jack pointed out. 'All right?'

He followed Moira out of the bedroom, but Chrissie stayed behind for a moment, giving unnecessary tuckings and touches to the blankets on the carry-cot. Nell had been in that mental hospital when the baby was born. But Chrissie had not forgotten; she had called the baby Rosemary, for remembrance.

Downstairs, Moira was getting the tea ready. Chrissie joined her in the kitchen. The porcelain sink which had replaced the old stone one had in its turn been removed and replaced by a stainless steel unit. Formica and chrome rendered the kitchen unrecognizable to Chrissie. Through a doorway she could see a range of gadgets lining the walls of what had been her mother's scullery.

'That's my utility,' Moira said, putting on her yellow

rubber gloves in order to fill the kettle.

'And how are the children?' Chrissie asked.

'We have very good reports. Of course it's a *great* sacrifice to send them away to boarding-school, but we feel it is in their best interests.'

She made the tea and pushed the steel tea trolley into what had been the parlour, and was now the lounge, where Jack was waiting.

'And are you enjoying your job in Scotland?' she asked him as she put a plate and paper napkin on to a coffee-table beside his chair.

'Oh yes, thanks,' he said. 'I'm working for a Norwegian firm of consultants supervising the construction of offshore oil rigs, you know.'

'It was a long way to have to move, all the way from Southampton to Scotland,' Moira said sympathetically.

'Well, we're used to the idea that we have to go where the work is. Really it all worked out very well. It's good to get to grips with big marine works again; any work connected with the sea is unpredictable and I do enjoy the challenge of it.'

Chrissie listened to him; the warmth in his voice was reassuring. She wondered sometimes, but in the past year Jack's confidence in himself had slowly built itself up. Time and work had wrought their miracle. All the same, the wound was still unhealed, and she wasn't going to have Moira probing it.

'We're meeting Nell off the four-ten train in Bragton,' she said. 'She decided against driving up.'

'She was ill a long time, wasn't she?' Moira said. 'We were very sorry, Derek and I. What exactly was wrong? I've always wondered.'

'She's overworked rather,' Chrissie said vaguely. 'She just needed a good rest.'

'She must have been the best part of a year off work,' Moira pointed out lugubriously.

'Well, two terms. But college was very good about it. She was due for a break, anyway.'

'She's given up that house she bought, so I'm told.'

'Yes, she lives in college now. It's easier, really. She doesn't have to cook.'

Moira sighed. 'Yes,' she said, 'cooking is very tiring. Men don't realize.'

She sipped her tea and then bethought her of something else.

'What happened to that gentleman, the one we thought she might marry?'

'I think they decided against it,' Chrissie said, even more vaguely.

'Not that I'd dream of asking, of course. She doesn't confide in us. But it's as well to know how the land lies, isn't it, when people are coming, I mean. I wouldn't want to say the wrong thing.'

Chrissie made non-committal noises. Moira replenished tea cups, Jack ate biscuits noisily.

'I suppose they had a – disagreement?' Moira said quietly to Chrissie. She was going to say row, but gentility intervened.

'I suppose so.'

'And how is Derek enjoying life?' Jack asked heartily. 'No regrets about giving up farming?'

'Oh dear me, no. It's the wisest thing he ever did.'

'I'm glad it's worked out well.'

'He has regular hours, you see, now, on the machinery side. It's not like animals. He gets home at half-past five, so we can enjoy our evenings.'

Jack looked at his watch.

'I think we should be going, Chrissie,' he said. 'Is it all right if we leave the baby here, Moira? I promise she won't wake.'

'Very well, I'll lend an ear.'

'We'll call in at the pub, Chrissie, on the way, to let them know we've arrived.'

'Oh, not a pub, Jack!' Moira sounded quite shocked. 'The Curlew's not a pub any more. More a roadhouse, really.'

Nell sat in the corner seat of her empty compartment staring out of the window. The grey and green countryside slipped past, sheep stared uncompromisingly back at her, telegraph wires dipped up and down, up and down. Coming back has been a mistake, she thought dully. I know that before I have even arrived.

She had put too much hope on this return to Netherby. She had thought that the joy she had once felt in this land, the sense of belonging, might flow again in her and carry her back to life. But she looked at it and felt nothing at all.

She had felt nothing for a long time. She was better, of course. It was all behind her: the electric shock treatment, the drugs, the awful group-therapy sessions. All in the past. Her mind was alive and well. She had worked conscientiously this term, marking essays, preparing lectures, giving tutorials. More than that: she had encouraged, admonished, joked. She had given a good imitation of living.

But she was dead, dead. This is what hell is, she thought, this deadness at the centre of one's being. Hell is the cessation of love. I look at this countryside of my childhood without love, at my friends without love, at my books without love, and I do my work without love. I have tried; I have worked and worked, I have pretended to live so that the pretence might become reality, but it is hopeless.

She could not even hope to escape into oblivion, as she had tried to do in her despair last year. The return to health had brought with it the responsibility to live. But nobody could call it living. She contemplated the remaining years of her life with sick dread.

Sometimes she tried to rouse herself from this limbo by remembering, hoping to feel some emotion, even if it was only pain. She thought about the house, The Lonely House, which she had loved, but she felt nothing. It was sold, it was seen to, finished. She recalled the ignominy of her departure from it – common knowledge in the area now, thanks to the kindly garrulity of the Odgers. But she felt no spasm of humiliation, just a dull acceptance. She could even recall Gregory Nansen with the same despairing acceptance. When he had written to tell her that he was getting married she had felt only that this was part of the pattern of things, part of the desolation of her life. She didn't blame him in any way. He was getting on, he said, over forty now, and he wanted to settle down and have children. He knew her views on these matters and wished her well in her chosen life-style. The American woman whom he was marrying in the spring, had, he explained, no ambitions other than to be his wife and a mother to his children.

Nell contemplated the wreckage of her life without emotion, just as she saw this countryside without either joy or sorrow. There seemed to be some barrier, some thickness, some grey mist, between her and what she contemplated that blocked all feeling, all reaction.

So she sat staring listlessly out of the train window until

it drew into Bragton Station.

Chrissie and Jack greeted her warmly and she was grateful to them in a theoretical kind of way. They chattered brightly as they drove along the winding road between the high dry-stone walls from Bragton to Netherby. She tried to respond, aware that she felt nothing for them apart from this dutiful gratitude.

When they were almost in the village the road suddenly widened. New walls had been built of imitation stones bonded together with cement. 'Whatever have they done that for?' she asked, surprised.

'Road widening scheme,' Jack said. 'There's so many tourists now and the bigger buses couldn't take that corner.'

She looked out for the hump-backed bridge over the beck. It had gone, they were approaching a new bridge with concrete slabs and a metal parapet.

'The old bridge couldn't take the traffic,' Jack explained.

Once over the bridge there was an unexpected rush of new houses, so brightly painted that they seemed to jump out at her.

Nell stared at them, alarmed and bewildered. 'Where's the village gone?' she asked.

Jack laughed. 'Still there,' he said, 'although admittedly the approach to it isn't recognizable.'

Then they were round the corner and there was the church where Jack and Chrissie were married. She sighed with relief that the moment of nightmare was over. It had startled her. Her heart was thumping.

'The Curlew's altered, too,' Jack warned.

Even so, it was a shock. The village green had gone and been replaced by a car park. The whole front of the pub had changed, the flowerbeds, the old bench, the cobbles, all gone. There was a new sun lounge, dismal in December, looking out over an expanse of asphalt.

'We'll drop your luggage in,' Jack said, 'and then go along to collect Rosemary, shall we?'

She had an impression of stuffiness and patterned carpets and plastic flowers and of her room, tiny and obviously partitioned out of a much larger room. At least they'd left a little lead-paned window looking out over the back, she noticed as she dumped her things quickly and went to rejoin Jack and Chrissie in the hall.

'We thought we'd walk along,' Jack said. 'All right by you?'

'I'd like that,' Nell said. 'I could do with stretching my legs.'

Double yellow lines marked both sides of the village street.

'It's impossible to find anywhere to park in the summer,' Jack said. 'And the car park's always full.'

Facing them on the other side of what had once been the green was a supermarket.

'Oh, Chrissie,' Nell cried out. 'Drinkwater's shop!'

'Pulled down five years ago – you haven't been for a long while, have you?'

'No.'

She wondered if Chrissie remembered the hundreds of times they had shopped for Aunt Liz, the smell of oats and paper and dust, the time the vicar's wife had been routed by old Drinkwater. She could see her now, standing there clutching her flowers and basket of fruit.

They turned left to walk the short distance to the Newboulds' farm. The old houses which had once faced each other across the narrow street had all been pulled down. Council bungalows had been built, set well back from the road with a wide area of asphalt in front of them. There was a pavement, too, made of chipped stone set in concrete.

'Whatever do they do that for?' Chrissie asked. 'It's awful to walk on.'

'Architects' rural,' Jack told her. 'It costs about five pounds a square foot.'

It was almost dark when they reached Derek's house, but Nell could see the concrete slabs where the cobbles used to be and the ugly expanse of glass like a square hole in the long low building, where once the little windows had been set in perfect harmony. In panic she thought of what the inside of the house might reveal, and had to force herself to go in when Moira opened the door. She was relieved when Jack and Chrissie said they must just collect the baby and go. She followed them upstairs and into the bedroom which she had once shared with Chrissie.

The dark oak floor was covered with a fitted carpet now, and the uneven walls had disappeared behind fitted cupboards which might have belonged to millions of homes. She remembered the huge mahogany wardrobe in front of whose long glass Aunt Liz had stood on Chrissie's wedding day.

'It's nice, the vanitory set, isn't it?' Moira asked, coming in the door behind her.

Vanity? Sanitary? Ah, it was that little wash-basin in the corner set in brown Formica. She bestowed upon it what she hoped would pass for an approving look. 'Yes, *very* nice,' she said.

The only thing that remained unchanged in this room was the view of the hills, for the window had been allowed to remain, although no branches or twigs tapped against its panes.

'We took out the climbing pear and rose,' Moira said. 'So bad for the pointing, we were told.'

Nell thought of the years she had lain there, under that window. There were twin beds now, with fitted covers and matching headboards. On one of those beds, in a carry-cot, Chrissie's baby lay sleeping.

'What do you think of your latest niece, Nell?' Jack asked her.

She roused herself and went over to the carry-cot to look at Chrissie's baby. Rosemary opened her eyes, looked with horror at the strange face above her and broke into roars of fright and rage. Jack scooped up the carry-cot and made for the door, and they all followed him down the stairs.

'I'll go to bed early, if you'll excuse me,' Nell said after dinner. She was exhausted by the effort of mealtime conversation. She wanted desperately to be alone. She had thought that nothing could be worse than the limbo she had been living in, but at least she had been able to keep going dully and without embarrassment. Now this pilgrimage was bringing not comfort but pain, dreadful and undisguisable.

'All right, Nell, we shan't be long,' Chrissie said, walking with her to the lounge.

'Good lord,' Jack said as they passed the side door to the bar, 'isn't that Derek in there?'

One of the maids, a distant Newbould relation, heard his comment and said, 'Yes, that's Derek Newbould. He comes in every night.'

Derek was standing leaning on the counter, in profile to them. He looked remarkably unchanged, Nell noticed. He still had that bull-like, uncontrolled look that had frightened her as a child. But the powerful frame had filled out and the face was fleshy.

He looked up, and recognition dawned in the bloodshot eyes. But not before she had seen the despair and emptiness of his gaze.

'Well, well, it's my old sis,' he exclaimed. 'Come along in, all of you. This round's on me. It needs celebrating, this does.'

There was no escape. He kissed Chrissie and Nell and shook hands with Jack. They arranged themselves around a little wooden table and Derek ordered drinks.

'Moira told me you'd arrived,' he said. 'Wish you could stay with us, but you know how it is.'

His voice was thick. 'Oh, we quite understand,' Chrissie said.

'Got the old bitch of a la-di-da mother-in-law coming to-morrow,' Derek said. 'And the old boy. Got nothing against the old boy. He's all right, he is. Forks out for the kids to go away to public school.'

'That's very generous,' Jack said.

'The old bitch doesn't want them under my influence, I can tell you that,' Derek said. 'That's the truth of it.'

'Oh, come . . .'

'Don't come me,' Derek said. 'I could tell you a thing or two.'

They drank in silence. Then Jack asked about work. 'Bloody marvellous, money for jam,' Derek said dolefully.

'Not affected by the recession?'

Derek shrugged. 'Maybe,' he said.

Jack looked around the room. 'There's been some changes here,' he said, 'and in the rest of Netherby.'

'For the worse,' Derek said.

'We all think that as we get older,' Chrissie told him.

Derek drained his glass and looked at them. He seemed about to make a speech. Then, 'Same again?' he enquired.

They refused. 'Let me get you one,' Jack offered, ignoring Chrissie's warning glance.

'Whisky,' her brother said briefly.

He drank it and then looked at each of them in turn.

'You remember my father?' he asked suddenly.

They nodded.

'There was a man,' he said. 'There was a man.'

He shook his head. 'They don't make them like that any more.'

He drained the glass.

'My father,' he went on, 'had self-respect. He didn't owe

anybody a living and he didn't have to kowtow to nobody, neither. My God, he worked! Winter and summer and all the hours of day and night; but he was strong. He knew it all, all about the land and animals. He walked straight. Nobody told him what to do.'

'But Derek,' Chrissie interrupted, 'you've chosen something different.'

'Shall I tell you what I've chosen, Chrissie? I've chosen the right to be pushed about and paid a salary. And if I play up to all the right people, I'll get on. I'll get promotion. And another thing,' he went on sarcastically, 'I have my evenings free. I can enjoy my family more than my dad could. Do you hear that, Chrissie? I've more time for my son and daughter than our dad had. It's good, isn't it? You should see with what respect they look at me, the toffee-nosed little sods.'

He glared about the bar, bull-like with his bloodshot eyes, thick neck and shoulders and blunt features under the thick thatch of coarse hair. A powerful wreck.

'I'll walk home with you, Derek,' Jack volunteered. 'Nell and Chrissie want to get off to bed.'

'I'm not going yet,' Derek said. 'You go on up. Don't mind me.'

In the end Nell left the three of them in the bar, and went upstairs alone.

She scarcely slept that night. The room was stuffy; turning off the radiator did nothing to reduce the central heating. The turmoil in her mind made her feverish. She shouldn't have come back. She had thought it was bad enough to live in a limbo but now she had lost that deadness which had at least enabled her to keep going last term. It had been a blessed thing, she realized, for now it seemed to her that it wasn't just her own life which was ravaged; the whole world seemed beyond hope. The George Newboulds had been replaced by men like her cousin Derek. It need not have been so. Outside pressures had brought it about. It was happening in every sphere of life. The mentality of the market place had invaded the professions. Doctors on strike; it would have been unthinkable a decade ago. Would the police soon stand by and watch the innocent being attacked, in order to get more money? There was no reason why not. The old decencies were gone; the responsibility lay heavily on those who had helped destroy them, but they did not notice it. They bore it lightly. They had traded in integrity and self-respect for the things which money could buy. Some, like Derek, knew it had been a bad bargain.

She thought about Derek and Moira. They had brought it on themselves; we all construct our own tragedies. Moira made life bearable by filling it up with futile domesticity, Derek with drink. It was a poor if traditional prop. Her father drank himself to death because reality was not bearable. Our weaknesses get us in the end; they are lethal.

In the worst hour of the night she realized that she had at least regained despair and with it the possibility of escape to oblivion. This time she would make a better job of self-slaughter. Only the possibility of suicide makes life bearable. With this thought she fell into a deep sleep.

She awoke to broad daylight. It was nearly nine o'clock. She got up and drew back the curtain.

A shock went through her. She stared out in disbelief. All the time she had been lying there, snow had been falling, silently, steadily. It lay thick and white over everything, making a deep porthole of the little window, framing the view of the white paddock at the back of the pub and the little fields beyond, which rose gently to the hills. Everything was very still.

A curious light suffused everything. The sun was not powerful enough to make the snow sparkle; it was still very low in the sky. But the whole world seemed to glow. Above the whiteness of the snow the air was tinted with an orange warmth. She gazed out at it with awe. It was a moment of wonder and she had thought life held no more of them.

When she got downstairs, Chrissie and Jack were just finishing breakfast.

'You don't mind, do you, Nell?' Chrissie asked. 'I had to get on before Rosemary wakes up.'

'Of course not. Were you very late last night?'

'No, Jack took Derek home about an hour after you left us. But do you know, we saw him this morning and he looked as right as rain.'

'Yes, he was going past just as we looked out at the front door, soon after eight,' Jack explained. 'He was off to work, so perhaps things aren't as bad as we thought.'

'We're going into Bragton to finish the Christmas shopping,' Chrissie said as she and Jack got up. 'Do you want to come? I expect you'd rather go for a walk.'

Nell nodded. 'Yes, I'll go up the dale,' she said.

'I thought so. You haven't changed.'

But everything else has.

Afterwards she went upstairs to get her coat and called in on Jack and Chrissie on her way down. Their bedroom door was open. The baby was lying on the bed, kicking. Chrissie and Jack were looking down at her and they seemed to be suffused in a most extraordinarily tender glow. Nell stood in the doorway, baffled by it, not sure if it was light reflected off the snow which gave them this radiance. But when they turned towards her, she saw that it was not the light from the window, for they had their backs towards it and, though their faces were in the shadow, they still had this light on them.

'I'm going for a walk,' she said awkwardly. Feeling like an intruder, she who didn't belong to this love-world.

'All right,' Chrissie said, the light still flowing from her. 'Thanks for letting us know.'

They were a normal, everyday kind of couple, who said and did normal everyday things. They were familiar to her. Yet they were strange and extraordinary as they stood there looking down at their child, touched by this light. It was as if – but she shied away from the idea as extravagant even as it came into her mind – it was as if they were touched by something divine.

She left them, after an ordinary everyday exchange of farewells, and walked out into the street. It was very quiet this morning in Netherby under the snow. Her footsteps were muffled as she walked past the new houses and bungalows. She averted her eyes as she passed the Newboulds' farm, instinctively protecting herself from fresh pain. She started up the lane. Even through the snow she could feel that it had been surfaced with tarmacadam, presumably for the convenience of the tourists' cars. She passed some new warehouses which she had glimpsed yesterday afternoon, garish concrete buildings roofed with corrugated iron. Then there was a dump for old cars.

She walked steadily on. Beyond the point where the lane narrowed, and began its steep and winding way up to the head of the beck, the tarmacadam stopped. She could feel the unevenness of the lane again under her feet, as it used to be. Ice crackled as she stepped on tiny frozen pools and puddles lying in the ruts invisible under the snow.

She climbed further, looking at the familiar outline of the

hills. This didn't change, it didn't change. Once she had thought that *Thus it was, Is now,* was a dreadful thought, barring progress. Now it seemed a comfort. The hills of her childhood could not change. Uncle George had lived and that could not change. Between these walls she had walked with her father, on this bank they had sat together. It was all so familiar, this land where she had grown up, that it seemed as if it must have something of herself in it. She looked at it with a kind of self-recognition.

The sun was higher in the sky now, lighting up the tops of the hills. She stood still, resting, looking up at them, and she remembered the light she had seen on Chrissie's face and Jack's as they looked down at their child. She remembered the way she had fought for the baby. Once, once in her life, she realized, she had done something good. She had done it without calculation or rational thought. She had done it because she had to. Forces outside herself had impelled her to it. It came to her that a world in which such a thing could happen could not possibly be devoid of hope.

She stood for a long time feeling hope strengthening in her. It was not a fantasy, not a whim. Frail, maybe, but real as a rose. She turned her back on the hills and forced herself to face the village, which had been so scarred and spoilt. But the snow lay thick and glowing on that, too, turning the new houses and garish bungalows into white mounds which blended gently into the rest of the village. The corrugated roof of the warehouse was a pure sheet of white on whose convolutions the sun sparkled. Even the gaps in the dry-stone walls, which no craftsman now repaired, were hidden.

With a strange sense of wakening she gazed about her, at the village below, the hills beyond. Hope continued to grow in her like a flower. She could go back, start again. There would be other moments of wonder. Not yet, but later. It was a time for healing now, not for doing.

As she stood there she felt the air beginning to stir. Soon the wind would rise and whip the snow into new patterns, swirling it away from the centres of the fields, piling it up into great drifts, sculpting them into fantastic new shapes. But not yet. Now was the moment of stillness and white peace when the snow lay like a blessing across the dale, mantling ugliness and obliterating all human scars.

Journey to Guyana

The author gives a vivid picture of the country's many-sided life: its multi-racial population and amazingly varied terrain. She describes too her everyday domestic life in Guyana, setting up home, making a garden, going to market. She tells of adventures – and some misadventures – into the Interior and of encounters with the different races which make up the Guyanese nation. She analyses the problems which confront it, which are many and grave, but behind all this she portrays a diverse people, full of resourcefulness, good humour and charm.

"A vivid and affectionate account of the country. The book is intelligent, readable and humorous." *The Times*

"For intelligent sensitivity puts most travel books in the shade . . . frequently wildly funny. There is nothing to beat a good travel book for painless learning. Added to which, this one is very well written." *Network*

"A great deal more than a travel book . . . an absorbing study." *Western Morning News*

"Humour and honesty shine through with the intensity of the Georgetown sun." *Evening News*

"A bargain." *Daily Telegraph*

Published by Hill House Publications at £4.95

ISBN 0 9513565 0 X

The Kingdom of the Rose

Eglantine Thorpe's mother predicted that no one would love her, by which she meant that her plain, bluestocking daughter would not make a good marriage. In that, at least, Mrs Thorpe was proved right.

Born in 1896, Eglantine belonged to that generation of women whose men were killed in the First World War. Also, like so many of them, she had to battle to win for herself a good education and a career. And when, years later, she wanted to marry, she had to choose between marriage and her job, for the law as it then was did not allow her to have both.

As England was shaken by two world wars, strikes, unemployment, political and technological change, Eglantine and others like her fought for those rights which women nowadays take for granted, such as the freedom to decide for themselves whether to marry, have children, study, enter a profession or go into politics. But for them it was a long struggle and they were often mocked for their pains. Contemporary women owe them a great debt: Eglantine Thorpe, the "rose" of the title, is a heroine too long unsung.

She first appeared as a minor character in *Snow in Winter* but the strength of her personality was such that the author had to explore it to the full and give Eglantine a book of her own. A historian as well as an accomplished novelist, Margaret Bacon has not only created a vivid and endearing character, but has also thrown into dramatic perspective the major events of this century and caught the distinctive flavour of each decade. Older readers will re-live many of their experiences in the book's pages and younger ones will discover much that they did not know about the lives of their mothers and grandmothers. More than a novel, *The Kingdom of the Rose* is an accurate and moving portrait of England in the twentieth century.

"Margaret Bacon has such intelligent writing sensitivity that the concept of reading fiction fades away into the feel of real drama." *Yorkshire Post*

Available from:
Hill House Publications
4 Shrivenham Road, Highworth
Nr. Swindon, Wiltshire SN6 7BZ
Price £4.95